ABOUT THE AUTHOR

Cathryn Hein is a best-selling author of rural romance and romantic adventure novels, a Romance Writers of Australia Romantic Book of the Year finalist with *Santa and the Saddler*, and a regular Australian Romance Reader Awards finalist.

A South Australian country girl by birth, Cathryn loves nothing more than a rugged rural hero who's as good with his heart as he is with his hands, which is probably why she writes them! Her romances are warm and emotional, and feature themes that don't flinch from the tougher side of life but are often happily tempered by the antics of naughty animals. Her aim is to make you smile, sigh, and perhaps sniffle a little, but most of all feel wonderful.

Cathryn lives in Newcastle, Australia with her partner of many years, Jim. When she's not writing, she plays golf (ineptly), cooks (well), and in football season barracks (rowdily) for her beloved Sydney Swans AFL team.

To discover more about Cathryn and her books, visit cathrynhein.com

Facebook: facebook.com/cathrynhein
Twitter: @CathrynHein

Also by Cathryn Hein

Rural Romance
Elsa's Stand
The Country Girl
Chrissy and the Burroughs Boy
Wayward Heart
Santa and the Saddler
April's Rainbow
Summer and the Groomsman
The Falls
Rocking Horse Hill
Heartland
Heart of the Valley
The Horseman's Promise

Romantic Adventure
The French Prize

The Falls

CATHRYN HEIN

First published 2015

This edition published by Cathryn Hein 2018

ISBN 9780648000594

Cover Art by Kellie Dennis at Book Cover by Design www.bookcoverbydesign.co.uk

For Jim

ONE

THE ENTRANCE SHOULD HAVE TOLD her this was no ordinary property. Teagan brushed a lock of lank hair back from her sweaty forehead and checked the lettering again. *Falls Farm* was spelled out across the open wings of the gate in beautifully formed wrought iron. Definitely the right place. Two kilometres from the village shops, as Ness had directed.

It was the stock grid and the 'Beware of the Ram' sign nailed to the brick column to her left that had Teagan confused. As far as she knew, Aunt Vanessa didn't run stock. She owned a couple of hundred or so acres overrun with kikuyu and God knows what else. Probably feral goats or hobby-farm escapees. A nightmare, in other words. But apparently that was normal for the Falls Valley. The once rich grazing land was now home to even richer Pitt Street farmers from Sydney and horsey types who had no idea about pasture management. Or much else, given the state of some of the properties Teagan had passed. Perfect post and rail fences, sweeping tree-lined entrances, enormous mansions, and bloody awful paddocks.

With a shrug, Teagan put the Landcruiser into gear and followed the steep bitumen drive upwards. So what if everything was a mess? She wasn't here to be a farmer.

At the top of the slope, the road took a last curve before opening on to a large brick-paved yard. A pale lemon-and-grey timber cottage with a wide, welcoming verandah fenced by a single rail and dotted with armchairs occupied the very peak of the hill. A matching grey post and rail fence surrounded a capeweed-infested lawn and garden, yellow flowers bright in the late-afternoon sun. From an open wrought-iron gate, decorated in the same pattern and lettering as those at the entrance, a paved path ran towards a set of timber steps. Teagan turned off the car and studied the front door, expecting her aunt to walk out at any moment and greet Teagan with spread arms and a smile that always made the world seem to glow with her special brand of personal warmth.

It was good to be here.

And heartbreaking.

Teagan closed her eyes and rested her forehead against the steering wheel as another wave of hurt threatened to overwhelm her. Twelve hundred kilometres from South Australia's lower south-east to the rolling rural fringes of Sydney that tickled the Blue Mountains' feet and the loss and betrayal remained as strong as when she'd left Levenham the day before. Maybe even worse.

Hot tears prickled. She swallowed them away. Teagan might be a complete headcase but that was one piece of her screwed-up life she'd prefer to keep to herself. She squeezed her eyes closed and pressed her head harder against the steering wheel as she felt the dark slick of despair begin its oily, insidious creep.

Not now. Please not now.

An almighty crunch shot her upright. Teagan released a high-pitched yelp and attempted to scramble away from the driver's door only to be jammed in place as the seatbelt locked. The ute shuddered from whatever had crashed into it. Her ears rang with the hideous noise of the impact. The aftermath sounded even worse: her breath ragged and heartbeat pounding against the sudden stillness.

Quiet reigned, broken only by the metallic pings of the cooling engine and resettling ute. Teagan stared at the driver's side window as, with a rattle and scrape, one corner of the glass dropped a centimetre in its frame and caught. A light wind brushed the triangle of space, freshening the car's stale interior with a waft of eucalyptus. She blinked and blinked again, her lips parted in disbelief.

Movement had Teagan refocusing. A broad behind appeared, followed by more rust-tinged fleece as the sheep backed away. A set of thick curled horns were next, followed by an extremely ugly head. Vacant blue-grey eyes lifted upwards, and for a moment Teagan thought she saw the ram's mouth quiver as though attempting to smother a smile.

Her jaw tightened. She was grimy from the long drive, exhausted and fractious thanks to a nervous night camped in her swag in the tray of her ute at a Hume Highway truckstop, and furious with a universe that seemed intent on swindling her out of everything she'd ever held dear. A psychotic ram was *it*.

She pulled the door handle and gave the panel a kick. The ute door swung open with a groan. The ram backed up a couple more steps and lowered its head.

'Oh, no you don't, you little shit.'

The ram charged, but Teagan had been around sheep and cattle all her life. She dodged to the side and snatched at a horn, hooking her hand around the rough surface and gripping tight. Her stiff muscles protested at the force of the ram's fightback. It shook its head in fury and released a deep bleat, then attempted to butt her leg.

Teagan jerked on the horn. 'Cut it out!'

They eyed one another, panting. Mongrel merino cross, she guessed. Likely hand-reared and feral because of it.

Keeping a forceful grip on the ram's horn, Teagan fired a look at her ute. A large round dent hollowed the driver's door. To her horror, her throat thickened at the sight. Heat began to needle her eyes. She swallowed and breathed hard, forcing the approaching tears away.

She would *not* cry over her ute. And she certainly wouldn't cry over anything some stupid pet ram had done.

As if sensing her fury, the ram made a deep guttural noise that it probably thought sounded tough but made Teagan wish she had a castrating knife. Although it was far too late for that. The ram had balls like the pendulum of a grandfather clock. Only hairier.

'Oh, shut up,' she said instead, kneeing its head aside.

Teagan glanced at the house and frowned. Where the hell was her aunt? She stared at the large, open-bay machinery shed to the right of the main yard. A sporty-looking Alpha Romeo occupied the middle bay, a ride-on mower and other junk another. The third housed a battered aluminium horse float. Where the paving ended, a fissured red-clay-and-gravel track cut past the main yard and house before disappearing down the far side of the hill.

The ram yanked against her hold but Teagan maintained her grip. She hunted for a pen to house the animal while she searched for Ness, and spotted what appeared to be a horse enclosure behind the shed.

'Come on, you,' she said to the ram, steeling her legs for the haul ahead.

'Teagan! Darling!'

It was five years since Teagan had last seen her aunt, and if it was possible for someone to become more womanly with age, Ness had achieved it. She skipped across the front lawn in a voluptuous display of curves, cleavage and legs, all set off magnificently thanks to a tight-bodiced cobalt-blue dress with a sweetheart neckline, and weirdly, a pair of thick pink socks and boots.

Ness radiated against the muted eucalyptus background of Falls Farm like a lit-up show ride. Gloriously rich, dark-red curls bobbed around her lightly freckled face. Her full lips were parted in a wide welcoming smile that added becoming crinkles around her delight-filled blue eyes. Rounded hips seemed to swing with each step.

'Darling!' She spread her arms to expose a creamy and very full décolletage, spiking envy into Teagan's less-endowed chest. It was as if buxom beauty had flowered on Vanessa's side of the genetic tree and spread no further. 'You made it!'

Teagan adored her aunt, but seeing a woman over twenty years her senior skip towards her like Marilyn Monroe on steroids when she felt like utter crap plummeted her already fragile mood to rock-bottom.

She pointed towards her ute. 'Your ram attacked my car.'

Ness halted at the sheep's side and rolled her painted lips together as she surveyed the damage. She regarded Teagan sideways from under mascara-darkened lashes, eyes still sparkling. 'Well, yes. He is, you know, a ram.'

'Not funny, Ness.'

Her aunt leaned across the sheep and quirked a finely plucked eyebrow. 'Not even a little?'

Teagan rubbed her face and tried to find her sense of humour, but it had been stolen away along with everything else she'd once loved.

Ness touched her arm. 'I'm sorry about your car, darling. I was so excited about your arrival that I forgot to lock Merlin up.'

'Merlin? His name is Merlin?'

'Merlin the Magic Ram.' Ness placed a hand on the sheep's head and gave him an affectionate rub. 'So named by the family who bottle-raised him after he was abandoned by his mother. They thought him cute until he started bowling over the children. Then it was either the chop or here, and I couldn't stand by and let the poor thing be slaughtered for doing what comes naturally. It's hardly fair. He has his moments, I admit, but I've grown quite fond of him.'

The ram sniffed Vanessa's knee, lifting the skirt of her dress slightly to expose more smooth white leg. His nose wrinkling, Merlin raised his head and curled his top lip before releasing another throaty bleat.

'Oh, be quiet, you stinky old goat. Here,' Vanessa said, grabbing a horn, 'let me sort him out. You look like you could do with a wash and a drink. There's a fresh jug of margarita in the fridge. Help yourself.'

Leaving her bemused niece, she marched the ram towards the

yard Teagan had spied earlier, Merlin bunting and bellyaching the entire way.

Not for the first time, Teagan wondered how Ness and her mother could be sisters. It wasn't just the difference in their ages – twelve years thanks to Vanessa's unplanned arrival – it was their completely different perspectives on life. Teagan's mother was a typical conservative farmer's wife. Penny Bliss wore practical clothes, kept her hair short and nails blunt, applied makeup only on special occasions, and buried any sensuality she might possess somewhere Teagan had never seen. She hadn't even been able to confront her husband when she'd suspected him of spending hours trawling internet porn sites. The shame had been too much for her.

Ness, on the other hand, dressed and acted like an Italian film siren, albeit with dark-red hair and pale, Celtic skin. She liked good food, wine and cocktails, enjoyed foreign films, spoke French and Italian, was rarely seen without makeup, and dressed in ultra-feminine clothes. She was also a double divorcee whose mysterious past in Europe made Teagan's mother's lips purse in disapproval at any mention of the subject. Which had naturally left a teenage Teagan completely in awe of her aunt and her exotic life.

Now, as a twenty-nine-year-old adult whose own life was exotic only for the mess it was in, she couldn't help feeling envious. But she was also grateful. Ness was nothing if not big-hearted. When Teagan had learned the truth about the disaster her father had brought on her family, Falls Farm had seemed the perfect place to run.

Teagan just hadn't counted on a horny, fat-headed ram to spoil the welcome.

A hot shower and a tumbler of soury-sweet margarita did wonders for Teagan's mood. Suddenly, the late afternoon seemed to brighten, and even the sunny swathes of capeweed flowers across Vanessa's lawn looked pretty instead of rampant. Following her aunt's cue she rested her feet on a cushion-topped cane stool and settled back to sip her drink while the day dipped towards evening.

The view from the verandah was nothing special, but what it lacked in beauty it made up for in serenity. The steep hill on which the house was perched kept them above the racket of the busy road below. A dense plantation of eucalypts running the length of the slope added another layer of screening. Bellbirds populated the branches, their sweet song filling the atmosphere. Occasionally, a male whipbird would split the air with its distinctive long whipcrack call, his partner following with her *choo-choo*. West of the house, where the land tumbled down a ragged paddock to a line of lush scrub that followed a rambling creek, even more birdcalls echoed.

Teagan closed her eyes and thought of Pinehaven, the only home she'd ever known, now lost to her, and how it would sound without her there. Whether the land would be weighted and hollow with failure the way she was. Its fauna made mute by the burden of sorrow. The rustle of grass and trees a melancholy, tuneless whisper.

They were stupid thoughts, for their pointlessness more than anything. Yet the questions remained in Teagan's mind, mingling with the ever-present anger and grief.

Ness seemed content to let her enjoy the quiet. They'd chatted about her trip as Ness had helped cart her pathetic possessions to the house, the subject of Teagan's parents only briefly touched on. Halfway through the second trip an overweight fluffy mutt, shoulders and back stained and reeking of something very dead, had bounced from the back of the house and bounded around Teagan with her tongue flapping. Ness had shooed her away, but the dog – a labradoodle called Saffron, or Saffy for short because of her golden coat – had kept up her welcome dance, retreating only when Ness had dumped Teagan's suitcase on the top step of the verandah, plucked up a hose and jetted it at the dog.

At which point, Ness had announced there was also an amiable and most definitely unstinky cat hovering somewhere for Teagan to make friends with, two female guinea pigs named Betty and Wilma, and a piebald horse called Claudia. All of which had come into Vanessa's care because they'd been dumped by their owners, were strays, or, in Claudia's case, rescued from cruelty.

The parallels between her own desperate arrival at Falls Farm and her aunt's menagerie, Teagan didn't wish to contemplate.

To Teagan's surprise, the house had proved much larger than it appeared from the front. Thanks to a modern extension, the cottage opened up at the rear into a vast living area, featuring a modernist, scallop-shaped fireplace kept hanging in space only via its flue, around which three well-padded two-seater sofas were arranged. Two large bedrooms, one with full ensuite, and an office, ran off the main area, along with another bathroom and toilet. Parallel wings extended the house outwards to more rooms. Between the wings and beyond ran an inviting deck, accessed from the living area by a set of glass-and-timber concertina doors. The deck ended in an infinity-edged pool that offered a soothing view over the small valley and densely canopied creek below.

Noting the outdoor lounge, gas heaters and hooded stainless-steel barbecue, Teagan had expected Ness to settle into that comfortable area for drinks. But when she'd padded into the kitchen after her shower, her aunt had directed her to the cushioned cane setting on the front verandah.

'It's peaceful here,' said Teagan, opening her eyes and taking another sip of her drink. 'Very quiet.'

Ness gave a secretive smile. 'For the moment.'

Teagan threw her a sideways look but Ness didn't elaborate.

'Did you want to ring Penny?'

Teagan shook her head.

'Teagan, darling, she's your mum.'

The sympathy and concern in Vanessa's voice made Teagan look away, breathing through her nose with her mouth held firmly shut. 'I don't want to speak to Mum. Or Dad. Not yet.'

'Do you mind if I call? They'll want to know you arrived safely.'

Teagan turned back, anger igniting. 'I'm not sixteen.'

Ness gave her a raised-eyebrow look that intimated Teagan may no longer be a teenager but she was definitely acting like one. 'Sixteen or sixty, age doesn't stop parents from worrying about their children.' When Teagan remained mute, Ness stood and rested a hand on her shoulder. 'You can't blame your parents forever. People aren't perfect, they make mistakes.'

Something Teagan knew too well. 'I know. I just . . .' She shook her head. Maybe later. Now was too soon. The way she felt, forever would be.

Her aunt squeezed her fingers and let go. Teagan listened to the creak of floorboards as Ness made her way inside, and swallowed another gulp of margarita. Her aunt's soft voice drifted from the house. She thought of her mum, the pathetic way she'd stood at the door of the tiny renovated timber worker's cottage Teagan had occupied at Pinehaven, wringing her hands as she apologised again for her husband's deeds and her own ignorance, while Teagan had dumped clothes into duffle bags and seethed with fury.

After multiple warnings, most of which Teagan was unaware of, the bank had foreclosed on Pinehaven, her beloved home. Not because the property couldn't sustain a family or be profitable. But because her father, for reasons no one could understand and that he would not deign to explain, had been suckered into buying a program for trading in a share derivative that Teagan had never heard of. For hours he'd shut himself away, monitoring, tapping, following his path to riches, while her mother had done nothing and the scam artists who'd sold him the program had shared high fives and clapped their greedy hands with glee.

Naturally, the promised riches never came. Only a slow siphoning of the farm's income and equity until, in desperation, Teagan was asked to loan her preciously saved cash. Like a fool she'd handed it over, not for one moment guessing the real situation. She'd thought they were having a bad run. It seemed unfathomable, but without access to the books, she'd had to take Graham Bliss's word for it. One loan followed another until, after a year of unbelievable stress and anxiety, of fights, lies and secrets, the worst happened. He lost it all.

And so did she.

If it hadn't gone on for so long, if her parents hadn't manipulated and used her and duped her so badly, perhaps she could have forgiven them, but the betrayal, when it came, was simply too overwhelming. They'd gambled her home, all that she'd loved, and lost it. Forgiveness would be long coming, if ever.

She finished her drink and reached for the margarita jug, ice cubes clunking as they hit the tumbler.

Ness settled back into her seat. Teagan expected her to pass on some message, but her aunt remained quiet, her head tilted slightly as though listening for a signal. A smile flickered. 'Here they come.'

The sound of a car had Teagan turning back towards the drive. A pale-blue Ford Falcon rattled into view. A man waved from behind the windscreen and braked next to Teagan's Landcruiser. He bent to gather something from his seat and pushed open the door.

Ness stood and placed one hand on a verandah post. 'Col, how lovely to see you.'

Col shuffled up the concrete path towards the house, a carton of eggs tucked under one arm. The fading sun glinted off a skull devoid of hair and covered with age spots. His washed-out stubbies were so brief that with each step he exposed a slither of scarlet jocks. 'Had some spare eggs. Thought you might like some.'

'You know I always welcome your eggs, Col.' Ness reached down to take the carton. 'They're so much better than supermarket ones.'

'Don't know why you don't get yourself some chooks. I could source you some bantams. No trouble.'

'That's very kind, but I think I have more than enough animals. And I'm not sure if Blanche would cope.'

Col suddenly noticed Teagan in the shadows. His bushy grey eyebrows shot up. 'Hello.'

'How rude of me. Colin Walker, this is my niece, Teagan, up from South Australia.'

He gave Teagan a nod before turning glowing grey eyes back on Ness. 'Your niece? You could be sisters!'

Teagan's polite smile fell, but Col didn't seem to notice the insult.

'You're too sweet. Oh,' said Ness, glancing towards the drive, 'here's Antonio.'

Col's expression turned vinegary as he watched an aging white van with a faded Australia Post symbol on the side pull up next to his Ford. 'What's he doing here?'

A curly-haired, well-built man with olive skin emerged and strode to the verandah. '*Bella!*' He grinned widely at Ness, before shooting Col a distasteful look. 'Colin.'

'Tony.'

Antonio looked across at Teagan, and the grin returned in force. '*Due bella donne!*'

Teagan twinkled her fingers. The margaritas were making her feel silly. 'Hi.'

'My niece, Teagan,' said Ness. 'From South Australia.'

Antonio nodded in approval. 'Come to visit your aunt? She'll keep you entertained.' From his broad Australian accent, the Italian Stallion routine was over.

'I'm sure she will.' She already was. Entertained and more than a little tipsy on tasty margaritas.

Antonio turned back to Ness and passed her a wad of stapled paper. '*The Falls Express*, hot off the press.'

'You didn't have to. I could've picked it up tomorrow.'

Antonio shrugged. 'It was on my way.' He clapped his hands together and rubbed them, then gave Col a meaningful stare that was returned with one just as meaning-filled back.

Ness shot Teagan a sly wink. 'Can I offer you gentlemen a drink?'

The two men regarded one another, each clearly wanting the other to leave. When neither budged, they both shook their heads.

'Best be off,' said Antonio.

'Maggie'll be waiting,' muttered Col.

Ness smiled and waved them farewell, observing the duo as they walked back to their cars, swaggers aggressive, heads butted as they argued quietly.

'What was all that about?' asked Teagan.

'That,' said Ness, her voice cheery with humour, 'was just the start.'

As soon as Col and Antonio disappeared, another car arrived, quickly followed by another. Again, both callers were men, one bearing news that could have easily been delivered by phone, the other carrying a box of vegetables.

Ness greeted them both with delight, careful to introduce Teagan, but they weren't interested in Teagan, only her aunt, and with each visitor Teagan's already fragile ego crumbled a little bit further. Taking the contents of the margarita jug down with it.

'Oh dear,' said Vanessa, observing her niece as Teagan wove her way inside for the loo. 'Perhaps I shouldn't have mixed that third jug.'

'You didn't tell me she was coming.'

Vanessa turned back to Domenic Ashe. He leaned casually against a verandah post dressed in his usual expensively tailored suit and handcrafted shoes. His tie was loose and a shadow of stubble was forming around his jaw. She wasn't fooled by the relaxed pose or the end-of-day slackening of deportment. Dom had the edginess of a man who wanted something. At least he'd scared off all the others. Her admirers were all incredibly sweet, but the attention didn't make life easy in the village.

'I only found out myself two days ago.' She winced as a crash sounded from the house. 'Poor thing was so uptight on her arrival I thought a few drinks would do her good.'

'No fat to absorb the alcohol.'

'She is thin, isn't she?' Teagan's appearance had been a shock. Her fractious manner even more so. 'I'll have to fatten her up.'

'Give the girl some womanly curves like you? You'll have all the young bucks on your doorstep, as well as the old.'

She rolled the ice cubes in her drink and took a sip, assessing him over the rim. 'And which category do you fit into?'

His blue eyes held hers. 'Not young, not old. Just right.'

'Ah, a Goldilocks man.' She deliberately broke eye contact and checked the yard. 'Speaking of golden locks, where's my stinky dog? Saffy!'

On cue, the labradoodle bounded out from the thick scrub to the right of the house. Her coat was matted with more of whatever she'd discovered to roll in. The reek could be smelt from the verandah.

'Jesus,' said Dom, turning away.

Vanessa sighed. 'A job for tomorrow. I really can't face that right now.'

The screen door creaked open. Teagan stumbled through before collapsing back onto her wicker armchair.

'Are you okay, darling?'

'Fine,' said Teagan, reaching for her margarita glass. Vanessa had laid out bowls of dips, warmed homemade focaccia, marinated olives, tangy *giardiniera*, cheese and shaved Parma ham, but her niece had shown no interest in food.

'How long do you plan to stay in The Falls, Teagan?' asked Dom, spreading pesto on a piece of bread.

She shrugged. 'Depends.'

'You should try this,' he said, raising the bread before tucking it into his mouth and chewing.

Vanessa watched his jaw work. He had one of those chiselled manly faces that fascinated.

'On what?'

Teagan shrugged again and stared blankly across the yard with the sort of hollowed-out look you'd expect from a trauma victim. Vanessa's heart wrenched for her. The poor darling really was in a state. Completely on edge and horribly thin. Penny's rotten husband had a lot to answer for.

Dom exchanged a look with her, but Vanessa could only shake her head. Teagan would need time and patience. Poking an olive with a toothpick, Dom stepped to Vanessa's side. When he spoke again his voice was low. 'You know that plan I've been considering?'

Vanessa nodded. Dom's plan to expand The Falls Wellness Centre, his exclusive and highly profitable health retreat on the other side of town favoured by the rich, famous, burnt out and addicted, wasn't new. He'd been contemplating it for months.

'I've decided to go ahead. Lodged the development application with the council this afternoon.'

'I hope you're prepared for a battle then.'

'It might not turn out that way. With your help.'

Her mouth thinned. She had no influence over the people who mattered in The Falls. In fact, there were wives in the area who would gleefully oppose anything Vanessa supported, purely on principle.

'You flatter me,' she said, sauntering to the table to refill her glass before Teagan scoffed the entire jug. Goodness, the girl could drink. Although, looking at her owlish eyes, she doubted her niece would last much longer.

'You're very flatterable,' said Dom, catching her eye and holding it in a way that made her stomach flutter and consider, for the thousandth time, whether she should just say to hell with it and sleep with him. But that way lay heartache. Her days of being a rich man's toy were over.

Teagan flopped her head drunkenly to the side and narrowed her eyes. 'Are you coming on to my aunt?'

'Not at all,' answered Dom smoothly. 'I'm simply trying to enlist her help with a project of mine.'

'Sure you are.'

'Dom's looking to expand his health retreat,' said Vanessa. 'Apparently there's a shortage of places for celebs to get clean.'

'Not all of the centre's clients are addicts,' explained Dom, swapping to the persuasive businessman's voice that Vanessa secretly disliked for all that it reminded her of. 'We treat a range of disorders, with a focus on healing our client's bodies, minds and spirits, through a holistic approach.'

Teagan's eyes began to cross. Or perhaps she was trying to roll them, Vanessa wasn't sure. As Dom continued, Teagan slid further down her chair.

'We're looking to upgrade the spa and treatment rooms. But increased privacy is my number-one priority. The centre's international clients demand complete anonymity, which means more specialised accommodation and upgraded security.'

With his last word, Teagan slid completely onto the floor.

Vanessa tried not to laugh at Dom's expression. 'I don't think Teagan is your target market.'

'So it appears.'

Vanessa sighed and grabbed one of Teagan's arms. For a thin girl she was surprisingly muscled and weighty. 'Where's Lucas when I need him?'

Dom draped Teagan's other arm over his shoulder and hoisted. 'Are you casting aspersions on my manliness?'

'Darling, no one is as manly as that boy.'

Together, they carted a jelly-legged and mumbling Teagan off to bed.

'She's very pretty,' said Dom from the door as Vanessa tucked Teagan in and placed a plastic glass of water on the bedside table and a bucket by the bed.

Vanessa regarded her niece with a mixture of fondness and worry. 'I get the feeling no one has told her that for a long time, least of all herself. Isn't that sad?' She kissed Teagan's forehead and left the door ajar in case she woke in the night and needed help. 'Not that she'd believe it anyway. She's very down, poor love.'

'She's come to the right place then.'

'I hope so.' She left Teagan to her snuffles and headed out to the verandah. 'Otherwise the centre might have another patient.'

He threw her a sharp glance. 'That bad?'

'I don't know.' Vanessa looked back over her shoulder, frowning. 'She worries me.'

'If you need help, Nessie, I'm here. So is the centre.'

She began clearing food. Dom would do anything if he thought it would get her into his bed, but she had no inclination to put herself in a position where she owed him, unless left with no choice. Rich men called in their debts, as she knew too well.

'Things could get ugly in the village, Dom,' she said, changing topic to the expansion. 'I don't want to take sides.'

'You know this is good for The Falls.'

'No. I know this is good for you.'

He stopped her as she tried to slide past him into the house. His hand felt hot on her waist and drove another heat lower. He tilted his head until their mouths were close, the air sizzling with their attraction. In the warm colours of dusk his voice sounded like honey. His eyes were alight with hunger. 'Don't you trust me?'

For three husky breaths Vanessa felt her want surge against her will. Then self-preservation had her laughing and twisting away.

'Not a scrap, Domenic Ashe. Not a scrap.'

TWO

TEAGAN SNIFFED. Screwing up her nose, she squeezed her eyes even more tightly closed. The stink kept coming. Gingerly, she eased one eyelid open. A pair of evil-looking, iceberg-blue eyes with narrow inhuman pupils stared back at her. She opened the other eye. And screeched as her brain finally registered that there was a hairless alien thing sitting on her bed blowing fish breath into her face.

In a flurry of sheets and doona she backpedalled up the bed like an Olympic cyclist. Jammed against the wall, she panted and stared. The thing meowed and attempted to crawl closer but Teagan wasn't having any of it. With a lurch she threw herself out of bed and rolled with a thump onto the floorboards.

The cat jumped lithely down to join her, skinny body creepily sinuous, as if it possessed bones made of gelatine. Teagan shuddered and stared at it, fighting an urge to hold two fingers up in a makeshift cross. She had never seen an animal so ugly, or so demonic. And its breath reeked.

She opened and closed her mouth, tasting fur and sourness. People in glass houses . . .

A knock sounded at the door. Ness called out and, after a pause, carefully pushed the door open.

She peered around the edge with a worried expression. 'I heard a thump.' She spied Teagan on the floor. 'Teagan, darling, are you all right?'

'Fine.' Notwithstanding a pounding head and mouth like a century-old septic tank. 'But I think your cat has some sort of disease.' She regarded it with distaste. God, what a horror.

Normally she didn't mind cats. She was rather fond of most animals, except this was a spooky huge-eyed mutant with disgusting breath, ears that stuck up like a gremlin's and a frown to match, and skin like a newborn extra-terrestrial.

'Oh,' said Ness, coming in to scoop up the cat, 'this is Blanche. I can assure you she's completely healthy. She's a sphinx cat. They look like this, which, I have to admit, is a bit of an acquired taste, but she's wonderfully friendly and curious.' She tickled the cat's chin. 'I'm sorry she disturbed you. She was just saying hello.'

'With fish breath.'

Ness arched a single eyebrow at her.

Teagan rubbed her face. 'I know, I know.'

'How are you feeling?'

'Average.'

'Paracetamol?'

Teagan nodded. 'And coffee. But I'll make it.'

'Go and have a shower and brush your teeth first. I promise you'll feel much better. Then we can have a nice cuppa and you and I can sit on the verandah and discuss what we're going to do with you.'

'Shoot me?'

'No guns on Falls Farm and a tad drastic. Plus Penny would kill me if I let anything happen to you.' She smiled. 'Nothing is ever that bad, Teagan. Believe me.'

She left Teagan with instructions that there was plenty of shampoo and conditioner and body wash in the shower, a new tooth-brush and tube of toothpaste on the vanity, and a fluffy towel hanging up in readiness. Kindness that only made Teagan shed tears of hungover misery for five solid minutes the moment the door closed.

A shower and clean teeth did indeed do wonders. Teagan almost felt normal when she padded out of the bedroom dressed in a pair of fresh jeans and a thin wool jumper, both of which had seen better days. No point dressing up. She wasn't about to go parading about the village, or anywhere else. And, bar a few 'best' outfits, most of her clothes were in the same state. Ragged and worn out, like her.

Ness was busy with an impressively sleek espresso machine when Teagan reached the kitchen. She looked up from her milk frothing and nodded towards the granite bench. 'Paracetamol and water all ready for you.'

Teagan sank down onto a squishy leather-topped chrome stool and took her medicine. The headache was only at the edges of her mind now but still strong enough to be unpleasant. 'I'm sorry about last night.' She winced as a memory surfaced. 'I was rude, wasn't I? To your friend. The good-looking blond one.'

'I wouldn't worry about Domenic. He's unoffendable.'

'Is he your . . .' Teagan took a breath to think of the right word for a male friend who might also come with benefits. She may have been drunk last night, but even she hadn't missed the way Domenic had looked at her aunt.

'Boyfriend?' Laughing, Ness pushed a large, beautifully frothed latte towards her. 'No, darling. Dom is not my boyfriend.'

'Just another member of your fan club then,' said Teagan, inhaling the delicious scent of good coffee. A girl could get used to this. All she ever had at home was instant or tea. Proper coffee was relegated to very rare cafe outings in Levenham or when she visited her friend, Emily Wallace-Jones, at Rocking Horse Hill.

Ness joined her at the bench. Even crossing the kitchen she sashayed with siren sexiness, and Teagan once again wondered where her aunt's genes had come from. Teagan certainly hadn't inherited any of the good ones.

'Dom would be horrified to hear you put him in the same category as Col.'

Teagan grinned. 'You mean he doesn't wear red jocks?'

'I suspect Dom is more a Hugo Boss or Armani trunks man, don't you?'

'You could always find out. He's very good-looking.'

Ness replied with an enigmatic smile and indicated the verandah. Teagan followed and was reminded again of her friend, Emily. Although her aunt was far more voluptuous, Ness and Em had that same innate class that saw them look stylish no matter what they wore. Today, Ness was dressed in tight navy capri pants with zips at the legs, a pair of pink strappy platform sandals and a stretchy pink twin-set that hugged her breasts and defined her tiny waist, and clashed spectacularly with her red hair.

Teagan wandered over to the top of the stairs to survey the land while her aunt eased down into a wicker chair and lounged back to put her feet up. Yesterday had been a blur of exhaustion, misery and margaritas. The long drive had given Teagan too much time to think. Too much time to alternate between festering in anger and sobbing with self-pitying misery.

Too much time to let the dark oily slick in.

The morning was one of those crunchy-cool ones, so crisp, fresh and sweet it was like biting into a new season's apple. The sky was gorgeous, an endless expanse of pristine azure, the air bush-scented and musical with bird chimes. Saffy lay on the flowery lawn asleep with her head on her paws. To the left, protected by a wire and timber cage, a couple of guinea pigs – one white, one black, tan and white – munched at a healthy pile of vegetables, their cheeks bulging cutely. Behind the hutch, body lowered and still like a stalking cheetah, crouched Blanche, watching them with cold, covetous eyes.

Teagan thought about chucking something at the cat but the verandah was devoid of suitable missiles. Figuring the guinea pigs were safe enough in their cage, she took a sip of coffee. 'How many acres did you say you had?'

'Originally it was two hundred and thirty but now it's just over a hundred and eighty. I sold off the smaller title last year.' Ness smiled. 'I didn't particularly want to but who am I to deny a wealthy man his Pitt Street farmer urges? The downside is that we have to put up with my new neighbour, Callum Albright, choppering in each weekend. Apparently he intends to immerse himself in village life, starting with the cricket club. That should make for some fun. Mark Dunkerton, the club president and team captain, is a complete obsessive. He won't take kindly to a blowhard like Callum throwing his weight around.'

'Sounds like you won't be short of entertainment come summer then.'

'We're never short of entertainment in The Falls, darling. You'll see that if you stay long enough.'

Pretending avid interest in the view, Teagan turned her back on her aunt and the elephant-sized opening she'd left.

What to do with her life? What a question. Teagan had no idea. She hadn't thought beyond getting the hell away from Pinehaven and the parents who'd betrayed her so badly. A few times during her escape she'd considered cutting across to the Newell Highway to keep heading north and even further away, but self-doubt and the need for a safe haven had kept her following the Hume towards Sydney.

The pause continued. Teagan could hear Ness shifting in her seat and bit her lip. The future she'd dreamed of was gone. She didn't have the heart to envision a new one.

'You're welcome to stay here for as long as you want, Teagan. You need time to rest and recover after all you've been through.'

The sympathy in her aunt's voice made Teagan's eyes fill. 'I'll pay board and rent.'

Ness waved the suggestion aside. 'You'll do no such thing.'

'I have to do something.'

'No. You don't.' Ness rose from her chair and came to tuck a limp strand of damp hair behind Teagan's ear. The gesture was so maternal and caring, such a reminder of another thing she'd lost, it made Teagan's throat turn gravelly. 'It's okay to be looked after, you know.'

'It's been so shit, Ness.'

'I know. But we'll make it better, I promise.'

'How?' Teagan let the tears fall properly now. 'Everything I loved is gone.'

'I know, darling,' said Ness as she enveloped Teagan into a soft, scented embrace. 'I know. But that doesn't mean you won't find new things to love.' She stroked her soothingly. 'Stay here and heal. The Falls worked for me. Let it work for you.'

Teagan was relaxing on the verandah in a half-doze when a ute pulled into the yard and continued past the house.

She frowned as it crossed towards the dirt track that led down the side of the house and wondered who felt they had the right to drive around Falls Farm as if they owned it. She thought she caught a wave from the driver, but the side windows were too tinted to see more than vague movement inside. The ute's back tray had been modified with two triangular-shaped galvanised steel bins, the pair forming a tent-like structure across the back, the steel so shiny it hurt the eyes to look at it.

Sitting up, Teagan followed its progress until it disappeared down the slope. She glanced at the house and at the main gate, unsure what to do. Ness had headed into the village with a newly washed and extremely petulant Saffy for a vet's appointment. Thanks to her penchant for raiding bins for food and digging up dead things, the labradoodle had torn a toenail and was walking with a painful limp. Teagan had offered to tie the stinky dog to the back of the ute and cart her in but Ness had refused. The local vet was a good friend who would enjoy a gossip, and Saffy would be fine in the Alfa after a good scrub.

Teagan regarded Blanche. The cat seemed to have taken an unnerving liking to her. 'Okay, ugly, who's that?'

In answer, Blanche formed her sinewy body into a question mark and began licking her genitals.

'God.' With a last, disgusted grimace, Teagan headed for the boots she'd put out to dry in the sun on the verandah steps. Bathing Saffy had left her soaked head to foot, while somehow, miraculously, Ness had remained without a splash on her.

She tugged on her boots and followed the ute's trail, poking her tongue out at Merlin as she passed his yard. The ram bleated and headbutted the gate. Teagan grinned at his temper. The ram should thank his lucky stars. If she had her way he'd be lamenting a loss far greater than his freedom.

The red clay track was scarred with deep fissures and Teagan kept to the grassy edges to save her ankles. Past a disused, dilapidated chook shed and a pile of old fence posts that was no doubt home to a dozen highly venomous snakes, the road rose to a crest. Each step opened up more of the western landscape to view. The distance was pretty – lush hills and verdant forest – but closer the bordering old barbed wire fence sagged in messy decline. The paddock behind was high with rank kikuyu and a nasty-looking woody weed with fat, hairy leaves that Teagan didn't recognise. Suspecting a noxious species, she made a mental note to find out what it was and how to kill it.

At the top of the slope she halted. The ute was parked near another run-down fence, this one timber. Both galvanised bin lids were up, making the ute appear like a silvery beetle about to launch into flight.

A man with golden blond hair tied back into a ponytail and wearing what looked to be a leather necklace with a pendant hanging from it was leading a fat piebald horse across the paddock using only a rope thrown around its neck. He wore jeans and a long-sleeved button-necked T-shirt that clung to a chest and arms muscled in a way she'd only ever seen in pictures of elite sportsmen. For a moment Teagan's breath suspended, caught in the absolute glory of him, then she pursed her lips and continued on. Vain, she judged. Vain and a hippy. A shame because even from a distance he was stunning.

His voice carried on the soft breeze, too low for Teagan to make out the words, but she recognised the soothing manner of a person used to being around horses. The horse's ears were twitching with interest, its walk stiff but calm and trusting. This must be the rescue horse, Claudia, that Ness had mentioned.

He was almost at the fence when he spied her. Immediately she was flashed with a starlight white-toothed grin that brought to mind an old toilet cleaner commercial where the loo blazed sparkling light each time someone opened the lid.

'Hi.' Somehow he managed to give the word an enticing deep drawl.

Teagan kept her own response cool. 'Hello.'

He patted the horse's woolly neck, unwound the rope and climbed through the fence. Close up he was even bigger and more muscled. Any wonder he fitted through the timber rails.

He passed her, eyes flicking up and down her body, the too-white grin still in place, and rummaged in one of the bins. 'Where the hell . . .'

Teagan crossed to pat Claudia and then wished she hadn't as a sudden ache for her pretty filly, Astra, pulsed in her chest. She'd sold her darling show horse to her friend Emily for far less than the animal was worth. Em would have readily paid more, but that was all the cash she'd had on hand, and Teagan had refused more anyway. Em had done enough, taking her horse on, looking after the sale of Teagan's float and equestrian gear. Letting her howl on her shoulder when the awful truth about Pinehaven finally came out, even though she had plenty of worries of her own.

The visitor stepped back and scratched his head in puzzlement. 'Sure it was there earlier.' He glanced her way. 'Don't suppose you have a halter handy?'

'There's probably one somewhere but I don't know where Ness keeps everything.'

'Doesn't matter.' He threw her the rope. 'She's a quiet old thing. This'll hold her.'

Teagan caught the rope. She looked at it and back to him, and propped on one hip. She had a fair idea who he was now, but the way he was acting had her hackles up. 'And you are?'

He grinned another annoyingly bright smile. How did anyone get teeth like that? Teagan brushed and flossed regularly, had kept regular check-ups since childhood, and her teeth had never once looked like his.

Bleached. Had to be. The big pendant-wearing ponce.

'I could ask the same of you,' he said.

She kept her chin high and her gaze unimpressed. 'You first.'

He tilted his head to one side. The glint in his clear blue eyes displayed his amusement, which annoyed her even further. 'Red hair. Pale skin. Blue eyes.' He scanned up and down, a quirk to his mouth as if he knew how much this was irritating her. 'Pretty.' He drew the words out slowly. 'I'm guessing a relative.'

Teagan crossed her arms. At the twitch of his lips she dropped them again. Teeth gritted, she settled for twirling the rope like a small lasso. 'And?'

He returned to rummaging in the bin. 'And too skinny.'

Her ego, which had been floating a little thanks to his 'pretty' remark, collapsed.

He pulled out what looked like a pair of lederhosen but was, she recognised, a farrier's apron, and began fixing velcro strips. When the thick leather protective pads were strapped snug around his hips and thighs to the knees, he turned his back and walked around to the other side of the ute. The view from behind, and the way the apron sat, reminded Teagan of a cowboy stripper. Even with his jeans covering his bum there was no mistaking its tightness.

'So you're a farrier.'

'I am. A very good one.'

'Who goes by the name of . . .'

He sauntered lazily towards her, pushing up his sleeves. The sun caught his skin and made it gleam. Teagan's lip began to curl. Ponytail, necklace, bleached teeth and now body oil. What a wanker.

'Lucas Knight.' He held out a large hand.

She hesitated before taking, her grip as firm as his. He had man's hands, strong and work-roughened. 'Teagan Bliss.'

He grinned again. 'I bet you are.'

She snatched her hand back. 'Yeah, like I haven't heard that before.'

'Sorry,' he said, not sounding even remotely contrite. 'Couldn't help myself.' His gaze swept her hair. 'I have a thing for redheads.'

The compliment, if it was one, did nothing to improve her impression of him. All she could think was here stood another member of Vanessa's fan club. Her aunt was a complete testosterone magnet. Not that Teagan was remotely interested in Lucas or anyone else, but it was pretty deflating to know that a woman twenty years her senior could capture the attention of a man of this age and hotness.

'My aunt's not here right now.'

'Aunt? So I was right. Doesn't matter.' He studied her for a moment before indicating the horse. 'Have you met Claudia?'

Teagan shook her head.

He tousled the horse's forelock. 'Sweet old thing. Came from a hobby farm up the mountains. Owners bought her for their daughter to ride, but she lost interest after a while and poor Claudia was left to go to seed. When she broke down with laminitis they didn't want to pay the vet bills. Claudia was going to the knackers when your aunt heard about her and came to the rescue.'

Teagan leaned on the fence to study Claudia's hooves. Despite not being tied up, the horse seemed content to stand in the sunshine while they talked about her, tail swishing, eyes sleepy-lidded.

'Do you know anything about horses?' he asked.

'A bit.'

'So you know what laminitis is?'

She threw him a look and then softened it. How was he to know she'd been around horses since childhood? 'How far had her pedal bone descended?'

If he was surprised, Lucas didn't show it. 'Not too far. She still had plenty of sole depth left. She was in specially buttressed shoes for a while. We're past that now and it's a matter of keeping the hoof trimmed properly to make sure the structure keeps growing the right way.'

Teagan stroked Claudia's cheek. The pain the animal must have gone through was horrible to think about. She'd never seen a foundered horse herself but had read and heard enough about the disease to know it was agony for them. Laminitis occurred when the laminae of tissue connecting the pedal bone to the hoof became inflamed. Left untreated the bone could shift so much it penetrated the horse's hoof. Usually it was a side effect of severe obesity, but injury and poisoning could also be the cause.

'Must've cost Ness a fortune in vet bills.'

'I doubt it. Bunny would've done it as a favour, like I did.'

'Bunny?'

'Yeah. Local vet Bunny James. She's great.'

Teagan regarded him, suspicion curdling. 'So you looked after Claudia for free?'

He shrugged. 'I don't like to see anything in pain.'

Teagan returned her gaze to Claudia's hooves. Interesting. Perhaps he wasn't as big a wanker as she'd thought. When it came to animals anyway. Then again, he could have been trying to impress Ness.

'I just need to give her a quick trim.' He glanced at the sky. 'Do you have time to hold her for me? She probably won't move, but I don't want to have to chase her around if I can help it. I'm meant to be on another job.'

'So why are you here then?'

'Passing by.' He winked. 'And Tony de Vitis mentioned there was a gorgeous new redhead in town. Thought I'd better take a look.'

The cheeky sod had known who she was all along. She added another label to her list of first impressions. Game player. Teagan hated people like that, even when they came as exquisitely packaged as Lucas Knight.

Still, the day was fine and she had nothing else to do, and she could think of worse ways to spend half an hour. He might have a long list of dubious characteristics, but a good perve was a good perve. And Lucas Knight was exceptional.

Vanessa stroked Saffy's head as the labradoodle began to whine.

'Don't be such a sook,' admonished the vet before addressing Vanessa. 'It's not too severe. I'll clip it off and clean it up. I won't put her on antibiotics at this point, but if there's any sign of infection bring her back in.' She ruffled the dog's ears and cupped her jaw to stare at Saffy's face. 'Are you going to behave or will we need to muzzle you?'

'She'll be fine. I'll hold her.'

Bunny James nodded and rummaged for antiseptic and nail clippers. At a metre eighty in height, with short, spiked platinum hair, swimmer's shoulders and legs like a gazelle, the only rabbity thing about Bunny was her small turned-up nose. The rest of her was pure glamazon. Vanessa could only assume that her parents had had no inkling of how their daughter would turn out when they'd named her.

'How's Claudia?' asked Bunny as she set to work.

Vanessa cuddled Saffy's head as the dog whinged. 'Putting on weight again. I'll have to start locking her up. Which reminds me, I forgot to tell Teagan that Lucas said he'd try to call in today.'

'She arrived safe then?'

Saffy gave a sharp yelp as her damaged toenail was removed.

'Shh. You'll feel better now. Safe in body, if you ignore how thin she is, but definitely not in mind. The poor darling's a wreck. Graham has a lot to answer for, I tell you. As for my sister . . .' Vanessa shook her head in disgust. The next time she saw Penny it wasn't going to be pretty. It was bad enough that Penny had done her best to keep Vanessa out of her niece's and nephew's lives, but to know she'd allowed this mess to happen . . .

'What are you going to do with her?'

'I don't know. Feed her up, mostly. Find something for her to feel passionate about again. She'd put all her energy into Pinehaven and now it's gone she's completely lost.'

Bunny straightened and patted Saffy. 'There, all done. You could put her to work on Falls Farm. God knows the place needs it.'

'No thanks. Teagan has had quite enough of being treated like a slave. Did I mention that they hadn't paid her in months? She admitted this morning she'd even loaned them money. Eighty grand all up. Every dollar she'd ever saved. I could throttle Graham.' She sighed. What was done was done. Her role now was to make things better. 'She'll need a job eventually. For her own self-esteem, if not for money.'

'You could always try marrying her off to some rich idiot. Callum might be a good start. He's an idiot but he's still a loaded idiot.' Bunny scooped up Saffy and lowered her from the examination table as though she was a chihuahua instead of a twenty-five-kilogram labradoodle. 'Worked for you. Twice.' She grinned and put her finger to her bottom lip, cocking her head. 'Or was it three times? You've always been a bit vague about Mr Italy.'

Vanessa lifted her chin and sniffed. 'That was a civil union, so technically never a marriage.'

'Marriage or not, you didn't do too badly out of it.'

'Timoteo was very generous, but that's the sort of man he is.'

'What a life you've had.' Bunny looked despondently at the door. 'And here's me, stuck in a nowhere village, spending my days poking fingers up animal's bums when what I should be doing is swanning around Europe collecting rich husbands.'

'It wasn't all it sounds.'

Bunny lifted a pale eyebrow.

Vanessa grinned. 'Oh, all right. It was fun.'

Except that wasn't strictly the truth. Most of the time, when the thrill of whirlwind romance had worn off, she'd discovered what a whore must feel like. She'd been young, a stupid romantic who believed in fairytales and the sweet whispers of her lovers. She'd married because she believed they loved her as much as she loved them. Instead, Vanessa had turned not into an equal, but into a wealthy man's trophy. An alluring but untouchable purchase to be paraded on their arm when it suited, while they continued to do what they pleased. Until Timoteo, love had never been on their agenda.

Some days were enormously exciting. Vanessa travelled extensively, met fascinating and sometimes powerful people, wore beautiful, tailored clothes and lived between a series of incredible country and city houses that boasted both staff and spectacular scenery. She skied the French or Italian Alps in winter, yachted the Mediterranean in summer. She even had amazing sex, for the men she fell for were alpha males who took great pride in everything they did. Other days were pure heartbreak and despair. It took Timoteo to make her realise how short she was selling herself, how vacant her rich life really was.

As her fortieth birthday rushed closer, Vanessa began to desire more than parties and endless travel. She wanted a normal home, full of laughter, her own and her children's. Although he already had near-adult offspring from a previous marriage, Timoteo did his best to grant her that wish but their ages, and his hectic business schedule, worked against them. When their attempts at pregnancy failed, Vanessa realised she'd left it too late, an understanding that left her tired and, for the first time in twenty years, longing for the relaxed comfort and freedom of Australia. With deep sadness, Timoteo had let her go. It had taken some searching but thanks to him, his generosity and kindness, she'd eventually found The Falls and with it peace with herself.

Admirers existed here, too, but at least she felt safe and had the strength to fend them all off. Even Domenic who, with his dark-blond sexiness, chisel-jawed determination and easy masculinity, made her nostrils flare with want and her heart thud with longing.

She gathered up Saffy's lead. 'Thanks. Why don't you come around for drinks later this week?'

'Can you invite Lucas, too?'

'Darling, you wouldn't be able to handle him.'

Bunny's shoulders slumped. 'You're right. I wouldn't. I'd probably lay there stroking him like a puppy and then fall asleep.'

'Never mind. There's always Mark.' She stood on tiptoe to kiss Bunny's cheek. 'Thursday for sangria?'

'Okay, unless . . .' She flicked a hand towards the examination table. 'You know.'

'I know.' Vanessa knew not to hold Bunny to anything.

With a sympathetic parting smile she urged Saffy forward with her shin, pleased to see the dog's limp had eased considerably. Janice, Bunny's rather frightening old-school receptionist, had the bill already made up. Vanessa paid with a smile that wasn't returned. Like many older married women in the village whose husbands had taken to dropping into Falls Farm, Janice wasn't a fan.

Vanessa kept her head high and her smile in place. It wasn't her fault they visited. She didn't encourage any of them beyond politeness. She didn't flirt or do anything that could possibly be construed as husband stealing. Nor, since moving to The Falls, had she ever indulged in a single relationship with anyone remotely local. Yet the siren reputation stuck.

Outside, she breathed in deliciously bread-scented air. The village shops were designed in a horseshoe. Bunny's practice took up one end, the bottle shop the other. Between them thrived a bakery, a butcher, a newsagent, a doctor's surgery, a chemist, and a small IGA supermarket. Further down the road was an aging service station, the

Rural Fire Brigade and the town's bowling club, which also served as headquarters for the local cricket and rugby teams.

She caught a 'Ciao, bella!' and turned to see Antonio waving to her from the door of the newsagency.

She waved back only to see his cheerful smile collapse. Like a mouse skittering into its hole, Tony darted back into the shop, leaving her waving at nothing. Her smile thinned. She didn't need to look to know what had happened.

Bending to give Saffy a quick pat, Vanessa determinedly set a pleasant expression then straightened and turned. 'Kathleen, how are you?'

The old lady regarded her with a frosty expression. As a widow in her seventies the woman shouldn't have cared a whit about competition, yet Vanessa always felt as though they were in one. 'I'm well. And yourself?'

'Can't complain. Though poor Saffy would think otherwise, I'm sure.'

They both regarded the dog. Saffy ignored them. Her big brown pleading eyes were focused longingly on the bakery door.

'No,' said Vanessa.

The dog glanced at her, furry eyebrows drawing together in a canine *aww, Mum.*

'One sausage roll won't hurt.' Without waiting for a reply, Kathleen Ferguson wheeled and strode purposely back to her bakery.

'Now look what you've done,' hissed Vanessa, but Saffy was already straining at her leash. Vanessa hated denying animals, and the dog had suffered Bunny's treatment admirably. She held up a finger. 'One. And you'd better eat it fast.'

Saffy gave her a loopy-tongued grin that spoke of 'as if there was any other way'.

She followed Kathleen's ramrod-straight back across the carpark. It was quiet, that lull between morning smoko and the lunch rush and, except for the spaces in front of Bunny's and the doctor's, the carpark was barely occupied. Vanessa tied up Saffy outside the bakery, hitched her handbag up onto her shoulder and pushed through the vinyl fly strips protecting the entrance.

Kathleen was behind the counter, already retrieving a sausage roll from the warmer. Vanessa made a show of inspecting the pastry display cabinets. The vanilla slices looked impressively thick. A bit of creamy custard would do Teagan good.

'I suppose you've heard?' said the old lady.

'Heard what?'

'That man's plans.'

Vanessa feigned innocence. 'What plans would they be?'

'Apparently, he wants to build a giant brick wall around the place so we can't see what he does there.' She tapped her nose. 'I know though.' She angled forward conspiratorially and dropped her voice, lips pursed. 'Enemas.'

'Isn't that what the late Princess of Wales practised?'

The pucker deepened. Kathleen Ferguson was a true royalist, having curtsied as a girl to the Queen during her 1954 Australian tour. The thought of a princess having an enema was something she would never want to contemplate. Vanessa suspected that Kathleen believed royals never needed the loo.

'Completely different,' Kathleen snapped, sliding the paper-wrapped sausage roll across the counter. 'Her Royal Highness went to a private practitioner, not some unregulated so-called clinic over-run with drug-addled pop stars.'

'The centre is open to the public. Perhaps you could book in for a day spa and see for yourself what goes on. I'll take two vanilla slices as well, thank you.'

Vanessa was usually careful not to take sides when it came to Domenic and his Wellness Centre, but today the insinuation that he was running some sort of dodgy enterprise rankled. Domenic was a businessman whose only belief was in profit. Something the Wellness Centre excelled at generating and not something he would put at risk through unethical practices.

'And have my brain washed? I think not.' Kathleen sniffed and snatched up a pair of pastry tongs, opening and closing them in a series of vicious nips. 'I'd rather be dead than give a single penny to that man.'

It would take more than a penny to get into the Wellness Centre. While the centre was open to anyone who could pay, very few had the means. The prices were exorbitant. Vanessa had been several times, each a birthday or Christmas gift from Domenic. At first she'd been too curious about the facilities and treatments on offer not to accept. Afterwards, the sheer indulgence of it kept her going back. Plus she'd made sure they were kept even with return gifts.

'Domenic has done quite a bit for the community. The rugby club would've folded without his sponsorship.'

'Rubbish. They would've found another sponsor.'

Vanessa handed over a note and gathered up her goods. She'd had enough. 'I'm sorry, I really have to dash. Saffy had a rather stressful visit to Bunny. I should get her home.'

As she gave her the change, Kathleen's hand gripped hers. 'We must stop him.'

'It's just a fence, Kathleen.'

'It's a start,' she replied, nodding knowingly. 'That's what the people of Dachau used to tell themselves about the camp fence.'

When things deteriorated to mentioning the Nazis it was definitely time to leave. Vanessa tugged her hand free and with a tight smile walked out rapidly. She stopped beside Saffy and breathed in hard, only faintly registering the dog's excited nudges.

Kathleen Ferguson was the bellwether of the village. If she was getting worked up about a brick fence and invoking the Nazi clause, there was no telling what she'd be like when she heard about the expansion.

Life in The Falls was about to get very entertaining indeed.

THREE

TEAGAN RUBBED a grimy forearm across her forehead. Despite the mild morning, she was sweaty and it wasn't pleasant. Her pores leached a disagreeable combination of sour margarita, horse, dead possum and ancient dust.

Lucas had departed as cheerfully as he'd arrived, leaving her with nothing to do except to return to the verandah and the cane chair. She'd tried to relax with her aunt's copy of *The Falls Express*, but after a few minutes had become fidgety. The last time Teagan had sat around doing nothing was over a year ago, and that had only been because she'd had the flu and could hardly raise the energy to shuffle to the toilet.

Now here she was, a glorious mid-August day, healthy-ish if you ignored the hangover, and with not a thing to do beyond fantasising about Lucas Knight's deliciously taut muscles and cheeky winks. Except there was plenty. And it was making her twitchy.

Which was why, after using her nose to track down the source of Saffy's decaying scent roll and burying it, Teagan was now rummaging through Vanessa's shed looking for fencing tools. In half an hour, all she'd managed was to become filthy. Apart from Merlin, who scarcely counted, the place appeared to be devoid of anything remotely farm related.

Annoyed, she left the shed to check the merino's water. The stupid animal had knocked his bucket over but that hadn't really surprised her. The ram should be out in a paddock instead of locked in a horse yard, but none of the paddocks appeared sheep proof. Claudia's was probably the best of the lot, but Teagan wasn't sure about putting a ram in with the horse, especially one recovering from laminitis. What if Merlin became aggressive and attacked her? One bunt and Claudia could fracture a cannon bone. Then there'd be no saving her.

'What are we going to do with you?' she asked the ram, but Merlin was too busy headbutting the gate. The gate was timber and attached to the gatepost via two hinges. With each collision the bolts rattled and bounced. The top bolt had already slid out far enough to be at risk of falling out. She narrowed her eyes, wondering if he knew. Impossible. Sheep had brains the size of peas.

Sighing, she headed back to the shed, this time in search of a hammer to pound the bolt back into place, only to pause at the sound of an approaching car.

'Darling!' yelled Ness through the wound-down window of her sporty Alfa, before grunting as Saffy climbed onto her lap and hung out her golden head in flappy-tongued greeting. With effort, Ness pushed the dog back onto the passenger seat.

Teagan sauntered over. 'How did she go?'

'Fine.' Ness reached behind to the rear and held up some paper bags. 'Come have morning tea.' She suddenly registered Teagan's state. 'Goodness, what have you been up to?'

'Looking for fencing gear.' Merlin's gate gave another loud clank. 'And a hammer.'

Vanessa's eyes widened, her mouth popping as she clearly envisioned a swift bonk on the head for her ram.

'Not for that. Although it is tempting after what he did to my ute.' Teagan gestured towards the yard. 'The hinge bolts are loose.'

'Oh, yes.' The threat to Merlin over, Ness returned to cheerful pride. 'It's a trick he's learned.'

'Seriously?'

'Mmm. He's a clever thing, for a sheep. Probably why he was named Merlin.'

At the sound of his name Merlin released a throaty baa. Teagan regarded the ram with grudging admiration.

'Leave him,' said Ness. 'He'll be fine. Come up to the house. I bought you a vanilla slice to go with your coffee. They make decent pastries at the bakery.'

Teagan stepped aside as her aunt parked in the shed and alighted, Saffy following. The dog yelped as she landed on her sore paw.

'Serves you right,' Teagan said, crouching to give the animal a comforting hug. She cupped Saffy's snout and regarded her eye to eye. 'That's what happens when you go digging up dead possums.'

Saffy rewarded her with a lick on the chin and happy dog grin that made Teagan laugh and ruffle Saffy's ears, and wish human wrong-doings were so easily forgiven.

'Is that what it was?' said Ness, gathering her bag off the seat and joining Teagan. They crossed the yard, the sunshine warm and sweet. 'Poor thing. I wonder what killed it.'

'Probably a fox or cat.' Teagan threw Blanche a suspicious look as she passed, but the ugly creature took no notice. The cat was too busy observing Betty and Wilma. It was unlikely to be her anyway. Blanche seemed more of a house cat, and too small and thin-skinned to take on a clawed possum, whereas a defenceless guinea pig was perfectly sized.

'The farrier was here earlier,' Teagan said when they had their coffees and were back on the verandah. She wondered if Ness ever used the back deck. It was beautiful out there, private and peaceful, but for some reason her aunt preferred the front of the house.

'Oh good. He's a lovely boy.' Ness gave her a pointed sideways glance. 'Very decorative.'

'Bit of a wanker though, isn't he?' probed Teagan, torn between hoping he was and the feeling that he wasn't. The more she'd chatted to him the more normal and unaffected he'd seemed, to the point where she'd found herself liking him. Quite a lot, which was not an ideal outcome. It'd be nice to have her initial impression proved right and to have a reason to push those muscles and cheeky grin out of her head.

'Lucas?' Ness blinked several times.

Teagan forced herself to take a bite of vanilla slice. She'd never been a fan of the squishy custardy treat, but she didn't want to appear ungrateful after Vanessa's thoughtfulness, and eating gave her time to think of a way to respond to her aunt's incredulity. She swallowed, surprised to find the slice wasn't bad. 'He was all oiled up. And those teeth.'

Ness laughed and tore off a flaky piece of pastry for Saffy. 'I think you'll find that's sunscreen. As for his teeth, aren't they amazing?' Her expression turned slightly dreamy. 'If only I was twenty years younger.'

'He did make a point of saying he had a thing for redheads.'

'Did he?' Ness appeared genuinely astonished. 'He's never mentioned it.'

'Another one for your fan club?'

'Might I remind you, Teagan darling, that you are also a fine redhead.'

'Who doesn't have your assets.' Teagan poked a finger into the yellow filling of her slice and gouged out a lump. She inspected the creamy sample before scraping it on the side of her plate, her interest suddenly gone. 'He said I was too skinny.'

Her aunt frowned then quickly smiled when she caught Teagan noticing. 'He was telling the truth. But we'll work on that.' She took a sip of coffee. 'He's single, you know.'

'Figures.'

Vanessa's eyebrows shot up.

'Necklace, over-pumped body. Has to be gay.'

Her aunt spluttered into her latte glass. 'Lucas? Gay? I would wager my car that man is a more red-blooded heterosexual than Merlin.'

Heterosexual. Bugger. Surely he had faults? Like kinky sex fiendishness or something.

'Bound to be a man-whore then.'

Ness let out a long sigh. 'Teagan, Teagan, Teagan, what on earth has made you so cynical?'

Teagan stared at the eucalypt treetops, thinking of Pinehaven, of the thick-trunked old gums lining the drive to the house, a symbol of its solidity and permanence. How, when her brother was still at home, the place used to be. Productive, lush, envied. Her home.

A home her dad had effectively gambled away.

She shrugged and turned her head, not wanting Ness to see the build-up of tears in her eyes as she remembered the acres of prime grazing land gone to ruin. The way the kangaroos from the adjacent State Forest barely bothered to cross the boundary to feed anymore. The absolute heartbreak of it all.

'Darling,' said Ness, reaching across to touch her shoulder, 'it'll be okay.'

'Sure it will.' She cleared her throat and forced herself to sound upbeat. 'I thought I could do a few things around the place. Repair a few fences.' She tilted her head towards the creek. 'That paddock could do with slashing, too, and that woody weed looks like trouble.'

Ness pursed her lips. 'You're here to relax not work.'

Relax? Teagan wasn't sure she knew how to do that anymore. Relaxing meant thinking, and that never led anywhere good.

'Sitting around is making me tense. Do you have any fencing gear? Wire strainers?' At Vanessa's 'you're kidding' expression, she added a hopeful, 'Pliers?'

'I don't think so. If I need anything done there's usually someone willing to help.'

'The fan club?'

'They're very handy. Although, I always insist on paying them.' Ness paused. 'Just not in the way they hope.'

They looked at one another and laughed.

'How on earth are you related to my mother?' asked Teagan. 'You couldn't be less alike if you tried.'

'I'm sure Penny's wondered that often herself.' Ness watched Blanche delicately walk the rail, tail flexing like a lemur's as it helped her balance. Although, from the glaze in her aunt's eyes, Ness was clearly elsewhere. 'If she only knew.'

'Knew what?'

Ness blinked and refocused. 'That it was her fault I turned out the way I did.'

Intrigued, Teagan shifted to incline forward. 'How?'

'You'll laugh.'

'Probably.' She grinned. 'But I'll do it nicely.'

'When I was twelve, Penny brought home a box of books she'd picked up at a jumble sale. There were all sorts of things in that box, from cookbooks to Ian Flemings to crochet patterns. But hiding at the bottom were a stack of Mills and Boon romances. Penny showed them to Mum, who told her to put them on the bonfire heap.'

'And you stole them off.'

'I did indeed.' The smug memory of her daring tugged at Vanessa's mouth. 'Those books took me on the most breathtaking adventures imaginable. I rode camels with sexy sheiks, drove the Tuscan hills with Italian millionaires, was wined and dined by the British heirs of banking empires.' She sank back and closed her eyes in a way that made Teagan envious of all the emotion she'd experienced. 'I fell in love, dozens of times. You have no idea.'

No, Teagan didn't. The last time she'd been properly in love was age seventeen, with a young dairy farming lad from Port Andrews, south of Levenham. When that inevitably and painfully ended, as so many teenage romances did, her relationships became casual. As time passed and opportunities to meet decent single men became fewer, and Em's disappointments and her other friend Jasmine's disastrous affairs made her warier, the flings petered out. For the last five years there'd been nothing. Teagan thought she'd learned to live with it, but now the thought of all that missed passion made her feel even emptier.

'Those stories gave me dreams I was determined to chase. So I did. The moment I'd saved enough for a plane ticket I was gone.' Ness sobered. 'Unfortunately, my leaving broke Dad's heart. He was a darling man, so kind, and being so much younger I was always his baby girl.' Her voice quietened. 'Your mother never really forgave me for that.'

This was news to Teagan. 'I thought it was the multiple marriages she couldn't forgive you for.'

'No, it was the way I hurt Dad, but they didn't help.'

Teagan rested her head against her chair. 'I wish I could turn back time. Do what you did. What Owen did.' At the mention of her brother's name her heart gave a squeeze of jealousy and regret. Leaving home to backpack around Europe had shown Owen not only new horizons, but love and happiness. Things that might have been Teagan's too, had her dreams been bigger. 'But I could never bring myself to leave the farm.'

'Now you have.' Ness reached across to pat her arm. 'Which means from here on in it's all adventure.'

'Have you heard?'

Lucas turned to the man who'd snuck up behind him and suppressed a sigh as he recognised Colin Walker. He kept his body half facing the bowling club's old-fashioned Formica-and-timber bar, not rude but not welcoming either. It was Saturday night. All he wanted was a quiet beer and a relax. Col had a way of making him want to drink too much of the former and destroying any hope of the latter.

'How are you, Col?'

Col ignored the greeting, grey eyes bulging with overexcitement. 'Kathleen was right. The fence was just the start.'

Lucas took a good swallow of beer. The Wellness Centre. The locals either loved or hated it. Even though his daughter, Margaret, worked there as a cleaner, Col stood firmly in the hate camp. More thanks to his sycophantic relationship with Kath Ferguson than any rational consideration.

He glanced over at the cricket club sign-up desk, where Dunks sat with his cashbox, paperwork and pen poised, attempting to look professional and captain-like in his blue baggy cap and Falls Falcons blue-and-gold polo shirt. The club's redesigned logo – a swooping bird with a stump in its mouth – was embroidered boldly over one chest. Behind him hung the club's new banner, also in blue-and-gold livery.

All thanks to the Wellness Centre. Not that Col gave a shit.

Another breathless proclamation broke the bowling club's amiable quiet. 'Word's getting around.'

Lucas didn't want to ask. He just wanted to enjoy his beer and think about Teagan Bliss for a while, but until he did, Col wouldn't leave him alone. 'What word would that be, Col?'

'Expansion.' Col fairly hissed each syllable.

Lucas shrugged. 'More work for Maggie then. You'll be able to take the van to Yamba again.' And give his long-suffering daughter some peace. Thanks to Col taking up residence in her backyard in his clapped-out caravan, the poor woman hadn't had a life of her own since. But she was a kind-hearted sort and an only child, and felt it her duty to take care of her father.

'What?' said Col, confused. 'No!'

He sidled even closer. Lucas tried to stop himself looking down but couldn't. Sure enough, Col was in his shrunken stubbies, skinny legs sticking out like a pair of petrified twigs.

'You know what this means.'

'Let me guess. More cricket club members?'

Col finally realised Lucas was taking the piss out of him. 'This is serious, boy. Our village has been over-run by them as it is.'

As he finished the sentence, one of 'them' waltzed into the club and walked up to Dunks.

'This where we sign up for the cricket team? Only I need to be quick. Chopper's waiting.'

Lucas heard the air seething through Col's false teeth as he sucked in outraged breaths. Meanwhile, Dunks had the papers out and a pen in the man's hand before he could blink.

Vanessa's venture capitalist neighbour Callum Albright. Though Lucas had only met him once, Vanessa had warned him and Dunks that Callum intended to join the Falcons and there was no mistaking that arrogant stance or the superior manner in which he swept his gaze around the bowlo. Here stood a man who thought he mattered. The massive architect-designed pile he'd built yelled the same with its full-sized pool, tennis court and helipad. Not that any of those features could be seen from the road. Callum at least had some discretion, which was just as well according to some locals. Blow-ins like him could keep their cocaine-snorting parties to themselves.

Lucas couldn't care less how the bloke viewed himself, but he did think it a shame that what was once productive farmland was now reduced to a rich man's playground, although that could be said for most of The Falls. It rankled, too, that Vanessa had chosen to sell rather than lease the property to someone who'd use it properly. Deep down Lucas couldn't blame her, not when he'd heard the money on offer, but still.

Callum caught Lucas's gaze on one of his sweeps. Lucas raised his glass. The bloke was to be his teammate, after all. He received a cool nod in reply before Callum returned once more to his paperwork, signed with a flourish and strode back out.

As soon as the door swung closed, Lucas wandered over to Dunks, Col shuffling and chuntering behind.

'That makes seven,' said Dunks, eyeing the list and scratching worriedly at his five-o'clock shadow.

'We'll get there.' Lucas winked at Col. 'Col here could play in slips.'

Col's hand immediately went to his back, the very back that had supposedly kept him on a disability pension for years while his wife had worked her guts out to support the family. 'Couldn't possibly. Terrible back.'

Lucas shared a look with Dunks. Everyone knew Col did cash work on the sly at a vegie farm in the next valley. 'Tony coughed up yet?'

Dunks shook his head and stared morosely at the cashbox.

'I don't think he's going to. Always thought he was full of it.'

'I'll have a word. Want a beer?'

At Dunks's nod, Lucas escaped to the bar, relieved when Col stayed behind. The old boy appeared harmless at first glance, but he was a gossiping old git with nothing better to do than stir up trouble. The Falls would be a peaceful place if not for the likes of Col and Kathleen Ferguson.

Lucas chatted with Arnie the barman about horseracing as he waited for their beers. For some reason everyone seemed to think Lucas was good for tips, but he had no interest in racing beyond the income it brought his farrier business. He didn't do much with the thoroughbred industry these days anyway. Mostly he dealt with hobby and performance horses. They were far more lucrative, although the owners could be pains in the arse.

Lucas didn't mind making conversation. Arnie had been around in the district even longer than Col and knew everything, in partic-ular the virtue of discretion. The club was dowdy and old-fashioned, with commemorative boards dating from the fifties lining the walls, worn carpet and mismatched furniture. But Lucas liked its commu-nity feel. Its air of country welcome and unpretentiousness. It reminded him a bit of his nan and pop's old place in the outer western Sydney suburb of St Marys.

The club door opened again as Lucas returned with the beers.

He and Dunks stared at it hopefully but the new arrival turned out to be Bunny.

She grinned and strode over. 'How are my favourite toyboys?'

They both grinned back, while Col, who was still hovering, scowled. Bunny might be over fifty, but she was a fine specimen of womanhood, didn't tolerate crap and could drink like a man. Swore like one too when the mood took her. On first meeting, Bunny had made no secret of her interest in Lucas. He'd been tempted and told her so, which had made subsequent encounters flirty affairs. But he'd quickly learned how fast gossip travelled around the valley and decided to keep his nose clean. Bunny hadn't minded. She hadn't really expected him to take up the offer and had better luck with Dunks, who was at that time newly divorced and with his ex-wife, Angela, having majority custody of their two girls, finding single life and an empty house lonely. Despite their age difference, the pair had enjoyed a couple of flings. Dunks said she'd worn him out so much he could barely get out of bed the next morning. Which was funny because Vanessa had mentioned that Bunny had said the same of Dunks.

Bunny flipped around the clipboard containing the sign-up sheet and gave it a quick scan. 'Never mind, Cherub,' she said, using the nickname she'd given Dunks when they'd started shagging and which, to Lucas's bemusement, his mate didn't appear to mind in the slightest. 'It's early days.'

Dunks tossed down his pen and reached for his beer. 'I need to have the full team in to the association by next month.'

Bunny patted his head. 'I'll ask around.' She turned to Lucas. 'How was Claudia?'

'Good. She's coming on well.'

She nodded, but he could see the sparkle in her eye and knew the next question would be about Falls Farm's new arrival.

Instead, Col butted his way in, speckled head aglow under the club's fluoro lights. 'Have you heard?'

'It's a fence, Col,' said Lucas, not bothering to hide his exasperation. 'Not the bloody Berlin Wall.'

'No! The rest.'

Bunny flicked a look at Lucas and settled her features into concerned interest. With Col spending so much time hanging around the village shops, pouncing on unsuspecting locals and the occasional bewildered outsider, she understood the game better than anyone. 'What rest?'

'Expansion!'

'Of what? The ozone layer? Some soapie star's boobs?' Bunny ducked her head to peer closer and sucked in a mock-shock breath. 'Not the caravan?'

Col was practically flapping and cawing in frustration. 'The Wellness Centre!'

'Really? Bloody brilliant. I might get some extra work and be able to put on another vet.' She kept her expression serious. 'Those pop tarts take their toy dogs everywhere. I could offer a doggy day spa. Maybe rehab for mutts with attachment issues, and there's bound to be the odd drug-addicted Shih tzu among them.' She snuck a sly wink at Lucas before concentrating back on Col. 'Thanks for the heads-up. I'll ring Dom tomorrow.'

Dunks feigned deep interest in his receipt book, his shoulders shaking. Col's face was turning puce, his mouth puckering into folds so tight they were almost bloodless. Without the wink and Dom reference, Lucas would have laughed out loud, but his focus was on Bunny. There was something in that look and wink that put him on alert.

'We don't want more of their sort around here!'

'I agree,' said Lucas, 'drug-addicted Shih tzus are a menace.'

Dunks burst out laughing which only set off Bunny. Col shot a filthy glance at each of them before stomping off, muttering under his breath.

'Oh,' said Bunny, wiping her eyes. 'That was mean.'

'Stupid little fuck deserves it,' said Dunks.

'Is it true, do you think?' Bunny asked them. 'Vanessa was in this morning and she never mentioned anything. Out of anyone she'd be sure to know.'

Lucas shrugged. 'Wouldn't surprise me.'

Dunks pointed at his chest and the falcon logo. 'He didn't do this for nothing.'

'No,' said Bunny. 'Dom's not the sort to do anything without a reason.'

Only if that reason was himself, but Lucas kept that thought contained.

They mused for a moment before Bunny tapped the sign-up sheet. 'I'm up at Belgravia on Monday. I'll see if I can't kick some bums.' She tugged up the sleeves of her jumper and began folding up the cuffs of her shirt. 'Anyway, if you're desperate I can always dig out my whites.'

Both men looked at her.

'Didn't you know?' She glanced from Dunks to Lucas and back again, a glint in her eye. 'I was in the Southern Stars. Won the World Cup back in the late eighties. I might be old but I bet I still know how to swing a bat.' And with that she strolled off.

Dunks looked at Lucas and then down at his sign-up sheet. A heartbeat later he was on his feet and hurrying after her.

'I'll man the desk, then,' Lucas called in his wake, grinning. He'd bet a week's pay those two would end up in bed tonight. Nothing turned Dunks on more than cricket.

Lucas sat down and picked up the pen, tapping it against the seven names on the sheet. Bunny was right, it was still early days. The same thing had happened last year. Dunks had been almost in tears, certain his beloved cricket team was going to fold, when there was a flurry of last-minute names. The season was still a month away. People's minds were on the rugby finals. As soon as the grand final was run, they'd be right.

Lucas continued to tap the pen, thinking of his day. Specifically, of Falls Farm and the girl he'd met.

The entire encounter had been an intriguing mix of dismissal and sexual spark. Teagan was pretty, really pretty, with glorious red hair that blazed copper and bronze and made him think of wisp-fine metal wire turned magically into silk. Her eyes were blue and cool, her features sharp and delicate, her skin pale and dappled with freckles.

She was like Vanessa but not. Where Vanessa was all sexy curves and kindness, the sort of woman whose pillowy breasts you wanted to bury your face in, Teagan was more angular and far too thin. Even so her figure was attractive, with straight shoulders that tapered to a narrow waist before flaring to slim hips. Her breasts were small but possessed the roundness and height of pert perfection. As for her legs, they were like a colt's, long and slender, and made for wrapping around a man's hips.

Though she didn't seem to be aware of it, Teagan had inherited her aunt's innate sexiness. It wasn't the same, not even close, but it smouldered. Vanessa wore her sexuality with the confidence of a mature woman who knew who she was and what she wanted. Teagan's was unselfconscious, earthy and enigmatic, and as hot as hell because of it.

The stir in his groin when she'd twirled the lead rope like a contrary cowgirl had forced him to look away and pretend deep interest in his hunt for a halter. With her jeans slung low around her hips, the movement had caused her thin jumper to rise up and expose a sliver of creamy flesh. The purity of that strip was mesmerising, and he'd been swamped with the stupid notion that touching her would be like touching something pristine and flawless, a body created just for him.

Not that that was ever going to happen anytime soon. Unlike many women on first meeting, Teagan hadn't simpered or leered once, something he found refreshing, if odd. That his looks were above average was a truth Lucas had understood since boyhood. Except for a few over-hormoned incidents during adolescence, he'd made sure not to let it go to his head, in particular when he'd learned his colouring was all due to his bastard of a father. It affected others sometimes though, and not in a way he enjoyed, leaving him occasionally resentful of the dumbness of their behaviour. Just because he'd won some sort of genetic lottery didn't make him special or blessed. Take away his attractive exterior and Lucas was just another bloke. Which was why he preferred to hang around people like Dunks and Vanessa, who took him for who he was.

There was no question that Teagan had noticed – he'd caught her checking out his arse, and casting sly glances over his arms and chest – but her overall dismissal of him wasn't contrived. She genuinely seemed to think he was a bit of a dick. Which was annoying as much as it was unusual. Lucas prided himself on being a good person. Being a prick was his father's way, not his.

Which meant that, if what Vanessa had told him was true about what her old man had done, he and Teagan at least had something in common: both their fathers were arseholes.

He finished his beer and stood. It was time for home. And maybe a dream or two about a sexy, creamy-skinned redhead.

FOUR

TEAGAN SAT on the top verandah step with her phone in her lap and her hands over her face. The phone call with her friend, Jasmine, telling her about Emily had left Teagan shaken and desperate to return home. There'd been an accident, a terrible one, but at least Em was safe. Beyond offering their love, there was nothing she or Jas could do. And home wasn't home anymore. Not now Pinehaven was lost.

She picked up the mobile and dialled Em's number. As expected it went straight to voicemail. She left a message, passing on her love and apologising for not being there. Em would understand. They'd talked about families long into the night before Teagan had left. About the messiness of them, and the power they had to hurt like nothing else.

Blanche snaked her silvery body around Teagan's legs, cheek rubbing sensually against her calf. She resisted the urge to edge the cat off the step and shifted aside instead, hoping it'd take the hint. The animal still gave her the shivers. Its resemblance to something from a horror film was quite uncanny. Any moment she expected polyps to start popping along its back and bursting. Last night she'd made sure her bedroom door was firmly shut, yet this morning Teagan had again woken with fish breath in her face. At first she'd thought the cat really was an alien, capable of teletransportation, until a hunt around had revealed the bedroom window was ajar and a corner of the fly screen unsecured.

When Teagan still refused to play, Blanche tossed her a severe look and skulked off to torment Betty and Wilma. Poor guinea pigs. It's a wonder they had any nerves left with that thing licking its lips at them all day.

Teagan leaned back on her elbows and turned her face to the sky in an attempt to ease the cold sadness from her bones. One thing about this place she appreciated was the sun. Here it was late winter and the weather was simply beautiful. No doubt in the summer, when the days turned muggy and the temperature stretched into the high thirties for days on end, she'd come to hate it, but for now she'd take it for what it was – glorious.

After a minute or two, Teagan sat up again. She scanned the front garden before stretching her gaze further afield. The slack wire of the front fence caught her attention. Her leg began to jig.

The screen door opened. Ness emerged with a tray containing glass latte mugs and the results of a baking session.

'Daydreaming? That's a good sign,' she said as Teagan rose to join her.

'Not quite.' Teagan settled into her cane chair and nodded at the tray. 'They look great.'

On a plate sat four cupcakes decorated with thick cream cheese and lemon icing. Teagan didn't have a particularly sweet tooth, but her aunt meant well. Dutifully, she picked one up and took a nibble. Like yesterday's vanilla slice, she found it surprisingly comforting.

'I hope your mind wasn't on fencing again.'

Teagan screwed up her nose.

'Darling, what did I say?'

She waved towards the lawn. 'At least let me do something with that.'

'But what would Betty and Wilma eat?'

'They're hardly starving.' This morning the two guinea pigs were chomping their way through half a broccoli head and a couple of kiwi fruit. Every time Teagan looked they were eating.

'Bunny said they like dandelion. That's why I've let the lawn go.'

Teagan rolled her head to the side to look at Ness.

Lifting her chin, Ness picked up a cupcake and began to pick at the paper case with fingernails the colour of ripe strawberries that perfectly matched her lipstick, loafers and snug-fitting T-shirt. 'That's my excuse and I'm sticking to it.'

'I need to do something, Ness. If you won't let me fix the lawn it'll have to be the fences.' And sooner rather than later. Only that morning Merlin had managed to bash his way out of his yard. He'd ambushed Teagan as she was patting Claudia good morning. Only a triumph-filled warning bleat had saved her from being pummelled into the timber fence.

At Vanessa's suggestion he'd been left on the loose and was now patrolling the yard like a woolly Doberman, pausing occasionally to regard the house with predatory eyes. Religious callers had been spotted in The Falls. Merlin might be a complete psycho but he was also a marvellous guard ram.

'You could go for a swim. It'll be a little cool, but a few laps will warm you up.'

'No bathers.'

'So go nude. I do. Or just wear your underpants. No one will see.'

Given the frequency of visitors to Falls Farm, Teagan wasn't so sure about that. 'And for the rest of the day?'

Ness took a slow sip of coffee.

'I can't keep sitting around doing nothing. I'll go mad.'

Ness put down her cup and sighed. 'There's a farm and produce store at Wilmington, in the next valley. I'll take you there Monday and you can book up what you need on my account.' She threw Teagan a stern look. 'But you will stop for morning and afternoon tea, and take a proper lunch break. Do I make myself clear?'

'Perfectly.'

Ness jutted a finger. 'And no weekends.'

Teagan was saved from answering by a car chugging up the drive.

Ness let out a groan as a pale-blue Falcon drove through the gate and rattled to a stop outside the house fence. She plastered a smile and rose, the high-waisted ecru linen trousers and bright top outlining her womanly figure. Merlin, who was picking young shoots near the shed, lifted his head.

'Colin,' she called sweetly, 'what a nice surprise.'

'Have you heard?'

Ness barely blinked. 'Heard what?'

Merlin let out an excited croak and lowered his horns.

'Oh, just the alarm,' remarked Teagan as the sheep broke into a gallop.

Colin turned, and with a yelp shot through the gate and banged it shut, retreating up the path backwards as a foiled Merlin skidded to a halt and stood panting on the other side of the fence.

'Sorry, Col,' said Ness with faultless sincerity. 'I should've warned you Merlin was out. Anyway, you were saying? What is it I've meant to have heard?'

Deciding he was safe, Col swung around and gripped the stair rail. His bald pate was completely aglow, his age spots bright in contrast, giving the unfortunate image of something having pooed all over his head. 'Expansion!'

'Oh, is Maggie finally allowing you to attach an annex to your caravan? How wonderful. You'll be able to hold canasta nights with Kathleen.'

'No.' Colin stamped his foot, causing the loose flesh of his leg to ripple in a wash of hairy wrinkles. 'The centre!'

'Goodness, are you sure? I thought it was just a fence.'

Colin's jowls wobbled as he shook his head. 'No, much worse than that. Much, much worse. Kathleen has seen the development application. New private accommodation, a hydrotherapy suite' – he uttered the words as though describing a home for lepers – 'and a complete detoxification centre.' He glanced around with narrowed eyes and lowered his voice. 'Druggies.'

'Really?' Ness clapped her hands together and placed the edges against her mouth. 'Goodness.'

Assuming from her tone that she was on his side, Colin nodded. 'We have to stop him.'

'But the fence will keep us safe, surely?'

'They have ways of escaping.' Colin tapped his nose. 'Sneaky, those druggies.'

'Bit like rams,' murmured Teagan.

'Yes.' A twitch ticked at the corner of Vanessa's mouth but she remained stoic. 'Yes, I've heard that.'

Teagan only just managed to hold in her laughter. Her aunt was incredible. The entire thing was a whole lot of rubbish, but Colin was one of those busybody types that deserved a tease.

'He never told you?'

Ness lifted her chin and sniffed. 'Domenic and I never discuss business.'

Teagan coughed on a cake crumb. Admittedly, Friday night was a bit vague, but she had a distinct memory of Dom asking Ness for help with his plans for the Wellness Centre.

'Are you all right, darling?'

'Fine,' Teagan squeaked, her eyes watering. 'Went down the wrong way.'

Col began to wring his hands. 'What are we going to do?'

Ness released a long sigh. 'Domenic is a wealthy man, Colin, who I'm sure has already done his homework and has the council onside. I'm not certain there's much we can do.' Her gaze drifted upwards as though calling on a higher power for inspiration. A finger slowly rose to her lips. 'Unless . . .'

Colin jigged with hope.

Ness paused, then nodded to herself as though decided. Her hand dropped and her shoulders straightened. 'Talk to Kathleen. She'll know what to do.'

Bewilderment turned Colin's face hangdog and his voice whiny. 'But it was Kathleen who told me to talk to you.'

Ness spread her hands. 'I'm afraid you need an old head for this, Colin. Someone who understands exactly where one fence can lead.' She regarded him sternly. 'In situations like these you need wisdom and prudence. I'm afraid I'm liable to become too hot-headed. And hotheads make mistakes. The village needs people like you, Colin. People with fortitude, who can make a stand, bring others into their learned fold.'

Colin sucked on his false teeth. 'You're right.' He puffed out his chest. 'Definitely one for wise heads. I'll get on it right away.' With a gallant half-bow, he scuttled off.

Ness remained at the top of the verandah stairs like a general having sent her soldier into battle. As soon as the car disappeared down the slope, Merlin in hot pursuit, she bent double and released a roar of laughter.

Teagan could only watch in wonder. 'You're amazing, you know that?'

When Ness had finished laughing and collapsed back into her chair, she sat for a long moment with a smile on her face. Then she sobered and sighed. 'I suppose I should call Dom.'

'What for? He'll figure it out soon enough.'

Ness turned to her. 'A word of advice. If anyone asks, don't take sides. The Falls isn't like Levenham. It's a lot smaller and a lot more intense. Things like this have a way of getting out of hand. And believe me, you don't want to be caught up in the whirlwind if they do.'

Teagan spent the remainder of Sunday with deep purpose. She walked the entire property, notebook in hand, making a shopping list and setting priorities.

She was beginning to alter her opinion of Falls Farm. On first look it seemed a rundown property on a series of unproductive slopes, with poor improvements and half the place left to return to scrub. But closer inspection revealed good alluvial soils and remnants of what must have once been productive pasture.

The creek, although eroded in some parts, was pretty, its water gurgling like a contented baby as it flowed shallowly over the worn rocks below. Teagan had even discovered a bower bird's nest in the scrub on the opposite side, the bird's carefully arranged hoard of treasures made even brighter thanks to its collection of sky-blue bottle tops, washed, she guessed, down the waterway from the road. And a sad indictment of how far even the smallest piece of tossed rubbish could spread. Many of the plants appeared native. Cabbage and swamp gums were common, as were acacias, but there were a few plants she didn't recognise or like the look of, along with a nasty stand of lantana that would need to be dealt with.

The fences were uniformly appalling. Claudia's was by far the least dilapidated, but that wasn't saying much. Other than the main gate and the house fence, with their expensive wrought-iron decoration, Ness appeared to have spent nothing on the others. Although she had to concede that her aunt probably couldn't see the point when the only animals being contained were a laminitis-affected horse and a randy ram.

Satisfied that she had herself organised, Teagan collected a bucket of brushes from the shed and carried it down to Claudia's paddock. The afternoon was closing, the air cooling with it, but insects still maintained their industrious hum and the scrub's bellbirds continued their sweet piping. Her thoughts drifted to Astra, her heart squeezing at the pain of their separation. If only Teagan could have brought her along.

The horse was more than a pretty showhorse, she was a friend. Steady and forgiving. Astra had been the one Teagan had sobbed her heart out to this last year, whose nuzzles had helped keep her despair at bay when it had threatened to smother her completely. She hoped the filly wasn't too distressed or giving Jas too much trouble. In the aftermath of the drama surrounding the Wallace-Jones family, Astra had been temporarily relocated from Rocking Horse Hill, along with Em's horse, Lod, to Jasmine's small acreage near Admella Beach.

Teagan grimaced and swept a body brush over Claudia's thick coat. Astra wasn't hers now anyway. She was Em's. Time to forget about her, like she needed to with Pinehaven.

So easy to think. So impossible to do.

'Not quite in the same league, are you, Claudia?' But the piebald was a lovely old thing regardless. Gentle-natured and with a constitution tough enough to survive terrible privations and injury.

The sound of an engine had her looking up the hill. Lucas's ute appeared at the crest and coasted down towards her.

'G'day,' he said, emerging from his car with a twinkling smile. His hair was loose today, swept back from his forehead and brushing almost to his shoulders. The necklace was still in place – a sort of Art Nouveau swirl made of hammered steel. She'd been intrigued by it yesterday and itched to ask what the design meant, but guardedness had kept her quiet.

'Hello.' She gave Claudia's rump another sweep of the brush. 'Come to check on your patient again?'

Lucas folded his arms across the top rail. 'Something like that.'

Teagan waited for him to comment further but he seemed in no hurry for conversation. She carried on, trying not to feel self-conscious under his scrutiny, but the memory of his 'too skinny' comment had risen and she wished she'd worn a baggy work shirt instead of the old soft tee that cupped her hollow belly and hung loose around her collarbone.

Claudia's tail was a mess of tangles. Teagan swapped the body brush for a comb and settled into sorting it out.

'You must miss your horse,' Lucas said finally.

She clenched her teeth, wishing she'd never mentioned Astra to him. The pain was still too acute. Only bringing up her parents would have been worse. 'I do but she's not mine anymore.'

'I bet she still is.' He patted the left side of his chest. 'In your heart.'

The truth of the observation resurrected all the agony of her loss. A rough ache settled in her throat. Talk would only expose it. Keeping her head down, she let his words melt unanswered into the afternoon, and concentrated on a particularly tricky knot woven with twigs.

'I could help you find another one, if you wanted.'

She had to swallow hard before it felt safe to talk. 'Thanks, but I'll be okay.' She let the knot drop. It would have to be cut out. She crouched at the bucket and dug for a knife or scissors, eyes darting to the fence and back, trying to get a feel for what he wanted. Surely Lucas Knight had better things to do than talk to her.

'Too soon?'

'Yeah. Plus I don't know how long I'll be here for.'

A *whuppa-whuppa* sound clouded the air. They both looked up, tracking the noise as it came closer. A blood-red helicopter appeared. It flew low over the farm before turning a sharp left and was lost past the tree line of the creek.

'Do you like cricket?' Lucas asked suddenly.

'It's okay.' Teagan paused and resumed her hunt for something sharp. 'My brother, Owen, used to play when he lived at home. Club cricket, not grade. I used to watch him occasionally.' Her hand closed around the handle of a bot knife, a special tool for scraping bot fly eggs off a horse's coat. She held it up and ran her thumb over the edge. Too pitted and worn. She tossed it back and regarded Lucas again. 'I prefer football. Much better for a perve.'

'Not impressed by the thunder of a fast bowler?'

'Hard to beat a good full forward.'

He frowned and then understood. 'Australian rules football. I forgot you were from the south. It's mostly rugby up here.'

'I take it you're a fast bowler, then.'

'Medium pace. The team workhorse.' He grinned in a way that seemed to ignite the afternoon, straight, pure and loaded with genuine good humour. A bloke who found the world a pretty damn happy place. 'My job is to grind them down with boredom.'

'I couldn't imagine you being boring.'

'I can be all sorts of things, if I try.'

'Hmm,' she answered, undecided if he was flirting. He couldn't be. Not genuinely. Not with her. Teagan was dirty, smelled like horse and was wearing the ugliest T-shirt imaginable.

She retrieved the comb from the bucket and rose to tug it through Claudia's knot, accidentally tearing out a couple of long white hairs in the process. The horse shuffled. She shushed her and stroked her rump, the discomfort she'd caused the horse making her feel even more flustered.

Teagan couldn't help a quick fantasy of Lucas playing sport. He possessed the sort of body that spoke of prowess as well as power. Boring would never be in his repertoire. He certainly didn't look boring today in those snug-fitting faded jeans. God, the man was built. He had a nice profile, too. Kind of noble, with his hair smoothed back. All the better to regard her with dancing blue eyes that seemed to soak her up.

'Did you want Claudia? I'm just mucking about here.'

'Actually, it's you I'm after.'

Teagan stilled, blinking. 'Me?'

Lucas shot her another of his dazzling grins. 'Yep. You're meant to be up at the house. Afternoon drinks.'

At the mention of drinks Teagan winced. Her aunt was proving a formidable mixologist. Last night it had been fruit-and-mint-filled jugs of Pimms, a drink Teagan had never had before but which proved rather addictive. 'Not margaritas I hope.'

'No. That's a Friday special. Vanessa's Sunday special is kir royale.' Clocking her clueless expression, he explained. 'Champagne with a dash of cassis. It's good.' He shoved his hands in his pockets and tilted his head. 'Come on.'

Teagan regarded the knot and gave up. She'd return with scissors tomorrow and cut it out. Not that it'd be noticeable. Claudia had more than enough tail hair to cover the gap.

Lucas didn't push when she refused a lift back in his ute. Teagan wanted time to recover from her discomposure and the pathetic disappointment that his appearance was thanks to Vanessa's invitation. Something that must happen often given how familiar he was with her aunt's cocktail-hour schedule. A teensy part of Teagan had hoped Lucas was there to see her, but she should have known that was ridiculous. Yet he had a way of looking at her with a tease in his eye and a grin that made her stomach flip-flop, and kept fuelling the dumb thought that they might represent a modicum of interest.

A champagne bucket and bottle of dangerously purple liqueur was already laid out on the table when Teagan arrived at the verandah. Lucas was resting comfortably against the rail, while Ness lounged in her cane chair with one slim leg crossed over the other. She'd changed into jeans and a pair of very high-heeled cork-soled mules. Her fitted shirt was unbuttoned just enough for a teasing hint of cleavage. From his vantage point, Lucas had to be scoring more than a hint.

The knowledge tightened Teagan's insecurity further.

'Darling, how did you get on?'

'Okay.' She tugged her notebook from her back pocket. 'I made a list.'

'Teagan's going to repair my fences,' Ness said to Lucas. 'She might need a hand.'

'I've been fixing fences since I was a kid. I'll be fine.'

Lucas held her eye. 'I don't mind helping.'

'Never pass up the help of a strong man, Teagan.'

A statement that caused Teagan to peek at Lucas's arms, the way his biceps stretched the sleeves of his polo shirt, the power of his forearms. Even his hands seemed fit. How could any woman work with that around?

'Like I said, I'll be fine. Excuse me a moment,' she said, pulling open the screen door. 'I smell like Claudia and need to wash up.'

In the bathroom she rested her forehead against the cool tiles. How utterly mortifying to be treated like a gauche teenager who needed her aunt to play matchmaker. Fantasies were one thing but Teagan didn't want a relationship. With Lucas or anyone else. Not with her head the way it was.

When she returned the drinks were poured, and a bowl of olives was on the table. Ness handed her and then Lucas a champagne flute and picked up her own, raising it in a toast. She smiled at Teagan. 'To new beginnings.'

Lucas winked. 'Definitely.'

Teagan took a long gulp of champagne and turned away, feigning interest in Merlin's headbutting activity. The ram was back in his yard and up to his old tricks. His dedication to the task was impressive.

'Col been around?' asked Lucas.

Ness sighed. 'This morning. He could barely contain himself.'

'Same as in the club last night. Bunny strung him along a beauty. Said she was going to ring Dom about providing rehabilitation services for drug-addled Shih tzus and pets with attachment issues.'

'Ah, Bunny, I so love that woman.' Ness took a thoughtful sip of champagne. 'Although it's not a bad idea. Dom probably has clients nutty enough to go for it.'

'She could run feline yoga classes.'

'Or reiki for Rottweilers.'

'Polarity therapy for pugs.'

'Aromatherapy for Afghans.'

The pair of them cracked up. Teagan dipped her head, feeling left out and devoid of charm. Blanche tiptoed her way along the rail towards her. She was the ugliest cat imaginable, but Teagan felt a strange urge to cuddle her to her chest. Before the cat could reach her, she turned back to the others. She wasn't that needy yet.

'Did you know she played for the Australian women's cricket team?' Lucas's voice was full of admiration.

'Of course. She won a World Cup.'

'You never said.'

'I figured you knew. Certainly I thought Mark would have.'

'Nope. None of us had a clue until last night. Dunks is beside himself.'

'I can imagine.' Ness smiled at the thought. 'Those two are made for one another, if only they could see it.'

'Give them time, they'll work it out.' Lucas took a sip of his drink. Teagan watched the movement, thinking how incongruous his big hand appeared around the flute's delicate stem. There were scars and nicks on his skin, as she'd expect for a farrier, but other marks, too. Small pale scars that extended up his forearms and looked more like burns. 'So what did you tell Col?'

'I told him this needed wise heads and to talk to Kathleen. That ought to help keep a lid on things for a while. With a bit of luck they'll simply sit around complaining until it's too late.'

'I'm guessing it's too late already. If he's submitted the DA.' He addressed Teagan. 'Have you seen it yet, the Wellness Centre?'

She shook her head. 'I haven't been anywhere except here.'

'Not even into the village?'

'Not yet.'

'Gird your loins. It's a festering hive of intrigue and misdeeds.'

Ness poked him with her toe. 'Stop it. The Falls is a perfectly nice place.'

'If you don't count Colin.' He addressed Teagan again. 'So you haven't even seen the actual falls yet, the waterfall the village is named after? It's worth a visit. I'll take you to see it, if you want.'

Convinced he was being polite and didn't mean it, Teagan gave a noncommittal nod.

The dozy quiet of evening was broken by a chopper sounding overhead.

Ness grimaced at the sound. 'Callum heading back to town, I imagine. Pity he wouldn't stay there.'

'At least he put his name down and paid his dues,' said Lucas.

'Which is more than can be said for some. Anyway, you're the one who sold him the block.'

'Something I'm beginning to regret.'

A loud honk had them looking towards the drive. The chopper had drowned out the car's arrival and now a sleek black Mercedes that Teagan recognised from Friday night was purring into the yard.

Dom alighted and strode towards the verandah, taking the steps two at a time, like a man arriving home. He nodded at Teagan, addressing her as he made his way to Ness. 'Feeling better?'

'Yes thanks.' She cleared her throat. 'And thanks for . . .' She waved vaguely towards the house.

'No problem. My business gives me plenty of experience in handling that sort of thing.'

Teagan could feel Lucas's questioning gaze but kept her eyes averted. Margarita night was something she was in no hurry to discuss. Especially with him.

Dom bent to kiss Ness on the cheek before nodding coolly at Lucas. 'Lucas.'

'Domenic,' Lucas replied even more coolly in return.

Ness was already tugging the champagne bottle from the ice bucket. 'Kir?'

Dom glanced at Lucas before nodding. 'Thank you.'

'You stay here.' She touched the back of his hand. 'Talk to Teagan and Lucas while I fetch a glass.'

He smiled briefly as though acquiescing, only to take Vanessa's elbow when she rose and escort her into the house, head bent closely towards hers. Teagan followed their progress with a frown, not liking the intense expression on Dom's face. She hoped he wasn't about to make accusations about whoever spilled his expansion plans, but his voice was too low for her to make out the words.

She glanced at Lucas. His gaze was also on Ness and Dom, his expression hostile as they disappeared from view. He downed the rest of his kir in one gulp and placed the empty flute on the table, easy manner and sparkling humour gone. Teagan stared into her drink. So that was the way it went. Lucas would rather retreat than bear witness to the seductive charm of a rival.

'Let me know if you need a hand with the fencing,' he said. 'My place is just up the road. I can easily swing by when things are quiet. I don't mind helping out with the heavy stuff for half an hour or so.'

'Thanks, but I really should be okay.'

'Tough girl, huh?'

'That's me.' She struck a brief muscleman pose that made him chuckle but didn't change his mind about staying.

She watched him pause to pat Saffy as he passed and crouch quickly to inspect Betty and Wilma. Then he opened his ute door and raised his hand a final time in farewell.

Ness emerged with a tray of more food as the ute's tail-lights fell away. Her lips thinned. 'I really wish he wouldn't do that.' She set down the tray, snatched the champagne flute from Dom's hand and filled it. A trickle of cassis followed. Her tone clearly annoyed, she said, 'I don't know what it is between you two, but whatever it is, it's silly and I wish you'd stop.'

But Dom was staring towards the drive with a strange expression and didn't answer.

FIVE

'THESE,' said Vanessa, after ordering Teagan to slow down, 'are our village shops. The bakery is lovely. Kathleen Ferguson, who serves most days, is not. Actually, that's probably a little unkind. She's just a small-minded busybody like Col, who hates change.'

Teagan laughed. 'That's hardly an improvement.'

'I know. I'm sorry, but the woman rubs me up the wrong way and sometimes it's a terrible effort to maintain my temper.'

Vanessa pointed across the bitumen carpark, still glistening and puddled from the remains of Sunday night's showers. In a few hours, it'd be dull once more thanks to another unseasonably warm day. Vanessa was glad for it. Sunshine always made life brighter, and if anyone needed brightening up it was Teagan.

'That's Bunny's practice. You'll meet her Thursday night. She's coming around for drinks. Assuming she isn't waylaid, of course. Vets are notorious for being late. That's the newsagent-cum-post office, which Antonio, bless him, half-heartedly runs. The IGA belongs to Gus and Debbie Anderson. Nice couple, the sort that volunteer for everything even though they don't have time. Country folk from way back who had to sell their farm when they couldn't last another

drought. Poor darlings, they must miss it.' Realising the reminder
she'd just given Teagan, Vanessa quickly indicated the chemist and
doctor's surgery. 'Perfectly serviceable for an emergency, but I prefer
my own doctor in town. More than happy to get you an appointment
if you need one.'

'I'm not planning on getting sick.'

'None of us ever do, but these things happen.' Vanessa held back
on saying she suspected deeply that Teagan already was ill, maybe
not in body but definitely in mind. Although, to be fair, her niece
seemed a little cheerier this morning. Perhaps all she needed was
some undisturbed sleep.

Certainly the charcoal smudges of fatigue beneath her eyes
weren't as harsh, and the worry lines – so distressing to see on
someone so young and pretty – had eased. But three days after arrival
Teagan still wasn't eating well, picking at her food and poking it into
the edges of her plate, and she was consuming alcohol with little
restraint. Vanessa hoped she wouldn't have to resort to going dry. She
so enjoyed her cocktails and company. It reminded her of the joyful
days of her past, before things had turned sour and sad. And dinner
without wine was too uncivilised to contemplate.

She continued her narrative, careful to keep the worry out of her
voice. 'The takeaway is run by Antonio's sister. She's nice, too,
although unfortunately not a fan of mine. If you ever need to drop in
for fish and chips perhaps it's best not to mention that you're staying
at Falls Farm. I wouldn't put it past her to spit in the batter.'

She pointed out the rural fire brigade and the bowling club, and a
few of her favourite locals' houses until the village passed and the
road went back to eighty kilometres an hour. Suddenly, a two-metre-
high, barbed-wire-topped cyclone fence began to stretch down the
side of the road. Inside it, a thick stand of lilly-pilly formed a lush
hedge, offering only short glimpses of the manicured property
beyond. The fence ended, replaced by a large rendered brick wall
that continued for fifty metres before sweeping inwards to form the
entrance to a large driveway. Tall wrought gates topped with brass

fleur-de-lis spikes stood closed. A plaque on the wall – matched on the opposite wing of the entrance where the wall continued – spelled out 'The Falls Wellness Centre' in shiny brass lettering. Below, in smaller print, ran the line, 'By Appointment Only'.

Teagan let out a whistle and hunched over the steering wheel for a closer look. 'Bloody hell.'

Vanessa's reaction had been similar when she'd first spied the centre eleven years ago. It was far less established then and under different management, but still impressive. Impressiveness that took on new meaning under Dom's captaincy.

His vision was broad and inspired. He had the innate ability to recognise and fulfil clients' desires. Women, in particular, who comprised the majority of his business. He understood their need for privacy and luxury, as well as the scope to find healing. Vanessa had learned long ago that women possessed a limitless capacity to lay burdens on themselves. Dom, with his astute eye and attention to detail, had created a place where they could ease those loads in a way that made them feel strong instead of weak.

Although hidden from the road, the complex radiated out from the property's original historic homestead. A large, very modern reception building welcomed guests as though they were checking into an exclusive hotel. From there, clients were escorted by their personal attendant to their suite inside the homestead or to one of the hidden villas that dotted the pristine, designer-landscaped grounds. Depending on their requirements, guests were free to range and relax, availing themselves of the centre's various spa facilities and activity studios, or were guided through a tailored treatment program.

While most staff were skilled in natural therapies, the centre also boasted trained medical staff, including nurses, psychologists, and a full-time doctor, with specialist practitioners available on call. Although not well-publicised, this formed the more serious side of the business, where the focus was on addiction and mental health issues, and which accounted for Dom's obsession with confidentiality. It was much easier for someone to cover up treatment of a serious disorder with the airy proclamation that they were enjoying a week or more of pampered luxury. Without insider knowledge, no one could prove otherwise.

It seemed odd to have this exclusive, privacy-obsessed centre so close to a village where everyone knew everyone else's business. But as had been proven over the weekend, even the best-kept secrets can leak out. Most of the professional staff lived elsewhere, in the McMansions of the ever-expanding western suburbs or up in the bush-coated mountains, and travelled to work. The more menial positions tended to be filled by locals. A place of the centre's size required a brigade of cleaners and cooks and gardeners. All staff were bound by strict confidentiality agreements, and those Dom currently employed tended to be the more reliable of the locals. With the expansion he might be forced to take on others he'd previously rejected, the ones with fewer scruples. Sadly, The Falls wasn't short on those.

As they cruised past, an approaching black Humvee with heavily tinted windows slowed and indicated. Triggered by remote, the gate began to ease open. Teagan decelerated even further as the two cars passed, staring out the side window with her mouth slightly agape. Smiling, Vanessa waved at the driver, Andrejus, who remained stony-faced behind the windscreen. She dropped her hand. Andrejus was a sweet man, but deeply professional when on a job and unlikely to have recognised her in the battered Landcruiser anyway.

Out of curiosity, she used the side mirror to watch the Humvee turn into the centre's drive and slide through the gates, Teagan doing the same in the rear-vision mirror. They wouldn't see anyone. Whoever the arrival was, their identity would be hidden all the way to their private room.

'Another of Domenic's famous clients?' asked Teagan, speeding up.

'Probably. Although he has had the occasional North Shore bride check in with her bridesmaids for a few days of indulgence.'

'Sounds like fun.'

'I wouldn't be so sure about that. With the exception of Dom's private quarters, the centre is strictly alcohol-free.' She laughed at Teagan's screwed-up nose. 'I know, but it's proved rather necessary. A few years ago one of Dom's more desperate clients was caught glugging from a bottle of alcohol rub used in massage therapy. Had to be rushed off for a stomach pump. Now even the mouthwash is alcohol-free.'

Teagan gave a shudder. 'I can't imagine ever being that desperate. Have you been inside?'

'Only to use the spa facilities. Dom treats me to a pamper session every year for my birthday and occasionally at Christmas. It's beautiful. Complete indulgence. Very quiet too, like being in your own private palace. Dom said they provide group therapy with certain drug- and alcohol-treatment programs, but mostly it's just you and the staff who are all quiet as church mice.'

'What do you have done?'

Vanessa waved a hand. 'Oh, the usual. Sauna, spa, massage. I did have one of the naturopaths try to talk me into a coffee enema once. Colonic hydrotherapy they call it.'

'Yuck.'

'Quite. Coffee is for oral consumption only.' She stroked a finger along the dirty window. 'Although Dom said some cancer sufferers find it beneficial as a complementary treatment. It helps them cope with the pain. I guess if you were in that position you'd try anything for relief. Poor loves.'

'Sounds like quackery to me. I mean, there's no scientific basis for this stuff so why encourage it?'

Vanessa frowned at Teagan's unsympathetic tone. She may not have had that much to do with her niece over the years, but she'd never remembered her like this. Teagan had always been a kind child, especially with animals. As a little girl, whenever Vanessa visited, Teagan could barely wait to show her aunt around the farm. She'd tug on her hand and demand her aunt come see her pony, newly dropped lambs or calves, or one of the working dog's bundle of squirming puppies. And all the time she would babble about her friends and their horses, asking if Vanessa had any pets in Italy, what her life was like, if she could come visit. She was a darling girl, happy and carefree.

So different to the thin, anxious woman sitting next to her.

'Perhaps it is quackery,' said Vanessa. 'But a lot of people are happy to pay a lot of money for the centre's holistic approach to health and wellbeing, including the use of non-conventional therapies. And, really, if it makes them feel better within themselves, who are we to judge?'

'Yeah, but if it's all bullshit . . .' Teagan stared at the road, mouth thin and her hands tense on the wheel. 'Remember Nanny Bliss?' She glanced at Vanessa to check if she did. Although Vanessa had had very little to do with Graham's family, she nodded, curious as to where this was going. 'She was into all that stuff. Cupboards full of powders and pills. Forced it on to Pop too. Fat lot of good it did them. Pop died of a massive stroke and she ended up in a home with Alzheimer's. The way she died was horrible.'

'One didn't cause the other, Teagan.'

'I'm not saying that it did. But that doesn't take away from the fact it was a complete waste of money. Not to mention hope.' She jerked her chin toward the centre's fence. 'Do you think Dom believes in all that rubbish?'

'Oh yes. If it earns money, Dom believes.'

Her niece gave a grunt of disgust.

'It's a business. He provides a service people want and they're willing to pay a lot for it.'

'Still a rip-off though, isn't it? Like Dad with his contracts for difference. The company he got involved in? They told him they had a sure-fire program able to predict market movements. All he had to do was buy in on the contracts at the right time to take advantage of the arbitrage effect. Naturally, they got a cut of every transaction, regardless of whether it was a gain or loss.' She shook her head, her tone unforgiving and harsh. 'Anyone could've seen it was no better than gambling.' She gestured towards the endless stretch of cyclone wire and lilly-pilly hedge. 'They were preying on people's vulnerabilities and ignorance, just like in there. It's wrong.'

'Maybe. But we're all adults. With free will to make our own decisions whether they're good or bad.'

Teagan brushed a hand across her forehead. 'I know.' She breathed out a long breath. 'It just makes me so angry. How could he be so stupid? How could Mum? And to take me down with them?' She wrung her hands around the wheel, mouth like a slit, a crack forming in her voice. 'I know they're my parents, Ness, that I'm meant to love them, but right now all I feel is bitter. I hate them for what they did even more that I hate the rip-off merchants who sucked Dad into this mess.'

Pained by the distress that seemed to leach from her niece in sour waves, Vanessa reached across the ute to curl her hand around Teagan's tense forearm.

'Don't do this. Don't let yourself be defined by what happened. Think of all you can start rebuilding.'

Tears sparkled. Teagan cleared her throat as though embarrassed and took several deep breaths before glancing across the ute with a pleading expression that made Vanessa want to hug her as she had when her niece was a little girl. 'Like what?'

Vanessa smiled as though she possessed all the answers in the world. She indicated the road and the turnoff to Wilmington, where the farm supplies store was located. 'Fences, darling. Fences!'

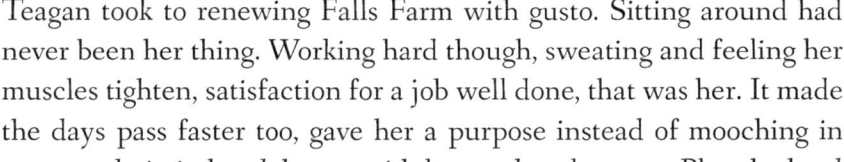

Teagan took to renewing Falls Farm with gusto. Sitting around had never been her thing. Working hard though, sweating and feeling her muscles tighten, satisfaction for a job well done, that was her. It made the days pass faster too, gave her a purpose instead of mooching in anger and victimhood, heavy with loss and uselessness. Plus the hard work made her end-of-day swim and cocktails feel earned instead of lazy and decadent.

Too nervous to skinny-dip, she wore knickers and a lycra singlet top until, after a day trip into the Sydney CBD on Wednesday, Ness returned with a white designer-label bikini. Teagan was more of a plain black racing swimsuit girl, and the bikini was embarrassingly brief, but she was grateful for her aunt's thoughtfulness. Regarding herself in the mirror, she had to concede it didn't look too bad. The colour gave her skin a lush pink hue instead of its usual vampire white, and brought out highlights in her red hair. Only her bony rib cage and hips spoiled the picture and made her look aside, biting her lip.

Teagan still couldn't get over the weather up here. The nights remained cool but the days were absolutely glorious, with temperatures in the low to mid twenties. Ness said those maximums were unusual for the time of year, but neither of them was complaining, nor were the animals from the way they took to lazing around in the sun. Although Blanche, the evil-minded thing, multi-tasked, diligently combining her sunbaking with guinea-pig tormenting.

Teagan started work not long after dawn and learned quickly to take her promised breaks. If she forgot, Ness would stomp to wherever she was labouring and order her to down tools, standing grumpily with her hands on her hips until Teagan obeyed. Given the early starts, her aunt refused to let her work beyond afternoon tea, no matter how she pleaded. Which left nothing else to do but to either play with Claudia or the other animals, or swim.

Today, she'd finished repairing the fence behind the main shed and now Merlin was free to roam in his own paddock. How long that would last Teagan wasn't sure. The rabid ram was already attacking the gateposts in an attempt to loosen them. But she'd used ringlock for the rest of the fence, straining it tight, and any attack saw Merlin bounce off, much to his bleaty frustration.

After a quick wash, Teagan headed for her room to put on the bikini, using a chock to hold her door closed. Ness had promised to find someone to fix the faulty latch but so far nothing had been done. Ready, she opened the door and immediately held out a foot as Blanche attempted to dart inside. She toed the cat away, trying not to shudder at the way it drooped over her foot like a piece of slime. It was as if the thing had no bones at all.

The water was bliss, warm enough to be pleasant but cool enough to soak away the heat and hard work of the day. She swam laps before gliding to the middle to lie on her back with her eyes closed in an effort to clear her thoughts. She sang songs in her head, concentrated on the metallic pings of the water, yet no matter how she tried, her mind remained filled with memories of Pinehaven.

And each passing image brought another slow leak of tears.

'Mind if I join you?'

Teagan splashed and turned in fright, swallowing a gush of water as she did. She emerged coughing and hacking with her hair plastered over the front of her face, cutting off her vision. She swept it back, only for the pound in her heart to hammer even worse when she saw who stood at the edge of the pool.

She opened her mouth and shut it, then looked around in a panic. Her towel was thrown over the far seat of the outdoor setting. She'd have to walk a good five metres in her bikini to fetch it, exposing every bony inch of her underweight frame to Lucas.

'Don't worry,' he said, in his deep, smile-filled voice. 'I grew out of peeing in the pool. You're safe.'

She glanced back at him again and found herself repeating her gormless cod-mouth gape, only this time it wasn't due to shock. The man had abs. A full-on six pack. And hair. A sexy line of it that traced across his chest and down to the top of his board shorts. For some reason she'd expected him to be hairless. One of those blokes who went for waxing because it made his muscles stand out better. But here he was, radiating manliness like Adonis come to life.

Ness appeared through the French doors, looking even more glamorous than normal in an exquisitely cut white shift dress with black lace detail at the waist, towering black-and-white heels, and a silver-and-diamond tennis bracelet that shot kaleidoscope sparks with each swing of her arm. 'Sorry, darling, I hope you don't mind. Lucas sometimes comes over for a swim after a busy day. You don't mind sharing, do you?'

Teagan shrugged, pretending nonchalance when all she could think about was how fast she could escape the pool without Lucas noticing. 'Not at all.'

What else could she say? This wasn't her house. This wasn't even meant to be her life.

Lucas gave her a knowing look before rounding the pool to the deep end and diving in with a graceful arc. She retreated to the side and watched him swim three laps, his stroke smooth and easy, his kick strong. She glanced at Ness but her aunt wasn't watching Lucas, she was watching Teagan, a kind smile on her face. Then with a flash-filled wave she clip-clopped off on her high heels, leaving Teagan alone with Lucas.

He glided to a stop at the wall opposite and scraped his long hair away from his face. 'You've been working hard by the looks of things.'

'There's a lot that needs doing. And I want to help my aunt.'

'Not because you're bored?'

She fanned the water in front of her and watched the ripples. How did he know that? She continued to concentrate on the water, the way the sun caught the tiny waves and refracted it in rainbow colours. But the man across from her made the natural world seem faded and drab, drawing her gaze in fish-dart glances.

His jaw showed a shadow of pale stubble. Droplets clung to his long eyelashes and reflected sunlight from the water made his blue eyes seem even brighter. The power of his looks made Teagan even more self-conscious. She crossed one arm over her chest to grip the opposite shoulder, feeling naked and vulnerable.

He tilted his head. 'You should come out with me one morning.'

'Why?'

'Check out the area. Get some horse time in.'

'Thanks, but I have Claudia.'

He carried on as though her coolness meant nothing. 'I'm heading up to Belgravia tomorrow. It's an equestrian centre not far from here. Showjumpers, performance horses. Full service agistment for ponies and hacks. They do trail riding, too. Want to come?'

Teagan shook her head. An equestrian centre would only make her feel worse about her lot. As Ness said, she needed to rebuild, look to the future, not wallow.

In a smooth glide, Lucas crossed the pool to join her against the wall. God, he was stunning to look at. Almost too vivid, too fantasy-land. She turned away, wishing he'd disappear to somewhere else. Wishing she could do the same, but her jutting bones had her anchored.

He rested his head back. For several seconds he said nothing, then he rolled to the side to look at her. 'I'm not what you think.'

She raised her eyebrows at him. 'Mind reader, are you?'

'Maybe.' He smiled lazily. 'You think I'm a bit of a wanker.'

Embarrassment crawled from her belly all the way to her neck and face. Ness had been talking. She closed her arm tighter over her chest, fingers digging into her shoulder as she focused hard on the pool's infinity edge, studying the surreal merge of water and space.

He remained quiet, waiting. Only the water ripples and birdsong tuning the air. This was ridiculous. So what if he was good-looking. She had more gumption than this.

Teagan dropped her arm and rolled her head in a mirror pose to Lucas. 'And are you?'

A quirk tilted his lips. He pressed closer. 'Sometimes. But I prefer the real thing.'

His breath teased the moisture on her skin, shooting goosebumps over her flesh. His eyes slid to her mouth and the waterline where her breasts bobbed, pebbled nipples pushing against the thin fabric of her bikini. A look that made her heart rear and thump down before tearing into a panicked, breath-stealing gallop.

The urge to cover up was enormous, as was the urge to bolt from the fear he'd unleashed. Fear of this not being real, of being used, of being rejected in a world where she already had no place. Instead she firmed her chin and tilted it up. 'Don't we all.' And with that, she duck-dived to the bottom of the pool and swam as far as she could underwater. When she broke the surface, Lucas was close by.

She glared at him, whipped words defending her racing feelings. 'Do you mind?'

'Mind what?'

'I'm trying to enjoy a swim.'

'And I'm trying to enjoy you.'

'You? Enjoy me?'

'Yeah, why not?'

'Because you're,' she waved a finger at his face and chest, at his unreal looks and body, at the sheer impossibility of him, 'you, that's why.'

'And? Teagan, I'm just your average bloke.'

She rolled her eyes. 'Who just happens to look like a movie star.'

'You think so? Which one?'

Teagan couldn't help it, his cheek was too much. She laughed and splashed water at him. 'Idiot.'

Smug that he'd at last penetrated her prickly exterior, Lucas grinned. Sweeping a muscled arm through the water, he caught her hand. 'Come on. Life's too short to live it worrying about crap that doesn't count. Have some fun.' He swept her backwards. They drifted on their backs, staring at the sky.

The enormous blue expanse brought on another wave of vulnerability. This time she had no defence, only truth. 'I'm not sure I know how anymore.'

'Then let me show you.'

'Wouldn't you rather be playing with my aunt?'

'No.'

'Isn't that why you're here though?'

'No.' He lowered his legs to float vertically. Remembering her fleshless frame, currently on full exposure, Teagan quickly followed suit. 'Vanessa and I are friends, nothing more.' He cupped the point of her shoulder. 'I prefer to play in my own age group.'

'Ageist.'

He drifted closer, gaze dropping to her mouth. 'Yeah.'

Teagan's insides buzzed so violently it was as though someone had plugged her into a power socket. How the hell did this happen? How was it even possible? Yet Lucas was surveying her with heart-stopping intensity, as if this weren't some indolent afternoon game but serious.

He floated even closer, only to draw away at the clatter of heels on timber.

'Oh.' Ness smiled broadly, obviously delighted by what she'd witnessed. 'Sorry. I just wanted to mention that Bunny's arrived. But you two darlings take your time.' She made a shooing motion, as though telling them to get back on with it. 'Bunny and I have plenty to catch up on.' She gave another tinkly wave and clattered off.

Teagan glanced at her towel then back at Lucas. No way was she staying now. Not after that embarrassing near miss. 'You can get out first.'

He shook his head. 'Can't.'

'Why not?'

He looked down at himself and back up, one eyebrow raised.

'You're kidding?'

'Nope.'

Teagan didn't know whether to be flattered, excited or appalled that his mind had even drifted in that direction when she was still trying to get her head around the idea that one, Lucas wasn't interested in Vanessa, and two, he might actually want to kiss her. Then Teagan remembered his 'too skinny' comment and what little hope she'd harnessed deflated. One look at her xylophone ribs and he'd be put off for life.

'I can't get out either.'

He blinked several times, his confused, little-boy-lost frown strangely appealing. 'Did I miss something?' Nose slightly screwed up, he eyed the water where she floated. 'Like a penis or something?'

'No!'

'Then what?'

Teagan's face burned. 'My bikini's too brief.'

That made him laugh. 'That's a matter of opinion.'

'You can see everything,' she mumbled, refusing to look at him.

He stopped grinning. The tease disappeared from his voice and his tone became gentle. 'Hey.'

'It's not pretty. My hips stick out.'

He shrugged. 'They're just bones. I have a good enough imagination to picture what you'll be like with meat on them.' Suddenly he grinned another sparkle-toothed smile. 'I'll let you feel mine if you let me feel yours.'

She splashed water at him. 'Cut it out.' She stared morosely at her towel. It was either stay here and have whatever was going on between them escalate into something ridiculous, not to mention dangerous, or make a run for it. She held up a finger. 'Don't look. I mean it.'

'Come on, Teags, a bloke's allowed to perve.'

'It's Teagan, *Lukey*, and there's nothing to perve at. Anyway, you're the one who said I was too skinny.'

'You are.' He said it without a scrap of apology. 'But that won't last forever.'

She shook her head. 'You really know how to flatter a girl, don't you?'

'Yup.'

She made a twirling motion with her hand. 'Turn away!'

He rolled his eyes and did as he was told. As soon as his back was turned Teagan hoisted herself out of the water and ran as fast as she could without slipping for her towel. When she looked up he was watching.

He shrugged, not even remotely contrite. 'You should've made me promise.'

SIX

THE FALLS WAS, Teagan decided, bloody weird.

There was country friendliness and interest, and then there was The Falls version.

A ten-minute job, that's all it should have been. A quick drive into the village to check Vanessa's post-office box, grab a couple of litres of milk from the IGA, and some dinner rolls from the bakery. Forty minutes later she was still stuck.

The IGA had been fine. The Andersons were her kind of people – rural to their bootstraps. Polite and welcoming without wanting to know everything. Teagan had spent a calming fifteen minutes or so chatting about farming and the weather, the affinity between them immediate.

The newsagent-cum-post office was also fine. Antonio de Vitis was charming and flirty, but in an amusing way that signalled it was simply a game he played to pass the time and make people feel good. The sort of man who smiled often and loved to tease. He also possessed a quick wit that revealed intelligence lurking behind that light-hearted manner. Teagan warmed to him a lot.

'A born-and-bred local,' he told Teagan with a wink when she'd asked where he was from. 'But don't hold that against me.' Then he'd hunched across the counter like a conspirator, hand held up to shield his mouth. 'We're not all inbred. Although I can't rightly say for Colin Walker.' Then he'd groaned and quickly leaned back, muttering under his breath, '*Lupus in fabula*,' followed by a wry, 'Speak of the devil.'

And that moment had proved to be her downfall.

Teagan had taken one look at Colin's purpose-filled countenance and attempted to bolt, but the old man was too wily.

'Teagan,' he said, hovering in the shop's doorway, blocking her escape. 'You're just the person.'

Startled, Teagan could only manage a dumb, 'Eh?'

Col took her elbow and guided her deeper into the shop. She threw a panicked look at Tony but he was too busy grinning in relief that it was her under fire instead of him.

'Your aunt,' said Col.

'What about her?'

'Very good woman. Smart.'

'Our Col's always been a brains-before-boobs bloke,' said Tony, winking at Teagan.

Colin ignored him. 'Influential, too. There are some in this town who look up to her.'

Teagan raised her eyebrows, wondering where the hell this was going.

'But it appears she isn't taking this business with the Wellness Centre seriously enough.'

Teagan held up her hands and tried to reach for the mail she'd left on the counter, but Col put in a nifty sidestep and braced against it, bony spotted hand splayed next to the envelopes as though ready to play 'Snap' should she try to grab them. Frustrated, she had to force herself to stay calm when what she really wanted was to snatch up the mail and scamper as fast as possible to her ute.

'Nothing to do with me. As for my aunt, her mind is her own. If you want to change her opinion, you'll have to talk to her yourself.'

'Have you seen it?'

'Seen what?'

Col flapped an arm as though she was a complete idiot. 'The centre!'

She folded her arms, cocked a hip and pursed her lips, hoping Col would take the hint that she wasn't interested in Falls politics. Her voice was as hostile as she could make it. 'I drove past.'

'Then you'll understand that we can't have this sort of thing in our valley.'

'Why not? If rich people want to waste their money on quackery that's their problem.' Temper lost, in a lightning move she plucked up Vanessa's mail from the counter before Col could react, and waggled it at Tony. 'Thanks. I'll catch you tomorrow.' Although if Col remained at large she had a good mind to let Ness resume the mail run. Confident he was wrong-footed enough not to block her exit again, she paused to address him, her voice clear. 'I'm just visiting. Village politics has nothing to do with me.'

She strode out as quickly as she could but the tell-tale shuffle of Col's feet followed. Teagan glanced at the bakery, wondering if she could forego the bread and charge for the farm instead, but she'd promised Ness the rolls. She glanced at Bunny's surgery. There was always sanctuary there if Col became too insistent. Bunny had been nice enough when they'd met the previous week, but Teagan had the impression of a no-nonsense woman possessing little patience for people like Col. At least the vet had declared Blanche perfectly well when Teagan had complained about her breath. Apparently it was normal cat breath. Which, in Teagan's opinion, had to be the only normal thing about the creature. The cat's strange affection for Teagan certainly wasn't.

With a sigh, she strode for the bakery.

It smelled of yeast and good things, which was where the pleasantness ended. The thin old lady behind the counter regarded her with a combination of suspicion and interest. She was tall, with short silvery hair sporting curls as tight as her puckered mouth. 'You must be Vanessa's niece then.'

'Mmm,' said Teagan, hoping the non-committal answer would keep her from having her rolls spat on. The woman might not be like Tony's sister from the takeaway, but Teagan didn't like the look of her at all. And from the unfriendly tone, she wasn't a fan of Vanessa's either. 'Could I please have half a dozen dinner rolls?'

The old lady continued with her moue and didn't move.

The plastic fly strips protecting the entrance rattled as Colin burst through. He pointed, panting. 'It's her.'

'Yes, Colin. I determined that.'

'Teagan,' muttered Teagan, raising her eyes heavenward. 'My name is Teagan.'

'This is Kathleen Ferguson,' said Colin, scuttling closer and puffing out his chest as though it was himself he was describing. 'Seventh-generation Falls resident. Family's been here nearly since Blaxland, Wentworth and Lawson.'

'Impressive.' She pointed desperately to the wire racks behind Kathleen Ferguson, where her prizes lay. 'Six dinner rolls, please?'

Kathleen didn't even twitch. 'Seems your aunt is backing the expansion.'

Teagan's shoulders sagged as she realised her predicament. Colin was hovering close, ready to block her exit, while Kathleen held her locked with those piercing grey eyes. A massive urge to tell them both to bugger off rose inside her, but the last thing Teagan wanted was to make trouble for Ness, and although it might only be temporary, The Falls was her home for the moment, too.

'I have no idea if she's backing it or not. She might be, she might not be. I don't ask. It's none of my business.'

Kathleen's gaze sharpened along with her mouth. 'Perhaps not, but it's assuredly hers.'

'I can't see how.' Teagan again pointed at the racks and tried not to sound pleading. 'Six rolls?'

'Do you have any idea what sort of people we'll get in here?'

continued Kathleen. 'Drug addicts. Drunks. The ment-ally disturbed.' She spread out the syllables as though Teagan were an imbecile.
'This is a good area. Traditional.'

Kathleen nodded as though agreeing with herself. Feeling a
weird Pavlovian urge to follow suit, Teagan slapped a hand to her jaw
as though resting her head on her palm, and gripped tight to stop
herself.

'Do you know how expensive land is here now, thanks to all these
blow-ins? They go to that place, have a few crystals waved over their
heads, drink wheatgrass smoothies and God knows what else, then
next thing they're buying land and building some monstrosity on it.'

Teagan dropped her arm. 'Look, I'm just new in town.'

'Exactly.'

She blinked at the cryptic statement. The morning was disappearing quickly up its own rear, and for what? All she wanted were
six bloody rolls. Frustration made her words harsh and defensive.
'What's that supposed to mean?'

Kathleen gave a derisory sniff before addressing Col. 'Waste of
time. The girl couldn't care less.'

Col hopped from foot to foot, wringing his hands. 'We have
to try.'

Kathleen refocused on Teagan with distaste. 'That man is ruining
our valley with his charlatanism.'

'Charlatanism?'

Colin sidled closer, nodding vigorously. 'Charlatanism.'

Leaning away, Teagan regarded him with a mixture of horror and
disbelief. God, it was like being dumped into some sort of quirky
foreign TV show where the townspeople had gone mad from
isolation.

'Look, it's all rubbish as far as I'm concerned, but if rich people
with more money than sense want to waste their lives on enemas or
whatever, that's not my concern. What *is* my concern is six dinner
rolls. This lifetime, if you don't mind.'

'Happy to see people ripped off, are you?'

'No, but —'

Kathleen pointed a finger. 'You watch that Domenic Ashe. He's got your aunt curled around his finger.'

'No one has Ness curled anywhere. Now, can I *please* have my rolls!'

Kathleen gave her a hard look before finally turning to the racks and loading a paper bag with rolls. Teagan paid quickly, and, without a goodbye or acknowledgement of either local, shot out the door and jogged for her ute, catching a glimpse of Tony laughing in the doorway of his shop as she passed.

Vanessa listened to Teagan's account of her time in the village with dismay. Being collared by Colin and Kathleen about the centre was the last thing Teagan needed. As for the part about Dom having Vanessa curled around his finger, well. She'd have words to say about that in good time. She was no one's patsy, least of all a man's.

'That pair is nothing but trouble. Colin's harmless on his own, but when he teams up with Kathleen Ferguson they cause all sorts of problems.'

'What's it all about anyway?' Setting her elbow on the bench, Teagan flopped her chin into her hand. 'I mean, what goes on behind the centre's walls hardly affects them. I understand the land-price problem, and I can even appreciate that they don't like seeing the village change, but we're what? Ten kilometres from the suburban fringes of Sydney? The Falls is hardly the country anymore.'

'It's about small-mindedness and clinging to the past, among other things.' Vanessa sighed and turned on the espresso machine. 'The land the centre is on was owned by Kathleen's family. Had been practically since settlement.'

'Wow.'

'Quite. Being female, naturally she didn't get anything. Her brother inherited it all, but as with so many places around here someone came along and made him an offer he couldn't refuse. It was meant to be a golf course and day spa initially, with a housing development incorporated, but that all fell through. Only the spa ended up being developed alongside the original homestead, no thanks, I'm sure, to Kathleen's intervention with the council. But that was when the council was mostly made up of conservatives. Things are different now. It's more progressive. As you pointed out, the city is moving ever outwards. This valley can't stay isolated forever.'

Vanessa turned back to load the filter head with coffee. 'The people who originally owned the spa used to let Kathleen visit and walk around whenever she liked. Dom put a stop to that the moment he took over.'

'You kind of can't blame her.' Teagan slid off her stool and headed for the fridge. Vanessa smiled her thanks as her niece placed the milk on the bench. She leaned back against it, arms folded and contemplative. 'It'd be like me and Pinehaven if I was still in Levenham. I'd probably sneak in for a look around, too.' She shrugged. 'It's hard to let places go.'

'Perhaps, but it's people that really matter. Whatever you think of the services Dom provides, a lot of people have been helped by the centre. The privacy he ensures means they undergo treatment for their addictions or problems without fear of being tormented by the media or anyone else.'

She tamped down the coffee and locked the head on to the machine, then set a stainless-steel jug under the steam nozzle. The hiss of steam put a momentary stop to conversation. As she worked, Vanessa wondered if now wasn't a good time to address more deeply some of the issues they'd only danced around.

'There's another reason Kathleen is bitter, too.' She glanced at Teagan and smiled. 'I'll tell you when I've finished making our coffee, but never forget that people's motivations are often complex. Nor do they always make sense. Humans are very strange, complicated creatures.'

Teagan sucked on her bottom lip and contemplated her feet. 'You're talking about Mum and Dad.'

'I'm talking about all of us.' Vanessa lightly touched Teagan's arm. 'Why don't you go outside and enjoy the sun while I finish up?'

When the coffees were made, Vanessa placed them on a tray with some of the orange-and-poppy-seed syrup cakes she'd made earlier that morning. Despite her best cooking efforts, her niece still wasn't eating enough to put on weight. One look at Teagan when she had finally emerged on the verandah on Thursday night and Bunny had half-jokingly offered to inject her with steroids to increase her appetite. Having seen her in her bikini, rib bones corrugating under her pale skin, Vanessa had been tempted to take Bunny up on the offer.

She stared towards the front door. What she feared Teagan really required was a trip to the doctor and a prescription for antidepressants. Yet with Teagan so deep in denial Vanessa knew that would be resisted at all costs. All Vanessa could do was try to feed her up, cultivate a positive environment and hope that the poor darling would find her own way out of the darkness.

The idea made her think of Lucas, the way his gaze had followed Teagan while they'd enjoyed their sangria. If ever there was a man to light the way it was Lucas Knight. Vanessa was sure they'd been about to kiss when she'd interrupted them in the pool, and had quickly made herself scarce, but a few minutes later Lucas was out on the verandah, Teagan remaining somewhere inside. He'd batted aside Bunny's tease about being a fast mover with a riposte about her and Mark Dunkerton, and that had been the end of it. When Teagan had joined them again, she spent most of her time as far from Lucas as possible. Retreating with her drink to the end of the verandah where she'd stood staring at the sunset wearing that awful hollow expression that made Vanessa's heart clench.

She pushed open the door. Teagan was in her cane chair with her legs tucked up and her arms wrapped around her knees, glaring at

Blanche. The cat circled below, head tilted up in disapproval, which she voiced with loud meows.

'She really has taken a shine to you, hasn't she?'

'Unfortunately.' Teagan's mouth twitched in apology. 'Sorry. I'm just not a cat person. And Blanche is . . .'

'An acquired taste, I know. But she means no harm.'

'Tell that to Betty and Wilma.'

She handed Teagan her latte and edged the plate of cupcakes towards her as well, pleased when her niece picked one up. There was enough sugar in that cake to give an elephant diabetes.

'So what's the rest of the story with Kathleen Ferguson?'

Vanessa sipped and settled back. 'Not long after Dom took over the centre a druggie tried to hold up the bakery when Kathleen was there on her own. Turned out he was one of Dom's clients. Walked all the way into the village barefoot, completely off his trolley. Sniffed the bakery and that was it.'

'Must've given her a shocking fright.'

'I imagine it did. I used to feel sorry for her until I learned she accepted a without-prejudice offer from Dom to keep it out of the news. Turns out the druggie was the lead singer of some band that had just made it big. She could've made rather a mess if she wanted, but Dom bought her off with hush money.'

Teagan puffed out her cheeks in amazement.

'Yes, I would never have thought it of her either, but I imagine the offer was substantial and apparently Kathleen was struggling financially at the time. Perhaps she didn't have a lot of choice.'

'That must've hurt. No wonder she hates Dom and the centre.'

'Yes. Hurt pride is an ugly thing.' Vanessa picked up a cupcake and smiled as Saffy immediately appeared by her side. The labradoodle placed a paw on the seat edge and gave Vanessa her best starving animal impression. Remembering Bunny's warnings about overfeeding, she waggled a finger. 'None for you, darling. Vet's orders.'

Saffy immediately padded to Teagan, only to be chased off by a hissing Blanche.

Teagan rolled her eyes at the cat before picking off a tiny piece of cake and eating it. 'So how did Dom end up with the centre?'

'Without the housing development to keep the cash rolling in, the developer got into financial difficulty and had to sell. Dom already had a successful facility at North Ryde and was looking to expand. The Falls property was perfect.'

'I bet it didn't come cheap.'

'No. I always wondered where he got the backing but he's a smart operator. I also suspect he has friends in interesting places.'

'Druggie rock stars?'

Vanessa laughed. 'Even druggie rock stars need to invest their money somewhere. And that particular man is now very much rehabilitated. Like I said, Dom does good work.'

Teagan spent a moment contemplating her cake. The rate she was going, crumb by crumb, the thing would never get eaten. 'You like him, don't you?'

Vanessa thought for a moment, wondering how to answer. She did like Dom, a great deal. He was smart, sexy, and would sometimes catch her with a look that made her stomach lurch and heart race. Men like him were also ruthless and covetous, and that made him trouble. 'It's a funny thing, liking a man. He's so like my exes. An alpha male who thinks he'll get his way simply by the force of his personality.'

Teagan frowned. 'So you don't like him?'

'No, I do. Quite a lot as it happens, but I also see his warts far more clearly than he could ever imagine.' She tilted her almost finished cake at Teagan. 'You should be careful around him, too.'

'Somehow I don't think he's interested in me.'

'Perhaps not in that way, but never underestimate what a man like that will do to achieve his own ends. If he thinks he can get to me through you, he'll try.'

Teagan sighed and put her cake down. It looked like a mouse had been nibbling at it. She dropped her head back on the chair, gaze turning empty. 'I came here to escape secrets and games but it seems everyone's playing them.'

'Not everyone. Bunny doesn't. I don't.' She paused. 'Neither does Lucas.'

Teagan rolled her head sideways to face Vanessa. 'You sure about that?'

'As I can be.'

'Huh,' said Teagan. 'We'll see.'

Lucas sucked on his beer and stared unhappily around. When Vanessa had invited him over for a Saturday barbecue he'd thought it would be just him, and maybe Bunny and Dunks, perhaps even Dom. Instead, he'd encountered a yard full of cars and what felt like half the village indulging in Vanessa's fruit-laden jugs of Pimms, or plucking beers from ice-filled buckets.

He stood near the far edge of the pool, catching the last of the afternoon sun's rays and people-watching. Dunks hovered by Bunny, feigning ordinary friendship when it was obvious to everyone from the hot looks they kept sharing that they were shagging every moment they could get. Dom was hanging around Vanessa as he always did, sort of protective and watchful. Tony was joking with the Andersons, while flicking his ever-seeing gaze around the others. The rest were gathered in pairs and threes on the deck, chattering happily. But it was Callum Albright who concerned Lucas most. He'd barely left Teagan's side since his arrival. Not that she seemed appreciative of the fact. From the mutinous look on her face Callum's attention peeved her as much as it did Lucas.

Callum's strident look-at-me voice kept rising above the general hubbub, usually when he was talking about himself. Apparently, after twelve years on the waitlist, he'd scored himself membership of the Sydney Cricket Ground and was boasting about the matches he planned to attend this summer. In the past, Dunks would have been sucking right up, but Bunny kept whispering in his ear, and the two kept throwing Callum what-a-fuckwit looks and giggling like teenagers. Teagan could only manage the what-a-fuckwit part.

He took another suck of beer and wondered whether he should rescue her, but the idea that she might not regard it as rescuing held him back. When it came to women he was usually confident. Not so with her. Although there was one thing he was certain of, he sure as hell wanted to continue what they'd started in the pool.

To his further annoyance Dom had put himself in charge of the barbecue, normally Lucas's job. It was childish to feel irked by something so trivial but he did. Most guests had dressed in casual gear. Even Callum had donned checked shorts, a polo shirt and deck shoes. Dom though, as always, had to remain that cut above, wearing dark-blue chinos and a white shirt with the sleeves rolled up. Lucas had hoped he'd get fat splatters all over himself, but Vanessa had hooked an apron over Dom's head as protection. His only satisfaction was the deeply uncool quote on the apron's front: Sausage Master.

Dom took it in his stride, making a joke, but Lucas bet that inside he wasn't impressed. Perhaps that's why Vanessa had put the apron on him in the first place. She could be sly like that. It was one of the reasons he liked her so much.

He glanced again at Teagan and decided it was time to live up to his Knight surname, whether she wanted it or not. He sauntered over. Her relief was palpable when she noticed his approach.

'Lucas.' Callum gave him an unnecessarily chummy thump on the back. 'I was just about to tell Teagan about my plans for Elysium.'

'I can't wait,' she said through gritted teeth, causing Lucas to grin behind his beer.

'Big plans, are they?'

Callum kept his focus on Teagan. 'Looking at starting a sheep stud.'

'Had much experience with sheep?' she asked.

'A bit.' Which Lucas suspected was an outright lie, but Callum wasn't a man who liked to look ignorant.

Lucas shot her a glance and saw that she'd picked the fib, too. 'You've met Merlin, haven't you? Vanessa's prize ram.'

'Not yet. Stud, is he?'

'He certainly thinks so,' said Teagan. 'Merino. Fine wool. Good staple length. Maybe you could borrow his services. I'm sure Ness wouldn't mind.'

'I'd have to check him out first.'

'Of course,' said Teagan. 'Nothing quite like a hands-on feel of the testicles. I do it often myself. Good way to check the virility of man and beast.'

Callum nearly choked on his drink.

Though her mouth twitched at the corners, Teagan kept her composure. 'Excuse me, I must go and help Ness.'

Lucas watched her leave. She was wearing green shorts and a cream T-shirt which would have appeared plain on anyone else but on Teagan looked healthy and wholesome. Her hair was long, loose and hung softly around her shoulders. Though slim, she was broad-shouldered, tapering to a narrow waist and hips that swayed, not with Vanessa's overt womanliness, but just enough to be tantalising all the same.

'She's a sort,' said Callum. 'Not quite in her aunt's class, but not bad.'

Lucas felt his jaw flex. 'She is.'

'Doesn't say much. Probably shy. I hear farm girls are like that. I wonder if she likes cricket.' He pursed his lips, thinking. 'Night out at the SCG. One dayer. That'd make a good date.'

For some reason, Lucas looked towards Dom. According to Bunny, Vanessa had been tempted with all manner of treats after Dom had first met her, but as far as Lucas knew, with the exception of a few spa sessions, she'd rejected them all. She'd rejected Callum a few times, too. He hoped Teagan was made of the same stuff.

Callum followed his gaze. 'Dom's pretty tight with Vanessa these days.'

A bitter edge belied the casual words. Lucas wondered exactly how hard Callum had tried with Vanessa. Harder than Vanessa let on if that tone was anything to go by.

'You're a proper local. How do you feel about this Wellness Centre business? Seems to be causing a bit of a stir. That old bird in the bakery, Kathleen Ferguson, nearly chewed my ear off the other day about it.'

Lucas took a careful mouthful of his beer. The centre wasn't something he wanted to discuss. 'It'll bring more employment to the area.'

'That's what I told her. Didn't that set her off.' He shook his head. 'It's a wonder that business survives the way she treats customers.'

'Only bakery in town. And they make good pies.'

'They do. But you only have to drive to Wilmington and there's that chain bakery.'

'Most of us try to shop local when we can. If we don't support the village we'll end up with nothing.'

'That may be so,' said Callum, reverting to his pompous dickhead voice, 'but I, for one, don't enjoy being told how to think. And that Colin's a fucking menace. Why can't his wife buy him a pair of shorts that fit?'

'Probably because she's dead.' A comment to which even Callum didn't have a comeback. Besides, it was hardly a new question. Practically everyone in the village had asked the same at least once. All anyone could work out was that, much like Merlin, Col liked showing off his assets.

As the drinks and food flowed, people began to loosen up. Even with a few beers under his belt Lucas couldn't get into the mood. Dom had decided to use the evening as an opportunity to get people onside and was waxing lyrical about the benefits The Falls would experience from the centre's expansion. He didn't want to listen to Dom's plans. He'd heard enough of them before. Dom didn't give a shit about The Falls. The man didn't do anything unless it was for himself.

He snuck out to the front verandah and down the steps to where Wilma and Betty were feeding. The guinea pigs were funny. All beady eyes and triangle-shaped snouts. These two had silky hair and when excited jumped up and down like fat jack-in-the-boxes. The first experience of it had had him turning to Vanessa and Bunny in alarm until Bunny had explained what it was. Popcorning was the term, which was exactly what it was like. If anything could lighten his sour mood it was bouncing guinea pigs.

He reached into the cage and took out Wilma, the white one. Betty was cute but Wilma enjoyed a tickle more.

He'd made the cage for Vanessa as a gift. Before then the little rodents were housed in a plastic wader pool filled with shredded paper, with chicken wire over the top to keep Blanche and other predators out. Bunny had promised it was fine, as long as the bedding was changed regularly and the pigs had tunnels and other spaces in which to hide. But Lucas was a sucker when it came to animals and he'd thought it a bit mean that they didn't have grass underfoot. Now their house was wheeled to a different spot on the lawn every couple of days. The pigs had greenery and soft footing, and Vanessa, who hated mowing, used it as an excuse not to.

He smiled as Wilma tried to crawl up his chest, her little claws scrabbling against his T-shirt.

'I bet if I took a video of that and posted it on YouTube it'd go viral.'

He looked up to see Teagan watching him from the steps.

She walked down. 'Can't say I blame you for escaping. If I hear one more word about Callum's helipad or Dom's hydrotherapy suite I'll scream.' She lifted out Betty and attempted to stroke the pig's head, but Betty was already letting out squawks and struggling. Teagan sighed and put her back in the cage.

Lucas did the same with Wilma and closed the cage lid, making sure the latch was properly fixed. Blanche was stalking nearby and the cat had been spotted more than once trying to flick the latch open. 'Not impressed by your new friend?' He nodded to the far side of the yard where a low-slung black car was parked. 'That's his Maserati over there.'

Teagan gave it a perfunctory glance before looking down to where Blanche was curling around her legs. 'He's okay.'

He ducked his head a little to draw her eye. 'Bit of a wanker?'

Catching his tease, she smiled in a way that made his pulse pump and wish it was him rubbing against her instead of Blanche.

'Possibly. Probably. Do you think we could con him into feeling Merlin's balls?'

'I suspect you'd be able to con Callum into anything.'

She crossed her arms and rolled her eyes. 'Hardly.'

'Come on. Don't tell me you didn't notice.'

She appeared genuinely puzzled. 'Notice what?'

'He's interested in you.'

'Don't be daft. He's just being friendly so he can get to Ness.'

It was Lucas's turn to roll his eyes. 'Have a bit of confidence in your own attractiveness.'

'Right. Sure. This from the man who called me too skinny.'

'You are.'

'There you go.'

'You're hard work, you know that?'

Suddenly, she rubbed her hand across her face. 'I don't mean to be. It's just everything.' She dropped her hand, her expression twisting. 'I don't know what I'm doing here. I don't belong, and these people.' She swept her arm back towards the house. 'It's like they're all playing games. Trying to outdo each other. Telling lies to make themselves look good.'

'Not Vanessa.' He moved closer, wanting to kiss that look of anguish away. 'Or me. Takes energy I'd rather channel elsewhere.'

She eyed him sceptically but didn't step back. The last of the sun touched her hair, burnishing it. Lucas resisted an urge to stroke the strands, feel them flow like molten copper through his fingers. 'I didn't mean Ness. She's always been straightforward with me.'

'And I haven't?'

'Hard to tell. We only met two weeks ago.'

'You could always get to know me better.'

'I could.'

Their voices were getting quieter with each word. The air began to hush like it had in the pool. Everything felt stretched, as though someone had taken the world and pulled it from either end.

He leaned close, lowering his voice to a seductive murmur. 'Want to make a start?'

For a second he thought he had her. Her gaze dipped to his mouth, causing his heart to skitter, then a burst of laughter sounded from the house. With a blink the moment was lost.

Her voice returned to normal. 'Given the mess my life's in right now that might be one complication too many.'

'I'm not complicated. I'm the easiest bloke here.'

She raised an eyebrow.

'You know what I mean. Look, Teagan, I shoe horses for a living and don't make a bad income from it. I have a house on twenty acres down the road that I take care of pretty well. I'm single, never been married. Been properly head over heels in love exactly three times but they never worked out for the usual reasons. None of which has anything to do with me being a wanker. I don't have a criminal record, in fact I've only been done for speeding twice and that was when I was young and stupid. For fun I play cricket and I also muck around with blacksmithing. I'm house-trained. And,' he cast his gaze over her hair and parted lips, before settling it onto her widening eyes, 'I really do have a thing for redheads.'

'Wow. That was quite a speech.'

Surprised at himself, he grinned. 'It was, wasn't it? But the million-dollar question is, was it convincing?'

She held two fingers to her mouth and tap-danced them against her lips. 'Convincing? I'm not sure.'

Lucas could tell from the crinkle around her eyes that she was teasing. 'But you're intrigued?'

'Perhaps.'

'Enough to come around with me for a morning?'

More laughter sounded from the house. She glanced towards it and rubbed at her neck before finally returning her focus to him. 'All right.'

Lucas flipped a mental bird towards Callum. 'Wednesday work for you?'

She nodded and began to walk up the verandah stairs. She paused at the top. 'No funny business.' Her hand went to the screen door handle then she stopped and pointed. 'Promise.'

So she'd learned her lesson from the pool. He wanted to laugh, instead he placed his palm across his chest. 'Promise.' He gave her his best innocent-boy smile, knowing from experience the effect it had on women. 'What sort of bloke do you think I am?'

'That,' she said, tugging the screen door open, 'is something I'm still trying to figure out.'

SEVEN

NO QUESTION, Lucas Knight was walking, talking woman bait. Man bait, too, given the unashamed lust-filled ogles of some of his clients. Teagan had been around farriers and horsey people all her life, and never had she seen a person attract a crowd the way he did.

As they'd arranged, he'd picked her up on Wednesday at six am and driven to a large racing stables fifteen or so kilometres south of The Falls, where the landscape was a strange mishmash of agriculture, light industry and creeping housing development. Teagan swore every single strapper in the place made an excuse to saunter by for a gander. She was sure Lucas noticed – it would be impossible not to – but it didn't seem to bother him. He'd either look up and offer a quick cheery g'day or carry on working.

A couple of the stable girls tossed her sullen looks that spoke of deep envy and dislike. Though the waves of hostility rattled her fragile self-esteem, she forced herself to match them with a steady, neutral gaze. Teagan didn't want the day ruined by their wrong thoughts. Besides, she wasn't competition for anyone. Lucas might be action-movie-star attractive and on the surface a good, honest bloke, but his interest in her was too surreal to be believed. Besides, she wasn't in a trusting enough state of mind for any form of relationship. She wasn't optimistic that she ever would be again.

From the racing stables they called in on a small acreage with a monster-sized house sprawled across the middle to shoe the owner's daughter's dressage horses. They were stunning animals, sleek and pampered, although surprisingly obedient. Teagan guessed it had cost a lot of money to train them. The entire place reeked of money.

Though still early in the day, the girl's equally sleek and pampered mother had been joined by two other women, all in their forties, who spent the entire time lounging around the pristine yards trying to capture Lucas's attention. When Lucas paused to remove his jumper, the collective intake of breath nearly had Teagan breaking out in laughter, but a cautioning glance from Lucas kept it inside. He'd warned her on the journey over that this might happen, and hadn't sounded happy about it either but accepted it as his lot. If a few bored housewives getting their jollies was the price of keeping his business going then so be it. Like everyone else, he had a mortgage and bills to pay and couldn't afford to be precious.

'Doesn't it make you feel like a piece of meat though?' she asked as they drove to his next appointment.

He shrugged. 'Not really. It's only annoying when they get in the way.'

'So you like being slobbered over by a bunch of cougars?'

He took his eyes off the bitumen for a second to throw her an amused glance. They were on one of the thin, crumbly-edged roads that seemed to wind like snakes across the region between the broader main road ladders, all of which Lucas appeared to be highly familiar with. 'Wouldn't you?'

'The middle-aged male equivalent?' She affected a shudder. 'No thanks.'

'Who's being ageist now?'

Teagan shut up. He had a point.

'They're harmless.' He lifted his palm from the wheel, his voice taking on a slightly tired tone that revealed how he really felt. 'Most of the time.'

'I take it from that you've had to fend off your fair share of offers.'

'A few.'

'That must be tricky.'

'It's not easy.'

He smiled a little, which made Teagan wonder if he'd accepted any of the proposals. Not all his admirers would be like the women they'd just left. He'd encounter plenty of women his own age, riders or strappers who were single and offering no-strings-attached sex. A quick bit of fun against his ute or a stable wall, the sun kissing them as rough hands played over soft skin and breaths came fast, mingling in pleasure.

For some reason the image made her irritable. She shifted onto her left hip and stared out the window to concentrate on the passing scenery, wishing the vision of Lucas and his expert, exploring hands away. Annoyingly, it lingered.

'So how did you get started as a farrier?' she asked, trying for another distraction.

'I didn't really know what I wanted to do when I finished school. I wasn't stupid but I wasn't very academic either, so uni was out. Figured I'd do an apprenticeship of some sort but they were pretty thin on the ground. To fill in I took a job in a racing stables near Warwick Farm. Discovered I really liked working with horses but I was too big to be a jockey and stable work paid like crap, so there didn't seem to be much of a future there for me.

'One morning I got talking to the farrier. He told me about a TAFE course I could do. I looked into it further and signed up. Did vocational work with a couple of master farriers while I studied then four years later I was out on my own. Started working around the valley and never looked back. Not many professionals around these days, so it's been a steady business over the years. Plus I get to work outside, doing something I enjoy and am good at.' He winked at her. 'I even have groupies.'

'So it seems.' Teagan took a moment to tame her thoughts which were running rampant again thanks to that wink. 'You probably shouldn't have asked me along today. I'm likely ruining your business.'

'Nah. It'll just make me look more unattainable. Women love that.'

She laughed and rested her head back. 'God, you're conceited.'

'What? You don't have fantasies about men you can't have?'

'None of your business.' But she softened it with a teasing 'wouldn't you like to know' tone.

'Shame. I wouldn't mind knowing your fantasies.' The cheeky wink he followed that with left her insides skipping and a warm flush blooming across her skin. Then he refocused on the road and turned serious. 'I'm just trying make the most of things while I'm still young and fit. There'll come a point later on when I won't be able to do this anymore. My back will have gone or I'll have suffered an injury. It happens a lot in my profession. I may as well make the most of it while I can. Tomorrow I might be stuffed.'

'Then what would you do?'

'I'd make things.'

Intrigued, Teagan shifted around from the window to look at him properly. 'What sort of things?'

He tapped his necklace. 'Things like this. Other stuff, too. Home-decorator pieces. Garden sculptures. The margins are great and if things get slow I could go back to doing bigger ironwork. Commission projects. Like I did for Vanessa with her gates.'

'That's *your* work?'

'Uh-huh. That's how I got to know her. She wanted someone to design gates for the farm. Bunny knew I had my own forge and put her in touch.'

'I didn't realise.' The admiration in her voice was sincere. Lucas had real talent. 'They're amazing. Really beautiful.'

'Thanks.' He caught her gaze for an extended moment before looking away, but Teagan saw the genuine pleasure her praise had brought and was surprised by how much it thrilled her. That despite her inner darkness she'd created something lovely in someone else.

'There's a living to be made if I can get a name for myself.'

'I bet. Would you miss the horses at all?'

'Yeah, but I can always get one of my own. Anyway, by then I'll probably be married, have kids. Maybe they'll want to ride.'

'You have it all worked out, don't you?'

'Not really. I've yet to find a girl who'll take me on.' His expression left her unsure if he was serious. It seemed unfathomable that Lucas Knight would struggle to find anyone to fall in love with him, yet his mouth had a grim tilt and his gaze seemed to hold a distant edge.

'Come on, you have women throwing themselves at you the moment you open your door.'

'They're not exactly the right girls.'

'Then what constitutes a right one?' The moment the question was out itchy heat began to crawl up her neck. It made her sound like she wanted to be the right girl, when that was stupid. Sure, Teagan could do with a friend, but anything else was beyond her, the pool incident notwithstanding. Lucas was only playing games anyway.

He didn't seem to notice her discomfort. 'Someone who takes me for who I am inside and doesn't spend all day blowing smoke up my arse. Someone who doesn't mind a bit of dirt under their nails or on me.' He flicked a glance towards her head. 'Red hair.'

'Not skinny.'

'Not skinny would be good. You women are weird about your weight. Most of the time you think you're too fat when the truth is blokes like something to grab hold of. Bums and boobs and other fleshy bits.'

Eyes narrowing, she angled closer. 'Are you sure you aren't secretly in love with my aunt?'

'Nah. I'm ageist, remember?'

Teagan laughed and sat back to stare once again out at the surroundings. Lucas had explained that most of his work was to the south and north. Unlike when he first started, these days he had only a few clients in the valley. The demographics had changed. A lot of city people had bought land and built large houses hoping to enjoy a tree change. Wealthy retirees abounded along with urban types like Callum with money and no children, and an urge for a country retreat. Even Bunny's business had altered focus, from livestock and horses to mainly small animals.

In the Wilmington Valley south of The Falls, where the land was less rolling, racing yards, a few studs and equestrian centres flourished. The fences were treated or painted timber. Glossy-coated animals grazed on well-managed pastures, the paddocks protected with windbreaks and dotted with steel shelters.

This was the sort of place Teagan had expected Ness to live in. Her aunt was glamorous, independently wealthy and well-connected. Hanging with stud owners and famous racehorse trainers seemed far more her than an underutilised farm in a hidden valley beset with eccentric villagers.

Although glancing at Lucas, she could see the appeal. Dom was extremely good-looking, too. In fact, they almost looked alike. Both tall, with dark-blond hair and blue eyes, and skin that took on a tan instead of freckling. Lucas, though, was huge in comparison, and with his big scarred hands, rumbling voice and easy laugh, much earthier. Dom was all lean metro polish and smooth talk, careful of every word he uttered. Clever with his manipulative language and hypnotic gaze.

Their next stop was a miniature horse stud owned by a gentleman called Peter Somersby, who had to be the campest man Teagan had ever encountered. He practically minced across the yard towards the ute, arms open wide to Lucas in greeting.

'Lucas, you sublime creature. You're so good to me!'

For an awkward moment, Teagan thought Peter was going to kiss him. Then he spied Teagan. He tucked in his chin, and, with a waggle of his finger, he admonished Lucas with a pouty 'you naughty boy' look before prancing his way towards her.

'And who is this adorable girl? Don't tell me you found yourself a redhead at last?'

'This is Teagan Bliss,' said Lucas. 'Vanessa's niece.'

Peter clapped. 'The glorious Vanessa! How utterly wonderful.' He appraised Teagan with appreciation. 'Aren't you a pretty thing. But one would expect that. Such good genes.'

Peter held out a floppy hand towards her. Teagan took it, trying to smile above the awful limp-wristed shake.

'I cannot express how jealous I am of you, dear.' He clutched his hands together under his chin. 'Oh, to be able to stroke that divine body!'

'Give it a rest,' said Lucas, but his tone was amused.

Peter sighed and rolled his eyes. 'He has *no* idea what he's missing. Such a waste.'

Recovered from the onslaught of rampant affectation, Teagan grinned.

With a wink, Peter minced off towards the end of the stables.

'Don't pay any attention to the gay act,' said Lucas. 'Peter's worked in theatre all his life. He can make you believe what he wants.'

'So he's not gay?'

'Dunno. He might be bi. But with two ex-wives and four kids he's definitely not averse to having sex with women.'

'So . . .'

'His way of testing how judgemental you are. Plus he loves acting. I came here once when he was in rehearsals for *Othello*. Suddenly, he starts quoting Shakespeare, something about dying upon a kiss. Next thing I know he's stabbed himself. Scared the crap out of me. I was on my knees dialling Triple Zero and he starts laughing. I could've stabbed him myself.'

As Lucas spoke, Peter led a tiny horse, not much bigger than Saffy, out of the end stable.

'Bloody hell,' she said. 'It's like a dog.'

'Unfortunately, not quite as good-natured,' said Lucas quietly. 'But Peter adores his horses.'

Peter beamed at Teagan. 'This is Marielle Maison, my best mare.' He ran a perfectly manicured hand down the tiny horse's tufted mane. 'Isn't she a treasure?'

'Mmm,' said Teagan, unsure how else to answer. What the hell were you meant to do with it? She let the horse scent her fingers before rubbing at the tiny white star on her forehead. 'Are they for children to ride?'

Peter's hand flew to his chest, eyes bulging in indignation. 'They're not toys!' He gave a sniff. 'They're stud animals of the highest breeding. I would never let an irresponsible child near one of my darlings.'

'O-kaaay.' Teagan looked at Lucas, but he was enjoying the exchange far too much to help her out. 'So . . . not to be difficult, but what are they for?'

'For connoisseurs, of course. Equine aesthetes like myself.'

'Teagan's a horse girl,' said Lucas, finally taking pity on her. 'Show horses.'

'Was. I had to sell my horse, sadly.'

At the news Peter was all sympathy. 'Oh, you poor sweetheart. I would simply *die* if I had to give up any of my darlings.'

'How many do you have?'

'Six. My stallion, Barnabas, three mares, Chester – the gelding who was my first mini and got me hooked – and a young filly I recently purchased from another breeder.' His expression turned soppy. 'My babies.'

'Right,' said Lucas. 'Best crack on.'

His predictions about the tiny horse's manners proved correct. Thoroughly spoiled by her owner, the mare skittered and danced, and even sank her teeth into Lucas's arm when he tried to pull her leg forward to work on the toe of her near fore hoof, the reason they'd been called out. The mare had a break in the hoof from lashing out and hitting a wall. Not serious, Lucas said after an inspection, but in need of a tidy. Teagan would have swatted the vicious little thing, but Lucas barely reacted, hampered, she supposed, by a hovering Peter.

When he'd finished, Peter did his best to coax Lucas into the house, but Lucas politely refused. 'I'm due at Belgravia in half an hour.'

'You work too hard.'

'Nothing wrong with a bit of hard work.' He patted Peter's back and winked in a way that probably melted Peter as much as it did Teagan. 'You should try it sometime.'

'You take care, gorgeous girl. And give my love to your aunt. I must give her a call. Such a classy lady.'

'You should come around for drinks one afternoon,' said Lucas. 'Vanessa would enjoy seeing you.'

'You know, I might just do that.' He pressed a finger to his chin. 'If I recall, Friday's margarita night. I might pop by then. Perhaps the divine Bunny will grace us with her presence, too.' He clapped his hands. 'And that utterly stunning man, Domenic.' He slid a look at Lucas. 'You are, of course, my favourite, but Domenic is more my age.'

'Everyone's an ageist,' said Teagan as they drove off, which earned her a cheeky grin from Lucas.

'Only way to be, babe,' he said with a look that made her feel suddenly gushy and silly. God, she had to get a grip. 'Only way to be.'

Lucas poked his head around the corner of Belgravia's office door. Nick was at his desk, staring morosely at his computer screen. Trays of paperwork overflowed around him. A coffee mug with a dead fly floating in the top sat forgotten by his elbow.

Lucas rapped on the doorframe. The coffee sloshed dangerously as Nick was jolted out of his contemplation.

'Sorry,' Lucas said, walking into the room. 'Thought you would've heard the car.'

Nick reached across to briefly shake his hand before indicating the monitor. 'Too bloody caught up in this. Sucks you in, this stuff. Like a black hole.'

'Don't I know it. How're things otherwise?'

'Shit. Bloody staff.'

Which was what Lucas had expected him to say. Finding reliable stable staff was the biggest problem Nick faced. Anyone with experience and sense was snapped up by the racing stables and other properties in Wilmington and further south. Nick wasn't in a position to pay above-award rates, which meant Belgravia tended to be lumped with beginners or the useless.

'I might be able to help if you need someone.'

Nick looked up at him in hope.

'Vanessa's niece. Arrived a couple of weeks ago from South Australia. Farm girl. Plenty of experience with horses. Can't stand sitting around so she's been keeping herself occupied fixing Vanessa's fences.'

At the mention of Vanessa, Nick perked up. 'Does she look like Vanessa?'

'Sort of. Red hair at least.' Lucas tapped the desk. 'I thought you wanted someone who could work. Stick a Vanessa in here and nothing would get done.'

Nick glanced at the monitor and then at his paperwork. 'I can only offer part-time.'

'That'd probably suit.' He began walking to the door. 'She's outside. Why don't you come and ask her?'

As he and Nick emerged from the office, a skinny, heavily pimpled lad who looked about twelve but was probably seventeen, was attempting to lead a skittery horse across the brick yard. Teagan was out of the car, bum against the bull bar, watching the action.

One of the female stablehands was leaning on a broom, teasing the kid. 'You don't have the muscles, Bart.'

'Shut up.'

She was right though. The young lad was struggling to hold the horse, which had a bee in its bonnet about something.

Recognising the animal, Lucas glanced at Nick and made a face. 'Not him.'

'Sorry. Cast a shoe yesterday.'

'Shit.' Lucas ran a hand over his head. This could get ugly and he was rather hoping he'd make it through the day without meeting any of his nemesis horses. Diablo was likely to show him up in front of Teagan. Peter's little shit of a mare had nearly done it with her bite, but he'd kept his calm. Anyway, it was never the horse's fault. It was fear that usually caused them to play up.

He crossed to Teagan. 'I might need your help.'

'Sure.' She nodded towards the horse. 'That him?'

'Yeah. Diablo. Worst horse in the place.' As he spoke the horse yanked hard against the boy's hold, who cried out as the rope slithered across his palm and left a friction burn. Sensing freedom, the horse began to trot away before breaking into a joyous buck and then canter.

Nick raced to shut the yard gate. Horses poked their noses over stable doors. The girl dropped her broom. The boy stood staring at his hand.

'For fuck's sake, don't let him trip on it!' yelled Nick too late. The loose lead rope caught under the horse's off fore. With a jerk of Diablo's head the clip attaching the lead to the halter snapped, giving him even more freedom.

Spooked, Diablo careered from one end of the yard to the other, slithering dangerously across the pavers as he changed direction. He propped at one end and released a hysterical neigh before streaking towards the now closed gate. Nick stood in front, frantically waving his arms. For a moment it looked like Diablo was going to attempt to jump both him and the gate, but at the last moment the horse skidded and lithely sprinted back towards the other horses.

He trotted back and forth in front of the stables, snorting and head-tossing, before finally settling to an agitated walk. Nick approached with quiet steps. The horse matched him step for step but backwards until he was caught quivering in the stable block corner, watching them all with wild eyes. Nick had almost reached him when Diablo took a sneaky sidestep and barged straight past. He trotted to the far end of the block, where a water tank was pressed between the wall and yard fence and close to Lucas's ute. Diablo paused to snatch at some grass growing around its base, facing his attackers as he chewed.

Teagan stepped towards him, talking in soothing low tones. 'Look at you, you big idiot. What a show-off, huh?' She kept the flow of talk coming as she walked, all in a calm, even voice that belied her actual words. 'Think you're something, don't you? But you've got nothing on my Astra. She's the prettiest horse there is. Bit stupid like you, admittedly, but she'll come round. Just needs to grow up. All legs and energy and teenage brain.'

Diablo's ears twitched. His head lowered, nostrils flaring as he watched her. He pawed the ground with one hoof but Teagan kept coming. Lucas exchanged a glance with Nick. The stable girl went to move closer, but Nick jerked his head, indicating for her to stay back.

Finally, Teagan made it to the horse's side. She let him sniff her hand and stroked his soft muzzle. She didn't reach for his halter, just kept talking in that soothing voice, telling him what an idiot he was, how Astra would run rings around him. The horse began to relax. He bunted her head and snuffled through her hair. She grabbed the check piece of his halter and turned around, leading the puppy-like horse back towards the young boy.

'Thanks,' he said, eyeing Diablo warily before clipping another lead on.

She shrugged. 'He's just like my old horse. Completely fractious. They get these things in their brains for no reason at all. You just have to talk to them.' She stroked the animal's sweaty neck. She turned to Nick. 'How old is he?'

'Only three.'

'Off the track, I suppose?'

'Bred to win the Golden Slipper but he never made the cut.' He nodded towards the horse's groin. 'Which is why he was given the cut. Didn't improve his temper though.'

'It's hard to get them over their nerves. My Astra's the same. Was. Was the same.' She caught Nick's unsaid question. 'A horse I recently sold.'

Clearly impressed, Nick cast a keen look at Lucas, who gave an imperceptible nod. He spoke casually, as if afraid Teagan would career off like Diablo if he sounded too desperate. 'Lucas mentioned you've experience working with horses.'

'Only my own. But I've been riding since I could walk.' She stroked Diablo and whispered something to him. 'Funny things, but I can't help but love them.' She addressed Nick again. 'Sorry, I'm Teagan.'

Nick shook her hand. 'Pleased to meet you. So you're new to the area?'

'Sort of. Visiting my aunt. Vanessa Rogers. You no doubt know her. Seems everyone does around here.'

'I do. Quite well.' Lucas tried not to sigh as Nick's voice gave away his Vanessa lust.

Catching it, Teagan gave Nick a tight smile before turning to Lucas. 'Sorry. You probably need to get to work.'

'So do you.' He indicated Diablo. 'You can hold him for me.'

Erin, the stable girl, hovered around as he worked, filling Teagan in on the owner's plans of a showjumping career for Diablo, a plan that she clearly disapproved of. How the owner was one of those rich, fairweather people who sold their horses on the moment they didn't perform. Diablo was likely to end up at the knackers if he didn't learn to behave. He'd thrown the shoe not long after throwing his rider, losing both up on the property's steep back hills. The idea being that if she took the horse up and down them enough, tiring him out, he'd be too stuffed to play up when she took him back to the riding ring. Clearly a strategy that had failed.

'Poor baby,' said Teagan, stroking him. 'He's too young for that. I turned my Astra out for eight months after I bought her. She was like a puppy, legs going everywhere. Only knew stop and go. Still only knows two speeds, but we're getting there.' She gave an irritated sigh. '*Were* getting there, I mean. A friend owns her now. It's a long road for these animals. They need patience, not the guts flogged out of them.'

'Couldn't agree more,' said Nick, sidling up as Lucas patted Diablo and began stripping off his leather apron. He glanced at Teagan. She was watching him again, mouth slightly open. So she liked him in his leathers? Interesting. Made him wonder what she'd be like if she saw him at work in his forge.

Nick addressed Teagan. 'Look, I had one of my staff quit on me yesterday. Ran off with her boyfriend.' He lifted his arms from his sides and looked skywards. 'What is it about horse girls? Always running off with men. Most of them losers.'

'Not this horse girl,' said Teagan.

'Some men are worth running off with,' said Erin, throwing Lucas a hot glance.

'You.' Nick pointed at her, then jerked his thumb towards the stables. 'Work.' He turned back to Teagan. 'I have a part-time vacancy. Six am until twelve, Monday to Saturday. Award rates. Interested?'

Teagan glanced at Lucas and then at Diablo. 'I don't know. I've only been here a couple of weeks. I still have a heap of stuff to sort at my aunt's.'

'You said yourself you'd need a job eventually,' said Lucas. 'That you didn't want to keep sponging off Vanessa.'

Teagan bit her lip. 'Can I get back to you?'

Nick handed her a card. 'Mobile number's the best. Don't leave it too long. I can't afford to be without staff for more than a few days.' He looked up at the two-storey, old colonial Georgian-style house perched halfway up the hill behind the yards. The sort of historic home that cost a fortune to heat and maintain. 'We've just had a baby. I spend enough time down here as it is.'

She fingered the card. 'I'll call. One way or another.'

Lucas glanced at her as they drove down Belgravia's long hill back towards the road. She kept alternating between staring at her hands and out the side window, dragging the point of her incisor over her lip. Horses grazed the paddock, most wearing their lighter day rugs. A few were snatching from a round bale feeder, ears pricking as the ute wheeled past. Looking after them and others would be Teagan's responsibility, if she chose to take it on.

'What's up?' he asked.

'I don't know.'

At the end of the drive, he braked and flicked the indicator. A few cars sped past. He pulled out behind them and waited until they were up to the limit before speaking again. 'Don't want the job?'

She shook her head and sighed. 'I honestly don't know. I love horses, I'd like to work with them. And you're right, I don't want to keep having to sponge off Ness, but it seems permanent, you know? Coming here was only meant to be temporary. A place to rest while I worked out what to do with myself.'

He glanced at her again. Teagan's lip was puffed where she'd been worrying it. The job offer seemed to genuinely trouble her.

'What would you do otherwise?'

'I don't know. Drive west or north. There're bound to be plenty of properties looking for workers. Lose myself out in the bush for a while.'

'Lonely.'

'I'm not exactly the world's most sociable person right now.'

'You're not doing too badly from what I've seen. Anyway, it's not like the job would be forever. You could give it a try and if you didn't like it look for something else.'

'Maybe,' she said doubtfully, staring back out the window. 'I'll talk to Ness.'

They drove back through the village. Lucas was tempted to stop and check his mail, but on spotting Col's battered Ford in the parking lot decided against it. It was lunchtime anyway. He had corned beef in the fridge. Some tomatoes and cheese, and homemade chutney that one of his clients had given him. All the workings for a good sandwich. Plus Lucas didn't want his time with Teagan to be over yet. What better way to extend it than to offer lunch?

He was about to ask her if she'd like to grab a bite to eat with him at Astonville when she spoke.

'Thanks for convincing me to come out with you. I had a nice time.'

'Good. I hoped you would.'

'I suppose I should get back to the farm now, let you get on with things?'

The way she spoke, the question in her voice, made him look at her. She was biting her lip again, her hands twisting together. 'Is that what you want?'

'Actually, no.' The words were shy, her sideways gaze low under her lashes. A pink hue was colouring her creamy, freckled skin. 'If you have the time, I'd really like to see your forge.'

She couldn't have asked for anything better.

EIGHT

TEAGAN HADN'T GIVEN MUCH THOUGHT to what Lucas's place would be like. She assumed it'd be similar to those of Owen's mates' she'd seen or Em's brother Digby's bachelor pad. A bit daggy. Perhaps even a little run down. Clean but not terribly tidy and full of boy's toys. What she found was quite different.

'It's not much, but it's mine.' He grinned as he braked near a paved, pergola-covered outdoor entertaining area at the rear of his house. 'Well, mine and the bank's.'

Teagan didn't quite know what to say. She'd been enchanted from the moment he'd turned into his drive and cruised slowly up the hill towards his home. His cottage was gorgeous. A sweet little stone building built into the side of a hill and surrounded by a well-maintained buffalo lawn and garden beds colourful with flowering shrubs. Tall trees swayed around the edges, offering shady respite and a partial screen from the road. The drive was neat gravel with shallow concrete guttering to catch rain and channel it to the small dam near the entrance.

'It's really lovely,' she said, meaning it. She smiled back at him. 'Not quite what I expected.'

'Yeah? What did you expect?'

'I don't know. Something more bachelory.'

'Uncared for, you mean?'

Not wanting to offend she shrugged lightly. 'Maybe not uncared for. Just more . . .'

'Untidy? Nah. I had to put up with enough of that when I was sharing. I like things neat.' He pushed open the ute door and waited until she'd also alighted to continue. 'Getting a mortgage focuses you. I've worked my arse off to own this place. I plan to look after it.' He tilted his head. 'Come on, I'll show you around.'

Teagan walked companionably alongside as Lucas pointed out the improvements he'd made over the past four years. Astonville, as the property had been once named and which he'd kept on, was a dump when he'd bought it, but if he wanted to buy in the valley, a dump was all he could afford. He'd laboured hard on the renovations, calling on mates like Dunks to help when he couldn't manage on his own. Begging and borrowing tools and equipment, cajoling extra labour in return for beers and barbies.

'The verandah was a killer,' he said as they walked along the garden at the front of the house. The view down through the trees to the road and across was richly pastoral, with a flock of brown-and-white Boer goats grazing the opposite hill, post and rail fences, and a eucalypt-lined driveway disappearing over the top. 'Had to replace the whole thing. Boards, posts. They were all rotted. The lacework I made myself.'

She could hear the pride in his voice. He deserved to be proud. The verandah's iron lacework was spectacular. Instead of the traditional spear tips, scrolling and regulated design, Lucas had created softly curving Art Nouveau forms and seductive organic shapes that seemed to sprout from the timber posts as though alive.

'You could make a fortune alone selling that lacework. It's amazing.'

The smile he gave her was dazzling, and not just because of his glowing white teeth. That she was impressed had made him happy.

She looked away as something flipped over inside her and brought back the memory of an emotion she hadn't experienced in years. An emotion pointless and unwanted, yet longed for all the same.

'Come and see this,' he said, grabbing her hand and holding it as he led her around the side of the house. The movement was as natural as it had been in the pool when he'd taken her hand and they'd floated on their backs, staring at the infinite sky.

She glanced down at their threaded fingers, not knowing what to think. Holding her hand said things. It implied their relationship was more than a growing friendship and she didn't know how to trust it. Or if she could. Teagan was a skinny, screwed-up redhead who belonged nowhere except a place that was lost to her. Lucas was a man with everything – ridiculous looks, friends, professional skill, a home he was proud of. He couldn't be serious about her. They were completely mismatched.

Still, she didn't pull her hand away.

He guided her beneath the pergola. Dormant vines were tucked against the bases of the uprights. They were thin-stemmed and young, but Teagan could imagine how gloriously cool and Mediterranean-like the setting would be in the summer, when the vines were established enough to twine across the roof and form a green protective canopy.

'More of your work?' she asked, nodding towards the timber-and-iron outdoor setting.

'Yep.'

'How do you find the time?'

He shrugged. 'My days vary. Sometimes I'm flat out, other days I only have one or two clients. Business tends to be seasonal, too. In the summer a lot of horses are turned out while everyone goes on holidays and I'm quieter, which means I have more time to spend on stuff for the house.'

Leaving the pergola, he crossed an open gravel space towards a small brick building attached to the end of an open bay farm shed.

Everything about Astonville was neat. No junk lying about. No unkempt lawn or shrubbery. Even the wood pile was tidy.

He let go of her to drag a set of keys from his pocket and Teagan couldn't help her pang of disappointment. He found the key he wanted and inserted it into the deadlock. The place was solid. Brick walls, thick timber struts and a corrugated-iron roof.

She stepped inside. The room was dark despite the bright sun creeping through the eaves. And there was a smell in the air. The scent of metal and something else she didn't recognise but which felt familiar all the same.

'Hang on, I'll give us some light.' He strode across the room and Teagan could see that the shed wasn't all brick. The left side housed a large steel sliding door. Lucas unlocked another bolt and began to push the door across.

Light flooded in, exposing his workshop.

'So this is your forge,' she said, taking in the space.

'Not a proper one. But it does the job for now.' He placed his hands on his hips and looked around. Again that sign of pride. 'One day I'll have it set up properly. Can't quite afford everything at the moment.'

Teagan began to wander, fingering things as she walked. A large gas forge with a flue reaching to the roof dominated the room. Solid racks containing steel sheets, rods and tubing of various size and diameter occupied one wall. Anvils – one enormous, the other smaller – stood mounted at waist height on log plinths. Tools were hooked onto special frames on the walls, all well cared for and stored neatly. Along another wall, stretched a steel-and-timber bench with pieces of sculpted and shaped metal in various stages of completion.

There were books, too. On a galvanised bookshelf behind the door. She walked over to study the covers. The books about metal-work she'd expected but not the titles covering design and art. She pulled out a hardcover volume on Art Nouveau style and flicked through the pages before looking up at him.

Lucas was watching her closely. 'I use them for ideas. I'm not,' he scratched his cheek, 'you know, real arty-farty.'

'Could've fooled me.' She slid the book back and continued to nose around. At the far end of the bench was a small portable forge, about the size of a barbecue gas bottle. Nearby stood what looked like a jeweller's magnifying lamp on a flexible arm. Intrigued, she moved for a closer look. The mat beneath the magnifying glass held a shaped piece of silver with enamel inlays of incredible vibrancy. The artwork shone with a warmth that belied its metal-and-glass base.

She glanced at him. 'May I?'

He scraped his hands against his jeans and nodded.

Teagan picked up the pendant and studied it. The piece was circular. Inside, two stemmed silver flowers curled like yin and yang shapes around each other. The petals were enamelled in a deep red, the leaves emerald. A sky-blue background completed the filling. She could see areas requiring further polishing down, but even so, the craftsmanship was exquisite.

'I'm just playing around.'

'It's beautiful, Lucas. It really is.' She placed it down carefully, almost reverentially, giving the surface one last, lingering stroke before smiling at him. 'Does anyone else know you make these things?'

He shook his head and pointed to his necklace. 'Stuff like this everyone knows about.'

'But the jewellery?'

He held her gaze. 'You're the first.'

'I'm honoured.' She meant it, too. She drifted on, trying to act nonchalant when her heart was thumping fast. The hand he'd linked with hers had created this beauty. He was a big burly farrier, a man's man, and yet he created artwork so delicate and expressive it stole her breath. Lucas had surprised her in a way she couldn't have imagined. 'But you must have lots of visitors. Friends.'

Girlfriends. Women.

'Not really.'

She threw him a disbelieving look.

He rubbed his hand over the back of his neck. 'I tend to catch up with people on my rounds. Unless I've asked for a hand with something no one seems to bother calling in. When I'm home, I just want to kick back or work here anyway.'

'But you have that great entertainment area. You must've built that for something.'

'It'll get used. Eventually.'

She regarded him with folded arms, trying to work him out. None of this was as she'd expected. Lucas himself was proving nothing like she'd expected. 'You're a funny one.'

'Funny ha-ha or funny peculiar?'

'I'm not sure yet.'

'Don't puzzle too hard. I'm just your average bloke trying to sort out his place in the world. Come on, I'll show you the house.'

This time there was no offer of his hand. Teagan followed alongside, trying to kill the urge to reach for it. The man had heartbreaker written all over him, but when he'd held her hand earlier it had felt safe instead of insecure. A feeling she hadn't experienced since things had started going downhill at Pinehaven. Over the last eighteen months she'd been in a state of permanent anxiety. Then about six months ago the oily black slick had begun its ugly, whispering creep and Teagan had begun to feel unsafe even with her own thoughts. She still did.

But not today. Not with him.

Lucas pushed open the back door, letting her pass through before following behind. 'Kitchen's straight from the seventies. It's on my list to fix up. I burned most of my cash trying to get the place sound.'

The kitchen was as described, unfashionable but functional, with burnt-orange benchtops and splashbacks, and faux-walnut laminated cupboard doors. A large modern timber table dominated the area, newspaper spread open at one end, a pile of folded clothes at the other. In the centre was a metal bowl containing apples and a spotted banana. A wall clock ticked above a matching sideboard strewn with keys, mail, an empty iPod speaker dock and tablet computer.

'It's nice.' She nodded in approval. 'Homely.'

'Thanks.'

Teagan hunted for something else to say and couldn't think of anything. She licked her lips and grabbed at her upper arm, flicking a look from him to the lounge then towards the hall that ran dark to her left. The bedrooms would be down there. She swallowed and darted another peek his way.

He was studying her closely, hands in his pockets, a slight frown marking his brow.

Self-consciousness crawled over her shoulders and circled her chest and throat. She twitched a smile, wishing she could think of something, anything to say, but she'd been muted by awkwardness. Half of her was pleading for him to make a move. For him to smile one of his flirty grins and step close, tease her with glittering eyes that kept tracking to her mouth. The other half wanted to bolt for the door.

A smart person would do the latter. Teagan was too fragile for emotional games. All she wanted was some sort of normalcy, to find peace in her own thoughts. Playing around with Lucas wouldn't bring her that.

He pulled a hand from his pocket and scratched his cheek. 'What was your place like?'

The relief of conversation was huge. Even if it was about Pinehaven.

'Basic.' At his questioning look she elaborated. 'I lived in one of the farm's old worker's cottages. I had plans to do it up but never had the time or money. The main house was okay though. Mum and Dad renovated several years ago, when things were good. My brother still lived at home then.' Not wanting to let him see the despair mention of her lost home brought on, she folded her arms and strode to the end of the room. 'This is the lounge?'

A wall had been opened up so the kitchen fed straight into the space. A worn modular couch took up one corner. A mid-sized telly the other. A small pine bookshelf held more books, hardcovers from the looks of their spines.

'I don't use this much. Fixing it is a low priority.' He moved behind her and pointed to the fireplace. 'The old one was buggered, but I found this at a clearance sale up the mountains. Solid marble. Great, isn't it?'

'Yes. It is. Very.' The fireplace looked like it had come from a stately home. The columns either side were classically grand without being overdone, the broad mantel similar. Contrasting black-and-white stone gave it extra class.

'Carpet's stuffed. The floorboards aren't great either. I'm keeping an eye out for recycled timber to replace it. The room will look better with polished floors.'

'It won't be too cold in the winter?'

'Probably, but I'll buy rugs to help sort that.' He walked to the first of the lounge's two wide but short windows and peered out. 'I wouldn't mind knocking these bigger, but it'll probably cost too much.'

His mouth suddenly thinned as he spotted something, gaze hardening with it. Curious as to what had caused his abrupt change of expression, Teagan moved to look. A large black car was cruising along the road.

'That's the Wellness Centre's Humvee, isn't it?'

'Most likely.'

His tone and tension had her alert. She studied him, wondering. 'You really don't like Dom, do you?'

He shrugged. 'I'd have to care about him to feel anything, and I don't.'

The answer struck Teagan as odd. She waited for him to elaborate, but Lucas's attention remained on the Humvee until it disappeared around the bend.

He straightened and checked the clock on the mantel. 'I'd better get you home.'

The soft, smiling Lucas from the morning was gone. She'd said something wrong and now their time together was over. It shouldn't matter but it did. She hid her disappointment with briskness, talking as she took the initiative and strode back to the kitchen. 'Yes, I've work to do. I'm sure you have plenty to get on with, too.'

At the kitchen door she looked back. For a long moment he stayed at the window, his hands in his pockets and a brooding rigidity to his mouth and eyes. He glanced towards the lounge's other door, the one she assumed led to the rest of the house, then at the floor. Finally, he shook his head and with a slump of his shoulders followed.

Lucas kept quiet on the drive back to Falls Farm. He wanted to touch her. He'd wanted to all day. Then had come the house, the forge, Teagan's reaction to the pendant, and the urge to drag her to bed had become almost primitive in its intensity.

Whether she'd follow was another matter.

She hadn't pulled away when he'd taken her hand, but perhaps she'd felt she didn't have a choice. He'd gripped her firmly after all, and they were alone on his small property, surrounded by hills. The road was a good few hundred metres away. His neighbour's land was close but their houses weren't. Lucas was big, strong. No woman in her right mind would want to cause offence.

Besides, Lucas had promised her no funny business. He'd had every plan to ignore that directive, but the way she'd looked in the forge, when she'd spotted the silver pendant, touched it as though it was the most incredible thing she'd ever seen before lifting her amazed gaze to his, had made him reassess. This wasn't a bit of fun anymore. The way his heart had clenched watching her proved that. Why ruin what progress he'd made by trying to get her into bed? It'd only confirm what she thought of him.

The sight of the Humvee had wrecked his mood and the moment anyway. Fucking Dom.

'You're quiet,' she said, when they approached the turn for Falls Farm.

'Just thinking.'

'About what?'

'Not much. Work. What I have to do tomorrow.'

She nodded as though she understood and faced back to the window. The road was busy and he had to wait for a stream of cars. In a few minutes they'd be in the yard, their time together over. He might not get her alone again for days.

He should have made her lunch, stuff it.

An idea struck him. 'You haven't seen the waterfall, have you?'

'Not yet.'

He flicked his blinker off and, waving an apology to the driver caught behind him, pressed on the accelerator. Past the bowling club he indicated again and turned right down a worn bitumen road. The few houses along it quickly gave way to thick scrub. The road dipped and became dirt. Another kilometre on it swung around to the left and flattened, becoming narrower and more enveloped by trees with each turn of the wheels.

Lucas glanced at Teagan, checking for nerves. That she might be worried where he was taking her. She was observing closely, one hand on the dash as she peered into the thick scrub. Unlike in the kitchen, nothing about her face or body suggested anxiety. If anything she seemed eager.

The track curled to the right and opened up into a cul de sac edged with a low treated pine fence. Picnic tables that had seen better days lined a large deep pond beyond. In the summer the area was a popular spot with locals looking to cool off. Now, with the weather still mild and finding its spring step, the area appeared damp and isolated.

Lucas parked and turned off the engine. 'Right for a walk? The falls are a bit further up, beyond the pond.'

'Sure.'

He waited for her at the front of the ute and held out his hand in invitation. She glanced at it, her tongue darting slightly out to moisten her lips. For a second he thought she wasn't going to accept, then her slim palm was against his and his heart was thumping like it had in the forge.

'Not cold?' he asked as they dodged around a puddle.

'No.'

'Just say if you are. You can have my jumper.'

'I'm okay.'

The pond was teardrop shaped, fed by a small creek into the top. Lucas led her along a track that followed its course. Weak sun filtered through the tree canopy, leaving dappled light that moved and changed in an almost otherworldly play of colour and shadow. The air was full of noise – birds calling, frogs and the increasing, unmistakable sound of falling water. He smiled when Teagan caught it.

'It must be close,' she said, a thrill in her voice.

'Just up ahead.'

The track twisted left and opened up again. He halted, saying nothing, simply letting her drink in the beauty of it. She tilted her head back, eyes shiny with delight as she took in the view.

The waterfall wasn't spectacular or large, but it had a pristine prettiness that easily outstripped its lack of size. A small rock cliff rose in front of them, perhaps five metres in height. The cascade was small and gentle, the water falling in an easy bubbling stream to splash in another clear pool below. Trees overhung the edges and ferns dipped fronds like beachgoers testing their toes. Moss coated some of the rocks in colours so vivid they seemed painted on. The pond water rippled as though caressed by a breath.

Teagan's grip tightened on his. She turned to him, smiling. 'It's magical. The sort of place you expect a unicorn to come and drink at.'

He couldn't take his sight off her awe-parted mouth, her plump, moist lips. The way her breath made her chest rise. The colour of her cheeks, made pink with cold and perhaps something more.

Her own gaze dropped to his mouth. It lingered, briefly, before darting quickly away to the falls. A flush rose up her exposed neck, joining her stained cheeks. He wanted to press his mouth against it, taste the sweetness.

'Thanks for showing me. It's a special place.'

'You're welcome.'

They stood in front of the waterfall, holding hands, the tension between them as thick as the damp air. Several times he thought she was going to say something, only to remain silent.

He started to ask her if she'd like to come for a picnic here one day, but his stomach got in first, the thought of food inducing a loud rumble that had her raising her eyebrows at him.

'Sorry,' he said, wincing.

But she only laughed. 'Don't be. Mine was going in the car, too.'

'My fault. I should've offered you lunch. I had plenty of sandwich stuff.'

'It's okay. Ness usually makes me something. She's determined to fatten me up.'

The romance of the moment was gone. Lucas cast a last look at the waterfall and pond, and then at Teagan. 'Come on. We'd better get you back to the farm, and fed.'

The journey back was held in contemplative silence. Teagan kept her elbow propped against the door, hand curled near her mouth, gaze on the village and paddocks.

'It's martini night tonight,' she said as he indicated and turned into Vanessa's drive.

'Is that an invitation?'

'I doubt you need an invitation. Ness likes having you around.'

'What about you?'

She dropped her hand, a smile curving her mouth that made him curse his hesitation at the pool. He should have kissed her. He should have done a lot of things. 'As Ness says, you're very decorative.'

He laughed, turning through the second gate into the yard and braking. 'Glad I'm good for something.'

'After today, I get the feeling you're good for a lot of somethings.'

The tease in her voice made him stare at her. 'Teagan Bliss, are you flirting?'

The moment he saw her mouth drop Lucas knew he'd fucked up. She seemed horrified by the thought, as if there was something wrong with the attraction between them. Not understanding, he reached out to take her hand. 'Teagan . . .'

But she was unclicking her seatbelt and sliding away.

'Wonderful,' she said, pushing the door as though nothing had happened. 'Colin's here.'

Sure enough, Colin's old Ford was parked near the gate. Col was on the steps, twiggy, grey-haired legs on display.

'I can turn around. Whisk you back to Astonville.'

'I'd better stay. Ness looks like she needs rescuing.'

Lucas turned off the engine and undid his own seatbelt, but as he went to open the door, she twisted around.

'It's all right, you don't have to come in. I'm sure you have work to do.'

'No other appointments today. I might as well take a look at Claudia while I'm here.'

'You only saw her the other day.'

'Won't hurt to check her again.'

So it was a weak excuse, but he wasn't about to admit that he didn't want to leave her. Not with Colin loose. And he wanted to make certain Teagan talked to her aunt about Nick's offer. With two of them pushing, they might convince her to take it up.

Vanessa welcomed them with barely concealed relief. Arms wide and gesturing, and a voice higher and louder than normal. 'Darlings, did you have a good morning?'

'Great, thanks,' said Teagan as she attempted to sidle past Col with a polite, forced smile. She pointed towards the house as he tried to block her. 'Just need to . . .'

'We're protesting!' He thrust a whiskery chin at her, forcing her backwards into the handrail. 'The whole village!'

Lucas didn't need to ask what about. Talk of the expansion pissed him off enough as it was. Anything to do with Dom did, but the old fart was in Teagan's face and thanks to his own flirt comment she was backpedalling enough.

Not in the mood to put up with his shit, he turned on Col. 'The whole village? Including your daughter? The same daughter who just so happens to work at the centre? Who lets you camp in her drive, using her electricity for free? Electricity that she pays for with wages that she earns from Dom? Piss off, Col. You're talking out of your arse.'

Col's mouth opened and closed. Teagan regarded him with the same surprised, curiosity-laden look she'd given him at Astonville, when he'd made that reckless comment about Dom.

'Well,' said Col, finally finding his voice. 'Well!'

'Lucas didn't mean it,' said Vanessa, placing a hand on Col's arm and giving Lucas a meaningful look. 'Did you?'

Lucas considered before answering. Then he sighed. Village infighting was the last thing he wanted to be involved in, no matter how he felt about it. 'Sorry, Col. Your and Maggie's domestic arrangements are none of my business.'

'Too bloody right they're not.' Col was doing his best to sound outraged but he couldn't quite maintain eye contact. There was guilt in his manner, as if he knew the truth of Lucas's words. He addressed Vanessa. 'We'll see you at the rally?'

Vanessa shook her head. 'I'm sorry, Col. I can't take sides with this.'

The old man's mouth tightened. 'Kathleen said you'd say that.' He nodded at Vanessa and Teagan before scuttling past Lucas without acknowledgement.

As soon as the Ford was gone, Vanessa sagged into her chair. 'I thought I was never going to get rid of him.' She scraped her hair back from her face, looking unusually hassled. 'I know he means well, but I do wish they'd leave me out of it.'

'Is everyone really on their side?' asked Teagan, taking the other chair.

'Not everyone, but more than you'd imagine. I did a little canvassing myself. There are quite a few who believe the centre is big enough. Some of them would surprise you. It's not the villagers, but the absent landowners like Callum. The ones who come up here for weekend and holiday peace and quiet. They couldn't care less about escaping drug addicts, but they do care about maintaining their fairytale village. What they can't see is that the people who keep this fairytale village alive are the ones who live and shop here on a daily basis. And for that they need jobs. Dom's expansion could well provide those jobs.' She gave a tired sigh. 'Honestly, what harm is he doing?'

'Maybe some people believe their charlatan accusation.'

'I told you,' said Vanessa shortly. 'A load of rubbish.'

'Dom? A charlatan?' said Lucas. 'I doubt it.' Charlatanism smacked of not caring. The centre, making money from it, was the one thing that mattered to Domenic Ashe. He wouldn't dare risk the accusation.

Vanessa glanced at her watch. 'Is it too early for a drink?'

'One over lunch won't hurt,' said Teagan.

'Oh, darling, haven't you eaten?'

'My fault,' said Lucas.

'Well, there's a quiche inside and a bowl of salad. Dressing in the fridge, too. You two go help yourselves. And bring back that bottle of pinot gris in the door.'

'I'll get it,' said Teagan. 'You stay here and cheer Ness up.'

'A good morning?' asked Vanessa, shooing away Saffy who'd snuck onto the verandah to say hello. Her curly blonde coat was stained with something dark, half dried and foul-smelling. Saffy slunk off, casting reproachful looks between Lucas and her mistress. 'That dog!'

'She's just doing what dogs do.'

'I wish she'd do it with something better smelling.' Vanessa sat back and folded her hands under her chin. 'Well?'

'She was fine.'

'Are you sure? Only she looked a bit tense when you arrived.'

Unwilling to admit that was his doing, he shrugged. Besides, the reason for it was something he intended to explore himself.

Vanessa glanced at the screen door and lowered her voice. 'I'm worried about her, Lucas. This business with her family and the farm has affected her terribly. She's not as strong as you might think.' She looked suddenly back at him, concern lining her face. 'You wouldn't hurt her, would you?'

As she spoke, the sound of Teagan's footsteps carried from inside. The door pushed open and Teagan exited, carrying a tray containing two plates with a slice of quiche on each, cutlery and a bowl of salad glistening with dressing.

Teagan placed it down, throwing them both an unsteady smile, as if she knew she was the topic of conversation. 'I'll fetch the wine.'

He waited until she'd disappeared back inside before answering. 'Not if I can help it.'

Vanessa scanned his face for a long moment, then relaxed. 'No, I don't think you would. Which is just as well.'

'Oh, yeah?'

'I only have one niece. And I intend to look after her. Do bear that in mind.'

Although sweetly delivered, the message was clear. Hurt Teagan and he'd better watch his manhood.

Lucas refused wine but poured for the two women before settling down to his lunch.

'So,' said Vanessa, watching them eat. A frustrating exercise when it came to Teagan's picky forkfuls. For a girl who should have been starving, she ate like a fussy bird. 'Anything exciting happen on your rounds?'

Teagan spent a moment toying with her salad. 'I was offered a job.'

Vanessa set down her wineglass and tipped forward excitedly. When Lucas had mentioned taking Teagan out on his rounds they'd hoped this would happen, but neither was certain how she'd react after the loss of her own horse.

'Don't tell me, Belgravia.' When Teagan nodded, Vanessa clapped her hands. 'But that's perfect, darling. Nick's a wonderful man and his wife, Stacey, is a total sweetheart. She's just had the most adorable baby. They could do with someone reliable like you around. The agencies keep sending them kids who don't want to work or keep running off. To be fair the pay isn't great, but the youth of today do seem to possess a terrible sense of entitlement.'

'It's only part-time. Six mornings a week.'

'But that's even more perfect. You don't need to be working yourself to the bone. You've had quite enough of that for one lifetime.' She reached across to cover Teagan's hand with her own. 'You're going to take it, aren't you, darling?'

'I don't know. I'd hoped to find something a bit more, you know, farmy.'

'That could come,' said Lucas. 'Belgravia's a fairly big property. Nick's always complaining that he doesn't have time to manage it the way it should be. Owners keep getting in the way and with Stacey busy with the baby he'll have even less time. You might start as just a stablehand, but prove yourself and who knows where it could end up.'

She kept looking at her plate, fork twisting in her rocket salad. 'I don't really know that much about pasture management up here though.'

'Oh, darling, don't be silly. Clever girl like you would have that worked out in no time.'

They waited while Teagan considered. Lucas's stomach felt tight. A single yes would mean she'd stay on, at least for a while. And he wanted her to. Badly.

Her fork went down. She reached for her wine and drank, then looked from her aunt to him. A slow, cautious smile eased across her mouth.

'I suppose I could give it a try.'

NINE

TEAGAN SLUMPED on a fencepost and blew out a breath. Her first day on the job and she was already carrying an extra load thanks to Erin deciding to take an impromptu day off.

To give him his due, Nick had been pitching in as well, but with sixteen stables to clean, checks of all the paddock-agisted horses, plus change of rugs for those owners who'd paid for the extra service, feeds to be doled out and an enormous yard to be swept, the work felt never-ending.

And Teagan didn't mind a bit.

Charged by two glasses of wine and Vanessa's and Lucas's encouragement, she'd phoned Nick back that same afternoon to accept his offer. When he'd asked if she'd mind starting the next day, Teagan had hesitated for several seconds and, unable to think of a reason not to, had responded with an 'Okay, sure. Why not?' Words that had earned her a smothering hug from Ness and an intense eye-meet from Lucas that had given her heart a momentary attack of the hiccups.

As Ness claimed, Nick had so far proved to be a decent man. He had a calmness that came from being around flighty horses and even more temperamental owners. Nothing seemed to faze him, although when, after an hour of waiting, it became clear that Erin wasn't going to show, he'd succumbed to a fit of swearing, followed by a hefty kick at a hay bale. Teagan had looked on warily until he'd glanced up, saw her watching and grinned.

'Sorry. Had to get that out of my system.'

Teagan had nodded, still cautious, but with his temper relieved Nick simply got on with it.

Belgravia was nestled in a pretty part of the valley on four hundred acres of rolling countryside. The stable-kept horses were generally sweet-natured, with only Diablo and one other acting like prima donnas. Most were smaller types. Little been-there-done-that horses and ponies purchased at great expense by doting, well-off parents for their offspring to ride on weekends. The paddock agisted horses tended to be owned by locals or people from the encroaching suburban swathe who loved horses but couldn't afford their own acreage.

Much of the area around the stables had been levelled, with the historic homestead overlooking the yard and front paddocks from its perch on the hill like a grand old lady. A magnificent garden formed a colourful skirt below that was, according to Nick, Stacey's pride and joy. Apart from baby Oliver who, despite only being capable of pooing like a scouring foal, howling like a demon, projectile milk vomiting like Linda Blair in *The Exorcist*, and depriving even Stacey's deaf old fox terrier of sleep, had somehow now become king of their world.

The comment had been made with an edge to Nick's voice that had made Teagan look at him sharply. But the bags under Nick's eyes suggested he was indeed suffering deep, new-father fatigue, a situation not helped by his staff problems. Given the circumstances, he was coping better than Teagan thought most men would.

There were two full-sized arenas, one spanned by a large steel open-sided roof, the other laid out with multi-coloured showjumps. Nick was a qualified instructor and coach, who'd had a solid career as a professional showjumper in Europe before meeting Stacey and returning to Australia to set up stables and training facilities on the property she'd inherited from her grandfather.

Some owners also paid a premium to have their horses exercised during the week. Nick employed riders for that, who usually rode a mount while leading one or two others around the property's trails. When the first had turned up, wearing worn jodhpurs and half-chaps, Teagan had experienced a twinge of envy. She missed riding. She missed the feel of wind in her hair and the sheer heart-bursting exhilaration of directing half a tonne of powerful animal. Nick had suggested she might be able to ride once she'd proved herself, but Teagan didn't hold out any hope. There was too much other work that needed doing.

Although she was meant to knock off at twelve, Teagan hung around to help Nick with the last of the paddock feeds and rug changes. Work kept her mind off Pinehaven and the worry about what was happening with it. All the things she was missing, the life she'd lost. It also stopped her thinking about Lucas Knight and her confused feelings for him. Feelings she was trying her hardest to suppress.

'Who'll help you with the evening feeds and rugs?' she asked as Nick rubbed his brow and stared morosely towards the stables.

'Toby usually helps,' he said, referring to one of his owners who received discounted rates in exchange for work around the farm.

'I could come back if you need.'

He shook his head. 'You've put in enough today. I can't have Vanessa thinking I'm exploiting you. She'd have my balls.' He grinned and waggled his eyebrows. 'Not that I'd say no if she asked for them.'

'I'm sure your wife would have something to say about that.'

At Teagan's tone he held up his palms. 'Just kidding.'

Sure he was. Joke or not, there was no escaping the desire in his voice. Half the bloody valley seemed to lust after her aunt. Why should he be any different? She threw the last of the hay to a dish-faced pony whose mane and tail seemed to take up more space than her body. 'Same time tomorrow?'

'Yep.' He regarded her seriously. 'And thanks. You're a lifesaver.'

Teagan drove back to Falls Farm with her stomach rumbling. They'd barely had time to stop for a drink of water, let alone morning tea, and thanks to her staying late it was getting close to two. She'd promised Ness to check the mail on her way home and planned a quick stop, but one look at the bakery had her stomach growling even more. Kathleen Ferguson might be a pain in the bum but she knew how to make a meat pie. And the carpark was thankfully empty of Colin's Ford.

There were new posters in the windows of the chemist and doctor's surgery. Angry yellow lettering on a harsh black background. 'Save The Falls From The Wall' read one. 'Keep The Falls Family' read another. The bakery's poster was three times the size of the others, almost covering the entire window. Teagan read the outraged message, 'The Falls Is for All, Not Just the Rich', with its call below to join the Falls Union Progress Association, and rolled her eyes.

'I hear you've found yourself some work up at Belgravia,' the old lady remarked without so much as a hello to precede it.

'Yep.'

'Nick isn't a bad fellow for a blow-in. Wife's family has been here for over a hundred years, of course. Young Stacey knows what's what.'

Teagan took that to mean that Stacey wasn't in favour of the Wellness Centre's expansion. 'Could I have a plain pie, please. And a sausage roll.' Saffy adored them. Ness swore she only suffered the bakery because her dog had a terrible addiction to Kathleen Ferguson's sausage rolls, but Teagan knew her aunt felt the same as Lucas. Without local support, they wouldn't have any shops in the village.

'Suppose that Domenic has been visiting?'

Teagan shrugged. She wasn't going to get into this game. Anyway, she hadn't seen Dom since the barbecue.

Kathleen gave her a pucker-mouthed look. 'Like I said before, all you young people care about is yourselves.'

Teagan regarded her coldly. 'You don't know anything about me, Mrs Ferguson. But I'll tell you something. Right now I'm hungry and would like some lunch. If you can't accommodate that simple request I'll truck across the carpark and buy something from the takeaway. Up to you.'

Kathleen's expression turned sour but she snapped open a paper bag and plucked up a pair of tongs. The pie and sausage roll ready, she laid them on the counter and held out a wrinkly hand for Teagan's note.

'You know,' said Teagan, handing it over, 'you really would do better if you bothered being pleasant.'

The change was slapped onto the counter in surly silence.

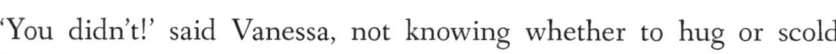

'You didn't!' said Vanessa, not knowing whether to hug or scold Teagan.

'I did.' Despite her laughter, her niece at least looked contrite about what she'd done. So she should. There was enough hostility trembling through The Falls without Teagan adding to it. 'Sorry. I know I shouldn't have, but she's been rubbing me up the wrong way.'

'She does that to a lot of people.' Despite her misgivings, Vanessa smiled. 'You never know, it might actually teach her to be nicer, although I doubt it. I fear our Kathleen simply isn't made that way.'

She sank back and put her feet up. The weather was gloriously lazy and it was nice to sit on the verandah and chat after the morning she'd had. It seemed every year her investments grew more and more complicated. That was the trouble with owning commercial property when you lived halfway around the world. It would be so much easier to sell the lot and consolidate her holdings, but with the eurozone in the state it was she'd take too much of a loss. Besides, the properties remained good earners.

'So what're you going to do for the rest of the day? The pool will be lovely after all the sun it's had.'

Teagan took another bite of her pie and sent a cascade of flaky crumbs over her front. She chewed, eyes narrowed as she looked past the shed. 'I asked Nick about that weed. He said it's wild tobacco. Nasty stuff apparently. I thought I could start cutting it back.'

'I think you have to spray it, too. Or paint the stems. I remember Lucas offering to take care of it for me.' Vanessa kept her voice innocent, though her gaze slid slyly to Teagan. 'He's such a sweet boy.'

Teagan studied the thick gravy of her pie and didn't say anything for a while. She peeled a bit more paper down but didn't eat. Instead, she picked at a few crumbs and dropped them on the verandah to a delighted Saffy. 'He's nice, isn't he? I mean, genuinely nice.'

'Very. Which is interesting, isn't it? You'd think he'd be one of those men who think they're God's gift, but he's not like that at all.'

'He must have faults though.'

'Of course he has faults. Everyone does.' Vanessa thought for a moment. 'I'm just not quite sure what Lucas's are yet.' She smiled. 'But I'll leave that for you to find out.'

Teagan put the half-eaten pie down on the table and rubbed her face. 'I don't know if I want to go there.'

'Why on earth not? Darling, you said yourself he's nice. And, let's face it, he's hardly tiring to look at.'

'But that's the thing, isn't it? What does a bloke like that want with me? I mean, look at me.' She indicated her face and body. 'I'm not exactly you.'

'And nor should you want to be!' Vanessa wanted to growl in frustration. Her niece seemed to have no concept of how attractive she was. '*Vive la différence*, darling. You're beautiful in your own right. Lucas certainly seems to think so. He couldn't take his eyes off you yesterday.'

From Teagan's expression she didn't seem convinced. 'It's just a thing. He's not serious.'

'What makes you think that?'

Teagan picked up her pie again and inspected it, then sighed, peeled off the paper and handed the remaining half to Saffy, who sucked it in so fast it was as if she'd inhaled it. 'I don't know.'

Vanessa waited for her to elaborate but Teagan remained silent, stroking a grateful Saffy's head. Her stare had a hollowness that worried Vanessa deeply. As though her niece's thoughts had disappeared into somewhere so abyssal she couldn't climb out.

'Teagan, darling. What is it?'

'I just don't feel like I can trust anyone these days. I mean, look at all the married blokes who come round here. Remember my friend Jasmine? She's having her heart torn inside out because the man she thought was single turned out to be married, and now she's too in love to let him go. Even this morning Nick made a comment. The man has just had a baby, for God's sake.' She looked aside, biting her lip. Her eyes were shiny with unshed tears. Vanessa resisted the urge to leap up and crush her to her chest. Talk was the only way to uncover Teagan's terrible malaise.

'That doesn't mean Lucas is the same.'

'How can I believe that when the man I trusted most turned out to be the biggest liar and cheat of them all?'

'Oh, sweetheart. Not all men are like your father.'

Teagan said nothing.

'I know you're heartbroken by what happened, darling, but that will pass in time. Please don't let it stop you from finding happiness.' When she still didn't respond, Vanessa tried another tack. 'Lucas is a good man, an honest one. He'd never hurt you.'

'Come on, Ness. He had women and men throwing themselves at him yesterday.'

'And did he respond to any of them?'

Teagan looked away.

Vanessa spoke gently. 'I think your answer lies there. Give him a chance, darling. Let him make you smile again.'

Teagan's only response was a tight, 'I'll think about it.'

The conversation left Vanessa troubled and unsure how to proceed. Going through life carrying so much hurt, not trusting anyone's motives was a terrible way to exist. Rotten, rotten Graham. Vanessa could have cried for the damage her brother-in-law had caused.

The problem kept her occupied through to the next day without a solution. Her only hope was to play a little matchmaking.

At five-thirty on Friday, Vanessa prepared a jug of margarita and took it outside along with a series of heavy tumblers, before heading back for a dish of warmed olives. She smiled at the arrival of a car, hoping it was Bunny. A few minutes of her unique company would put things to rights. Her friend never minced words, and Vanessa could do with some no-nonsense womanly advice.

'What a day!' exclaimed Bunny as she clomped into the kitchen and flopped down onto one of the stools. 'I love my job, I really do, but it seriously challenges my faith in humanity. This idiot brings his boxer in, tells me it was straining to shit for about two days. So he gets it into his head that it's constipated. What does he do? Buys a pack of chocolate laxatives from the supermarket, doles them out and leaves the dog to it. Wanders back outside later for a look and wonders why the dog's just about dead.'

'And was it?'

'What? Dead? No, but he's going to wish he was when he gets the bill.'

'I meant constipated.'

'No. Bloody thing had diarrhoea! Nothing was coming out because there was nothing to come out.' Bunny sprawled forward, pressed her cheek to the bench and let out a long, frustrated breath. 'What a fucktard.'

Vanessa stroked her hair. She really was the funniest lady. 'Some people shouldn't have pets.'

'Tell me about it.' Bunny let out another sigh and sat up. 'Is it drinky time yet? I'm a woman in need.'

'Give me one minute.' As Vanessa pulled the warming olives from the stove and poured them into a terracotta tapas dish, a soft knock sounded at the front screen door. Guessing who it was, she called out for him to come straight in.

Heavy footsteps sounded on the timber floor. Bunny suddenly sat up straighter, cheeks blooming with coy colour as she spotted Mark Dunkerton. 'Cherub. I didn't know you were coming.'

Mark blushed almost as deeply back. He nodded hello at Vanessa. 'Vanessa invited me. How's work?'

'Fine. The usual. Had an interesting case of herpes.'

Vanessa put her hand over her mouth to stop her choke of laughter as the blush drained from Mark's cheeks.

Bunny continued, oblivious. 'Owner nearly fainted when I told her. Let her hang on it for a while before I clarified it was canine herpes. I swear she thought her husband had been having it off with her pedigree Sheltie. How's our eleven coming along?'

Mark had to clear his throat before answering. 'Only nine.'

'But that's excellent news,' said Vanessa. 'You only have a couple to go.'

'Yeah, but there's no guarantee we'll make it.'

Deciding it was time to move the party outside, Vanessa lifted the bowl of olives and indicated the verandah. Mark held the door for her as she stepped out. She placed the olives on the table, noticing it took Bunny and Mark a fraction longer to emerge than it should have.

Pretending not to see that their cheeks were once more pink, she poured tumblers of margarita, and handed them over. They toasted one another before Vanessa settled down. Mark and Bunny stayed at the rail, arms brushing as they inspected the yard.

'Got a spare boot?' asked Bunny over her shoulder.

'What for?'

'Blanche is terrorising Betty and Wilma again.'

Mark tugged off his left boot and tossed it. There was a yowl and within seconds Blanche was curling around Vanessa's ankles, throwing dirty looks at Mark. But he and Bunny were too busy laughing to care. For a vet, Bunny sometimes had a remarkable way of dealing with animals.

Mark disappeared to fetch his boot, leaving them momentarily alone.

Bunny eyed Blanche as the cat sooked in Vanessa's arms. 'Good home for rescues, Falls Farm,' she said in that deceptive tone Vanessa had heard before. 'Just so happens —'

Vanessa held up her hand. 'Whatever you're going to ask the answer is no.'

Bunny carried on as though she hadn't spoken. '— I've heard of another animal in need. Sweet little thing. Shetland. Barely comes up to my knees. Local rescue found her. Terrible state. They're full up though. Would be awful if she had to be destroyed.'

'Surely it's not that drastic,' said Vanessa, her heart already softening as it always did when she heard about suffering animals.

'Looks like it.' Bunny actually sounded serious. She'd made plenty of past attempts to get Vanessa to take on another rescue horse, but mostly it was only as a joke. In the other serious cases, homes had been found.

Vanessa pursed her lips. 'What about Claudia? She might tread on her.'

'Claudia could do with the company. Horses are herd animals. They shouldn't be on their own. It's stressful for them. I've told you that before.'

'I don't know . . .'

'You've more than enough space and feed. And Teagan to give you a hand. She knows her way around horses. Nick said she's a bloody godsend. Can't praise her highly enough.'

Vanessa sighed and held up a finger. 'Only as a last resort. And only temporarily.'

Bunny grinned, happy she had her way. 'So how is our blue redhead?'

'Fine, fine,' said Vanessa, unwilling to comment further in front of Mark. 'She's off helping Nick with the evening feeds and rugs. Toby had an appointment and couldn't make it. Stacey would've helped but apparently Olly's being a complete horror.'

Conversation was suspended by a ute pulling in the drive. Lucas alighted looking even fitter and more casually sexy than usual in a pair of jeans and a snug-fitting polo shirt, his golden hair tied back in a neat ponytail. The darling boy really was keen. If only Teagan could learn to trust, she'd have the catch of a lifetime.

Lucas bounded up the steps, pausing by Mark to slap him on the shoulder. 'Dunks. Didn't expect to see you here. How's it hanging?'

'Good. You?'

'Not bad.' He winked at Bunny before crossing to kiss Vanessa hello and help himself to a drink, before nonchalantly looking around. 'Teagan having a swim, is she?'

'Still at Belgravia.' At his downcast expression Vanessa added, 'I'm sure she's not far away.'

Discussion drifted to the formation of the Falls Union Progress Association, which had become the talk of the village. The association was, it was deemed, a joke with only two members so far that Bunny knew of, although Kathleen and Colin were working hard at recruiting more and being cheeky about it. Bunny's receptionist, Janice, had already twice kicked Colin out of the surgery after catching him trying to stick a poster in the window. Tony de Vitis had done the same at the newsagency. The doctor and chemist were too busy to argue, and decided it was simply less painful in the long run to let Col have his way.

Vanessa had just returned from mixing another jug of cocktail when Teagan turned up. She hid a smile as anticipation lit Lucas's eyes. How sweet. He was suffering even worse than Mark was with Bunny.

Feeling smug at her matchmaking efforts, Vanessa regarded her friends with indulgence, only to be gripped seconds later with the realisation that in pairing them off she'd condemned herself to playing gooseberry. A sudden clench of sorrow and longing wrested her heart. The intensity of it surprised her, leaving her reaching for her drink to ease the thickness that had also affected her throat. Even when things were dire, she wasn't one to wallow in misery. Life was far too short. One skipped through it, not waded.

Yet without someone to share the joys of it with, what was the point?

Tossing the thought aside, she drank and joined in the chatter. Before long she was laughing at Bunny's quips and watching Lucas's and Teagan's hesitant moves around each other, silently egging her damaged niece to seize the evening and beyond. To take a chance on love and its potential wonders.

Even when Tony and her other admirers arrived to join in the fun, Vanessa still felt the loneliness. And her mind kept drifting to Dom.

TEN

KNACKERED DIDN'T BEGIN to express how Teagan felt. But it was a good kind of tiredness, the sort that came from a productive day's work and sense of achievement. Belgravia was hosting a dressage clinic that coming weekend, which meant catering for a large number of floats and horses, and having all the facilities pristine. She and Nick had been flat out, which was why she'd stayed behind even longer than normal to assist.

After a week on the job, she knew her way around and each day had Nick passing on more responsibility, trusting that Teagan could be relied on to complete any task with efficiency and diligence. It was still labouring though, and an underutilisation of her experience and skills, especially when there were 400 acres that needed better management. She might not be tertiary educated but Teagan had always prided herself on her self-learning. Farming had been her life and she'd studied the science of plant production and animal husbandry with the intensity of an agriculture honours student. Perhaps if she'd channelled that passion more broadly things would be different. But it was early days in her new position and as Lucas said, there was a good chance more would come with time.

The house was quiet. Ness was in the city for the day, and except for its menagerie of strays, Falls Farm was empty. Her aunt had disappeared into the CBD last week, too. Teagan wondered what Ness did there, who she saw. It was an onerous drive into the heart of Sydney, even in a sporty car like the Alfa. A solid hour, and that was only if the traffic behaved.

Teagan supposed she should play tourist around the harbour one day. Take in Sydney's famous bridge and Opera House. Venture up Sydney Tower and soak in the view. See what all the fuss was about. But she'd never been one for cities, nor was it something she thought she'd enjoy alone. Plus right now she preferred the numbing escape of work. Which is how she intended to spend what remained of the afternoon, as soon as she'd grabbed a belated bite to eat.

With the warming September weather, Vanessa's kikuyu back lawn had begun to sprout. The grass was ankle high, the thatch spongy. Vanessa's mower was a modern 4-stroke, but even it was struggling to cope. Teagan couldn't understand why until an inspection found the blades probably hadn't been sharpened or changed since purchase. A search of the shed for a steel file proved fruitless, leaving Teagan little choice but to labour on.

She tried to keep her mind blank as she pushed and puffed and sweated, but Lucas kept leaking in. He'd called into Belgravia that morning, and though she'd had more tasks to complete than she had time for, Teagan couldn't prevent herself from hovering nearby. She hadn't seen him since Friday night, when Bunny and Mark had provided most of the entertainment, and Lucas had kept throwing Teagan looks that had made her pulse jitter. For some reason Ness had been reserved that night, too. But when Teagan had asked the following morning if anything was up, she'd merely waved her hand and said something about feeling old.

Hard to believe. Ness had too much life in her to ever feel old.

Lucas was reshoeing one of the centre's expensive showjumpers when she'd caught sight of him. Erin had had charge of the lead, although loosely and with the barest attention on the horse. Her focus was Lucas. The young woman's overt ogling and flirts made Teagan's skin burn, which only made her more annoyed. She had no claim on Lucas. She didn't want one either.

Except that was a lie. The hyper-awareness she experienced whenever he was near, the fantasies that kept slipping into her daydreams, the longing that tugged whenever he looked at her, revealed how much she did want something with him. But why start a relationship that was only stupid anyway? Lucas would have his fun and then move on, and the ensuing hurt would sap what little strength she'd managed to stockpile since arrival. A risk she couldn't take.

Convinced it was for her own good, she'd slipped out of view before he could discover her watching. Now, in the heat of a lonely afternoon with her longing pulsing harder through her body than the mower's vibration, she wasn't so sure.

Teagan had just finished using Vanessa's equally poorly maintained brushcutter to trim the house's rear lawn edges and was scowling at the machine's rust-pitted blade when she heard a car door slam, followed by the rattle of heels on timber as someone ran up the steps.

The screen door opened and banged closed. Vanessa's voice hailed through the open French doors. 'Teagan! Darling!'

'Out the back, Ness!'

Her aunt's heels clacked as she made her way through the house and strode out onto the back patio. She looked stunning in a tightfitting cobalt-blue pencil skirt, enormous heels and a fitted white silk blouse.

'I thought you weren't meant to be back until late?' Teagan said, setting the cutter against the deck and making a mental note to ask at the ag store for brushcutter blades.

'I hadn't planned to be, but my meeting finished early and then I had a phone call.'

She halted near the pool, her face in shadow. Yesterday, while Teagan was at work, Lucas had helped Ness set a sail cloth over it, angled to let the morning sun warm the water yet keep the pool shaded when the UV was at its worst. The weather had heated up enough for the sail to come out of winter storage, and being a pair of pale-skinned redheads, both Ness and Teagan needed the sun protection.

'Have you finished, darling? Ready for a drink?'

Her voice had a strange quality. Sort of shrill and not quite right. Teagan studied her aunt. One hand was on the back of a chair, French-manicured nails tapping restlessly. Her posture was erect, her neck stretched as though stiff with tension. Something was up.

'Sure. Anything the matter?'

'I'll make us some gin and tonics, shall I? See you in a jiffy.' In a waft of expensive scent, Ness clacked back into the house.

Vanessa pushed a tumbler her niece's way. There was no easy way to do this, but a drink first might help ease the shock.

Goodness knows she needed one herself. If Vanessa hadn't had to drive, she would have ordered a fortifying cognac in the restaurant and downed it in one. No doubt Dom would have enjoyed that. Any excuse to delay her return to The Falls. She would bet her Alfa that his next move would have been to invite her to his Tamarama apartment. Perhaps indulge in another glass of wine while she enjoyed the ravishing view over the creamy beach below. Stay for the sunset, and more. The man was ridiculously transparent.

To be fair, she'd enjoyed their lunch. Dom was excellent company and possessed an astute business brain. It was a relief to discuss her property holdings and investment strategies with someone with no agenda. Vanessa had financial advisers that she respected, but they still earned commissions. Dom's only goal was to get her into bed.

After the strange feeling of need and loneliness she'd experienced the previous Friday night watching Lucas with Teagan and Bunny with Mark, she might well have taken him up on his offer. But the phone call had put paid to that.

Now she was back at Falls Farm about to turn her niece's world upside down again. Just when the poor darling's life was beginning to settle.

'Shall we go out onto the verandah?' Vanessa smiled, but it was shallow and false, and Teagan caught it.

'Ness, what's up? You're making me nervous.'

Her reply was an expression of dismay she couldn't conceal.

Teagan clutched her arm. 'Did something happen in town?'

'Please, darling,' she said, taking Teagan's elbow and steering her towards the door. 'Let's do this outside.'

Teagan swallowed, her eyes wide and frightened, but she nodded. As they settled on the edge of their seats, Vanessa whistled for Saffy, hoping the dog had managed to keep herself clean for once. She needed the animal's furry loyal comfort.

Saffy bounded out of the scrub and leapt up onto the verandah. Vanessa stroked her golden head and tutted at the burrs in her coat, relieved to find her dirty but unstinky.

'Please, Ness. You're scaring me.'

'In a minute, darling. Have a drink first.' She twitched her mouth into what she hoped was a more genuine smile, relieved when Teagan took a good gulp of her gin and tonic. Her niece winced at the potency of the mix but bravely took another long draught.

Teagan placed the tumbler down and rested her curled fists on either side of her seat. 'Now will you stop stalling and just tell me what's wrong?'

Vanessa sighed and let the silence hang for a moment as she formed her words. 'I had a phone call this afternoon.'

Teagan looked at her, her bottom teeth pulling on her upper lip as though trying to hold back tears. Her fists balled tighter, her elbows braced.

'From your mother.'

Rising fear made Teagan's voice high. 'Is she all right? Is it Dad?'

'No, no. They're both fine.'

Teagan's hand flew to her mouth. 'Not Owen. Please not Owen.'

'No! Everyone's fine.' Vanessa took a breath. This was going to hurt. 'I'm sorry, but . . .'

'But what?'

She closed her eyes for a moment.

Teagan's voice turned harsh. She thumped her fist on the table. Saffy whined at the sudden aggression. 'But what, Vanessa?'

'Penny has left Graham.'

'She left Dad?' Teagan slumped back, blowing air out between her lips. 'Well, I guess I shouldn't be surprised. I would've left him too after what he did. So where's she going to go?'

'That's the delicate issue,' said Vanessa, shifting nervously and taking another slug of gin. She really should have made her drink stronger. 'Your mother is coming to live here.'

Teagan held her head back and looked at the sky in despair, blinking away the sting of tears and swallowing the coarseness that scraped her throat. Falls Farm was meant to be her escape. Her chance to heal, to recover from the injustice she'd suffered, away from her parents. A place to stop being angry. To find peace.

But since her aunt's announcement a few days prior the little peace she'd found had been lost to a storm of temper and anguish.

'You all right?' asked Nick, staring at her worriedly.

'Yes, sorry.' She coughed and turned away to hide her shiny eyes. 'Bit tired.'

'Tell me about it.' He sighed heavily and went back to connecting the arena rake to the quad bike's towbar. Belgravia was quiet now in the haze of an orange sunset. Horses stamped and snorted in their stables, sounds echoed by the dressage clinic horses that had been left overnight in the yards. Further behind, where the forest trails started, birds squabbled and called as they roosted for the night.

Teagan dragged a hose as she continued checking the water buckets of the yarded animals, caressing velvety muzzles and affectionately tussling forelocks as she paused to fill those containers that needed topping up. The horses, with their simple needs and kind, long-lashed eyes helped control the worst of her despair. Life was so simple for them. Eat, drink, perform, sleep. No messy families. Nothing to worry about except the next meal.

She wasn't meant to be working – not this late – but after Vanessa's revelation she'd been avoiding her aunt. She'd been avoiding everyone, including her own thoughts. But they kept sneaking back, catching her unawares. Stinging her eyes with their unfairness.

She bit her lip against the ache and wished she could talk to her friend, Emily, but Em had her own troubles. Jasmine was an option, but Teagan had a feeling that Jas wouldn't give her the sympathy she craved. Teagan's own fault. Her intransigent attitude towards Jasmine's affair with a married man had affected their friendship and even Em's attempts to heal it had failed. Though they were still friends, the closeness they once shared was lost. Lucas crossed her mind, but she didn't want to lay her angst on him. Plus she was likely to bawl or say things she'd regret.

She filled the last bucket and coiled the hose. Nick was still raking the arena in preparation for tomorrow's lessons. She checked each of the stables, looking quickly over the half doors to check the animals were calm and resting with their haynets. Nothing much else to do. It was well after six on a Saturday night and past Vanessa's cocktail hour. Surely she was safe to return to the farm?

Teagan looked towards the sun as it made its final drop below the hills. For several seconds shadows laid claim to the land and goosebumps prickled her arms as the air suddenly cooled. A click and hum and the automatic lights came on, blazing the facilities in light once more. She picked up a yard broom and began to sweep.

'Go home,' ordered Nick as he switched off the quad bike's

engine. 'Vanessa will skin me if you stay any longer, and tomorrow's going to be just as bad.'

Teagan didn't work Sundays, but Nick had offered to pay double time. She'd accepted before he'd barely finished speaking. Come tomorrow anywhere would be better than Falls Farm.

She yawned and pushed the broom one more time before putting it back into its shed, hesitating before she let the handle go. Teagan forced her hand to release. Hiding here all night wasn't an option, and while she might be screwed up, she wasn't weak.

She drove to the farm slowly, eking out the minutes. The road wound narrowly and she passed the turnoff to Lucas's. Unable to help herself, she glanced up the drive towards the pretty cottage on the hill. The windows were dark. A little burst of hope that he'd be at the farm flickered before she extinguished it. What was the point? It was all too saccharine chick movie to be true. Men like Lucas didn't happen to women like her, and even she had enough self-awareness to know she wasn't good company for anyone at the moment.

She wasn't even good company for herself.

She turned into Falls Farm and rode the gullied track to the house. At the sight of Dom's sleek Mercedes she let out a breath. Good. Ness would be too occupied with him to force her into another of her 'little chats'.

It wasn't Vanessa's fault. Teagan understood that. Her mother was Vanessa's sister long before Teagan existed. Of course her loyalty lay there, but it still hurt, the desecration of her sanctuary.

She parked and stepped out. It was evening now and quiet, apart from a few late settling birds and calling insects. She swung her backpack on her shoulder and took a few steps towards the house, then changed her mind and took the side path towards Claudia and Mouse's paddock instead.

Ness had caved in to another plea from Bunny and the tiny pony had been duly delivered on Friday evening. After regarding her new companion with boggling eyes, Claudia had adopted her as though Mouse was her offspring, much to everyone's relief. The Shetland had simply carried on stuffing her stomach as if the attention was all she deserved.

Merlin released a frustrated bleat as she passed, his overstuffed woolly body ghost-grey behind his ringlock fencing. Another day and she would have paused to say hello, having developed, like Ness, a weird affection for the ram and his un-ovine-like wits. Today she wasn't in the mood for having her leg butted or her crotch nosed. At the sound of the sheep, Saffy tore out of the darkness, bounded around Teagan with her tongue lolling and her body reeking of something putrid, before galloping off on another nocturnal doggy mission.

At the top of the crest Teagan paused. Lucas's ute was parked near the gate. He was leaning on the fence, rising moonlight highlighting his loose shoulder-length hair. She wanted to turn around, but a painful yearn for friendship drew her forward.

He swivelled and regarded her as she approached, expression neutral.

'Hi,' she said, trying to sound normal.

'Hey. You look tired.'

'It's been a busy day.' She went to the gate and scratched Claudia's nose then crouched to reach through and tickle Mouse's. The pony was almost all hair. Mane sprouting like a wild paddock, tail so bushy it almost covered half her rump. Somewhere under the cascade of forelock, eyes were hidden. 'Everything okay with Claudia?' She assumed that's why he was here.

'She's fine. Mouse will take time.' He scraped the heel of one boot against the toe of the other. 'Ness told me about your mum.'

Teagan swallowed. The crusty lump was back.

'I'm sorry.'

'Why are you sorry? It's not your problem.' She closed her eyes and smacked her palm against the timber rail. Why did she have to be such a cow? 'Shit.'

Lucas didn't say anything.

She straightened and picked up her backpack. 'I should go to the house. Vanessa's probably wondering what happened to me.'

'Stay a minute?'

'Why?'

'I don't know. So we can talk maybe?'

'Look, Lucas, I'm in a bitch of a mood right now.' She stared at his shirt, fitted snug over his muscular chest. 'And I'm liable to cry all over you.'

'I don't mind.'

'I do.' She rubbed at her face. 'I just want a hot shower, a glass of wine, a bowl of something comforting and sleep.'

He stepped closer. 'Want company for all that?'

'I'm really bad company, Lucas. Really, really bad. My temper's so mean I don't even want to be with myself.' She slid him a look. 'What are you doing here anyway?'

He reached out to fondle Claudia's ears. 'Vanessa said you could do with a friend. So I'm here.'

'Oh, crap.' She turned her face away, tucking her tongue hard into the roof of her mouth, determined to keep the stinging tears at bay. As if the sheer force of the pressure would hold back the flood. A sob emerged. She jammed her fist into her mouth and bit.

'Come on.' Strong arms enveloped her. Cupping the back of her head, Lucas held her close, shushing into her ear as though she were a baby. The kindness only made her sob harder.

Finally, when her crying fit had moderated to unbecoming hiccups, she pulled away. Tear marks stained his polo shirt. She brushed at them pathetically. 'Look what I did.'

'Doesn't matter.'

Too mortified to lift her head, she continued to stare at his chest. 'I am such an embarrassment.'

'You're not. You're just upset. Happens to the best of us sometimes.'

'I can't ever imagine you crying into anyone's arms.'

'Believe me, I've done it.'

Smiling wetly, she looked up and immediately felt comforted by the compassion in his expression. The man was a bloody saint. 'She must've been a special girl.'

He smiled back. 'She was. She was my mum.'

The mention of his mum and his feelings about her sliced something cold through Teagan's heart. She sniffed and looked up the slope, towards the house. Tomorrow, Ness would make the long drive to the airport to pick up her sister and bring her back to Falls Farm. And Teagan would have to not only face, but live with, the woman whose faintheartedness had helped take so much from her.

Lucas took her hand. 'Don't think about it.'

'How did you know what I was thinking?'

'Your expression.' He shouldered her backpack. 'Come on, it's getting cold. Let's get you fed and watered and into bed. Tomorrow's going to be a big enough prick of a day as it is. You don't want to be facing it exhausted.'

ELEVEN

DUMB THOUGH IT SOUNDED, Lucas liked having Teagan cry on his chest. It made him feel needed. Even in the darkness, as they made their way back to the house, hand in hand, he could see how tired she was. Tired and hurt.

Vanessa had warned him in a phone call that Teagan wasn't taking Penny's imminent arrival well. She'd also asked for his help, which was why he'd waited for Teagan to come home, each passing minute of dusk making him fret that something had happened at Belgravia. Horses were unpredictable, accidents happened. He should have realised she was only hiding, extending the time before she had to return to Falls Farm.

He'd never seen Vanessa so troubled either. When Lucas arrived she'd been pacing the verandah with a large glass of wine instead of the usual Saturday-night Pimms. The moment he'd climbed the stairs she'd started, asking him if she'd done the right thing in offering refuge to her sister.

Lucas couldn't see how she could have done anything else. Penny had pleaded for sanctuary just as Teagan had done. How could Vanessa refuse?

It had occurred to him then that they could come to some sort of arrangement. After all, he had plenty of room at Astonville. Teagan could come and stay with him, but Vanessa had dismissed the suggestion. A sweet idea, and generous of him, but Teagan and her mother needed to make up. Whether Teagan wanted to or not.

Lucas wasn't convinced that lumping them together in the same house was the best way for them to reconcile. Not having had sisters, he didn't have firsthand experience of the dynamics of female relationships, but he'd had enough girlfriends and female interactions to get a general idea. The odds of things going smoothly were about as good as him making the Australian cricket team, but he kept that thought to himself. Now wasn't the time for negativity. And Vanessa might yet prove him wrong.

As he approached the steps he caught Dom's deep articulate voice. Stuffed if he knew what Vanessa saw in him. The bloke was good-looking and rich, but there was no getting away from the sort of man he was inside: an arsehole of the highest order.

His hand tightened on Teagan's, but she slipped from his grip.

'It's okay. You don't have to babysit me.'

He shrugged. 'You need someone to share that drink with.' They climbed up to the house, their tread slow and subdued. The door squeaked as Lucas held it open for Teagan. Immediately Dom's voice quietened.

'Teagan, darling.' Vanessa crossed from the kitchen. 'I was getting worried.'

'Busy day.' She nodded at Dom. 'Domenic.'

'If you don't mind me saying, you look a bit tired.'

She brushed hair from her forehead and let out a weary breath. 'Probably because I am.'

'Working seven days a week isn't healthy. For anyone,' said Dom. 'You should take it easy for a day. Indulge a little.' He glanced at Vanessa as though seeking approval to go on, and Lucas had the impression they'd been brewing something together. 'A day-spa session. Top-to-toe treatment. My treat.'

Vanessa clapped her hands and beamed at Teagan. 'What a good idea! It could be just what you need.'

'No thanks,' said Teagan. 'I'm too busy anyway.'

'Too busy for a full body massage and facial?' Dom tutted. 'You don't know what you're missing. Seriously, Teagan, on the house.'

'Sorry. Not interested.'

Dom shared a brief frown with Vanessa. 'Believe me, you'll feel like a new woman.'

Lucas wanted to wrap an arm around Teagan and steer her away. Instead, he did the next best thing and spoke for her in a hard-edged tone designed to end the conversation. 'She's not interested.'

Dom held his gaze, expression bland.

Teagan smiled wanly. 'Right now all I care about is a long shower.'

'Then go and enjoy one, darling.' Vanessa threw both Lucas and Dom a remonstrating look and ushered her out. 'There's beer in the fridge if you want, Lucas. More wine there, too. Dom, could you be a sweetheart and pour a glass for Teagan?'

'You're very protective,' said Dom as he raided the fridge. He handed Lucas a beer before reaching inside again for a bottle of chardonnay.

'Someone has to protect her from you.'

'I mean Teagan no harm.' His eye contact remained steady, unintimidated by the hostility in Lucas's voice. 'I mean no one harm.'

'Sure. Whatever.' He cracked his beer and wandered back out to the verandah. To his annoyance, Dom joined him.

'So how's business?'

He took a long draught of beer. 'Fine.'

'And everything else?'

'What do you care?'

Dom looked away. Lucas felt an immediate pang of guilt and was irritated by it. Being anywhere close to Dom irritated him. It annoyed him that the man was here now, trying it on with Vanessa. And worse, sucking up to Teagan.

He tilted the neck of his bottle towards Dom. 'I don't know what your agenda is, but I'm watching.'

Dom spread his hands in innocence. 'I told you. I have no agenda. I'm not the same man as before.' He paused, maintaining eye contact. 'I'd like you to see that.'

The door pushed open and Vanessa smiled at them both, although the fine lines at the corner of her mouth twitched with worry. 'I hope you two are playing nice.'

Dom turned his charming smile on his host. 'I always play nice.'

Lucas swung away and braced his forearms on the rail. He wished things were normal, the way they'd been before Dom had wormed his way into his life. Mostly they were, but in Dom's presence all he could think of was his mum and how she'd suffered. The way they both had; one with bitterness and then physical pain, the other with longing that had morphed into resentment.

'Did you manage to talk to Teagan?' Vanessa asked, moving to Lucas's side.

'A bit.'

'And?'

He picked at the bottle label, wishing he hadn't accepted the beer. Teagan was back safe and, he hoped, a bit comforted. He had no reason to be here, yet neither could he bring himself to leave. 'She's upset.'

Vanessa bit her lip. 'I feel so awful about all this, but how was I to know Penny was going to pull this stunt?' She blinked away tears. 'She's my sister. What am I supposed to do?'

'Hey,' said Dom, stretching his arm across her shoulders and folding her towards him. 'We'll work something out.'

Lucas's lip curled. What was it with this 'we' business? He didn't like the way Dom was holding Vanessa. It reminded him too much of how Lucas had held Teagan only a short while ago. Like it had meaning.

He took another slug of beer. 'I should go.'

'But, darling, you haven't had anything to eat.'

'I have food at home. Tell Teagan . . .'

What did he want to say to Teagan? That it'd be all right? That he'd help? That he could see she was a bit fucked up right now and didn't mind because he kind of understood where it came from? That his feelings had moved beyond base attraction to something else?

She wasn't ready for that. Especially now.

'Tell her I'm around if she needs someone to talk to.'

With an apologetic smile at Vanessa, Lucas dumped his beer and trotted down the stairs. Footsteps followed. Lucas clenched his jaw and kept his stride long. When he reached the car, he stopped and spun, chin jutted, fists clenched. 'What do you want?'

Dom ignored his aggression. 'You and I need to have a discussion.'

'I have nothing to discuss with you. Ever.'

Pain shot across Dom's face and was replaced with something harder. 'You can't keep pretending, Lucas.'

'Why not? I managed to pretend for thirty-two years already. What's another thirty-two matter?' He yanked open the door. Angry that he was leaving when he wanted to be there for Teagan. Even angrier that this prick had followed him to his car.

Dom grabbed the top of the door, preventing Lucas from closing it. He bent close, blue eyes dark with shadows. 'Whether you like it or not, I'm still your father.'

'No, Domenic,' he said, emphasising the syllables of his name, reminding the man of what he would never be in Lucas's mind. 'You're not. You never were from the start and you sure as hell aren't now. So take your false care and leave me the fuck alone.'

Vanessa frowned as Dom walked slowly back to the verandah. What was it with those two? That Lucas had no time for Dom she knew, but the confrontation she'd just witnessed seemed about to descend into a punch-up.

'Are you okay?' she asked, when Dom trudged up the stairs.

'Yes.' He smiled tightly. 'Just a business matter.'

'With Lucas?'

He made a dismissive gesture. 'Nothing important. Some iron work for the centre.'

Vanessa knew from his locked countenance that she shouldn't press, but her curiosity was on fire. 'He hasn't done it?'

'We're,' he hesitated, 'negotiating.'

'Interesting way of negotiating.'

Dom didn't answer. He sat and stared out into the night, a broody expression pinching his face. He looked troubled, a feeling that was hardly unique. Right now, the entire Falls Valley felt leaden with worry.

She sighed and picked up her wineglass, swirling the contents. 'This used to be such a peaceful place. I was so happy when I found it. It was exactly what I needed after Timoteo.'

'You make it sound like it's no longer so.'

'Things are changing. There's a bad wind blowing.' She put down her glass and rested her hands on her belly. 'Do you really have to expand the centre?'

'Even in its current form the rehab and private-therapy division returns three times the profit of the spa.' He leaned back, his face resuming its usual composure. 'It would be bad business not to expand on that, but to do so requires privacy and space. More areas where clients can be alone but secure. A place where they can receive treatment for their addictions and mental-health issues without stressing that they'll be photographed without makeup, looking fragile or, God forbid, normal. I have the means and location to provide that.'

Vanessa toyed with the stem of her wineglass. She wanted to drink some more, but she'd been indulging just a little too much these last few days. They all had. 'I hate to think of so much of the valley being fenced off.'

'I can understand your concern. And I agree, it does seem a shame, but the land is private property, to be developed as I choose within regulations and government ruling.'

He shifted to prop one elbow on the table and balance his head on his fingertips, his body open to her. The type of relaxed, trust-me pose he used when trying to convince her of his sincerity. Vanessa suspected that using deliberate, open body language was so second nature to Dom now he didn't realise he did it. Or that she noticed.

'I operate a business where customer satisfaction is paramount. Security was my number-one priority even before this, thanks to that incident at the bakery. Another breach and the centre's reputation, the very thing that makes it trusted and therefore profitable, would be under serious threat.'

'Perhaps you should solve the problem by buying an island instead.'

'A pleasant idea. Unfortunately, there aren't that many available.' He gazed into the distance, towards where Lucas's lights had faded. 'Besides, I want to be here.' He glanced back at her and smiled. 'One day, I'd like to live here permanently.'

Vanessa left that comment unanswered. She took a sip of chardonnay, wondering why Dom felt so sentimental about The Falls. Other than his business, he had no connection to the area or community. Perhaps he didn't need one. After all, she'd settled here and made it home. There was no reason why Dom couldn't, too.

As the same longing for companionship that had afflicted her days before squeezed her heart again, she found herself hoping strongly that he would. Afraid he might recognise her desire, Vanessa kept her focus on the surrounding rustling eucalypts. The breeze had lifted, and the air was redolent with the scents of the scrub. She wished she was in a better mood to enjoy it.

'I'm considering signing up for the Falcons.'

She regarded him with surprise. 'I didn't think you played cricket.'

Dom grimaced and scratched at his neck. 'I don't.'

His out-of-character sheepishness had her studying him closely. How fascinating. Dom was never one to allow himself to be shown up, yet here he was contemplating putting himself forward for exactly that to happen. There had to be a reason. Business? Surely not. Public opinion mattered, but the reality was the council or the Land and Environment Court would decide the fate of the centre. Which only left something personal, but what? It would take more than cricket heroics to entice Vanessa into his bed, as he was well aware. So who was he trying to impress?

She hid her curiosity with a smile. 'Mark will probably kiss you if you do. And Bunny. These days she's nearly as nutty about the team as Mark.'

'They make a good pair, don't they?'

'They do.'

He stretched across the table for her hand. 'Like us.'

'Not like us.' She gave the back of his hand a sympathetic pat and reached for her glass before he could trap her in his grip. 'Those two will last once they get over their hang-ups. You and I would only end up fighting.'

'Then making up for it in bed.'

Perhaps Dom found the idea appealing, but to Vanessa that sounded too much like the past. Relationships that used conflict to ignite passion were exhausting and bruising. She was a woman in her fifties, not a teenager. She wanted love, respect and comfort as well as good sex.

'You're forgetting I've been in relationships like that. I've learned that I need more than passion.'

His gaze stayed anchored on hers. 'And those needs are?'

Affected by the intensity of his look, she took a sip of wine before answering. 'Genuine love and affection. Friendship. The kind of deep caring that keeps people together long after the rest has passed its peak.'

'We have friendship.'

There was no denying that.

'I care for you, Nessie. More than I think you appreciate.' His eyes shone with reflected light and something else that made her heart thud. He dropped his voice. 'I can give you everything, including passion.'

'And when it's past its peak?'

'Who says that would ever happen?' He rose and stood in front of her with his hand held out. 'Come on, take a chance.'

Night sounds gathered in and merged with her hesitant breaths. Vanessa looked at his face, then his hand and back to the handsome contours of his features. Oh, it was tempting. Though she tried to deny it, Dom made her blood run faster, her skin prickle with sexual awareness. She longed for his touch. She wanted to know what it would be like to have those palms run over her body, to feel his lips on her skin, to merge together until everything was forgotten.

Footsteps sounded in the house. Vanessa blinked and breathed out. Her smile was shallow with relief and hidden disappointment. 'Not tonight.'

Dom's arm fell to his side. 'No, perhaps not. Another time then.'

Except with Penny arriving tomorrow there would unlikely be another time. Three women, all troubled in their own way, all with reconciliations to forge, rattling their tensions through the one house. Chances were it was going to get bitchy.

Another night might be a long time away.

TWELVE

TEAGAN WATCHED the last of the dressage-school attendees ease their cars and floats onto the main road. Training had ended hours ago, but Nick, being a good host, had put on a barbecue and drinks for those who didn't have far to journey or wanted to stay and chat. Stacey had brought the baby out for everyone to coo at. Sausage and onion aromas laced the air along with the comforting smell of horses and stables. The chatter had been amiable, horse talk and gossip, like Teagan had once enjoyed with Em and Jas when they gathered together.

She pushed a tangle of dusty hair off her face. God, she missed home. She missed her friends and Astra and Pinehaven. She even missed Levenham, with its familiar streets and faces, and a history and landscape she'd grown up with. The only thing she didn't miss was the weather.

Behind her folding chairs were being snapped shut. Little Olly went into his baby carrier. Nick glanced at her with eyebrows raised.

Teagan sucked on her lip. Time to go.

'See you Tuesday,' she called, earning a distracted wave from Stacey and a nod from Nick. She wished she'd rejected his offer of a day off but he'd been insistent. And she was tired; bone weary, heart-achingly exhausted. From work, fretfulness and restless nights that seemed to contain more conscious hours than sleep.

The lights of the verandah were on when she drove into Falls Farm. Moths flitted, casting shadows against the lemon-painted walls, reminding Teagan of the spots that appeared on damaged sepia-tinted cinema reels. Ness was in her favourite chair. The other was empty. The table, though, was set with an ice bucket of champagne and a bottle of Cassis. Kir royales for the Sunday cocktail ritual. Except the other two glasses on the table were empty. Only Ness had a drink.

Her aunt rose, tone and expression pure sympathy. Ness showing she knew why Teagan was so late. 'Darling.'

Teagan lowered her backpack. 'Is she here?'

'Inside.'

She stared at the screen door. Behind it, nothing moved in the house. Perhaps her mother was having a lie-down after a day spent in airports. She wondered where Penny had found the money to pay for the ticket. Stole it from Dad she hoped, although her generous aunt was the most likely source.

Ness placed a gentle hand on Teagan's upper arm. 'I'm afraid she's not in a good way.'

'And I am?' She scraped a palm down her face. She really needed to cut this victim crap. 'Sorry.'

'It's a difficult time for all of us.' Moving back to the table, Ness lifted a champagne flute. 'Drink?'

'I wouldn't mind a shower first. It's been a long day.'

'Of course.' She placed the flute down and crossed one arm over her chest, enfolding herself in a very un-Vanessa-like manner and blinking rapidly. 'I'm so sorry for this. I really am.'

'Oh, Ness.' Teagan wrapped her arms around her aunt. 'It's okay. I know you had no choice.' She maintained her hold, granting, if only for a brief moment, her big-hearted aunt the comfort of her under-standing.

She let go, and smiled as they both sniffed and swatted damp eyes. In her harrowed state she'd needed the hug as much as Ness had.

'Go have that shower. I'll fetch some nibblies for us all.'

Teagan pushed inside. She eyed the closed door of the guest area's other bedroom. Blanche sat in front of it, tail whipping across the polished timber, head tilted up in expectation.

'Fairweather friend,' she muttered, tossing the cat a dark look.

A bump echoed. Blanche's tail ceased its swish. As the door's handle began to turn, Teagan dashed into her room and held her back against the closed door, breathing hard with her eyes squeezed shut. She could do this. She could. All she needed was a moment to gather herself.

A latch clicked open and was quietly closed. Feet padded across the timber and then the screen door squealed. Good. Her mum was on the verandah. Respite would last a little longer.

The shower washed the grime, sweat and horse stink away and made Teagan feel cleaner but not much better. Nerves rattled her body as she dressed. She wished she'd said yes to Vanessa's offer of a drink and brought it in with her. Anything to take the edge off what would likely be an uncomfortable meeting.

Their farewell hadn't been pleasant. Penny had stood in the doorway of Teagan's cottage at Pinehaven, wringing her hands, while Teagan had dumped clothes into duffle bags and thrown less robust belongings into old suitcases. Though she'd kept her mouth shut, kept all her bitter, furious words inside, Teagan had boiled with resentment and deep hurt. When she'd deigned to look at her mother, the contact was brief and furious. Blame had hung like disturbed dust, thick and choking. Not once had Penny said sorry. Not once.

Maybe if she had Teagan wouldn't feel this way. Maybe the bitterness would stop eating acid trails through her soul. She slumped onto the bed and stared at the wall. God, she was being unreasonable. Why should her mum apologise? She'd done nothing wrong. It was all Dad. Dad and his computer and some stupid program he'd been suckered into buying, thinking he could raise enough money to entice her brother home from New Zealand.

How idiotic men were. Owen had found love, that's why he was in New Zealand. Not because his new wife's dad had a better property. But oh no, Graham Bliss had taken the selfish route, thinking it was all about the farm and money and nothing to do with his son's heart.

What about his daughter's heart? What about her money? What about her dreams?

Gone. The lot.

Teagan buried her face in her hands. What a bastard he was. What a complete bastard. No wonder she didn't trust anyone.

Her thoughts ran to Lucas, the way they'd stood together at The Falls, the way he'd looked at her in his forge. The tenderness with which he'd held her yesterday evening while she'd cried. Her heart ached to believe in him, but the cynic in her smouldered and spiralled smoke whispers in her ears. If her own father was capable of devastating her so calamitously, what damage could Lucas do if Teagan allowed herself to feel for him?

Better to stay distant. From everyone.

She took a moment to ensure her breathing was normal and her face and eyes had lost their stinging heat. Steady again, she dressed quickly in a pair of jeans and T-shirt and tied her wet hair back into a ponytail.

Her mum made a shaky stand when she walked out onto the verandah, steadying herself on the cane chair. 'Teagan.'

Shock caused Teagan to still. She flicked a peek at Ness, but her aunt was pouring drinks. Admittedly, Teagan hadn't been in a great state herself when she'd arrived at Falls Farm, but in the few weeks since she'd last seen her, Penny seemed to have disintegrated. Silver dominated the faded tones of her once red hair. The skin of her face had dropped like a fleshy landslide, stretching her jowls. Sorrow lines dug deep furrows around her mouth, and fat, bruise-coloured sacs hung under her eyes.

The collapse continued with her posture. Her spine and shoulders were slumped, her body defeated, all care gone. Everything about her screamed self-neglect. And she'd lost weight. A whole lot of weight.

Like mother, like daughter.

Teagan did her best to keep the horror from her voice and face. 'Hi, Mum. Good trip?'

Her mum hovered like she wanted a hug. Teagan glanced again at Ness, who was observing their reunion closely with her lips rolled together. At her subtle nod Teagan reached to give her mum a rapid, awkward embrace and clumsy, hesitant cheek kiss that had none of the intense emotion she'd shared with Ness only minutes before. They'd never been an affectionate family anyway. Not like Emily, whose familial devotion had, until recently, made get-togethers a much-loved ritual.

Contact made, she quickly moved on. 'Long day, I'm guessing.'

Penny wrung her hands in the same anguished way she had at Pinehaven. 'Yes. We had a delay coming out of Melbourne. Fog.'

Ness handed Teagan her glass, mouthing a thank you before addressing her sister. 'Penny darling, are you sure you won't have a drink? A small one to help you relax?'

'No, no.' She fluttered her hand, a nervous, jerky movement that made Ness frown. 'I'm fine, thank you.'

Teagan carried her glass to the verandah rail and leaned against it. Her mother surveyed her surroundings with a lost expression. Her shoulders hunched further. Collapsing back into her chair, she stared at her lap. Teagan looked away, her throat turning rough. She should have offered more but she wasn't capable. The wounds of loss, leaving and betrayal were too open.

'I'll get those nibblies,' said Ness. 'I'm sure you're both hungry.' As she passed Teagan she touched her forearm in a brief gesture of reassurance.

Teagan took a slug of her drink and stared through the dark at Betty and Wilma's hutch. The cocktail was slightly sweet and effervescent, a cheerful drink for summertime. The inappropriateness of it in the face of her mother's strange manner and awful appearance seemed wrong.

It was one of those peculiar nights she'd come to admire in the valley. Most evenings the temperature dropped rapidly as cool air cascaded from the ranges into the hollows. But tonight it remained balmy, the birds, insects and possums lively. The land had a happy life-filled ring to it. Yet on the verandah a bleak drama was playing out.

She wished it would end.

'Ness said you've left Dad.'

'Yes.'

Teagan nodded, searching for something else to add. 'How is he taking it?'

'Taking it?' Penny let out a laugh that sounded more like a sob. 'He's not.'

'What do you mean?'

'Your father lives in a dream world. He probably hasn't even realised I've gone.'

'Still wrapped in his computer, then?'

She nodded.

Teagan wasn't surprised. Even when their world was turning to shit his addict-intense dedication to the trading program hadn't wavered. 'Have you spoken to Owen?'

'Yes.'

'And?'

Penny shook her head. No sympathy from her brother it seemed. Teagan should have expected as much. On one level she couldn't blame Owen for not inviting his mother over to stay. They'd never been that kind of family and he had a new life now. A sweet new bride, a farm to work. And Owen was unlikely to have forgotten the fierce recriminations that had followed his announcement that he was relocating permanently to New Zealand.

How amazing that Teagan had once thought his move a positive thing. That this would be her opportunity to prove to her dad that she could take over the farm. But no matter how she protested, he'd been convinced she'd give it up the moment marriage and pregnancy came along. That her heart wasn't really in it. And what had she done? Instead of telling him where to shove his sexist attitude, she'd given up all chance of love and romance to prove him wrong.

Ness came back out with a tray of dips, pâté, pickled vegetables, and a basket of sliced French stick. Teagan and her mother regarded it with equal dismay.

'Some tapenade?'

Penny looked at her sister in confusion.

'Olive dip,' explained Ness kindly. 'It's very nice.'

Wrinkles formed across Penny's nose. Teagan suppressed a sigh of irritation. Her mother didn't go for fancy food. She rarely drank, and never wine. She didn't do anything remotely risky or exciting. She just followed meekly after her husband, straight into disaster.

Self-recognition had Teagan quickly turning to face the night again, her teeth jammed together. Finding fault with her mother was a bit rich when she'd suffered the same failings. Truth was they were both a pair of fools.

She took another slug of kir, desperate for the pain to go away, but since the news of her mother's arrival the scabs over her slowly healing cuts had been broken open. And they wouldn't stop stinging.

Ness fussed with food that nobody wanted, spreading bread with pâté, pushing dips and vegetables across the table, while the evening lay clotted and hushed around them.

Finally, Teagan broke the quiet.

'Why did you have to come here, Mum?' Her voice cracked on the words. 'I don't understand it. All those years you spent criticising Ness, holding her up as a bad example the moment I showed any interest in her life. Yet here is where you come?'

'Teagan, please,' said Ness. 'Not tonight.'

Penny's eyes were enormous and liquid, her face sagging into even more folds. She looked old and fragile and pathetically vulnerable. 'I had nowhere else.'

At the simplicity of her answer Teagan pressed her head against the verandah post and screwed her eyes shut. She hauled in several long breaths and straightened. 'I'm sorry. Ness is right. This isn't the time.'

Penny shook her head. 'No, you're right. I shouldn't have come. I'll find somewhere else tomorrow.'

'You will do no such thing!' Ness knelt by her sister's knees and clasped her hands. 'I promise you, Penny, it's fine. You're welcome here. For as long as you need.' She glanced at Teagan and back to her sister. 'We're all tired and emotional at the moment. It's been a tough few days for everyone, especially you. We'll talk tomorrow. Tonight is for rest.'

But her words were too late. The elephant had trumpeted and couldn't be ignored.

Sniffing and trembling, Penny raised her old-sad eyes to her daughter. 'I know I let you down. I know I should've encouraged you to think beyond the farm, experience a bit more of life, but you were so happy at Pinehaven. It was all you seemed to want, and when Owen left and didn't come home, I was scared I'd lose you, too. Then Graham, he . . . he started to change . . .'

It was the most they'd talked in a long time and the emotion of it was flailing Teagan inside and out. She wished she could relieve her mother of the anguish of it, but there were so many questions.

'Why didn't you stop him? He was gambling our lives away. Our futures.'

'Because I didn't know! I honestly didn't. I thought he was doing . . . other things.' Her voice fell to a whisper, her gaze falling with it. She crushed her lips together until they turned pale. 'I was ashamed. I hoped it would pass.'

'But the money, Mum. He took all the money.' Teagan slapped her hand on her chest. 'Money that I'd worked my guts out to save.'

'I didn't know. He said it was just a few thousand.'

'A few thousand? Mum, it was nearly eighty grand! Every cent I'd saved since school!' She looked away, breathing hard. Saying the sum out loud made her heart race, like she was having some sort of a panic attack. All that cash. Teagan was twenty-nine years old. How could she ever catch up?

'Please,' said Ness, 'why don't we leave this for now. Have a drink and something to eat and then sleep on it. We can talk in the morning. When we're all rested.'

'I have to work,' said Teagan.

Ness regarded her with dismay. 'But I thought you said Nick planned to give you Monday off to make up for the weekend.'

She shrugged, not liking herself for the lie, but the fluttery panic in her chest was frightening. She didn't want to talk tomorrow. Talk wouldn't solve the mess she was in. It would only remind her how deep the pit she'd fallen in was. 'He changed his mind.'

Vanessa's eyes narrowed. She didn't come out and call Teagan a liar, but Teagan could tell she wanted to. Lying had never been Teagan's forte and the fib was brazen. Her mother was too distressed to notice, but Ness had. No doubt there'd be a chat about it later. Later Teagan might be able to handle it. Right now she couldn't.

Penny stood, a slow, careful rise like an aching arthritic woman. 'I think I'll go to bed.' Her pleading gaze landed on Teagan. 'I didn't come here to ruin anything. I just thought . . .' She contorted her mouth as though holding in a sob and gave a weary wave of her hand. 'It doesn't matter.'

With a leaden weight in her belly, Teagan watched Ness escort her mum inside.

Ness returned and gathered up the untouched food. She held the tray in front of her while she addressed Teagan. 'I'm going to bed as well. It's been a trying day.'

'I might stay out here a while.'

'Brooding won't help.'

'I know.' She pointed to Saffy, parked on her haunches at Vanessa's feet, gazing big-eyed at the tray her mistress held. 'At least I'll have company.'

Ness's mouth parted as though she was about to say more, then she nodded. 'Try not to stay up too late. You need sleep, especially if you have to work tomorrow.' The last sentence was said with an edge. But Ness added nothing further, and after a meaningful eye meet, left Teagan to it.

When Ness had gone Teagan slumped on her seat with the last of her kir and her mobile phone. She stayed there for a long while, keeping company with Saffy and toying with the phone's screen. She needed to touch base with someone who understood what this last year had destroyed. Who remembered her as she once was, the happy girl who used to laugh and enjoy life, the Teagan who existed when her dream still lived. Someone who could promise her this anguish wasn't forever. That there was a way out of the pit.

She needed a friend, desperately.

Her call to Em went straight to voicemail. Another to Jas yielded the same result.

Which only left Lucas.

For a long time, as the night air began to swirl and cool around her ankles, and the creatures of The Falls squabbled and chirruped and chorused for mates, Teagan's thumb hovered over the little green dial icon. Until, finally, she placed the phone carefully down and gave into staring at the darkness. Alone.

THIRTEEN

LUCAS ANSWERED the knock at the door wearing only jeans and a sleepy expression. A white T-shirt hung loosely from one hand as though he'd scooped it up from the floor in passing. Teagan tried not to stare at the lightly haired curves of his chest, but her wits were as dulled as her spirit, and her jaw remained slack at the sight.

'Teagan.' He stepped out into the early morning. The sun had only begun to peek over the hills, but it tickled his skin, lighting the stubble on his chin and the smooth sheen of his developing tan. He held her shoulder, tilting his head to examine her face. 'Everything okay?'

'Fine. Fine.' Teagan squinted towards his forge and looked back to find him still studying her. She was sure her fake smile was like something out of a clown horror movie, but she kept it in place anyway. 'I know it's a bit rude of me to ask, but do you mind if I hang out here today?'

'Sure.' He began to pull his shirt over his head and drag it over his chest. Teagan wished he wouldn't. The sight of its broad muscularity, the certainty he'd let her bawl onto it if she asked, was reassuring. 'I have a few appointments this morning but they won't take long. Mondays are quiet.'

'I could do a few chores. Help out.'

'By the look of those bloodshot eyes, you'd be better off sleeping. Have you had breakfast?'

She shook her head.

'Come on, I'll make you some.'

She followed him into the kitchen and took a seat at the table while he filled the kettle and set about putting pans on the stove.

'Bacon and eggs okay?'

She nodded. Greasy comfort food would be perfect.

'Coffee or tea?'

Teagan thought for a moment. 'Tea would be good.' She rose. 'I can make it.'

'Nope.' He waved a spatula at her. 'My kitchen. You stay where you are.'

'At least let me set the table.'

'All right.' He began to point. 'Cutlery drawer, plates. Salt and pepper in the pantry, placemats there, too. Sauce in the fridge, if you want it.'

That was better. Something to make her feel less useless, although no less stupid. Why she'd lied about having to work today she still couldn't figure out. It was cowardly, but a day of talk, of rehashing all that pain, held zero appeal. Especially after last night. Except the lie had left her with a dilemma: either admit to it, pretend sickness, or find somewhere to hide out. The latter had seemed the easiest option, but morning had found her too exhausted to drive anywhere far. With the shops not opening for hours yet, a mall was off the list and a commute into the city held even less appeal. Which had left Astonville.

Lucas handed her a mug. She thanked him and sat back down. The tea steamed and she blew on it before sipping. The brew was hot and sweet and strong.

'Runny or hard?'

'What?'

'Your eggs. Runny or hard?'

'Oh. However they come.'

He raised an eyebrow.

'Runny.'

He grinned like he'd won some sort of a bet. 'I thought you might be.'

'Why? What makes me a runny-egg person?'

'Just a feeling. I like soft eggs, too.'

That didn't surprise her at all. Lucas might be hard in body, but he was proving surprisingly tender inside.

'I'm guessing last night with your mum didn't go well.'

'Not exactly.' She sighed and played with her mug handle. 'I said things I shouldn't have. Everyone was upset. Then Mum went to bed and Ness followed.'

'What did you do?'

'Spent most of the night on the verandah talking to Saffy.'

'Good dog, not much of a conversationalist though. You should've called me.'

'It was late.'

'Wouldn't have mattered. I would've come over, kept you company.'

Busy at the stove, Lucas's back was to her and she couldn't see his face, but she recognised the tightening in his voice.

'Lucas . . .'

He reached for a plate. 'It's what friends do.'

True, but friends didn't come in packages like this. Friends didn't nearly get it on in a pool or stand in front of a waterfall holding hands as if their togetherness was part of nature's beauty. Friends didn't have this electric force running between them.

Yet what was she here for if not that comfort?

'I mean it,' he said, placing a plate in front of her. 'You and me. Friendship. No strings.'

'I've never really had a male friend before.'

'You do now.'

The bacon smelled delicious, awakening her stomach. Other than some bread, sausage and onion at Nick's, she hadn't eaten since late yesterday afternoon.

'Eat,' he said, sitting down and pushing a tub of butter her way.

Teagan did as she was told, savouring her meal and sipping her sweet tea. Lucas didn't say much, apart from the usual questions about how her eggs were and did she want more toast. She helped him with the dishes, watching the morning continue its colourful rise through the kitchen window. It was companionable, standing here. Lucas with his arms plunged in suds, her with the tea towel, and for a moment she had a brief fantasy of what it would be like to wake at Astonville every morning. To stand beside him, smug from sex and a lovingly cooked breakfast, content with the knowledge that tomorrow would bring more of the same.

He handed her a pan, their fingers and gazes connecting for longer than necessary. Heat crept into her cheeks. She withdrew from him a little, head tilted to hide her eyes, hoping like hell her thoughts hadn't been obvious.

'What time's your first appointment?'

'Nine. But it's down near Camden so I'll have to leave around eight.' He glanced at the kitchen clock. 'Plenty of time.'

'For what?'

'Another cuppa.' He grinned. 'Why, did you have other ideas?'

'No,' she said, her voice as goaty as one of Merlin's bleats and her cheeks throbbing with heat. 'No, not at all. Another cuppa sounds good.'

At Lucas's suggestion they carried their mugs out into the crisp morning. The birds had already started up their greetings. The chime of bellbird calls came in surround sound, like constantly moving echoes. A cow mooed nearby and was answered by a horse's neigh. Noise from the road filtered up, commuters heading into the city.

Taking her cue from Lucas, Teagan lounged back on her outdoor chair and rested her legs on the table's thick central timber strut. She breathed in the scent of country life, of eucalyptus and dew, and the occasional waft of dung, and wished her mind could be as peaceful as this place.

'So what are you going to do about the situation with your mum?' he asked eventually.

A hollow feeling descended over her. She rubbed at her eyebrow. 'I don't know. Talk to her, I suppose. Try to sort it all out.'

'And then what?'

'Carry on as I was. Not much else I can do.'

'And if your mum decides to stay?' When she looked confused he continued. 'You're what, twenty-six, twenty-seven?'

'Twenty-nine.' She rolled her eyes. 'Old and cranky.'

'Hey, I'm not much older than you. And I don't feel remotely worn out.'

'That's because you're not human. You're descended from some sort of Greek god. Hardly fair.'

'Believe me, Teagan, my father isn't a god. Far from it.' He took a sip of tea. 'What I meant was that it'd be hard to stay living with your mum and aunt long-term.'

The notion wasn't appealing. 'I'll find somewhere to share. There's bound to be someone looking for a housemate or boarder.' She considered for a moment. 'I'm sure Nick mentioned he used to have live-in stablehands before they started ripping him off and getting up to no good. There's a flat above the tack room. It's not much, but I could ask.'

'Or you could move in here.' Lucas spoke without looking at her, his tone neutral, as if it was an offer he made every day.

Teagan stared at him. He couldn't be serious.

He shrugged, again as if it were of no consequence. 'There's a spare room with a queen-sized bed. I wouldn't ask for much in board, and we could share the shopping and chores.' He took another sip of tea. 'Just a thought.'

'But you hardly know me.'

'I know enough.'

'How do you know I'm domesticated? You like things neat. For all you know I could be completely feral around the house.'

He flopped his head towards her, his eyes rolled upwards.

'All right. So I'm not feral. But, Lucas,' she flicked a finger between them, 'you and me . . .' She shifted, uncomfortable.

'What? Afraid I'll ask for more than board as payment?' His mouth twisted. 'I'm not so thick that I can't tell when someone's not interested. Nor am I the sort of bloke who goes around harassing women. I was serious about us being friends. So you needn't worry about that. You'd be safe.'

Though welcome, his words left Teagan deflated. It was as if she'd imagined the chemistry between them. Perhaps she had. Perhaps it was wishful thinking, or him playing flirty games for the fun of it.

'Offer's there if you want.'

They lapsed back into silence, finishing their tea. It should have been awkward, and for a while it was, but as the minutes passed it began to feel okay. No pressure. No anxiety. Just companionship and the morning coming alive, spreading its glow over a place already polished by one man's care and pride.

'Don't you have any pets?' asked Teagan when she finally worked out what was missing from his home.

'I had a dog once. She died though. I never got around to replacing her, although Bunny keeps trying to fob animals onto me. She once tried to get me to take an alpaca.'

'It's a wonder Ness didn't end up with it.'

'She nearly did, but Bunny found a local hobby farmer who needed a mate for his own alpaca and off it went.'

'You should get a dog.' She nodded to herself. A farm, even a small one like this, wasn't right without a dog.

'I'll think about it.' He tossed out the dregs of his tea and rose. 'Come on, I'll show you the rest of the house and tell you where everything is. Did you bring a change of clothes?'

Teagan screwed up her nose. 'Why, do I smell?'

'No. I just thought you might like a shower after you have a sleep.' He touched her cheek lightly, causing her heart to somersault. 'You really do need bed. You look like shit.'

'Thanks,' she said, the somersault landing in a painful bellyflop. 'Just the compliment I needed.'

He grinned and winked. 'That's what friends are for.'

Lucas tried to keep his impatience at bay, but the horse he was shoeing was being a shit of the highest order. The moment Lucas went to nail the cleats, the bastard thing would drag its leg away, no matter how hard he clenched his thighs. Already he had a rip on one palm where a half-nailed cleat had caught and torn the flesh. It ached like a bastard too, dripping blood and making his grip slip further.

After yet another yank he gave up and ordered the owner to put a twitch on it.

Black-tempered, he stomped to his car and jerked open the first aid kit, not in the mood to be delicate. He tore open a pad and slapped it over the tear, then wrapped a gauze bandage around it, using his teeth to secure the knot tightly. It was only temporary and would get filthy in five minutes, but at least it would stop the bleeding.

Stroppiness wasn't his normal nature, but today he didn't want to be working. He wanted to be home, watching over Teagan. Taking care of her. Satisfying the protective instinct that seemed to pound his chest, Tarzan-like, whenever she was near. No choice though. A bloke had to earn money and he'd worked too hard to achieve all he had to let the bank snatch it back.

As he hammered and rasped he thought about her, wondering how much of the friend ploy she actually bought. He didn't buy it for a second himself so why should she? It was a dumb move, too. How the hell was he meant to keep up the pretence and his hands off her? He didn't want to be friends. He wanted more. A whole lot more.

The last time he'd felt like this was with Hayley, the RAAF dentist he'd met by chance in a sports store in Penrith a few years ago. She was super smart and gorgeous, if a little bit serious and reserved, and for four months it had been full-on. Both of them had been aware it might not last and he'd braced himself for it, but the knowledge hadn't stopped Lucas from falling hard. When Hayley announced she'd been posted to Queensland he'd been devastated and it had taken months before he considered dating again. Finding someone like Hayley though, had proven harder than he thought. Not that there hadn't been offers, just a dearth of the right ones. Plus between renovating the house and work, there hadn't been a lot of time for more than casual relationships, and even those had been few.

Now Teagan had walked into his life. Red hair, a bit funny, sexy as hell, possessing zero pretension and a passion for horses and country life. And what does he do? Tells her he only wants to be friends.

Idiot.

With the horse shod, he headed back towards home, passing through the village to check his post office box. It contained the usual: bills, bills and more bills, plus a bank statement and a newsletter from the Master Farriers Association. He sighed and tossed them through the ute's window onto the seat. Time to buy a lotto ticket.

Half a step inside the newsagent's and he regretted it. Tony was trying to sort mail and do his best to ignore Colin, but the old bugger was in full flight.

'Oh,' he said, breaking off mid-sentence and whizzing around before Lucas could sneak off. 'Good. You can sign up while you're here.'

A clipboard was immediately shoved under his nose, quickly followed by a pen.

Lucas stepped back, hands up. 'Just coming for a lotto ticket, Col. Not here to join schemes.'

Col made a sour face. 'And when our village is overrun with drug addicts and paparazzo?'

'Give it a rest,' muttered Tony, moving down the counter to serve Lucas. 'How many games?'

'What's it worth?'

'Twenty mill.'

'Better give us a full card then.'

A pen jabbed Lucas's ribs. 'You should pay attention. It's your livelihood at stake, too.'

Experience had taught him many times to keep his mouth shut, but Lucas couldn't help baiting. 'Can't see how, Col. Be good for business, I reckon. I mean, all those rich people, they'd want horses to ride, wouldn't they? Give it a year or two and Bunny and I could be raking it in.'

Tony had to turn away to hide his laughter as Col began to splutter. Lucas grinned and handed over a fifty, before inspecting the sheet of lotto numbers. What he'd do with that money. He could give up shoeing horses and muck around with blacksmithing full-time.

'You don't understand!'

'Did you just stamp your foot?'

Col blinked, bewildered. 'What?'

'Your foot. Did you stamp it?'

'I'm angry!' The clipboard was thrust out again. 'If you think anything of our village you'll sign.'

'Sign what?'

'The Fuckuppas,' said Tony.

Now it was Lucas's turn to blink while Colin worked his mouth in fury. The old man's speckled head was nearly scarlet.

'The Falls Union Progress Association,' explained Tony. 'Also known as the Fuckuppas.'

Laughter bubbled. Lucas tried to suppress it, but with Col still mouthing like a guppy and Tony desperately faking innocence there was no chance he could hold it in. He let out a great roar of laughter that set Col foot-stomping again, then off on some diatribe about thieving bastards who stole from rightful owners.

Suddenly things weren't quite so funny anymore. Hate him or not, the thieving bastard in question was still his father.

'You want to watch that temper,' warned Lucas. 'Bloke your age, high blood pressure, you could pop a vessel if you're not careful. Anyway, why don't you give poor Tony a break and stake out someone else's shop. In fact, why don't you just shut up and go home. And take your Fuckuppa bullshit with you. You're all for saving the village and the shops, but have a look at what you're doing. Scaring people away with your temper tantrums and stupid group. You're like a frigging scarecrow.'

Colin's guppy mouth turned into a cod's. Tony couldn't meet Lucas's eye.

Aware he'd overstepped the mark and, worse, done it in Dom's defence, Lucas bolted.

He drove out of the carpark one-handed, the other scraping his head in consternation. Since when did he defend his father? He didn't even like the prick, but there'd been something about the conversation they'd had by his ute that he hadn't been able to shake. A nagging feeling that Dom had meant every word.

Driving usually settled Lucas, but the confrontation had darkened his mood. Not quite the way he wanted to arrive home to Teagan. He'd wanted to be cheerful. Lift her spirits with his good humour. Maybe spend a bit more time talking, see what happened. Let the discussion turn intimate. Perhaps even slide into lazy afternoon sex, followed by a snooze and then more sex. He hadn't done that for ages.

But as the gates of Falls Farm neared worry lodged in his gut and wouldn't move. People didn't arrive on your doorstep at dawn unless there was something seriously troubling going on. A check with Vanessa to see what was up wouldn't hurt. Nor would mention of his offer of a room for Teagan either. He didn't want Vanessa taking it the wrong way. Besides, he was curious about Teagan's mum.

A thin elderly woman was stooped over Betty and Wilma's hutch when he entered the yard. As he pulled to a stop, she straightened, a white guinea pig in her arms, and he saw she wasn't as ancient as her bearing suggested. Teagan's mum, had to be. Lifeless, whitish hair retaining only a hint of copper, and sagging features, as if the personality behind them was crushed. Even so the familial resemblance was clear. In her day she must have been an attractive woman. She possessed Teagan's sharp, birdlike essence and eyes.

She stroked Wilma as she observed his approach.

'You must be Teagan's mum. I'm Lucas, a friend of Vanessa's.'

'Oh,' she said, 'hello. I'm Penny.' She waved vaguely behind her. 'Vanessa's inside, making lunch.'

He nodded at Wilma. The guinea pig was snuggled down making happy little high-pitched purrs in time with Penny's caresses. 'You've made a friend.'

'Yes.' She cuddled the pig closer. 'Sweet little thing, isn't she?'

Something pressed against his leg. Lucas looked down to see Blanche curling around his ankles. He pushed her away with his toe. 'Bugger off, Blanche.' At the look on Penny's face he smiled apologetically. 'Blanche has a hankering for guinea pig.'

'Oh,' said Penny again, her widening eyes making her look suddenly even more like Teagan.

Distracted, Lucas almost missed Blanche's sneaky move. He glanced down in time to catch the cat in the process of slithering through the open hutch door. Hunkered in the corner, Betty began shrieking hysterically.

'Oh, no you don't.' With a scoop he hoisted Blanche aside and slammed down the hatch. She landed on soft feet and bared her teeth.

Penny looked as though she was about to burst into tears. 'I'm so sorry. I didn't realise.'

'It's okay. You weren't to know. Blanche might act friendly but she's as cunning as they come.'

'Lucas!' Vanessa waved from the verandah. 'I've just made lunch. Did you want to stay?'

'Sorry. Need to get home.' He glanced at Penny and strode to the base of the steps. 'Do you have a minute?'

Vanessa understood his tone immediately. 'Of course.' She descended the stairs looking ridiculously girlish and sexy in a pair of faded skinny jeans, a pale-purple fitted T-shirt that followed every curve of her breasts, and matching suede flats. He couldn't blame Dom for wanting her. Any man with half a dose of testosterone would. She gently extracted Wilma from her sister's arms. 'Why don't you get ready for lunch? I won't be a minute.'

With childlike obedience, Penny wandered off.

Vanessa sighed. 'We were never close, you know, but it's awful to see her like this.'

'She looks pretty unhappy.'

'Yes. Even worse than when I collected her from the airport.' Her mouth thinned. 'Last night didn't help. Teagan and Penny had words and now she thinks she's not welcome here. That she's made every-thing worse. I've tried to tell her that's not true but she needs to hear it from Teagan.' Her gaze turned shrewd. 'I don't suppose you know where she is, because I know for a fact she's not at Belgravia.'

'At home. Turned up around six this morning. I don't think she got much sleep last night.'

'None of us did. It's all Graham's fault.' Vanessa let out a growl. 'I could throttle that man, I really could.'

'Listen, I told Teagan she could board with me if she wanted.'

Vanessa studied him but where he'd expected a cheeky dig he received coolness. 'Altruistic of you.'

'Just trying to help.'

'I'm sure.' Finally she smiled, although there wasn't a lot of humour behind it. Tiredness was sapping even her irrepressible sparkle. 'I suppose getting her into bed might help relieve some of that pent-up emotion.'

'Not happening. We're friends.'

She arched a thin eyebrow. 'Friends?'

'Yeah. And not the sort with benefits.' He winked. 'Yet.'

That brought on a laugh. 'You're playing hard to get? Oh, darling, I knew you were clever but that's naughty. Poor Teagan.'

He spread his arms. 'She can have me. All she has to do is ask.'

'But she won't.' Vanessa tapped his chest with a pale-purple fingernail. 'And you know it.'

Lucas turned serious. 'I don't think she knows what she wants right now. Seems safer to play the friend card. Work it from there.'

'I think you're right.' She gazed into the distance. 'It's all so horrible. So much pain and bitterness. But she and Penny need to talk it out. It's the only way.'

'I'll send her home after lunch.' He released an exaggerated sigh. 'There goes my chance for a bit of afternoon delight.'

She gave him an understanding pat. 'Poor darling.'

'Easy for you to say. You haven't been dreaming of her in that bikini these last couple of weeks.' He kissed her cheek. 'Hang in there. You'll all be fine.'

She squeezed his hand. 'Thanks, Lucas. You're a good boy.'

'I am. And what a bloody great bugger it is, too.'

FOURTEEN

TEAGAN ROLLED ONTO HER BACK, stretched and rubbed her eyes. She stared at the ceiling for a moment, blinking away the last of her sleepiness. With the curtains closed it was hard to tell what time it was but she doubted she'd slept for long. She wasn't good at sleeping these days. Hadn't been for quite some time, if she thought about it.

She shifted onto her side again, tucked her hands under her cheek and let her lids flutter closed. A floorboard creaked, too loud to be a normal house moan. Her eyes snapped open.

Lucas stood in the doorway. 'Sorry. I didn't mean to wake you.'

'You didn't. Not really. I'd just woken.' She sat up and rubbed at her mouth where an itch had formed and felt the crust of dried slobber. She quickly slid off the bed, angling away from him as she scrubbed furiously, hoping he hadn't noticed. Parting the curtains, she put on a bright, high voice. 'So what time is it?'

'After two.'

She let the curtains fall. 'You're kidding me.'

He shook his head.

'Shit,' she said, scraping her messy hair from her face and turning to tidy the rumpled bed. 'I've been asleep for hours.'

'You needed it. Now you'll need lunch. Corned beef, cheese and tomato sandwich okay with you?'

'Lucas, you don't have to. I can go buy us something.'

'Trust me, you don't want to be heading into the village right now. Not after what I just did to Col.'

'That sounds ominous.'

He grinned. 'He was hanging around Tony's, being a pest, so I said that for someone trying to save the village he was doing a fine job of sending its business owners broke.'

She grinned back. 'Oh dear. How did he take it?'

'Stamped his foot.' Lucas's laugh echoed off the hallway walls as he headed for the kitchen. 'I told him he needed to watch himself. Bloke of his age could pop a vessel.'

'You're mean.'

He turned while continuing to walk backwards, his palms held out, expression innocent. 'Me? Mean?'

'All right. A tease then.'

He spun back around and entered the kitchen, his voice so low she almost didn't catch the words. 'You don't know the half of it.'

Teagan wondered what he meant but chose not to ask. A more important urge had hit. 'Won't be a minute.'

By the time she'd finished in the bathroom and made it to the kitchen, Lucas had a board out, a slab of corned beef on a plate, a large block of tasty cheddar, and a couple of very ripe tomatoes set out in readiness along with an assortment of mustards and chutneys.

He held up a knife. 'Butter?'

'Thanks. I'll make us tea?'

'That'd be great.' He cut off a slice of butter and began to mash it on the board. Behind him the microwave beeped. 'Frozen bread, I'm afraid. I wasn't game to go into the bakery after Col.' He retrieved the plate and set about buttering, swearing when the butter tore at the soft slice. 'Butter tastes better but it's a pain in the arse from the fridge.'

'You could leave it out. Ness does.' She jiggled the teabags to help the tea along. 'Other than running into Col, how was your morning?'

'Okay.' He waved his hand at her. A wide plaster was strapped over the heel of his palm. 'Only one minor injury.'

'Do you get hurt a lot?'

'Sometimes. Been bitten and kicked a few times. Mostly it's rips and cuts, or being trodden on.' He shrugged. 'Nothing serious. The big one is watching your back with all the bending.'

'Good thing yours is so strong then.'

He winked at her, and a bolt of pure lust slammed her front on. 'Too right. Do you want hot English mustard, wholegrain, fruit chutney or hot tomato?'

Terrified of releasing an undignified squeak, she cleared her throat before answering. 'Hot English.'

'A girl after my own heart.'

Teagan concentrated on jiggling the teabags. His heart would be lovely but a pipe dream. The rest of him though . . .

With the sandwiches on two plates, Lucas trekked outside, holding the screen door open with his bum to allow Teagan through with the mugs.

'This area is so great,' she said as they settled at the outdoor setting. 'It'll be perfect when the vines are more mature.'

'That's the idea.'

Warm afternoon sun filtered through the pergola. No breeze rustled the trees or paddocks. Only a few industrious insects darted. The landscape had an indolent air as though it, too, had just roused from a snooze.

'Good to see you with an appetite.'

She swallowed. She hadn't meant to eat so fast, but her stomach had been twitching since she'd entered the kitchen and Lucas made a mean sandwich. 'Believe it or not, I like food. Or I used to. For some reason when everything went to pot I went off it.'

'Stress can have that effect.'

She took another bite and chewed. 'My friend, Emily is an amazing cook. All the women in her family are. You go to her place for dinner and it's like being in a restaurant.'

'You miss your friends?'

'Yeah. Yeah, I do.' She squinted at the cloudless sky. 'It's nice here though. The weather's unreal.'

'Not always. We get these filthy summer storms and it's bloody freezing in the winter.' He arranged his sandwich, ready for another bite. 'But I like it. Can't imagine living anywhere else now.'

Teagan finished off the last of her crust and picked up her mug of tea. 'Where were you from originally?'

'Mum and I moved around a bit when I was little but mostly we lived in St Marys.' When she looked at him blankly he smiled. 'Typical western Sydney suburb, east of Penrith up the Great Western Highway. We were happy there. Knew the neighbours. Mum had plenty of work.'

'What did she do?'

'Nail technician.' At Teagan's expression he smiled. 'Yeah, I know. She worked on human nails, I work on horses'. I didn't even think about that when I started. I just wanted to do something with horses. Becoming a farrier seemed a good idea. Turned out a smart choice, too.' He swept out an arm. 'Bought me this place. Took a bit of scrimping and saving, admittedly, but I got there in the end.'

'And your mum, is she still in St Marys?'

'Sort of.' His gaze slid downwards and he stared at the bite marks in his sandwich. 'She's in the cemetery there. She died a couple of years ago. Lung cancer. Never smoked a cigarette in her life. They say it might've been from the nail dust or the chemicals. She'd worked in beauty therapy since her late teens. Back in those days they never wore masks like you see now.'

'I'm sorry. That's really sad.'

'Yeah. Shit way to die.'

Teagan fingered the handle of her mug. From the way Lucas spoke, he'd adored his mum. 'And your dad?'

'Is an arsehole.'

So they had that in common. She wondered what his had done. Something pretty bad, by his tone and sour expression.

He finished the remainder of his sandwich and pushed his plate away. They sat sipping tea, listening to the quiet and occasional bird call. The hush brought back memories of Pinehaven, of spring there. The serenity of it. How, when Teagan went to its farthest reaches and stood still, it was as if nothing else existed in the world except her and nature.

She'd loved those special moments. The sense of peace, of belonging. The way her feet felt planted in the soil along with the pasture grasses. Roots that ran from her heart to the rich earth below. Roots that had been snapped off without warning and left to shrivel.

A month had passed since she'd taken her last step on Pinehaven, yet the agony of her loss felt sharper than ever.

Lucas broke the silence. 'Did you want a shower before you head home?'

'Worn out my welcome already?' She tried to sound amused but there was a catch in her voice.

'Hey, I did say you could board if you wanted.'

'I know.' She gnawed on her lip as she thought of her mother, of last night's distress. 'I've got to change the mower blades and a few other chores this arvo. May as well put off showering until they're done.' She stood and gathered plates and mugs and then stopped. 'You're really kind, you know that?'

'Learned it from my mum.'

'She must've been a good mum.'

'She was.'

At the pride and love in his voice Teagan dropped her head, fighting a horrible urge to cry.

He rose and wrapped his arms around her, his body solid and warm and comforting. 'You'll be all right.'

'You think?'

'I know.'

She sniffed. 'How?'

'Because,' he said, holding her away from him and winking, 'you have awesome friends to look after you.'

Lucas might have had faith, but Teagan's was rapidly running out. She, her mother and Ness were parked around Falls Farm's kitchen table, cooling coffees in front of them, and silence between.

'It's not so much the money, Mum,' said Teagan, digging her fingers into her temple where a headache was pounding. 'I would have – and did – give it gladly to save the farm. But it wasn't being used to save the farm. Dad was gambling it away. You must have had some inkling. Didn't a little bit of curiosity force you to look at the computer? He was spending hours on it.'

Penny pressed a sodden tissue to the tears that had barely stopped falling since the conversation started. She looked like Teagan felt: haggard, tired and depressed. 'I don't really know how to use it.'

'But you can send an email. You know what the desktop screen looks like? Surely you would've noticed the program?'

'The new computer wasn't like that. It had a new system. All bright tiles. App things.' She scrunched her face, bewildered. 'None of it made sense to me. Then he started turning the screen off whenever I walked in and snapping at me about not respecting his privacy.'

'But he was your husband. You laid in bed with him every night.' Teagan stared at her mother, not understanding. 'Why didn't you say anything?'

'I was scared!' More tears brimmed and spilled over. Penny made angry swipes at them. 'He wouldn't talk to me anyway. He'd just grouch and roll over.'

Teagan sighed and passed her a fresh tissue, then for something to do, stood and began to gather their mugs. Her mother's hadn't been touched.

'No, I'll look after that,' said Ness. 'You and Penny still have things to work through.'

Teagan didn't want to talk anymore. She wanted to go outside, breathe clean, fresh air. Play with Claudia and Mouse. Remove herself from this atmosphere of failure and despair.

What made the discussion more torturous was the recognition of her own culpability. For all the arguments, all the yelling at her father, Teagan hadn't marched into his office, switched on the computer and looked for herself either. The blame she was smothering her mother with was equally her own. Finding the words, the guts to admit that though, wasn't easy.

She rubbed her face and slumped back into her seat. 'I'm sorry, Mum. It's wrong to blame you. I didn't take action either. I should have.'

'But what could you have done?'

'I don't know. Walked in there when he was out?'

'He'd put a lock on the door, love.'

'Not until the end. There would've been a key somewhere. I could've kicked it in. I should have done something instead of burying my head in the sand, hoping it'd all be okay.' She let out a shaky breath. 'It's not as if I wasn't warned. Em kept telling me I needed to check the accounts, but every time I asked Dad did his nut. It was so much easier to let it slide. If anyone lacked guts, it was me.'

Feeling Vanessa's gaze, she looked up. Her aunt wore an approving smile. Teagan managed a tiny smile back then turned again to her mum and stretched out her hand.

Carefully, Penny reached across the table to take it.

'I'm sorry, Mum. For the things I said, the way I treated you. I know it's not your fault. I need to stop blaming you and you need to stop blaming yourself.'

Later, as Teagan laid back in the pool, floating and trying to relax, she realised how much better it felt to see her mum smile, to see the hope flare in her incredibly sad and defeated eyes. There was a lot to be said for forgiveness, and kindness. Maybe that's why Lucas practised it. For the reward. Or maybe he was just one of the world's good people.

She smiled to herself. Jasmine would tease so hard. So would Em. Teagan was always the cynical one, the one who was ready to condemn and blame, and saw the world a bit too black and white. Now look at her. A month in New South Wales and her cynicism was losing its prickly edge.

Had to be the weather.

Vanessa pursed her lips. 'Sorry, darling. She's not here right now. Anything I can help you with?'

'Not unless you want to be my date for the trivia night on Friday.' Callum let out a guffaw of laughter, as though the idea was ridiculous. 'No doubt Dom's already booked you up.'

She kept her voice sweet, while her brain whirred fast. So Callum was serious about pursuing Teagan. Well, she'd have to nip that in the bud. 'Actually, he hasn't. And Teagan has already been snaffled by Lucas.' Which was a lie. She had no idea if Lucas had asked Teagan to the cricket club's trivia night yet. He would be now though.

The guffawing ceased abruptly. 'But the email only went out a couple of minutes ago.'

'Insider knowledge, darling. He is vice-captain.' A sulky silence descended and Vanessa felt herself having a momentary burst of compassion. 'You could partner me.'

'Really?' Callum cleared his throat. 'I mean, that'd be great. I'll call by the farm and pick you up in the Maserati. Around six.'

'Come along earlier. We'll have margaritas to get us in the mood.' Goodness knows she'd need them.

Vanessa hung up, leaned back and tapped her pencil against her mouth. Then she picked up the phone and dialled Domenic.

He answered with a smile in his voice. 'My favourite girl.'

'You have other girls then?'

He laughed, a much nicer sound than Callum's self-important guffaw. 'Only you.'

Vanessa found herself smiling. 'Liar. But I am about to arrange a date for you.'

'Let me guess. The Falcons' trivia night.'

'The one and only.'

'You want me to partner Teagan,' he said without enthusiasm.

'Alas, Teagan's already booked for Lucas. You're partnering my sister.'

'I am?'

'You are.'

'Okay.' He drew the word out. 'In that case, who's escorting you?'

Aware this wasn't going to be received well, Vanessa winced as she said Callum's name.

There was an audible sucking in of breath. 'I see.'

'Only yourself to blame. You should've asked earlier.'

'I only got the email five minutes ago!'

'Well then,' said Vanessa, strangely pleased that Dom was so irked. 'You should've acted on it instead of assuming I'd partner you.'

'I would've thought that was a fair assumption to make, given our relationship.'

'Relationship? I wasn't aware we had one beyond friendship.'

'Don't play games, Nessie. It's annoying.' He paused. 'You don't really like him, do you?'

She smiled at the hint of uncertainty in his voice and twirled her pencil. 'He does fly a helicopter.' At Dom's *humph*, she relented a bit. 'Look, I really only accepted for Penny's sake. I didn't want her to be left out, and I don't think she's up to a night partnering someone as competitive as Callum in a trivia contest. He'd only be mean to her. You'll be kinder.'

'I will?'

'You know you will.'

He sighed. 'Only for you.'

'Thank you. Now, margaritas here at five and then we'll all head down to the club, okay?'

'Fine. Hang on.' A hand was placed over the receiver. Muffled voices filtered briefly before Dom came back clear. 'Sorry, I have to go. Anyway, consider me booked.'

'You're a good man.'

'Too good sometimes.' A smile returned to his voice. 'Bye, favourite girl.'

'Goodbye, Domenic.'

'Oh, and Nessie?'

'What?'

'You owe me.'

After ending the call, Vanessa stared out the window. Penny was wandering the yard, Wilma in her arms, Blanche stalking behind. She was staring vaguely, stroking the guinea pig's soft fur as she walked without direction. Her heart went out to her sister; she looked so alone. The talk with Teagan had helped at least. Vanessa knew Teagan wouldn't be able to hold onto her bitterness and blame. Not forever. That sort of ill-sentiment ate away at people. She suspected Lucas's influence. The boy was such a sweetheart.

Unlike Graham. Rotten man had called that morning, wanting to talk to Penny. Vanessa had fobbed him off as she had with his previous calls. Penny didn't need to hear from him right now. Not his whiny apologies that weren't apologies at all. Silly man was still insisting that if the bank had given him a few more weeks he could have traded his way out of the catastrophe he'd led his family into. It had taken all her fortitude to not swear at him.

What frightened her was the risk of Penny or Teagan picking up the phone. For the past week the women of Falls Farm had found a degree of harmony. It wasn't perfect, but the conversations they shared were mostly more relaxed than tense. A few words from Graham could resurrect all the hurt.

She watched Penny amble out of sight and picked up the phone again. A blast of music came over the line before the volume was quickly turned down and Lucas answered with his usual cheer.

'Sexiest single in The Falls.'

She laughed. The boy was gorgeous, inside and out. 'According to whom?'

'Me. How's things?'

'Good. You're driving. I can call back later.'

'Nah, it's all right. I'm on hands-free. Just about to turn into Nick's anyway.'

'Calling on Teagan?'

The click of an indicator carried over the line, the car's engine noise changing as Lucas geared down. 'Not specifically. Couple of ponies to shoe. She's a bonus.'

'I'm glad you think so because while you're there you can ask her to partner you to the trivia night.'

'Dunks sent the email out, did he? He said he was going to. I told him it was too short notice, but he reckons people won't mind. Not much else to do on a Friday night round here.' Vanessa heard the engine slow and then stop. 'I'll ask her as soon as she's free. You're partnering Dom, I take it?'

'No, Penny is. I'm afraid Callum beat Dom to it.'

Lucas let out a great laugh. 'Callum asked you?'

'Actually, he rang to ask Teagan, but I may have told a little fib about her availability.'

'Did he now?' The words had a menacing edge. 'Huh.' A heartbeat of contemplation and his voice returned to normal. 'You're a doll, you know that?'

'You just take care of her for me, Lucas. She's precious.'

'I will. So how did Dom take the news?'

'He was rather a good sport about it. Anyway, he'll be much

better for Penny. So drinks at the farm at five and then we'll head down at six?'

'Sure thing.'

'Oh, and darling?'

'What?'

'Have a chat to Mark when you get the chance. See if you can find out how serious he is about Bunny.'

'Serious, as far as I know. Although he won't admit it.'

Vanessa sighed. 'I thought as much.'

'What's up?'

'Bunny's convinced she's too old for him. That her job makes her too unreliable for someone with small children.'

'They're as bad as each other. Dunks is crazy about her but thinks she wouldn't want someone with all his baggage.'

'We need to do something.'

'Let them go. They'll sort it out.'

'That's the thing. I don't think they will, not without a nudge.'

'Just as well they have the best nudger in the valley watching out for them then.'

FIFTEEN

LUCAS REGARDED DOM SOURLY. Trust him to think of hiring a mini-van and using the Wellness Centre's driver, Andrejus, to cart them all from Falls Farm to the bowling club. He glanced across the bus at Callum, who was looking equally as peeved. Lucas bet Callum now wished he'd offered to ferry everyone in his chopper. Instead, he'd turned up at the farm in his black Maserati, expecting to impress, only to be outdone by an ugly white mini-van.

Although confident Teagan wasn't remotely interested in the self-important dickbrain, Lucas had stayed close during margarita hour. It only took a single 'fuck off' glare for his rival to get the message. Lucas might be a nobody, but he was a tall, muscled nobody and more than a match for a city-soft bloke like Callum Albright.

Foiled, Callum had then set his sights on Vanessa, who was looking incredible in towering heels and a snug-fitting scarlet dress that showed every curve of her voluptuous figure. She'd welcomed him with a kiss and her usual charm, which Callum appeared to interpret as meaning he was in with a chance, and Dom had not reacted too well.

Now they were all crammed into the mini-van, swaying and sweaty as the driver navigated the windy road into the village.

Teagan was in the window seat next to Lucas, her concentration on the passing landscape. He watched her for a moment, noting her fine profile, the cascade of freckles covering every surface. She'd left her hair out and it fell around her chin and shoulders in pretty copper feathers. Her hands were loose in her lap. A couple of scratches streaked the back of one. The nails were bitten to the quick, but her fingers were slender and elegant, like a pianist's. He wondered what they'd feel like, playing across his skin.

Lucas crept his hand across to mesh fingers with hers.

Her lips parted. She considered the connection for a few seconds before lifting her questioning gaze to his.

'You look nice,' he said.

Unlike Vanessa's overt femininity, Teagan's clothes were simple but appealing. Jeans and heeled brown boots with a matching leather belt, and a navy shirt made of some sort of silky material that brought out the blue of her irises and deepened the copper in her hair. She looked country and classy, and very, very pretty.

Surprise widened her eyes and colour flushed her cheeks. Lucas's heart gave an unexpected lurch. He liked her, wanted her, but that sensation went beyond both of those feelings.

'Vanessa's doing, but thank you.' She bit her lip and looked at their hands again. 'I hope you're not expecting miracles from me. I'm hopeless at trivia.'

'Join the club. Anyway, it's just for fun.'

That this was war and not fun was soon obvious once everyone settled down at their tables for trivia. As emcee and adjudicator, Dunks wasn't playing. Nor was Peter Somersby, who was acting as barrel girl and camping it up in a gold lamé suit that would have put Elvis to shame. On arrival, to the amazement of all, he'd announced his intention to sign up to the Falcons despite never having played any sport in his life. Dunks had immediately thrust a form under Peter's nose, asking why only after he'd signed. Peter had merely smiled slyly in Domenic's direction before expressing delight at being part of such a *talented* group and prancing off.

Much to his elation, Tony was teamed up with Bunny, who was looking particularly glamazonian in black leather trousers and a cream singlet top the same colour as her platinum-blonde hair. Nick was on baby duty, a towel over one shoulder as he burped Oliver and threw jealous looks at Stacey who, having spent the five days since the invitations had gone out expressing enough milk to last a hangover, was hopping into the wine. How they expected Olly to sleep through the racket that would follow was anyone's guess, but as Nick told Lucas, little Olly would just have to harden up and take one for the parental team.

The Andersons from the IGA were there as well, along with the rest of the cricket team, their wives or girlfriends, and a few roped-in friends and family, bringing the crowd to almost forty. But the couple that had surprised everyone was Col and Kathleen Ferguson, rocking up at the last minute to register, still exultant after their daily 'protest', which entailed marching back and forth across the entrance to the Wellness Centre, bearing ugly black-and-yellow placards and yelling slogans at passing cars. A sight deemed by many to be far more unsightly than any proposed fence could ever be. After tossing Dom unpleasant, sneering looks, they took position at the most outermost table, as far away as possible from the Falls Farm crowd.

Dunks tapped on the microphone and called them to attention. 'Welcome to the Falcons' trivia night, proudly sponsored by generous local business, The Falls Wellness Centre.'

Col and Kathleen let out a boo.

At the bar, the bowlo's regulars were leaning their elbows and watching with amusement. As soon as the boos were over the heckling started. 'Going to win a game this year?'

'Piss off, Jack,' said Dunks, forgetting he was emcee and the entire club could hear, then flushed crimson when he realised. 'Sorry.'

He coughed and glanced at Bunny, who smiled encouragement and caused Dunks to blush even deeper. Recovering, he carried on with explaining the night's format. Four rounds would follow, divided into entertainment, science, culture, and finally, the big one, sport. Scores would be tallied along the way but only rankings read out. So teams can enjoy a good tease, Dunks informed them.

Teagan bowed close to whisper, bringing with her a scent of something lightly floral. 'This is me saying sorry in advance.'

Lucas smiled, glad to see her relaxed, although that was probably more due to Teagan's margarita and wine consumption than him. 'We can both be hopeless together.' For a long moment her eyes held his. It was the same look she'd given him by the waterfall, shy and nervous but aware of what was brewing between them. As the connection lingered, his heart did an uncomfortable series of tumble-turns before breaking into racing speed. He drew a fraction closer, gaze sliding to her mouth, then Dunks began to speak and they both turned away.

'Right, let's get this show on the road. First up, entertainment.' Dunks grinned at the collective groan. 'Come on, I know you're all secret fans of Beyoncé and *The Bold and the Beautiful*.'

In an effort to calm his thumping heart, Lucas surveyed the room. Dom and Callum were feigning an ease that didn't fool anyone. Penny was fiddling nervously with her pencil. Vanessa was trying not to laugh at Peter Somersby, who had taken position behind Dom and Callum and was pointing between the two, pulling faces and shadow-boxing. Over the back, Col and Kathleen were sharing a smug look. Nick was busy making soft fart noises at Olly to keep him amused and not paying any attention at all.

'And no calling answers from the bar, or there'll be strife,' ordered Dunks loudly.

At another heckle, Bunny, who had drunk even more than Teagan, shot upright, hands on her hips. 'Strife meaning me, got it?' The heckles immediately ceased. She grinned at Dunks and blew him a kiss. 'Carry on, Cherub.'

The club erupted in laughter.

Dunks cleared his throat. 'Er, thanks, Bunny.' He took a moment to shuffle some pages before selecting one and straightening his shoulders. 'Everyone set?'

A collective 'yes' echoed back.

'First question.' He gave a wriggle of his eyebrows. 'What is the name of Beyoncé's and Jay Z's first baby?'

'How the hell are we supposed to know that?' was yelled out, followed by a puzzled, 'Who's Bee-on-say?'

Lucas looked at Teagan, who shrugged. 'Sorry. No idea. I didn't even know they were married.'

'It's bound to be something ridiculous. That's what those stars do, isn't it? Name their kids daft things like Moon Unit and Peaches.'

She pointed to their answer sheet. 'Put down,' she pursed her lips for a moment, 'Caterpillar. That's weird enough.'

'Caterpillar?'

'Got any other suggestions?'

She had a point. He wrote down Caterpillar and checked out the others at the table. Penny was whispering to Dom as he wrote. Vanessa was in charge of her and Callum's sheet but was still frowning and twiddling with her pencil, while Callum shot daggers at Dom. Col was reclining back with his hands behind his head as though he'd already won. Bunny was blowing more kisses at Dunks while Tony scribbled. The rest were shrugging and laughing.

The timer went. Dunks carried on with the next question, this time one about a movie that neither Lucas nor Teagan had seen and had no idea who the stars were.

'We're terrible,' said Teagan, laughing as another question resulted in another fabricated answer.

'Nah, we make a great team. We're both useless.'

With the final entertainment question over, Peter gallivanted between tables, collecting papers and camping it up to everyone's amusement except Kathleen's. Even Col wore a grin until it was shut down by Kathleen's puckered disapproval.

'Don't worry, we'll get them in the other categories,' Lucas promised Teagan. He stood and indicated her empty glass. 'Another?'

'Thanks. Although I've probably had too much.'

'Probably, but it's a trivia night. You're allowed to let your hair down.'

She glanced towards Nick, who was staring in horror at the nappy he'd just removed. 'I have to work in the morning.'

'How about we make a deal. You relax and play up as much as you want, I'll make sure you have an extra hand tomorrow.'

A small frown creased her brow as she considered. 'Why are you so nice to me?'

'It's what friends do.'

'Not because . . .' She grimaced and shook her lowered head. 'Doesn't matter.'

Lucas crouched down so he could look into her face. 'Stop thinking about stuff.' He shucked her under the chin. 'Now do as you're told and have some fun or I'll sic Bunny on to you.'

Bunny followed him to the bar. 'You and Teagan were looking pretty intimate just then.'

'I could say the same for you and Cherub when I passed.'

'I can't help it if my toyboy finds me irresistible.'

Lucas regarded her seriously. 'He doesn't want to be your toyboy, Bunny.'

Her face fell. 'Oh.' After a few seconds she perked up again. 'Never mind, it was good while it lasted.'

'What're you on about?'

'You just said he didn't want to be my toyboy.'

'Yeah, because he wants to be more, you twit.'

Delight glowed across her face. 'Really?' She smoothed her top, trying to be cool again. 'I mean, that's great. But I'm too old for him.'

Lucas wrapped an arm around her broad shoulders and gave a brief squeeze. 'Yeah, and he's got three kids and an ex-wife and a shit-load of baggage.'

'I know.' She stared miserably at the floor.

'You know, for a smart woman you're pretty thick. I meant that all that stuff makes you perfect for each other.'

'That's what Vanessa says.'

'Well maybe you should believe her.'

Bunny's eyes sought out Dunks. He was by himself, poring over the score sheets with a pencil stuck between his teeth and fingers tapping intently on a calculator. 'He's too good for me.'

'Bullshit. No one's too good for anyone. Just go for it.'

Bunny regarded Teagan, who had shifted across a seat to chat to Vanessa and Penny. Callum was in the line for the bar along with Dom, the two men standing deliberately apart. 'Maybe you should take your own advice.'

He shook his head. 'This one's a slow one.'

Bunny's gaze narrowed. 'Maybe, maybe not. Personally I think a good long shag would do her wonders.'

Lucas laughed. 'Is that your medical diagnosis?'

'Trust me,' said Bunny, hoisting her chin. 'I'm a vet.'

The evening carried on with more hilarity, hard thinking, and extravagant mincing by Peter. Dunks had done a brilliant job of compiling questions to suit all ages. After finishing last in the first round, Lucas and Teagan hit their straps in the second before slumping again in the third. But by round four they had risen to midfield. The top four comprised Vanessa and Callum, Dom and Penny, Bunny and Tony, with, to everyone's shock, Col and Kathleen as leaders.

Competitiveness hit the front-runners. Callum and Dom were eyeing each other off like a couple of circling bucks, oblivious to the eye rolls Vanessa was exchanging with her sister and Bunny. Lucas had lost count of Teagan's wine consumption and didn't care. She was at that giggly, touchy-feely state of intoxication that made her seem sweet and incredibly kissable. Something he was thinking seriously of trying at night's end.

As Dunks called the teams back for the start of round four, Lucas lazily stretched his arm across to lightly thumb lines over Teagan's back. For a moment she stiffened, then her posture loosened and she began to press against the pressure.

'Right,' said Dunks, glee in his eyes. 'Gird yourselves for the master round, the most important of all subjects and the one destined to sort the men from the boys,' he saluted Kathleen's way, 'and the young and clever from the old and wise.' He paused to lift his question sheet and scan the main contenders who were all huddled forward, intent and poker-faced. 'Question one in sport: How many gold medals did Australia win at the 2000 Olympics?'

Teagan groaned and flopped forward to rest her head on her arms. Laughing, Lucas pulled her back up and put his mouth close to her ear. 'I know this.'

'You do?'

'Yeah.' He picked up the pencil and wrote down sixteen. 'Told you we'd be right.'

He knew the next answer too, and the next. His chest began to puff with the admiring glances Teagan kept sending him. He slid his hand further up her spine and spent a few seconds toying with her silky hair before slipping his fingers underneath to stroke the tiny hairs at the back of her neck. Her mouth parted, and he felt her breathing become rapid. Glancing down, he caught the tiniest glimpse of an erect nipple against the silky thin fabric of her shirt. A throb started in his groin. Taking the van had been a mistake. With his ute in the carpark he could have driven her straight to Astonville.

He shifted uncomfortably and looked away, catching Vanessa's eye. She lifted a single finger and waved it slowly from side to side. His own ceased its caress. Vanessa was right. Only an arsehole would take advantage of a woman half-pissed. He didn't want that anyway. When it happened, Lucas wanted them both sober, not with their senses dulled by alcohol. With a subtle nod, he withdrew his hand and placed both arms on the table.

The final question of the night had competitors looking at one another and Dunks grinning in satisfaction. 'That'll sort you out,' he declared when a few protests were voiced.

As soon as the timer went off there were more groans. Lucas

folded his and Teagan's scoresheet and handed it over to Peter, who took it with a gameshow-hostess flourish before twirling on.

'We're on a ten-minute break while I add these up,' announced Dunks. 'And don't forget the raffle. This is your last chance to earn your choice of top-to-toe beauty treatment or remedial massage from one of the experts at our sponsors, the Wellness Centre.'

'Home for druggies, you mean,' yelled Kathleen, followed by a 'Hear, hear' from Col.

'This village wouldn't have a cricket team without the centre's help,' shot back Dunks. He nodded at Dom. 'The team and its supporters are very grateful for your sponsorship.'

Dom rose in a little half-bow. 'Happy to support the local community in any way I can.'

With a pro-Wellness Centre crowd and the club's majority regarding them with animosity, Col and Kathleen prudently kept their mouths shut.

Everyone wandered off for drinks and gossip. When Teagan made no move, Lucas remained seated, too.

'Enjoying yourself?' he asked.

'I am.' She suddenly looked surprised. 'I really am.'

He maintained eye contact. 'You should have good times more often.'

'I don't think my liver could take it.'

He tucked a loose tendril of hair behind her ear. 'You don't have to do it with booze.'

'What do you suggest then?'

There was a definite tease in her voice, reminding Lucas once again of their moment by the waterfall. So he'd silently agreed not to try anything. Stiff shit. No rules against laying some groundwork, but as Lucas began to lean in to say 'wouldn't you like to know' he caught the flash of a dark trouser leg out of the corner of his eye.

'How do you think you fared?' his father asked, smiling at them both.

'Hopeless,' said Teagan. 'But I hadn't expected anything else. How did you go with Mum? Not too badly by the rankings.'

'Your mother was a revelation.'

'Really?'

Dom nodded. 'Penny knew most of the entertainment questions and many of the culture ones. She also knew a few of the science questions.' He cast a look across the room to where Penny sat now with Bunny. 'We even muddled our way through sport.'

'Yeah, well, I guess she had a lot of time for magazine reading while Dad was ripping us off.' Teagan's hand flew to her mouth. 'God, sorry. I didn't mean to bitch like that.'

Lucas gave her arm a squeeze, wishing Dom would piss off. He threw him a pointed look, but Dom was in no hurry to leave.

'Have you given any thought to you and Penny coming to the Wellness Centre for a day?' he asked Teagan. 'I think your mother would enjoy it a great deal.'

Teagan looked across at Penny and down at her hands. 'It's not really our scene. I know other people believe in that stuff, but it's not for me. I doubt it's for Mum either.'

'You don't know until you try. Think about it. Please.'

Lucas watched Dom return to his seat, wondering what he was up to. Then his father bent across and exchanged a few words with Vanessa and his suspicions faded. A pamper session would be exactly the sort of treat Vanessa would try to organise for her sister and niece.

Dunks called them to attention. The night was closing, and a few participants were more than a little wobbly. People took their time coming back from the bar and finishing their conversations. Even Dunks was looking tired.

'First up, any last-minute raffle-ticket sales?' When there was no response he lifted up a box in which Peter had placed all the scrunched-up tickets. 'I'd like to call on the owner of the Wellness Centre, Domenic Ashe, Falcons sponsor and generous donor of this prize, to draw the winning ticket.' As Dom made his way to the table, Dunks continued. 'And just so you know, the raffle raised three hundred and sixty-five dollars. A big round of applause to yourselves for that.'

As he reached Dunks's side, Dom commandeered the microphone. 'As a gesture of personal support, I'd like to make that up to a thousand with a donation of another six hundred and thirty-five dollars.'

Callum's scowl was nearly as deep as Kathleen's and Col's. Lucas almost felt sorry for him. He was the one who'd signed up to play and yet here was Dom stealing all the glory with sponsorship, prize and cash donations, not to mention a mini-van and driver. Any counteroffer of Callum's at this point would only make him look like a wannabe. But Callum hadn't become a successful businessman for nothing. With a casual stretch, he placed one arm behind Vanessa's back and rotated his body towards her. The message was clear. Dom may have won that skirmish, but Callum was still the one with the girl.

To Dom's credit he remained outwardly cool. He dipped his hand into the box and shuffled around, making a show of picking a ticket right from the bottom. He opened the folded ticket and threw his head back with laughter.

Dunks plucked the ticket from him and grinned, his gaze zooming across to the farthest table. 'That's funny, Col. I don't recall you buying a ticket.'

Colin had the good grace to at least wriggle under Kathleen's furious stare. 'Bought it for young Maggie.'

'And your hard-working daughter shall receive,' said Dom, drawing an envelope from his pocket and crossing toward them. 'A top-to-toe spa session is hers. Unless you require a remedial massage?'

Colin thought for a moment. 'I do have a bit of trouble with my back.'

'Colin Walker, you will not accept that prize!'

Col jerked in fright at Kathleen's commanding tone. His lip trembled a little.

'Mrs Ferguson,' said Dom smoothly, 'I appreciate you're not the

Wellness Centre's greatest fan, but Col bought a ticket and has fairly won a prize. He's entitled to take it up.' He held the envelope out to Col. 'Your daughter is one of our most liked staff members. I'm sure she'd appreciate this prize very much. In fact, to encourage her to take it, I'll give her an extra day's holiday.'

He waggled the envelope. Colin hesitated and then snatched it, muttering a thanks and avoiding Kathleen's disgusted stare as the Falls Farm contingent let out a whoop and cheer.

'Right,' said Dunks. 'Now onto the trivia winners. Tight doesn't even begin to describe this competition. Only one point separated the top three going into the final round, and only one point separates the winner from the runner up.'

A murmur went around the bowlo.

'In third place, earning themselves a twenty-dollar bistro voucher, and proving that old heads can sometimes be wiser, Colin Walker and Kathleen Ferguson.'

The applause was embarrassing for its paucity, changing to laughter as Peter hammed it up in delivering their prize. After seizing it from Peter and ignoring Colin's outstretched hand, Kathleen neatly pocketed the envelope.

'We have some competitive people in our village, folks, and some clever ones by the looks,' continued Dunks. 'We have two very successful businessmen with us tonight who have made this an epic battle. What surprises me is that both not only seemed to know the main characters of *The Bold and the Beautiful*, but they also knew that Beyoncé and Jay Z's baby was called Blue Ivy.' He nodded knowingly, playing to the crowd. 'It seems our local businessmen have hidden depths.'

'More like clever partners,' yelled Bunny.

'Certainly the truth in my case,' yelled back Callum before Dom could say something similar. He gave Vanessa a deliberate squeeze and kissed her cheek. 'Beautiful and clever.'

Dom's amused expression didn't carry to his eyes.

'Without further ado, and with a prize of a fifty-dollar bistro voucher, the runners up are . . .'

Bunny slapped a drum roll on the table to add to the drama.

'Dom and Penny, which means tonight's winners of a hundred-dollar bistro voucher are Callum and Vanessa. Well done!'

Bunny began laughing so hard she fell off her chair. Dunks abandoned his microphone to help. Dom's expression was mutinous, Callum's ecstatic. Penny and Vanessa exchanged a look before laughing and rising to hug one another.

Lucas grinned at his father who, to his amazement, suddenly shrugged and held his palms up as if to say, c'est la vie, leaving Lucas to ponder if the gesture was real or for show. He suspected the latter, but Dom stood and shook Callum's hand, before kissing Vanessa.

He draped his arm around Penny, kissed her cheek and waved to the group. 'As thanks for coming along and adding to a great night for the Falls Falcons Cricket Club, I'd like you to join me at the bar for an hour when drinks will be on me. Thanks.' And in that single swoop, Callum's victory was once again stolen from his hands.

Lucas had to give it to his father, he knew how to take on a rival.

Pity he had no clue how to be a dad.

SIXTEEN

TEAGAN ROUSED and tried to roll over, but the sheets had her locked down tight. She screwed up her nose as her brain registered a terrible stench. She opened one eyelid and yelped as Blanche stared back, her hairless silvery brow heavily wrinkled as though in feline disapproval.

'Oh, go away,' she groaned and then groaned even louder as the alarm went off.

Reaching out an arm, Teagan banged her fingers around until she found the right button, the other hand pressed to her throbbing head. Her mouth was dry and disgusting, and as she came awake, she experienced the creepy, rising horror that she'd done something extremely embarrassing the night before.

A knock sounded and the door was pushed fully open. Lucas leaned against the jamb with his arms crossed, looking unfairly perky and sexy considering he was still wearing the previous night's clothes.

He nodded at Blanche. 'Nice bedmate. I thought you didn't like cats.'

'Someone forgot to tell Blanche that.' Teagan attempted to free herself from the tangle of sheets and stopped, hand once more across her forehead. 'Oh, God, my head.'

'Not much I can do about that right now. But if you get up, I'll take you home and give you my famous cure.'

'Cure?'

He grinned. 'Paracetamol, Berocca and a bacon-and-egg sandwich.'

From the roll her stomach gave, Teagan wasn't confident she'd keep any of those items down. She glanced at the clock. Five-fifteen a.m. She needed to get moving if she was to make it to work on time.

'Come on,' said Lucas, no trace of sympathy in his voice. 'The quicker you have a shower and get dressed the quicker I can get you home and a cure into you.'

'Why not cure me here?'

'I need to get Merlin into exile.'

'Merlin?'

'Long story. Are you going to make me carry you to the shower?'

Teagan waved him off, the movement causing more pain in her head. She shoved aside the blankets, tipping Blanche to the floor, disappointed when the cat made its usual elegant recovery in landing. She swung out of bed and stood, confused by the sight of her white bikini bundled wet on the floor. The horror that had been creeping around the edges of her consciousness struck in full force as she remembered. Both hands flew to her mouth.

This wasn't just bad. This was kill-me-now tragedy. Lucas coughed. 'Um, Teagan.'

'What?' Her voice came out a squeak.

He nodded towards her lower half.

Teagan looked down and what little self-esteem she had left shrivelled to the size of a dried pea. She slammed her hands over her bright-copper bush, whimpering as she hunted for something to cover herself. With only her bikini in sight, she launched back on the bed and buried herself in the sheets. 'Oh, *God!*'

'Shh, or you'll wake the house.' The sheet was pulled back from her head. 'Go and have that shower.'

He left her to her mortification. Teagan considered remaining in bed and sulking, but she couldn't leave Nick in the lurch. She needed this job, and she still had vague hopes of moving into his staff quarters. After last night, she sure as hell wouldn't be moving in with Lucas.

Although the shower had made her feel slightly better, Teagan could barely bring herself to look at Lucas as they drove to Astonville. Instead, she kept her head pressed against the cold side window, staring at the dark. Each time she closed her eyes another flash of last night manifested itself.

She groaned as a snippet of her pool conversation with Lucas filtered into her pulsing brain.

'What?'

'Did I . . .' She couldn't say it. It was far too shameful. She bit down on her knuckle.

'Proposition me last night?'

'Gnnnn.'

He laughed, which only made her feel worse. 'You did.'

Teagan closed her eyes and banged her head against the glass, trying to rid herself of her resurrected memories. Not only had she flashed him this morning, she now recalled, in excruciating detail, that she'd practically offered herself to him like some pink-and-white bikini-wrapped present.

She groaned again. 'I'm sorry.'

'For what?'

'Everything. Living.'

'Cut it out, Teagan. It's not that bad.'

'Yeah, right. Desperate tart last night, flasher this morning. Believe me, it's bad.'

'First up, I found your proposal last night flattering, and if it wasn't for the fact that you were one,' he held up a finger, 'hammered, and two,' he held up a second finger, 'in the same house as your mother, I might've taken you up on your offer. As for this morning,

I'm a bloke. I'm not about to knock back a flash from a cute redhead.' He grinned broadly. 'A true redhead, too.'

Teagan slapped her hands over her ears. 'No more, please. Can't you see I'm dying here?'

Lucas gave her thigh a reassuring squeeze. 'That's just your hang-over talking. Give it half an hour and it'll be fine.'

Forty minutes later, thanks to a dose of painkiller, an even stronger dose of vitamin B and a meal of greasy food, Teagan might have been feeling slightly less hung-over, but the misery of her humiliation remained.

She stood at the ute, waiting for Lucas to finish locking up. The rusted horse float they'd used to cart Merlin to Astonville was still attached, ready for return to Vanessa's shed. Merlin was at the gate of his new paddock, bleating grouchily at them, his dirty coat blushed peach in the rising light.

'Oh, shut up. You're lucky you aren't dog food already.' Although given Lucas's explanation of the ram's exploits last night, he still might be. Merlin had disgraced himself even more than Teagan, which was saying something. Pity there was no one to help her into exile, too.

She admired Lucas's broad silhouette as he made his way to the ute, wondering yet again how such a good person could reside in the sort of body that would normally encase an arrogant personality. Except he had no arrogance at all, simply an easy-going manner and kindness.

None of which she deserved.

She squashed her face into her palms. Every memory of last night was clear now; donning her bikini, parading in front of Lucas, teasing him to come and join her in the pool. Going off by herself to paddle drunkenly around until he'd finally appeared. Instead of joining her, he'd crouched at the pool's lip and suggested that it might be a good time for her to go to bed. Like a cheap street-walker she'd blinked her wet lashes and traced a finger over her cleavage before responding with a husky, 'Only if you'll join me.'

As any sane man would have done, he'd said no. Except that wasn't enough of a hint for Teagan. No, she had to attempt to drag him fully-clothed into the pool. When that had failed, she'd pouted and swum to the steps where she'd seductively – or so she'd thought at the time but in hindsight was more a drunken lurch – climbed out, hips wriggling like an entire worm farm had taken residence up her bum.

To Lucas's credit, he'd kept his cool and helped her to her room, after which things got hazy. She had a vague recollection of him searching her drawers for a top, and thrusting it at her, which would account for why she was wearing a daggy singlet to bed and not her nightie. As for who removed her bikini, she had no idea, although the heat in her cheeks had her believing it was Lucas.

A warm hand rested on her shoulder. 'You okay?'

'No.'

'Teagan, look at me.'

She dropped her hands.

He cupped her face. 'You have nothing to be embarrassed about, I promise.' He held her gaze for a moment, and she had the heart-stopping feeling he wanted to kiss her. She couldn't let that happen. Despite scrubbing her teeth both at Falls Farm in the shower and again after breakfast at Astonville using the spare toothbrush Lucas had given her, she was convinced her breath stank worse than Blanche's. A halitosis kiss would only make the day even worse.

The kiss never eventuated. Instead, Lucas ruffled her hair the way a brother would and strode around to the driver's door. 'Come on. The sooner we get Nick's work done the sooner we can get you home for a rest.'

At least that answered one question: the near-kiss thing was all in her imagination. He wasn't attracted to her and who could blame him? She was a mess, inside and out. Whatever existed between them was friendship and nothing more.

Nick greeted her with surprise. 'Bugger. I had a bet running with

Stace that you wouldn't show.' He peered at her closely and grinned. 'Was it worth it?'

'Not exactly.'

'You don't look so hot yourself,' said Lucas.

'Yeah, shit night.' He threw a pissed-off look towards the main house. 'Stace was rat-faced. Came home and put on an old DVD from her hen's night. Spent the next two hours doing karaoke to 'Dancing Queen'. I love her but the woman can't sing to save herself. Ended up with her squawking at one end of the house and Olly screaming at the other. When I mentioned something about being a responsible mother she flew at me then burst into tears.' He scratched his head, perplexed. 'Thought it was a reasonable question myself.'

'The joys of marriage and fatherhood, hey?'

'You wait until it's your turn and see how much fun it is. Anyway, we'd better get started. I've two lessons booked this morning.' He gave Lucas a hopeful look. 'I don't suppose you can help?'

'It's what I'm here for.'

'Thanks, Lucas. You're a mate.' Nick nodded at Teagan. 'I'm not sure how much good she'll be.' He held up a finger. 'No machinery and definitely no quad bike.'

An easy undertaking. Teagan couldn't guarantee she was up to managing a pooper-scooper let alone the quad bike.

The sun rose fast, beating down on Teagan's head and making her sweat. A good thing, Lucas promised. It'd help rid her body of the alcohol faster. By ten her headache had returned in all its pounding glory, but thanks to Lucas they were well underway. Nick had disappeared to give his lesson, leaving the two of them to work alone. If it weren't for her humiliation, it would almost be companionable.

They were done by eleven. Teagan was dead on her feet and reeking like a stale bar, while Lucas remained unfairly handsome and smelling of manliness and deodorant. Though technically she had an hour left to fill, Nick ordered her home, thanking Lucas for his help and promising to shout him a beer later.

Lucas was quiet and preoccupied as they followed Belgravia's long drive to the road. At the junction he braked but made no move to turn. He sat for a moment before angling to face Teagan. 'Do you want to hang out at Astonville for a while?'

'Probably not a great idea.' She looked at her hands. 'I need to get back to the farm and apologise to Ness and Mum for embarrassing them.'

'They were too busy dealing with Callum to be embarrassed.'

She stared for a bit longer at her bitten-down nails and scratch covered hands. It was nice of him to ask but he didn't really want her there. She stank, was a walking fiasco, and in the ragged edges of her mind, the black slick that had been dormant since her talk with Penny was once again beginning its nasty slither.

Because it knew, as she'd known from the moment he'd meshed his fingers with hers on the bus, and it was preparing to make it all worse.

She was falling for Lucas. And the broken heart that would inevitably follow was going to ruin her.

He smiled, his teeth white, his eyes warm and generous. 'I'll make you ham-and-cheese toasties.'

She swallowed, forcing the grit from her throat. 'Thanks, but I just need bed.' And a good long cry over her clapped-out, miserable life.

His contemplative regard kept her studying her hands until he finally let out a sigh, flicked on the indicator and turned out onto the road.

Vanessa padded out into the kitchen and blearily switched on the espresso machine. She stood with her hands on the counter, staring blankly across the dining room. Besides the usual creaks and moans, the house was quiet. Past the timber venetian blinds she caught glimpses of yet another fine day.

Fine for some. Not for others.

When the coffee machine was up to speed she set about making herself a double latte. Even that simple task felt like a Herculean effort. The clock read eleven, revealing she'd managed seven hours of sleep, but she felt as if she'd had two.

What was meant to be a night of fun and fundraising had descended into farce. Half the Falls Farm bus crew were plastered. The only sober ones were Lucas, who was keeping an eye on an uncharacteristically giggly Teagan, Nick, who was baby-minding, Dom, who, competitive whether over women or trivia contests, had kept sober, and Callum, who had to drive his Maserati home. The rest – Teagan, Bunny, Mark, Penny, Stacey, Peter and Tony – were raucous wrecks.

They'd arrived at the farm, ready to party on. Vanessa had fetched nibblies, bottles of red and white wine and glasses for everyone, and they'd milled on the verandah, enjoying the night air and an old seventies music compilation.

It was all highly convivial until Callum decided to leave. Feeling silly after a couple of glasses of wine, Vanessa had been conned into dancing to 'Kung-Fu Fighting' with Peter and Stacey. To her shock, Dom had joined them and the four had begun tittering like teenagers as they tried to outdo one another in karate moves. Unimpressed, Callum had declared he had an important meeting in the city in the morning and needed to go.

Vanessa had escorted him to his car, thanking him for a lovely evening and his excellent trivia knowledge. He'd started the Maserati and pressed the button to open the roof. Handel's *Zadok the Priest* poured from the speakers, which Vanessa would have found laughable for its kingly association and pretension had Callum not been so serious. He was standing with the door ajar, casually posed with his hand on the window edge, one leg in the car, one leg on the ground, halfway through asking her out for dinner when, just as the choir began its magnificent crescendo, an equally magnificent deep bleat had sounded.

Vanessa had had just enough time to whirl out the way when Merlin charged. He hit the Maserati door with an almighty crunch, slamming it against Callum's leg and tipping him backwards into an ungainly sprawl over the seats. Within seconds, Merlin was backing up for another go and only Vanessa's quick grab of a horn had prevented more damage to Callum or his precious car.

Chaos had then ensued. Callum was bellowing in pain. Penny, Bunny, Mark and Peter were clattering down the stairs to see what had happened. Despite Vanessa's appeal for help, Dom and Lucas were momentarily distracted by Teagan wandering out onto the verandah wearing her brief white bikini. Thanks to Merlin, who was fighting back, Vanessa was hamstrung and could only watch help-lessly as Bunny – extremely drunk but the only one present with any medical experience – took a vague look at Callum's leg before patting the poor man on the head and comforting him with a, 'There, there, it's only a broken fetlock. Just think, if you were a horse I'd have to get the humane killer out.' Mark then began wrenching at his hair, in a complete state over the potential loss of his number two batsman for at least six weeks, probably more. Only Penny had enough sobriety and sense to run for an ice bucket and a towel.

Finally, Dom and Lucas decided to pay attention, first extracting Callum from his car – which only made the suffering, humiliated man fume more, and then bellow even louder in rage when he spied the Maserati's crumpled door – before rescuing Vanessa and locking a fighting, bellyaching Merlin in his yard. Dom had then offered his minibus to take Callum to Nepean Hospital, rather than wait for an ambulance.

Vanessa, Dom, and a furious, panting, pain-addled Callum proceeded to spend three hours waiting in emergency along with a bunch of punchy drunks and other Friday night bedlam. The break turned out to be quite severe and would require surgery, forcing Callum, to his deep indignation, to be admitted. Having dismissed Andrejus when a long wait seemed unavoidable, Dom organised a taxi home for himself and Vanessa. The trip cost a ridiculous amount of money, but Vanessa was too tired to care, and Dom was more than happy to pay after witnessing the ignoble end to his rival's triumphant evening. He'd dropped her at the farm, leaving her with a tender goodbye kiss on the forehead and the promise that everything would be all right.

By then everyone was in bed, except for Lucas, who was stretched uncomfortably on the leather couch, snoring softly. After throwing a blanket over him, Vanessa wrote a quick note and tucked it under his keys on the coffee table, after which she collapsed gratefully into her own bed and fell into an exhausted but disturbed sleep.

Morning had found her feeling no less anxious.

Sipping as she went, Vanessa carried her latte outside. As glimpsed, the day was beautifully spring bright and nature-scented. Bees were springing from dandelion flower to dandelion flower. Saffy was on her back, paws curled, eyes closed in delight as she exposed her pale belly to the sun. Betty was chomping on a shiny red capsicum, her sweet cheeks stuffed like a chipmunk's, and from the surrounding scrub birds carolled and chimed.

It would have been idyllic if not for Callum's Maserati squatting like a menacing crow in the middle of the yard. No one had bothered to close its roof and now a couple of birds were perched on the seats, preening themselves and no doubt inflicting more damage. For a fleeting second, Vanessa considered remedying the problem and found she couldn't be bothered.

Bunny was slumped, red-eyed, on one of the verandah chairs. Penny was in another, feeding slices of kiwifruit to a very smug looking Wilma. Everyone else appeared to have disappeared home.

'That,' she said, letting the screen door bang behind her, 'was a most unfortunate evening.'

'Not for some,' said Bunny. 'I think your niece got lucky with our sweet Lucas. She was practically begging for it in the pool. Kept giving Cherub ideas, but I fobbed him off by saying you'd banned me from having sex in your house. I was too drunk anyway.'

Vanessa kicked a spare chair away from the too-harsh sunlight and into the shade before sinking down. 'Please don't tell me they had sex in the pool.'

'I think they took it to Teagan's room. Last I heard Lucas was dragging her off to bed. Lucky cow.'

'I doubt they had sex. Teagan wasn't in any state and Lucas isn't the type to take advantage. Anyway, he was asleep on the couch when I came in.'

'Bugger. That girl really needs to get herself laid.'

Penny suddenly rose, Wilma clutched tightly to her chest. 'I think I might visit Claudia and Mouse.'

Bunny winced. 'Sorry. I keep forgetting she's your daughter.'

Penny merely gave a tired wave and walked off. Vanessa followed her progress, noting the slow trudge and slumped shoulders. Penny had been so good last night, enjoying herself with Dom. Now, it seemed the poor darling was back to normal.

'So how's Merlin's latest victim?'

'Not good. He'll need surgery.' She closed her eyes. 'I should head to the hospital.'

'Leave him. He'll be all right.'

Vanessa opened her eyes and regarded the Maserati, wincing at the large, ram's-head-sized dent that marred its sleek lines. 'I'm not so sure about that. I suspect there's going to be a bit of fallout from last night, and it's not going to be pleasant.'

The last person Lucas expected to see driving into Astonville was his father. Nor was he in the right frame of mind to deal with Dom. The mood that had descended after Teagan's refusal of his invitation to hang out still lingered. Even the physical effort of spending the after-noon hammering steel in the sweltering heat of the forge hadn't purged it.

Last night in the club she'd been funny and sexy, slipping him shy, hopeful looks that had made his heart turn over and his blood thicken. All he'd wanted was the night to end so he could take her home and spend the rest of it exploring. Learning what turned her on, what made her gasp and shudder. He'd wanted to kiss her freckles, mouth, eyelids and more.

He'd wanted to trap the happy girl and keep her safe.

Instead, stupidly, he'd let her go too far. Now she was miserable with hangover and mortification, and couldn't meet his eye no matter how many reassurances Lucas gave that everything was fine. And it was his own fucking fault.

He stepped out onto the drive, slowly wiping his hands on a rag, and positioned himself with his legs apart while the Mercedes purred to a standstill.

'Lucas.'

'Dom.'

Lucas continued to rub his hands, waiting while Dom took in his surroundings. Finally his father looked at him.

'We have a problem.'

'We?'

'It's Vanessa.'

Lucas stopped his rubbing, a warning buzz vibrating through his skin. 'What about Vanessa?'

Dom pointed towards the side paddock where Merlin was grazing. 'Albright's demanding Merlin be destroyed as a dangerous animal. He's also making noises about suing over his broken ankle. There's also the damage to his Maserati, but that's the least of our problems.'

'So what's this got to do with me?'

'I need you to keep the ram hidden. For some reason Vanessa loves it. Bunny's going to talk to her council contact about the bylaws. I've instructed my solicitor to follow up as well.' Dom ran his hand through his blond hair. 'I'm not sure how we're going to handle his injury. It'll depend on Vanessa's public-liability insurance.'

'How's she taking it?'

'Shaken, upset. Albright's solicitor threatened her with all sorts of bullshit.' Suddenly Dom dug fingers into his brow. 'This is my doing.'

Lucas blinked in surprise. 'How?'

'Albright got it into his head that Vanessa liked him.'

'She thinks he's a fuckwit. Anyway, everyone knows you and her have a thing going.'

'Albright didn't. He's only here on the weekends and doesn't socialise much when he is. You know what she's like. Makes you feel like you're the centre of the universe. Now he's realised. Last night made a fool of him in more ways than one and he wants someone to pay.' Dom's expression turned stony, his voice dangerous. 'Albright can go at me the hardest he likes, but if that bastard thinks I'll stand back and let him harm a hair on her head, he's got another thing coming.'

'You really like her,' said Lucas, unable to hide his astonishment.

'No, Lucas,' said Dom steadily. 'I love her.'

The urge to say something smart, like 'God help her then' rolled through and disappeared. Lucas couldn't. His father might be an arsehole, but there was no mistaking the truth in his admission.

'So now what?'

'We wait for his next move. He might calm down yet, although I doubt it. Albright doesn't like losing.' He nodded towards Merlin's paddock. As if sensing their scrutiny, the ram looked up and released a guttural baa. 'Don't tell anyone where he is. Once Albright's learned he's no longer being kept at Falls Farm he'll be on the hunt. Literally.'

'He'll be safe here.'

Dom placed a hand on Lucas's shoulder. 'Thanks, son.'

Lucas shrugged the touch away. They might be thawing as men, thanks to the women in their lives, but that was going too far. 'This is for Vanessa, not you. And I'm not your son.'

Deliberately, he turned his back and stalked towards the forge.

It was some minutes before the Mercedes's engine started and purred out of the yard.

SEVENTEEN

TEAGAN SPENT Sunday clearing wild tobacco and an infestation of moth vine from a particularly weedy gully behind Claudia and Mouse's paddock. Work kept her from thinking too hard or hanging around the house, where every crevice seemed to echo her humiliation back at her.

Her apologies to Ness and Penny had been waved off as unnecessary, but that hadn't made Teagan feel any better. Nothing seemed to, and it was beginning to frighten her. Each time she sat still, dread that she might lose the precious happiness she'd been glimpsing of late would wrap cold tentacles around her heart and lungs and leave her breathless.

It was almost six when she trudged back up to the house. The birds were beginning to move and chatter. Saffy bounded beside Teagan as she navigated the slope. For a weak moment, as she pushed through the scrub around the creek, Teagan harboured the fantasy that she might find Lucas waiting at Claudia's gate, but the track was empty, the horse and pony elsewhere, and the dog remained her only company.

Just as well. Her stupid heart would only interpret his arrival as something more than it was and Teagan didn't need any more let-downs. She managed plenty of those on her own.

Her aunt was pacing the verandah with a tumbler of something in her hand that was definitely not a Sunday kir royale. Straight vodka from the colour. Perhaps gin. Dom was propped against a verandah post, arms crossed, watching her.

Ness reached the end of the verandah and whirled around. 'He's a feeble-brained, tiny-penised prat. Productive afternoon, darling?'

'Um, yes.'

'I could've told you that,' said Dom mildly as Ness clomped back towards him, each step a petulant stomp on the timber boards. She was wearing leather farm boots, thick socks and one of her fifties style button-through dresses that showed off her small waist and impressive décolletage. Little wonder Dom was mesmerised.

Teagan looked from him to Ness and back. 'What's happened?'

'There might be a problem with the farm's public liability insurance,' said Dom.

'What sort of a problem?'

Ness answered, halting with her weight on one hip, arm across her belly, and tipping forward as she waved her tumbler. 'The sort that doesn't cover dangerous animal attacks.'

'Dangerous animal attacks? But Merlin's a ram, not a Rottweiler!'

'Exactly,' she spat. 'Stupid, petty, pathetic, tiny-penised man.' She gave a theatrical shudder. 'Oh, how I loathe *little* men.'

Teagan blinked and wondered exactly how much her aunt had had to drink. This was not the calm, kind aunt she knew. Ness fairly radiated fury, yet instead of appearing red-faced and unattractive, she was magnificent. Breasts heaving, titian hair flying, and with a regal outraged beauty that, impossibly, rocketed her already sky-high sex appeal into the stratosphere.

She shot a glance at Dom, who was gazing at Ness with a mixture of indulgence and amusement. He didn't appear to be taking things as seriously as Ness. Then again, these weren't his finances at stake.

'But he did only break his ankle, didn't he?'

'It's quite a bad break,' answered Dom. 'Apparently he's in the middle of a major acquisition and his absence is problematic. There are fees. Loss of income. The total could be significant.'

Teagan's heart began to thud. 'How significant?'

'Enough to wipe out my investments,' said Ness, a sudden note of despair in her voice.

'It won't come to that, I promise.' Dom moved towards her. He plucked the tumbler from her hand and held it out for Teagan to take, before cradling Ness to his chest. He buried his face in her hair, his voice soft. 'I won't let Albright hurt you. You're safe. Nothing to worry about. I'll take care of it.'

'You can't. You're up to your eyeballs as it is.' She sniffed and let him hold her for several moments longer then stepped back, carefully flicking away moisture from beneath her lower lashes. She sniffed again and straightened her shoulders. 'I'll call Timoteo. I can trust him. He'll know what to do.'

There was a long tense silence that made Teagan wish she'd come in the back way. She shuffled towards the door but neither seemed to notice.

'So you'll trust him but not me?'

Vanessa's gaze dropped. 'That's not what I meant.'

'If only that were true.' Dom sighed and rubbed at his forehead. 'I don't know what more I can do to prove myself to you.'

'Dom, don't. Please.'

This intimacy wasn't Teagan's to witness. As quietly as possible, she opened the screen door, catching the last of Dom's words as she closed it carefully behind her.

'I know you've been through a lot. I know things haven't worked out in the past, but that doesn't mean it can't work this time. I care about you, Nessie. More than you can imagine.'

Teagan felt her throat thicken at the heartfelt sincerity of his words. She'd always considered Dom's attraction to her aunt as a bit of a joke. That, like most men of his ilk, she was simply another challenge to be conquered, but his words revealed it went so much deeper than that. He actually loved her.

How wonderful that must feel.

She found her mother in her room, carefully folding underwear into a monogrammed Louis Vuitton overnight bag that Ness must have loaned her. It took a few seconds for the implication of her activity to dawn. 'What are you doing?'

'Packing a few things.'

'Why? Where are you going?' A few weeks ago she'd never wanted to see her mother again. Now the thought of her leaving appalled Teagan.

Penny put down the nightdress she was about to fold and sat on the bed. 'Your father called this morning.'

At the mention of her father, panic set in. 'You can't go back to him, Mum. You can't.'

Penny looked up in surprise. 'I wasn't planning to. Not unless he gets help and changes.'

'Then why this?' Teagan pointed at the bag.

'I was so upset after Graham called, and with all the stress Vanessa is under thanks to that awful Callum, that Dom suggested this might be a good time for me to take a few days' rest at the Wellness Centre.'

'You're going to get coffee enemas?'

'I hope not!' Penny screwed up her nose. 'I won't be letting anyone near my bottom, thank you very much.' At Teagan's expression she smiled. 'But I will enjoy a massage and facial. Dom said I could also talk to the counsellors if I wished. He said all the centre's services and facilities are open to me.' She looked away, thoughtful. 'He's a good man inside, I think. And he adores Vanessa.'

That much was now obvious, but Teagan wasn't sure she liked the idea of her mother booking in to the Wellness Centre. Massages and facials were fine. She even felt a twinge of envy over such indulgence, but the centre's use of non-conventional therapies bothered her. Teagan believed in science, not wishy-washy new-age ideas based on anecdotal and untested evidence. It was false hope. She'd seen the damage that could do, and her mother was susceptible right now. As for enema-wielding naturopaths . . .

'I've never been pampered before,' said Penny a little wonderingly, as if the idea was something alien and amazing. 'Graham used to scoff at beauticians and things, and I never really had the time when you kids were growing up. Then after your brother left we never had the money.' She picked up the shirt again and began smoothing the folds. 'It'll be nice to do something just for me.'

Teagan joined her mum on the bed and draped an arm around her. 'Then I hope you have a wonderful time.'

'Why don't you come with me? Dom said he'd be happy to accommodate both of us.'

'It's a nice idea but I have to work.'

Her mother regarded her knowingly. 'Yes, and undoubtedly you have more important things on your mind. Lucas Knight perhaps?'

There was no hiding Teagan's longing. This was the woman who'd nursed her, treated her cuts and grazes, scared away the boogieman when Teagan had bad dreams. Their relationship hadn't always been smooth, but she was still her mother.

Penny squeezed her hand. 'He's a nice boy. Very handsome.'

'Too handsome. And far too good for me.'

'Nonsense. No one's too good when it comes to my daughter. And don't you forget it.'

The hug they shared after those words was the warmest Teagan could ever remember.

In the years since her arrival at Falls Farm Vanessa had never felt alone or lonely. Even if no one dropped by she had Saffy, Merlin and the other animals, the musical birds and a feeling of peace. She was safe here, beholden to no one. Independent. A woman in charge of her own destiny.

Callum had shattered that.

She'd slept badly Sunday night. Not helped by how much gin she'd imbibed. Vanessa enjoyed a drink, but she was usually careful never to overindulge. Classy women didn't lose their wits to alcohol, and she'd built her life on being classy, charming and smart. Now that over-inflated little egotist was threatening to take even that away from her.

Vanessa exhaled and resumed her assessment of her finances. It would be imprudent to sell the Andorra warehouse, it was too lucrative. The Provençal rental property would pain her greatly to lose. She and Didier had shared their most romantic moments there, in the days when they were happy. The view of Chateau Lacoste was spectacular at sunset. Which was why the villa was rarely vacant, even in the winter months. She checked her other holdings, calculating worth against earnings and sentimentality.

She sighed deeply and pressed her fingers to her temples. The commercial properties generated too much income, the other rentals held too many memories. Vanessa didn't want to relinquish any of them, but if she didn't make a decision she could lose Falls Farm. Out of all the places she'd lived, it was here she had sunk the deepest roots.

She wondered why that was. Dom? Bunny? The village with its dilapidated bowling club and struggling businesses but brave spirit? The picturesque landscape? She rolled her chair back and, crossing her arms, walked to the office window.

Merlin's yard and paddock were empty. He was a goaty old thing, but she delighted in his unique cunning and determination, and it was unfair that the animal should suffer for doing what came naturally. Everyone knew he was territorial and it wasn't as if she hadn't posted notice. There was even a sign on the gate proclaiming 'Beware of the ram'. A joke, admittedly, but the warning was still there. Yet it was counting against her. According to Callum's weasely solicitor –

another detestable *little* man – the sign was a clear indication that she knew Merlin was dangerous.

Dom promised the lawsuit threat was just that, a threat, and when she'd called Timoteo earlier, he'd agreed. The man was flexing his muscle, trying to put one over her. Give him time to calm down, then offer without-prejudice cash compensation and let that close the matter. A reasonable suggestion, but Vanessa couldn't shake the fear that Callum, in his pathetic pugnacity, wouldn't be satisfied. The man wanted vengeance.

Over a sheep and a woman who'd done nothing more than be polite.

Petty little tiny-penised twerp.

With a last forlorn glance at her computer screen she left the room to wander the empty house. It was nearing twelve. Teagan would be home soon. Perhaps they could drive to the old pub at Wilmington, enjoy a meal in the beer garden. The day was lovely and Vanessa craved distraction.

Blanche was on one of the cane chairs, preening herself. She paused to stroke her head. 'Getting yourself ready for Teagan?'

The cat allowed herself to be rubbed before returning to her concentrated licking.

Vanessa stepped out into the sun. Except for the last few patches where Betty and Wilma's cage had been positioned, the yard was yellow with dandelions. Bright and happy, the way Falls Farm should be.

The skirt of her summer dress swished around her knees as she walked the trail to Claudia and Mouse's paddock. They were at the back, grazing contentedly, tails flicking against flies. With the bush background, redolent with bird calls, the scene was peaceful. The air scented with eucalypt.

In all the places she'd lived overseas, nothing was like this. Not Provence, not Tuscany or Venice, not even Sicily, which she'd adored. This was home.

Dom had said the same last night as they'd sat on the verandah watching the sun fall. Teagan and Penny were inside, preparing a simple dinner. They'd all sensed the change between her and Dom. Until this crisis, Vanessa had never let him in. Never let him see her vulnerability. To him she was without fear, a woman who could take care of her own problems. Their relationship was a tease, nothing to be taken seriously even when her heart sometimes yearned for more. Her inner peace had been too hard-earned to let herself be beholden to another man. But Dom kept surprising her, not just with his offers to help but his understanding. His words that sounded so heartfelt, so honest. The way he held her. His hurt at her lack of trust.

This wasn't a man who wanted to possess an asset. This was a man whose feelings came from somewhere deep. A man who might truly love her.

A man she didn't know how to trust.

As word spread about Callum, the driveway at Falls Farm became almost as busy as the main road. Monday was relatively calm, but Tuesday cocktail hour saw the yard shunting cars like an inner-city taxi rank.

Bunny was always welcome, mainly for her ability to cheer up Ness with new epithets for Callum: Cockless Callum, Callum the Cocksucker, and Teagan's favourite, Callum All-dim instead of Albright. Tony from the newsagency arrived bearing an inflatable sheep to keep Ness company until Merlin returned home. Mark Dunkerton popped in regularly – usually on the tail of Bunny – as did Gus from the IGA, who, being a former farmer, thought the whole thing ridiculous. Peter Somersby sent flowers and a recording of himself singing a hilarious ditty called 'I Am Merlin, Hear Me Bleat' to the tune of Helen Reddy's 'I Am Woman'.

Others, like Col, were received coolly by everyone except Ness. While the events of Friday night had nothing to do with the Wellness

Centre's expansion, the Falls Farm crew were cognisant that whatever Dom was for, Callum would now be against. Col, thanks to his sycophantic relationship with Kathleen, partnership in the Fuckuppas, and easily manipulated nature, was an obvious recruit to spy. A suspicion validated by his many inquiries as to Merlin's whereabouts. The answer was the same no matter who asked: Merlin was incarcerated in a secure location for his own and others' safety.

Although he must have been busy himself and usually spent weekdays in the city, where it was easier to monitor his North Shore holdings, Dom had shifted operations to his office and apartment at the Wellness Centre, allowing him to spend more time at Falls Farm. Despite the intimacy between them on Sunday night, Ness had returned to her normal charming but arm's-length treatment of Dom. Teagan could see the hurt and confusion on his face whenever he thought Ness wasn't looking, and felt a pang of sympathy for him.

Penny was due home on Tuesday, but by Wednesday there was still no sign of her leaving the Wellness Centre. Teagan began to fret that she'd suffered something awful during one of Dom's weird therapies, but he promised her that was far from the case. Penny was having a wonderful time. The counsellors had advised that, given her issues, an extended stay would be appropriate, and Dom was happy to let her have it.

'Can I visit?' Teagan asked him on Thursday, when he informed her that Penny was staying until the end of the week.

'No. We don't allow it. It's important for our clients undergoing the type of counselling and therapy that your mother is having to work through their issues without interference.'

Teagan crossed her arms and narrowed her eyes. 'What, exactly, are these therapies?'

Dom didn't bite. 'Why don't you book yourself in and find out?'

She turned away. 'Thanks, but like I said before, not my thing.'

At the sound of a bang, they both looked towards the kitchen where Ness was mixing a jug of sangria. That lunchtime, Teagan had arrived home to discover Ness once again pacing the verandah in a fury. Scrunched in her fist was a printout of an email from Callum's solicitor stating that one of Dom's companies had paid compensation for the damage to Callum's Maserati. The demand for Merlin's destruction, however, remained.

Which part of the email upset Ness the most Teagan couldn't determine, but since its arrival her aunt's manner towards Dom had bordered on frosty. Teagan couldn't help feeling sorry for him. Even she could see Dom's actions were dictated by his deep care for Ness. When Lucas called by that evening, Teagan used the excuse that they needed to check on Claudia to give the couple time alone.

She left her arms loose on the off chance Lucas might want to take her hand while they walked, as he had on other occasions, but the moment they stepped off the verandah Lucas had shoved his fists into his jeans pockets and there they remained. She tried not to read anything into it but it was hard not to. Last week he would have held hands naturally. But that was before she'd made an idiot of herself.

The days were stretching longer as spring hit full bloom. Sunset was still thirty minutes or so away, the air holding warm. At Pine- haven it would be daylight for at least another hour yet. To stop herself brooding on Lucas, Teagan tried to picture her home, what was happening there. Wondering who was stealing the minutes and pleasures that should have been hers.

It didn't work. All she could think of was Lucas.

'I'm not Dom's greatest fan but I'm sure your mum's fine,' he said when she voiced her worry about Penny's extended stay at the Well- ness Centre. He leaned across the gate and rested on his arms, chin on the back of his hands. He turned his face, which shone golden in the falling sun, and tilted his head in invitation.

Teagan hesitated then settled next to him. This was the first time she'd been alone with Lucas since Saturday morning. Each day he called in to report on Merlin but didn't hang around. Ness dismissed it as some man-thing between him and Dom. Teagan knew otherwise. It was her. She was the one who'd got drunk and propositioned him and now her behaviour had become an embarrassment for them both.

But Lucas, being the kind person he was, felt obliged to maintain pretences.

She scratched at a rust patch with her thumbnail – the only one she hadn't chewed down – wanting to ask him about his day, what he'd been up to. If, despite what she'd done, they could still be friends. The thought of life without him, his steadiness, humour and strength of character, made her stomach clench.

'You okay?' he asked.

'Fine.'

'You're not saying much.'

'Neither are you.'

He shrugged. 'Not the best of days. Merlin got me this morning, the shit. I turned my back for a minute and bang, flat on my arse. Leg still aches. Then when I called into the bakery bloody Kathleen damn near chewed my ear off.' He reached out to pat Claudia, who'd sauntered over for a scratch. 'All I wanted was a bit of apple slice, instead I got an earful about what happens when we let people who have no respect for country life take over peaceful villages.'

'She sounds like she's on Vanessa's side.'

'I doubt it. It was Vanessa who sold Callum the land.'

They lapsed back into silence. Claudia wandered off to join Mouse. Their shadows were so long they were like wraiths chasing through the grass for darkness.

Lucas began to fidget. He tapped at the rail, twisted a loose piece of wire. 'Look, Teagan, about Friday night . . .'

Teagan gazed towards the creek, teeth jammed together, certain she knew where this was going. 'It's okay. You don't have to.'

'Don't have to what?'

'You know.' Not a chance in hell she was going to debase herself with details. She waved him off as though none of it mattered. 'Do the thing. It's not necessary. I'm okay with it.'

He stared at her as though he hadn't a clue what she was on about, then he frowned. 'I'm not sure we're on the same wavelength.'

His frown deepened further as footsteps sounded on the slope behind. Turning around, he let out a quiet 'Fuck.'

Teagan followed suit and released a breath. Thank God. Now she wouldn't have to carry on with this awkwardness. She stepped back from the gate.

Lucas reached for her, fingers brushing hers. 'No, don't. We haven't finished.'

'It's okay,' she said, withdrawing another step. 'We're all sorted.'

'No, we're not.' He stopped and with a growl turned instead on Dom. '*What?*'

'Could I have a quick word?'

'I'm busy.'

Dom remained unruffled. 'It won't take a minute.'

Lucas eyed him, mouth like closed scissors, sharp and steely. 'A minute is all I'm giving.'

Teagan looked from one to the other, not understanding the degree of their hostility. 'It's not Ness, is it?' She inhaled quickly as a thought arose. 'Or Mum?'

'No,' said Dom. 'They're both fine. This is a private matter.'

Private? Chewing her lip she glanced worriedly at Lucas.

'It's all right.' His harsh expression softened a little. 'We'll talk later, okay?'

She threw them both another look before walking on. At the top of the hill she turned around. The two men were facing one another. Lucas's arms were crossed, his stance aggressive. Dom looked more relaxed, gesturing as he explained something. She tried to catch a snippet of their conversation but their words were too quiet. With a final uneasy glance she trudged on.

'What?' said Lucas again, wanting to punch his father for interrupting him with Teagan. All week he'd been biding his time, giving her space. A few days for her to regain her equilibrium and realise she had nothing to be ashamed of. Everyone was too excited by Friday night's other misadventures to worry about hers anyway.

He could have cheered when she'd asked him to come with her to see Claudia. Here was his chance to admit that his friendship act had been just that. Ask if maybe her offer was still open. But he'd stuffed it up.

Teagan's distraction over her mother and his bad day had ruined the moment, and because he had no idea how Teagan would react he'd been nervous, uncertain whether to make it a joke or be serious.

What he hadn't expected was a riddle. What was it that he was supposed to know?

'It looks like the order for Merlin's destruction might get up,' said Dom.

'How?'

'I don't know. I'm looking into it. I suspect Albright's got someone on the council in his pocket.' He ran his palm over his mouth and chin in a tired gesture. 'Vanessa's refusal to reveal the ram's whereabouts to the council ranger didn't help.'

Lucas closed his eyes. He didn't know about the ranger. He was just an average working bloke of modest means, and as much as he wanted to help Vanessa, there were limits. 'Am I going to get caught up in this?'

'Not if I can help it.'

He turned away to stare morosely towards the hill, past which Astonville, and Merlin, lay. 'It's a sheep, for fuck's sake.'

'I know.'

He sighed and faced his father again. 'What if we move him outside of the council boundary? Someone will take him on, surely?'

'Probably. No doubt Bunny could find somewhere. Trouble is, the way Albright's acting he'll likely chase him down. He hates Merlin.' He swept the sole of a polished tan brogue over the track's loose stones. 'Although not as much as he hates me.'

'You in trouble, too?' Not that Lucas cared, but he thought he'd ask.

'No. But this fight with Albright could have implications for the centre.'

Of course. He should have realised Dom's priorities were always with himself. 'So that's what this is really about.'

'It's a consideration.' Dom regarded him steadily. 'I have a business, a good one that I've built over a long period. It's my job to protect it.'

'And people don't really come into it, do they?'

There was an assessing pause before Dom spoke. 'Fate gave your mother cancer, Lucas. Not me.'

'Maybe not. But you have no idea how she suffered, the sort of pain she was in. How she kept working even though she could barely get out of bed, because she couldn't afford to stop.' Lucas forced his voice to remain steady even though the memory yanked his guts. Dom needed to know what it was like. His mum, always so beautiful, wrecked by pain. The years it went on. The operations, radiotherapy and chemo. The false hope of remission. Then the final blow two and a half years ago when the doctors said it was back and there was nothing more they could do. 'You could've helped her.'

'I would have, had I known.'

'Bullshit.' He shook his head in disgust. 'You never gave a stuff about her or me.'

'Jesus, Lucas. How many times do I have to tell you? I knew nothing until after she was gone.'

Lucas began to march off. He'd heard this shit before.

'How was I meant to know she was pregnant? We'd split up. I'd sold the St Marys salon to fund the Chatswood day spa. Steph didn't like the new owners and went to work for someone else. I'd moved to the other side of town. Tell me, Lucas.' He gestured angrily. 'Come on. How was I meant to know?'

Lucas's stride stalled. Breathing hard, he closed his eyes against the possibility that Dom was telling the truth.

The reality was Lucas himself only found out who his father was just before his mum died, when she'd finally admitted the truth of his paternity. Not that he'd asked. He'd learned not to over the years because it upset her so much. Instead he'd let his imagination take over, filling it with boyhood fantasies about how great his dad would be. How they'd do things together, like play rugby or tool around with cars. The perfect dad.

Then she'd told him. After all those years of her not wanting him to find his father, she'd given him the opportunity. How ironic that they'd already crossed paths. Only briefly, through Vanessa, but he'd known Dom. Had even liked him. When Lucas asked why she'd kept it from him, she said it was for his own good. She didn't want him to be disappointed if he found his father to be not the man he hoped.

Lucas hadn't understood how that could be possible until she explained how Dom had dumped her when she no longer fitted in with his plans. That she was just western-suburbs scum to him, not good enough for his new eastern-suburbs life. How he'd left her to become some big-noting rich businessman who didn't want to know his origins anymore, his ambition too great for her. And her unborn son.

She'd made it sound like Dom had known she was pregnant. That he'd chosen to ignore Lucas's existence. It seemed to fit. After all, there'd been no birthday or Christmas presents, no cards, or maintenance money as far as Lucas was aware.

Only after she'd passed did Lucas discover that she'd also written to Dom. He never saw the letter; he only had Dom's word about what was in it. But he refused to believe that his mum was guilty of deliberately keeping knowledge of her son from Dom. That wasn't her. She was too loving, too kind-hearted for that degree of bitterness.

But that's exactly what his father said she'd done when Dom made his first overture. Lucas hadn't believed him. Couldn't believe him. Yet with each encounter like this, he was finding it harder and harder not to.

'That doesn't excuse what you did to her,' he said finally.

'You're right. It doesn't.'

To Lucas's surprise Dom sounded sincere.

Dom lifted his arms from his side and let them drop. 'I didn't realise she felt so strongly about the relationship. I was focused on building my business, making something of my life. Escaping the welfare cycle my family had been in for decades. I thought our relationship was casual. It wasn't, not to Steph, and my leaving hurt her more than I understood. We parted badly. Said things to each other people shouldn't.

'She didn't deserve that. But I also didn't deserve to have knowledge of you – a son I would have loved and looked after had I been given the chance – kept from me for nigh on thirty years. Yes, I've made mistakes, but despite what you think I'm not a complete bastard.'

Lucas stared at the dirt track. 'I'm not ready for this.'

'I know.'

Lucas looked up.

Dom's palms were open. 'I don't expect to suddenly be your father. But I would like to at least be a mate.'

He looked at his father, at the sky, up at the house, and wondered what harm there would be in it. There was another family out there to discover. Roots, ancestors. His mum was gone. One of her last acts was to reveal his father's name. Perhaps that meant she wanted them to know each other. Perhaps that meant she'd forgiven Dom.

Or regretted her own actions.

'I'll think about it.' Shoving his hands in his pockets he began to walk away, only to turn around several steps later. 'If you really want to be a mate, next time you see me and Teagan alone, don't interrupt.'

At that Dom threw his head back and laughed. 'I'll do my best.'

Even Lucas couldn't help his smile. Although he turned quickly away to stop Dom from noticing.

EIGHTEEN

VANESSA ROLLED her lips firmly together, trying not to laugh. To do so would be a grave error given the horror on her niece's face. Poor Teagan. In a way Vanessa couldn't blame her. Penny had gone rather over the top.

Teagan stood on the verandah, arms crossed and weight on one hip, voice low and slow with disbelief, while her mother sat like a blissed-out Buddha in her cane chair. 'You cannot be serious.'

'Oh,' said Penny, smacking her hands together like some sort of happy-clapping religious convert and beaming, 'but it was wonderful.'

'Enemas are not wonderful.'

Penny ceased her clapping and lifted her chin in defiance. 'Research has shown that colon hydrotherapy has excellent health benefits. Have you any idea how much waste lingers in the gut, putre-fying? All those toxins need cleaning out. I feel marvellous for it.'

'Whose research? Some quack's ramblings published on the internet, no doubt. The only reason you feel great is because you're pumped full of caffeine.'

Penny ignored her, driven by her good health and conversion to the holistic cause. 'And thanks to Dom's naturopath, Sienna, nearly all my menopausal symptoms have disappeared. She said mine were particularly severe. They'd put my entire body out of balance.' She smiled beatifically. 'She said that could've been why I didn't have the strength to confront Graham. I was simply too unwell in myself. Menopause isn't just a biological change, it's a spiritual change, too. By not embracing mine, by suppressing its natural empowerment, I caused an acute imbalance in my body's systems.'

'Mum, seriously, are you listening to yourself? You sound like a new-age religious convert!'

'More to the point, are you listening to me? I feel amazing, Teagan. The best I have in years. And if I keep up my program, each day will see me feeling even better.'

'Program?' Teagan narrowed her eyes. 'What else did they give you?'

Penny turned her face to the side, her chin again held aloft. 'None of your business.'

'Come on, you've come home fairly rattling with pills and potions. What are they?'

'Herbal remedies. Black cohosh. Some St Johns Wort.'

Teagan was almost spluttering. 'Black what?'

'Black cohosh. Native Americans have been using it for centuries.'

Teagan groaned and gave up, flopping onto a cane chair and rubbing her face. 'I knew this would happen. I knew it.'

Vanessa patted her hand. The poor darling, this really was a shock. 'You have to admit your mother looks well.'

'She does,' Teagan agreed. 'But five days of decent sleep, massages and being waited on hand and foot would make anyone feel amazing. Nothing to do with that cohosh rubbish, spiritual change or unbalanced systems.'

'Oh, be quiet,' snapped Penny. 'What would you know? You're hardly an expert.'

'Neither is your so-called natural therapist who's probably never been near a university let alone possesses any comprehension of the fundamentals of science. We're mammals, for God's sake. Not bloody fairy beings existing on another plane.' Teagan glared at Vanessa. 'This is all Dom's fault.'

Vanessa opened her mouth to defend Dom but Penny got in first. 'Don't you dare criticise Domenic. He's a wonderful man. And he's very pleased with my progress.' Her spine straightened and her voice ballooned with pride. 'In fact, he's offered me a position at the centre.'

Teagan rubbed her temple, a pained expression on her face. 'Doing what exactly?'

Penny slumped a fraction. 'Only cleaning to start with. But he says there's always potential for more. Perhaps, with study, even a therapist's position.'

Teagan made a half-choked noise, but before she could respond further Vanessa delivered a sharp toe-poke to her ankle. While Vanessa didn't mind a bit of healthy cynicism – she herself harboured the suspicion that half the treatments offered at the centre were of questionable benefit – undermining Penny's newfound happiness wasn't on.

Thankfully, Teagan got the hint.

Closing her eyes momentarily, she took a long slow breath. 'If that's what you want, Mum, then that's great. I wish you all the best. But even you have to admit this conversion is all a bit sudden. You've never shown any interest in alternative therapies before. Remember Nanny Bliss and all her pills? You used to laugh and say what a waste of money it was. And what about Mrs Fitzsimons who refused to have chemo and ended up doing that crackpot high-pH thing instead? She died in agony, poor woman. I clearly recall you saying that the people who ran that clinic should be shot.'

'They were victimising cancer sufferers. Graham's mother prescribed to mega-nutrient therapy, which is silly. This is different. These therapies have been around for thousands of years, helping people regain their health.'

'Then why aren't they part of conventional medicine, subject to the same scientific examination and government regulation as any other treatment?'

'Because the big pharmaceutical companies want to suppress them. They make too much money out of their patented drugs to allow alternative treatments to become mainstream.'

'They what?' Teagan pinched the bridge of her nose. 'Oh, Mum, who told you that?'

'My naturopath.'

'Then your naturopath is a complete wacko. This whole business stinks.'

Penny wouldn't be budged. 'You just refuse to believe.'

'Damn right I refuse,' said Teagan, providing good evidence to the inheritability of stubbornness.

Sensing a hiatus in the discussion, Vanessa rose. 'Well, darlings, I don't know about you, but it's past time for *my* personal therapy. One I'm sure my doctor would not prescribe either but does wonders for my wellbeing. Margaritas, anyone?'

'Not for me,' said Penny. 'I'm going to have some of my special cleanser.'

Teagan rolled her eyes.

A roll that only worsened when Penny returned to the verandah with a glass of something oily and alarmingly reminiscent of urine, and several pills of equally unappetising colour. Vanessa admired her sister's fortitude when a sip of the yellow liquid went down with only a slight wince. Though her admiration faded to concern at the range of vitamins and herbal pills she had lined up. There seemed an awful lot.

With every pill swallow, Teagan gave another shake of her head, but Vanessa could also tell she was truly worried.

As Vanessa poured margaritas for Teagan and herself, a car sounded in the driveway. Vanessa hoped it was Lucas arriving for a swim. Anything to distract Teagan and give her a chance to settle before Dom arrived. The temper she was in didn't bode well for a harmonious cocktail hour.

Unfortunately, the car turned out to be an aging blue Ford.

'Colin,' said Vanessa with all the warmth she could muster, 'how nice to see you.'

'Mrs Ferguson know you're here, Col?' asked Teagan, clearly in a combative mood.

Not looking at Teagan, Col mumbled a 'no' and thrust a carton of eggs towards Vanessa.

'Oh, eggs!' she said, using a delighted smile to hide her surprise at his answer. How fascinating. Col usually never did anything without Kathleen's imprimatur. 'You're such a darling man.'

'Knew you'd like some.' Col nodded at Penny before returning beady eyes to Vanessa. 'Any news on Merlin?'

'As far as I'm aware he's being well cared for.'

'As far as you're aware?' Col scratched at his head. 'So you haven't visited him?'

'No.' She slid a look towards Teagan and winked subtly before resetting her expression into deep earnestness. 'He's undergoing behaviour-management therapy. It's best I stay away lest he regresses.'

Col's grey eyes turned enormous. 'Therapy? For a sheep?'

'Yes. Merlin has been a valuable member of the Falls Farm menagerie. I feel he's worth it.'

He let out a whistle. 'You must really like that ram.'

'He's very special.' She gave a sad sniff, determined not to look at Teagan who, having at last shed her temper, now had her knees jammed up to her chest and her hand slammed across her mouth, trying not to laugh. 'He helped me through some difficult times. I'm terribly fond of him.'

Col patted her arm in sympathy. 'I'm sure he'll be allowed back soon.'

'I hope so. This affair is quite distressing.' She simulated brushing a tear from beneath her left eye. 'Thank you so much for the eggs. You know how I appreciate them.' She waved towards Penny's foul-looking drink. From this angle, the liquid looked even more urine-like. 'I'd offer you a glass of my new cocktail, but knowing how generous and caring you are, you're probably in a hurry to get home and help Maggie with dinner.'

He blinked at the glass, his mouth popping open as Penny raised it to her lips. 'Yes, right you are. Must dash.' He gave a wave and headed off.

The Ford disappeared down the drive and, for the first time since Penny's arrival home, the three women broke into raucous laughter. Which was how, a few minutes later, Lucas found them.

Surprised, he grinned in that infectious, radiant way he had. 'I'm guessing a private girls' joke. Laughter like that tends to only come at the expense of men.'

'Only one man,' said Vanessa, delighted to see that Lucas kept most of his attention on Teagan. With her cheeks pink and her smile wide, it was no wonder. When she wasn't looking anxious or being down on herself, her niece was extraordinarily pretty. 'And never you.' She held up her glass. 'Drink?'

'Thanks.' He turned to Penny. 'Look at you. You look great.'

Penny beamed at the compliment. 'I feel amazing.'

'You enjoyed yourself then?'

'It was wonderful. You have no idea.'

'Maybe I should book myself a session and find out,' he said, accepting a tumbler of margarita and groaning a little as he settled into a chair.

'Merlin?' asked Teagan.

He shook his head. 'Horse.'

'They do excellent massages at the centre,' said Penny, causing Teagan to raise her eyes heavenward as though praying for patience.

Fortunately Bunny chose that moment to arrive. Pausing only to give a rather startled look and flattering remark to Penny, Bunny let loose on Callum.

'I know who All-dim has onside at the council now. That fuck-tard Montague.'

'Dom says we don't need to worry about it,' said Vanessa. 'The *Companion Animals Act* was designed for dogs and cats, not sheep.'

Bunny remained unconvinced. 'There's a provision in the act for "any other animal that is prescribed by the regulations as a companion animal."'

'But that's hardly Merlin,' said Lucas.

'Montague believes there's a case to be made.'

Vanessa closed her eyes as she realised what a dunderhead she'd just been. Well, it served her right for being smart and teasing an old man.

Bunny arched forward in concern. 'What's the matter?'

'I am such a fool.'

'Why?' asked Teagan.

'I was just telling Col what a wonderful friend Merlin has been and how he's helped me through bad times. If he is spying for Callum, that little piece of intelligence will now go straight to your council fellow.' Her eyes began to sting. Such a silly thing, but she really was fond of that sheep. And it was so very wrong for him to be a pawn in a vain man's game. 'Poor Merlin. All he was doing was what came naturally. I'm so scared for him.'

Lucas placed his arm around her and squeezed. 'He'll be fine. No one's touching Merlin. They'll have to come through me first.'

Out of the corner of her eye, Vanessa glimpsed Teagan take a gulp of margarita and look away. Oh, dear. The last thing any of them needed was Teagan thinking the wrong thing about her and Lucas. Smiling at him gratefully, Vanessa shifted forward to reach for her own drink, forcing Lucas to drop his hold.

Bunny took over the conversation, but Vanessa could see Teagan's mood had again soured. She was staring moodily out at the trees, chewing a thumbnail. Vanessa let her be for a moment, considering how best to tackle the problem, then leaned across to whisper to Lucas.

'Time for a swim?'

Teagan hooked a slither of thumbnail between her front teeth and began to gnaw. It was stupid, this feeling. She hated herself for it, but it lingered like the oil in the bottom of her mum's glass.

Her aunt was over fifty, for crying out loud. Lucas was being his usual nice self. They'd known each other a long time. How could she possibly feel jealous? Yet the slimy feeling remained and her head was thick with negative whispers.

Ness didn't look her age. She was glamorous and classy and had a figure built for sin. What did Teagan have? A body like a plank, zero sophistication and the unerring ability to constantly make a total twit of herself.

She tugged at her thumbnail and felt a surge of sick pleasure when the nail tore too far. The sharp pain brought her back into focus. She wished it hadn't. Conversation had returned to the Wellness Centre.

'Think I'll go for a swim,' said Lucas, standing and wincing as he stretched. 'Might ease the pain in my back.' He looked at Teagan. 'Want to come?'

Teagan contemplated for a moment. It was either stay here and listen to more crap about the efficacy of gallbladder cleanses or join Lucas and the risk of him bringing up the trivia night again.

'Okay,' she said.

Lucas was swimming slow laps when Teagan padded out onto the deck in her bikini. She slid into the water and sat in the warmer shallows, admiring his easy stroke. He reached the deep end and stopped. Scraping his hair back from his face, he rested against the wall, one muscled arm raised to grip the pool's edge, and regarded her.

'What's up?'

'Nothing.'

He pushed off the wall and dived down. Teagan watched his body cut through the water until it reached the shallows and he resurfaced. He stayed lying in the water, balanced on his fingertips, head up.

The sun had dipped enough to sneak under the pool's protective sail. It caressed his skin, turning him golden and sparkling, and his blue eyes sky bright. Teagan wanted to look away, but he was too mesmerising. And she ached in that awful agonising way that only deep, hopeless want produced.

'You were laughing before, when I arrived.' He crept closer until he was level with her ankles. 'Now you seem upset. What's wrong?'

'It's nothing.'

'Doesn't look like it.' He tilted his head. 'Is it about Friday night, because —'

'No. It's not Friday night.' She breathed out. Friday night was not something she wanted to talk about. Ever. 'It's Mum.'

'What about her? She looks great.'

'She does, and I'm not criticising that, but she's come back with all these wacked-out ideas and drinking some slush that looks like wee. Plus they've given her all these weird pills. None of this stuff is regulated. They could have anything in them. And with all that's happened Mum's vulnerable right now.'

He smiled, trying to reassure her. 'I'm sure they're harmless.'

'Dad thought his stupid computer program was harmless, too, until it cost us the farm.'

'Come on, Teagan. It's hardly the same.'

She shook her head and looked away, biting her lip. Why did she feel on the verge of tears? This was ridiculous.

'Hey.' He took her hand under the water. 'What's really going on?'

'I hate seeing gullible people taken for a ride, Lucas. I hate it.'

'Because you were for so long?'

'Yes, because I was.' His fingers tightened as her throat caught and the words snagged. 'And so was Mum, and now she's being taken on another one, this time with her health. I'm not going to let it happen again. I have to protect her.'

'Look, I'm not in the habit of defending Dom, but I doubt he'd let anything bad happen to your mum. If nothing else, he cares too much about Vanessa for that.' He pressed a muscled shoulder against hers. 'You worry too much.'

Teagan said nothing. He didn't understand. No one did. It was because of her weakness, her cowardice, that they'd lost so much already.

'I was thinking,' said Lucas. 'Do you want to come over to my place for a while? Watch a movie or something?'

The idea of an evening alone with Lucas made her heartbeat quicken, but what was the point? It would only make her stupid crush worse. Besides, she wouldn't mind spending some time using Vanessa's computer to research some of the pills her mum was taking. Just to reassure herself that they weren't dangerous.

'Thanks, but I'd better stay here. Keep an eye on Mum.'

'She'll be fine. Vanessa's with her.'

'I know, but I want to Google some stuff. Check out what Mum's taking.'

'You can Google on my iPad.'

'It'll be easier on Ness's. That way I can show her anything I find straight away.'

'Right,' said Lucas, sounding pissed off. He released her fingers and rose out of the water like a Norse god to stand looking down at her. Annoyance dripped off him with the pool water.

Uncomfortable, she tried to make a joke. 'Not much of a friend, am I?'

'Friday night you wanted to be more than friends.'

She winced at the mention. Why couldn't he forget it, leave it alone? 'That was just drunk talk.'

'Drunk talk,' said Lucas, staring at her. Then he shook his head as if to clear it. 'I've got to go.'

'Oh. Okay.'

'I need to shift Merlin. He's too easy to spot where he is.'

'Yes. Of course.' She sucked in a breath, suddenly wishing she was going with him. So it would hurt, but the thought of not being with him hurt more. Except now it was too late. 'I'll see you later?'

Making a gesture that could have been yes or no, he walked up the pool steps, leaving her alone in shallows that suddenly felt cold.

Even in the calm sanctuary of Astonville, Lucas couldn't hold back his exasperation. What the fuck was wrong with Teagan? He'd practically spelled it out. *Come home with me.* How much clearer did he need to be? Sure, she was upset over Penny. After what her dad did he could sort of understand it, but Penny looked the best she had since she'd arrived at The Falls. Plus she had Vanessa there to keep an eye on things. And okay, so he wasn't egotistical enough to think he was completely irresistible. But still.

As for 'drunk talk', those two lousy words still stung. It was more than that, he knew it. And so did she, except she was too scared to acknowledge the fact. Why, he had no idea.

He ran his hand through his hair. Jesus, women were unfathomable.

Merlin didn't improve Lucas's temper. The ram was hell-bent on dislocating his knee. It took all his strength to keep the knuckle-headed creature out of bunting distance as he dragged him to the small paddock behind the forge. It wasn't ideal. A short wander behind the shed and any visitor would be able to spot the ram through the trees. In a few years the windbreak would be thicker, but for now the trees he'd planted were barely past sapling stage. Lucas hoped Merlin wouldn't ringbark or flatten them. He'd spent a fortune in water keeping them alive last summer.

After letting go of the ram's huge horn, he slid back through the gate and headed for the shed. Disappointment was pumping through his veins and he needed to sweat it out. He pushed the door open and turned on the lights. Soon it would be too dark to work properly, but the thought of going to the house alone didn't appeal.

He stalked over to the benchtop and picked up the silver pendant he'd been working on, a new design he'd thought Teagan might like. It was close to finished, the peacock-coloured enamel inlays buffed bright. All that was needed was some work on the silver curlicues and to fit a bale through which a chain could be threaded.

He turned it over in his fingers, thinking of her. The way she made him feel. Catching her laughing this afternoon was like watching some rare flower come into bloom. She was pretty before, but now that she was starting to put on weight she'd developed a sexiness to go with it. That it was unconscious and almost innocent made it even more powerful. His dreams were full of her in that white bikini. And out of it. Naked, in his bed. Red hair feathered over his pillow, an inviting smile on her face.

Getting her that way was proving harder than expected.

He walked to the door and stared down at his house and pergola, and experienced an unexpected jab of loneliness. The place felt barren. No family, no girlfriend. Just his own grumpy company.

Alone.

Except that wasn't quite true. He had a father. A father who wanted to have a relationship with his son. To be mates. The very thing he'd secretly longed for as a boy.

Lucas sighed and looked around. This was shit. He wasn't going to mope all night. He pulled his mobile from his pocket and called Dunks.

An hour later, showered and in clean jeans and a shirt, he was propped on a bar stool at the bowlo drinking beer with Dunks and wondering why he'd thought this was a good idea. His friend was even more of a misery guts than he was.

'Look on the bright side,' said Lucas. 'A least you're getting laid.'

But Dunks was too broody to see the positives. 'Why can't she stay the night? A couple of shags and she's off home.'

'Maybe she's worried about how she'll look in the morning. Maybe she snores.' He shrugged. 'You're asking the wrong bloke if you want to understand how women think. I haven't a frigging clue.'

Dunks took a long draught of beer and stared into the dregs. 'She says she's too old for me.'

'Seems to be doing a good job of keeping up so far.'

'That's what I told her. Anyway, I thought women were supposed to reach their peak at fifty.' He twirled a coaster. 'It's not just Bunny. Angela's being a bitch about it, too.'

'Probably jealous you're having fun with someone else.'

'She's threatening to apply for full-time custody.'

So that was the real problem. No wonder Dunks was upset. 'She won't get it. You're a great dad. No court would stop you from seeing your daughters.'

'Doesn't matter what the court says. She can make life pretty hard if she wants. The girls are only young. Wouldn't take much to poison them against me. She bitches enough as it is.'

'That's so fucking wrong.'

'Tell me something I don't know.'

Later that evening at home, feeling disturbed, Lucas pulled out his mum's old photo albums. Every page was stuffed with pictures of him as a happy boy. At school, at sport, playing in the yard. He flicked through the pages, feeling not just down but pissed off. He'd had a dad. One who said he would have wanted to be in Lucas's life, and she'd denied him that.

Lucas paused at a photo of him with his mum. She was crouched beside him, her arm tight around his body, her face turned to his. There was nothing but love in her expression, yet he couldn't help thinking of the tightness of her hold. As if Lucas was hers and no one else's. That her son wasn't for sharing.

She'd held extraordinary power and abused it just to punish Dom. Yet it was Lucas who'd been punished. Perhaps that's what she'd seen in the end, when she was close to dying. That she would be leaving Lucas with nothing, only the memory of her.

He shut the album and stared at the cover for a long while.

It wouldn't be easy, but maybe it was about time he started learning about his father.

NINETEEN

THANKS TO HER ONGOING IDIOCY, Teagan was in a gloom. Even Diablo affectionately snuffling his velvety muzzle through her hair didn't cheer her up.

Saturday and Sunday had passed with no visit from Lucas, when he usually poked his head in at the farm at least once over a weekend. Her own fault. She should have told the truth about her feelings instead of relying on the drunk defence, but watching Lucas put his arm around her aunt had brought on a bout of self-doubt and jealousy Teagan couldn't control.

A hundred times she'd thought about calling or sending him a text. She'd even slowed at the turnoff for Astonville, flicked the blinker on then flicked it straight back off again before accelerating past.

She was too uncertain of his reaction and too afraid of worsening the ache in her heart.

With a long sigh, she bent down to collect more manure into the pooper scooper. The woodchips in Diablo's stable were beginning to stale. Nick tried to keep to a schedule with changing the bedding, but some horses were simply messier than others. Diablo paced so much

he scattered his droppings and dug them in. She hurried along, the
smell of spoil reminding her too much of all the things she'd done to
mess up her own life. Pinehaven's loss still left a sharp pain in her
chest. Only on Sunday, feeling miserable in the wake of Lucas's lack
of contact, and like a masochist wanting to make it worse, she'd
checked the Levenham real estate listings and found a large promo-
tion for Pinehaven's upcoming auction. She'd been teary enough, but
that had left her bawling like a baby.

Teagan had finished the stable and was closing the gate when
Nick came jogging across the yard.

'Phone call,' he said, thrusting his mobile at her.

She regarded it with distrust. If someone wanted her surely
they'd call her direct? Then she remembered she'd left her own
phone charging back at Falls Farm.

Only when Nick waved the screen in front of her face did she
register his worried expression.

She snatched it out of his hand. 'Hello?'

'It's Vanessa. An ambulance is here for your mother.'

'Why? What's wrong?'

'I thought it was gastro but she kept getting worse.' Ness stifled a
sob. 'So I called the doctor. He rang the ambulance straight away.
She's really ill, Teagan.'

'Oh, God.'

'You'd better come home.'

'Yes. Yes, of course.'

'If we're gone, head to Nepean Hospital. I'll call you with the
details.'

When Ness hung up, Teagan swallowed and turned to Nick.
'It's Mum.'

He took the pooper scooper and phone from her hands and
pushed her. 'Go.'

The yard at Falls Farm was empty. Teagan picked up her phone
and immediately headed back out, steering one-handed as she called

Ness. Too bad if she was pulled over. The police could give her a bloody escort to the hospital.

'We're pulling into emergency now,' answered Ness without preamble. 'I'll see you soon.'

By the time Teagan arrived and found a park her mother had been taken away. Ness was pacing the emergency room, being ignored by the other people present who had their own worries.

Teagan grabbed her, fear making her rough. 'What did they say?'

'Nothing yet.' Ness's cheeks were pale, her eyes wide and liquid. 'I haven't heard anything.'

'But you must know something?'

'Only what the doctor said. Her blood pressure was too low and she was severely dehydrated. Which comes as no surprise. Everything was coming out of everywhere, poor thing.'

'Could it have been from all that stuff she was taking?'

'The doctor seemed to indicate as much. But, darling, there's no point jumping to conclusions until we see what they have to say.'

'It was that muck, I bet you.' Teagan stared towards the big doors, wanting to bash through them and demand what was going on. But all they could do was wait.

She rubbed her arms, feeling sick and angry and helpless. The antiseptic smell combined with the odour of humans under stress and the mustiness clinging to her clothes didn't help. If anything happened to her mum Teagan would never forgive herself. She should have gathered up all those pills and potions and flushed the lot down the toilet.

'I should have stopped her.'

'Teagan,' said Vanessa, reaching for her.

But Teagan veered away. She'd failed to act again, and this time over something far more precious than a farm. The shame of it was flailing her heart.

It seemed to take hours before someone came out to find them. A kind-mannered nurse finally led her and Ness to a bed where Penny lay. She was pale and deathly looking, her eyes closed, the lids greyish. Exhaustion dug deep lines through her skin. A tube was dripping something into her arm, another fed oxygen into her nose. Her breathing came slow, with a faint but frightening rattle.

'The doctor will be by in a moment,' said the nurse.

She and Ness stood at either end of Penny's feet, looking at her face, frightened by her fragility. Teagan wanted to wake her, to check this was really sleep and not unconsciousness. That she hadn't suffered more than the tubes and casual care indicated.

'Severe dehydration and electrolyte imbalance,' the doctor advised. 'Most likely from the cleansing program.' His tone revealed exactly what he thought of that therapy.

'But she'll be all right?' asked Teagan, skipping her focus between the doctor's and her mother's face.

'Yes. With rest.'

Teagan's shoulders sagged with relief. She moved forward to take her mum's hand while Ness asked a few more questions and the doctor hurried off to his other patients.

'They'll keep her in overnight at least, just to keep an eye on things,' said her aunt, sitting on the edge of the bed and reaching forward to brush a hank of greasy hair off Penny's forehead. 'I'm not surprised it was the cleanse. All that apple and grapefruit juice and Epsom salts, not to mention the olive oil. Her system simply couldn't digest it.'

'But why do it? She said she felt amazing after the centre. Why a cleanse? As far as I'm aware she has no history of liver or gallbladder problems.'

'Perhaps she thought it would make her feel even better.' Ness stroked the back of her hand over Penny's cheek. 'In her excitement she probably went a bit too far. Drank too much too quickly, added too much salt. I don't know.'

'She shouldn't have been doing it in the first place. She was a perfectly healthy woman before she went to that place. Now look what's happened.' Teagan curled a fist to her chest where a cold hole had formed. Her mother was *in hospital*. 'This is Dom and his stupid centre's fault.' And her own for letting her mother stay there for so long, getting brainwashed. It was meant to be for pampering. Instead she ended up seriously ill.

'You can't blame Dom or the centre staff. The fault is likely Penny's more than anyone else's.'

Teagan looked back at her mum and felt tears prickle.

'Teagan, look at me.' Ness was surveying her worriedly. 'This isn't the centre's fault. Nor is it Dom's. Or anyone else's. Surely you can see that?'

A soft moan had them both fixing back on the bed.

Teagan bent forward as her mother slowly roused. 'Hey, Mum.'

Penny stared unfocused before frowning in confusion. 'What?'

'You're in hospital,' explained Ness gently. 'You had a bad reaction to the cleanse. They're keeping you in for a while as a precaution, but you'll be fine.'

'I'm sorry.' Penny's face crumpled in on itself, contorted with pain and memory. 'So sorry.'

She began to sob, the sound heartbreaking. Teagan wanted to punch something. To hurt as her mum had been hurt.

'Hey,' said Ness. 'Shh. Don't be silly.' Ness leaned close to whisper to Teagan. 'I think she's upset about her bedroom.'

The thought only made Teagan feel worse. 'It's fine, Mum. You have nothing to be sorry for. You just get better. We'll look after everything else.'

Her words did nothing to ease her mother's distress. The tears flowed until exhaustion left her hollow and shrunken. Penny lay sunken into the pillow, staring at the ceiling and breathing rattled, ragged breaths while Teagan squeezed her hand and held back her own tears of guilt.

Finally, Penny cast sad eyes past Teagan and addressed her sister in a pathetic, needy voice. 'Does Graham know?'

Teagan stilled. Why would her mum care if her dad knew? She'd left him.

Ness used the edge of the blanket to tenderly wipe Penny's sodden cheeks. 'Do you want me to call him?'

Penny nodded, her mouth screwed up.

'I will when I get home.'

Teagan shot a sharp glare at her aunt. Why the hell had she agreed to do that?

Ness caught her gaze and held it steady, then she deliberately looked back at Penny. The message was clear: don't argue.

A fair call. A hospital wasn't the place. Later though, that would be something else.

A police car was parked outside the bakery when Lucas called into the village shops to check his mail. Probably ducking in for a pie, he decided, unlocking his post-office box and dragging out the contents. A bank statement. Better than a bill.

He headed into the newsagent's for a chat. Tony was on the phone but quickly rang off when he spotted Lucas.

'Have you heard?'

Tony's overexcited tone and bulging eyes told Lucas something big was up. 'Heard what?'

'The bakery. It was robbed this morning. Kathleen assaulted.'

Lucas stared out the door. He might not have much time for Kathleen Ferguson, but assaulting an old woman wasn't on. 'Do they know who did it?'

The Falls wasn't without its fair share of dropkicks. Nearly every shop in the village had been done over at least once since Lucas had moved to the area, and Bunny's practice had been hit even more times by idiots looking for drugs, although not with a lot of success. The practice was like Fort Knox. Bunny didn't tolerate crap.

'She's given a description. Col says it's the spitting image of that soapie star rumoured to have gone into rehab.' Tony pointed to the copies of women's magazines piled along the front racks. One cover showed a degenerate-looking bloke wearing a beanie and skinny jeans, striding down an urban footpath. A long-haired blonde with an oversized handbag hooked over one shoulder followed slightly behind, expression mutinous. *Splitsville?* the headline beneath read in large shouty print. Similar photos and tags graced the other magazines.

'He's at the Wellness Centre?'

'Who knows? You know how secretive that place is. Col swears it has to be him.'

'Col wouldn't know if his arse was on fire.'

'Can't argue with that. Still a bloody worry though.' Tony grimaced towards the bakery. 'She shouldn't be there that early by herself anyway.'

'Where was Heath?' asked Lucas, referring to the baker.

'Late. It was him who found her.'

Convenient. Heath was known as a bit of a punter with dodgy mates. Could have been one of them. Easy enough to set up. Lucas scratched at his neck, wondering why he didn't want it to be someone from the centre when he'd never cared previously. But that was before he'd stopped hating his father.

'Is she all right?'

'Yeah. Bruises mostly. Nothing serious.'

At that moment Bunny came jogging across the carpark, wearing spectacularly un-vet-like bright-purple scrubs. 'Lucas, have you heard?'

'I'm guessing everyone has by now.'

'Why would everyone know? Vanessa's only just phoned me.'

'Vanessa?' The seriousness of Bunny's tone and concerned expression set panic flaring. Something had happened. Something bad. 'Is it Teagan?'

She glanced at Tony and grabbed Lucas's elbow, steering him outside, past the takeaway and around the corner of the shops. An action that only worsened Lucas's fear.

'Jesus, Bunny. Just tell me.'

'It's Penny. She was taken to hospital this morning with severe dehydration. Sounds like she overdid the gallbladder cleanse she was doing.'

Lucas couldn't help his exhalation of relief at the mention of Penny's name instead of Teagan's. 'Is she all right?'

'Appears so. They're keeping her in for observation. Understandable given how low her blood pressure went.'

'Does Teagan know?'

'She's there now. Vanessa said she's pretty upset, blaming herself mostly.'

'It can hardly be Teagan's fault.'

'Try telling her that. Really, that girl needs to get laid.' She gave Lucas a blunt look.

Lucas scraped his hand over his hair. 'Trust me, I've tried.'

'Not hard enough, obviously.' When Lucas didn't answer she let out an exasperated sigh. 'You do realise she has the self-esteem of a maggot? Teagan just doesn't believe someone like you would be interested in someone like her. It's up to you to prove otherwise.'

'Like how?'

'I don't know. I'm a bloody vet not a psychologist. Try flexing those giant muscles of yours or something.' Bunny glanced at her watch. 'I have to go. Vanessa said they'd be home sometime after three. Mightn't hurt to call in.'

Lucas watched her jog back to the surgery, mulling over her news. Vanessa had mentioned before that Teagan wasn't as strong as she made out but perhaps he'd underestimated how much she kept hidden. That she was upset about her family and the loss of her home was obvious. She was grieving and out of sorts and needed a shoulder to cry on, but if it went deeper than that . . .

The thought left him wishing he'd pushed harder, spelled out his interest instead of confusing her with his stupid friend defence. He also had a strange urge to contact Dom and warn him about Kath

Ferguson and Penny, but the police would no doubt sort the former and Vanessa would look after the latter.

He turned back to the takeaway. Too late now for the homemade sandwich he'd planned. With his diary full for the afternoon he'd have to eat on the run.

By the time Lucas made it to Falls Farm it was close to six o'clock. He was tired, and his wrist hurt where he'd wrenched it trying to hold a bad-tempered racehorse, but crap timing or not he was determined this time to tell Teagan his feelings were for real.

Vanessa was on the verandah with a negroni, her Monday cocktail. Although dressed with her usual care, her makeup lacked precision and there were chips in her nail polish. Fatigue had left her eyes puffy. She smiled wanly and poured him a drink.

'Bunny told me about Penny. How is she?'

'On the mend. It was all horrible though.' Sliding a peek towards the house, she hunched towards him and dropped her voice. 'Teagan's been very quiet since we've been home. She blames herself terribly for what happened.' Vanessa sat back, her tone returning to normal. 'She's in the pool in case you were wondering.'

He was, but he had things he needed to check with Vanessa first and a drink to finish. For what he was about to lay open a bit of Dutch courage wouldn't hurt. 'Have you spoken to Dom?'

'Briefly. Just to advise him about Penny.'

'You heard about Kath Ferguson?'

Vanessa nodded, her expression anxious. 'I think Dom's quite worried about it. He'd never say, of course. But I could hear it in his voice.'

'It was probably a local. Wouldn't be the first time.'

'No. Still, accusations stick and the timing isn't good with the expansion going to council. Or this business with Callum and poor Merlin.' She forced a smile. 'I'm sure he'll sort it out. He's dealt with these sorts of crises before.'

The screen door opened. Teagan stood awkwardly with her hand on the jamb as though unsure whether to stay in or come out. She was wearing her white bikini and looked pale, fragile and huge-eyed.

'Hey,' he said. 'I heard about your mum. Thought I'd drop by and check she was okay.'

'Oh.' She glanced from him to Vanessa and back again, and bit her lip, still making no move to join them. 'Right.'

'Would you like a negroni?' Vanessa offered.

'No. I . . .' She glanced at Lucas and then at the timber floor. 'I might go back to the pool. Leave you to it. Thanks for asking about Mum. That was nice of you.'

Lucas stared as the screen door closed, before regarding Vanessa. 'What the hell was that about?'

Vanessa pursed her lips and blinked, as flummoxed as him. 'I have no idea.' She patted his arm. 'Why don't you go have a swim and find out?'

'I don't have my boardies.'

'Going commando these days, are you? How sexy of you, Lucas.'

That brought a smile. Of course he was wearing underwear. They weren't as safe as his boardies though, which covered things up. Stretchy trunks tended to show too much. And Teagan was wearing that white bikini.

'Go on. I promise to keep myself scarce. Although one rule.' She held up a finger. 'No sex in the pool.'

Lucas found Teagan floating on her back in the deep end, eyes closed, sunlit copper hair spilling brightly out from her head like a solar flare. She had a portable stereo playing and an unfamiliar but modern-sounding tune sweetened the air. He listened for a moment. The lyrics sounded Italian, the singer's voice husky. Romantic. His attention settled on Teagan, the curve of her waist, breasts and thighs, feeling himself rouse at the thought of stroking all that creamy, freckled skin.

Keeping his footsteps light, he padded to the edge of the pool and stripped off, then slipped into the water. The moment he entered

Teagan heard the disturbance and rolled over to stare at him. She drifted to the pool's edge and lifted her hand to grip the lip.

He swam breaststroke towards her, keeping his gaze on her troubled face. Anxiety clenched his gut. He wanted this to work.

Lucas floated in front of her, noting her huge eyes, her parted mouth, and knew talking wasn't the answer. She'd only evade and make excuses, and keep her desire hidden.

Not speaking, gaze burning into hers, he lifted his hand out of the water and placed it on Teagan's, anchoring them, then curled the other around her neck and drew her within breathing distance. One kiss landed softly at the very edge of her mouth. Another on the other side. The next was in the middle, soft at first and then opening into something harder and heartfelt.

The music and his touch spoke more than words could. Other than a soft moan Teagan didn't talk either. He pressed her against the pool's edge, firm against soft, his mouth exploring her lips, face and neck. His free hand caressing, feeling her shivers, the pebbling of her nipples.

'So much for drunk talk,' he murmured, pulling away. He didn't want to, but the way they were headed he was about to violate Vanessa's rule.

'I didn't want you to think . . .' She reddened and dug her front teeth into her bottom lip. 'You know.'

'Nope. I don't.'

'I wanted you to think I was okay about it. So you wouldn't feel obliged to do the let-me-down-gently thing. I was ashamed enough as it was.'

He caressed the soft skin below her bikini top. 'And now?'

Her eyes were wide with worry. And hope. Rolling her lips together, she shook her head.

'Teagan, look at me.' She hesitated then lifted her gaze to his.

'I want this. Have since we first met. It's real. Not an obligation.'

She frowned deeply and Lucas had a horrible lurching feeling she was going to start crying. This wasn't how he wanted things to go. He wanted her happy and smiling. Not upset.

'I thought you just wanted to be friends,' she said.

He grinned and nipped at her chin, exploring upwards until he could nibble at her mouth. 'We can do this and still be friends.'

She sucked in her breath and closed her eyes. He kissed her eyelids and forehead. Gentle touches designed to prove he meant it.

He found her mouth again. 'Come home with me.'

Uncertainty and longing pinched the corner of her eyes. She stared and stared, her breath coming in shallow little pants. A second passed, then another. If she said no this time he didn't think he'd be able to ask again. Then her head dropped and she stared at his chest, her cheeks blushing sweetly like sun-speckled peaches.

'It's been a long time.' She paused. 'A really long time.'

A thought clanged through Lucas. Did a long time mean never? Impossible. She was gorgeous, even if she couldn't see it herself. Men would have been chasing her since she was a teenager. 'How long?'

'Fvyrs.'

Lucas blinked. 'Did you just say five years?'

Teagan nodded, eyes darting everywhere as though looking for somewhere to crawl and hide.

He couldn't hide his grin. 'Worried you've forgotten how?'

'You must think I'm a freak.'

'Not even close.' He rested his hands on her waist, thumbs tracing lines over her skin. Measuring the places he planned to kiss and feel tremble. 'Good thing I'm fit.'

Her mouth quivered as she tried to smile through her nerves. 'Thinking of how fast you can run away?'

'No.' His lips closed in on hers. 'I'm thinking of all the catching up you have to do.'

TWENTY

TEAGAN ALMOST TURNED purple with mortification upon advising Ness she was going to Lucas's. The knowledge in her aunt's gaze revealed she knew exactly what Teagan was about to do, and made her feel like a squirmy teenager. With her mother in hospital it also felt wrong, as if she was being uncaring or disloyal. She'd mumbled as much to Lucas when they eventually made their way out of the pool and paused at her bedroom to throw on some clothes.

He'd stood in the doorway, jeans loose on his hips, water still speckling his bare shoulders. 'You want to pike out?'

'Yes.' She winced and pressed her fingers into her eyes. 'No.'

'You don't have to do this, Teagan.'

She did. After how he'd touched her in the pool, those exquisite teasing soft kisses, her body would go into mutiny if she pulled out now. The ache of longing in her heart had descended somewhere lower. She could no more deny it than her name. Never had she experienced lust on this level.

Lust and so much more.

She met his gaze. 'I want to.'

Lucas kept hold of her hand for most of the drive. At the suggestion she take her own car, he'd baulked. Too easy for her to chicken out, despite her promise, and he was fine with dropping her back in the morning. After all, he said with a wink, he was an early riser. In more ways than one.

That he smiled and joked helped. Teagan's nerves were fairly chattering by the time they reached Astonville, but Lucas did his best to make this seem normal, even if sleeping with the sexiest man on the planet was as far from normal for Teagan as she could get.

The joking stopped in the kitchen. He closed the door and used a finger to lift her lowered chin, his gaze intense, his voice reassuring. 'It'll be okay.'

'And if it's not?'

'It will be.' He smiled and kissed her softly, his touch a promise.

A few strides and they were in his room. She perched on the edge of the bed, hands in her lap, and chewed her lip, awkward with inexperience. The last time she'd had sex was in Pinehaven's shearing shed. A furtive and unsatisfying coupling with a shearer she'd felt not much more than mild attraction to. The sex was spoiled by the uncomfortable setting and fear of being caught.

This was adult. Serious. And the idea of afterwards cranked up her apprehension. What if Lucas didn't want her tomorrow? What if this was just a single night? The tension of it made her breath fast and unsteady, like her heartbeat.

Eyes trained on hers, Lucas peeled off his T-shirt and jeans then came to crouch at her knees. He took her hands. 'We don't have to do anything, if you don't want. We can just sleep.'

But she did. She wanted. More than anything.

In answer she slipped her hands from his and lifted the hem of her top, raising it slowly up her belly and breasts before tugging it over her head and throwing it to the floor. Her damp bikini lay beneath. Lucas's eyes flicked from her face to her breasts and back again. A power began to flood Teagan. Confidence. Slowly, she reached behind her neck for the bikini string and pulled. Holding the cups in place with her free hand, she drew on the remaining string.

For a couple of heady breaths she held the fabric in place, then carefully lowered her hand.

Lucas stared, saying nothing. He didn't need to. The desire lighting his face was enough. He stood, lifting her with him, and gently lowered her back onto the pillows before crawling alongside to brace himself on one elbow.

A finger traced over her belly. Soft swirls that made her skin pucker and something vibrate deep inside.

'You know the feeling when you hoped something was really good and then you see it and it's a million times better?' he said. 'That's the feeling I have right now.'

'Really?'

His focus returned to her breasts. 'Yeah.'

'They're not too small?'

A wicked grin crossed his face, making her insides leap. 'Not for my mouth.'

And in that moment, when his lips and tongue closed hot and hungry over her body, Teagan at last believed. It would be okay. Just as Lucas had promised.

Safe under his touch, she let go of all her fears and relished the pure joy of connecting with a man whose sole aim was to make her realise all she'd been missing. And want more.

Teagan smiled as a noise from the kitchen roused her and she remembered where she was. At Astonville, in Lucas's bed, feeling almost achy from the thorough lovemaking she'd enjoyed.

Unquestionably, the man knew what to do. Lucas made all her previous encounters look like adolescent fumblings in comparison. What struck her most was how fun he'd made it. Fun and silly and sexy, and uncaring of squelchy noises or misplaced limbs. She'd never really considered sex noisy and messy. But it was those things and more, deserving of laughter as well as passion.

He'd not only made her feel amazing, he'd made her feel good about her body, too. Under his burning gaze, the bleached Huon pine plank with two dark knots to show where her boobs were meant to be had become a thing of beauty, curves and desire.

And Lucas. Oh, Lucas. His body was a dream. Hard, soft, strong. Endlessly fascinating.

In a fit of delight and disbelief she wriggled, gripping handfuls of sheet as she drummed her heels onto the mattress.

So what if it all went pear-shaped. If telling her she deserved this was just a way to get laid. The hurt would be worth it for last night. A memory she could wrap up inside her and hold close to her heart for the rest of her life.

Fingers tickled the bottom of her foot through the sheet. 'What are you so excited about?'

She opened her eyes and stretched deliciously, the sheet falling away to expose her breasts. Lucas was wearing only trunks and carrying a mug of something steamy. 'You.'

His focus shifted. She liked the way he did that. The instant man-brain response to sexual stimuli. It made her feel beautiful.

He glanced at the mug and placed it on the bedside table. 'I made you tea. Are you hungry?'

Teagan was but she didn't feel like admitting it. Instead, she lowered her eyelids and regarded him with a sultry smile. The man was turning her into a complete tart. 'A bit.'

He stroked fingers along the bed, close to her rapidly heating body, an equally tartish look on his face. 'For cereal?'

'Is that all you have to offer?'

He grinned. 'What do you think?'

She sat up a little, reaching up to stroke the front of his bulging trunks. 'I think you have a whole lot to offer.'

'There I was thinking you were about to ask for sausage.'

She flopped back, giggling at the ridiculousness of the scene and held out a hand for him to take. 'Come here, sausage man.'

The tea went cold. Breakfast never happened. By the time they made it to the kitchen she was so late Lucas dropped her straight at Belgravia. The missed fifteen minutes made her feel guilty, but Nick didn't seem too perturbed. He took one look at her and another at Lucas, and rolled his eyes before ordering her to work.

Part of her felt guilty that she was even there. She should be at the hospital or at Falls Farm, helping Ness clean, but she'd already left Nick in the lurch yesterday, and with his staffing problems and her mum in no danger, more time off seemed unreasonable. The doctor had told her yesterday that there was a high likelihood Penny would be discharged later today anyway.

Under the jealous watch of Erin, Lucas dragged Teagan into an empty stable for a passionate kiss before departing with a promise to pick her up at twelve for the return trip to Falls Farm. Via a bedroom detour. A highly pleasurable thought, but she really needed to see her mum.

Morning tea had Nick relaying news of the attack on Kathleen Ferguson.

'I was all for the centre's expansion before this,' he said. 'Stacey was, too. Dom promised us a role in his new equine-therapy program. We've not done too badly in the past with starlets wanting riding lessons. Dom's always been good enough to recommend us. But this?' He tugged off his baseball cap and rubbed at his hair before donning it again. 'We can't have people being attacked. Especially the defenceless elderly.'

A sentiment Teagan could only agree with as the report set her heart hardening further against Dom and the centre, and her own remorse worsened.

Lucas arrived forty minutes late, full of apology and frustration. He'd been called to another equestrian establishment to the north to shoe a couple of ponies, only to find another two had been added to the schedule without notice, along with the demand for a bulk discount.

Nick patted him on the back. 'They're arseholes.'

'Yeah they are, but I'm not in a position to knock back the business.'

'Did you give them the discount?' asked Teagan in the car, when they were out of Nick's earshot.

'No. They weren't happy about it either, but they'd pissed me off and I wasn't about to budge. Besides, I'm a professional, not a bloody commodity trader.'

'Horse people can be like that.'

'Yeah, especially that lot.' He drummed his fingers on the wheel, still clearly unhappy. 'I mean, we're talking people who are professionals themselves – doctors, dentists, lawyers and the like. Imagine if you asked them for a bulk discount?'

'Did you tell them that?'

'Yeah, but they didn't seem to get it.'

'No one likes to be undervalued.' Something Teagan understood only too well, thanks to her father. But she didn't want to think about him right now.

'Have you heard from Vanessa?' he asked.

'Yes. She was just waiting for the doctor to give his okay to release Mum. She was going to call when she knew what time.'

Lucas reached across to tickle his fingers over her thigh. 'That's good news.'

'It is.'

A sly smile curled his mouth. 'For us, too.'

'Oh yes? And how would that be?'

'You'll need a shower before you see her.'

'I will. And I'm sure you need a good scrub after all your hard work this morning.'

'Be a pity to waste water by having separate showers.'

'It would. It's important to be kind to the environment.'

They glanced at one another and broke into laughter. Teagan

thought her heart would burst with the surge of joy their banter delivered. The niceness of him, the easy sexiness, amazed her. And he'd chosen her. Probably only momentarily, but it was wonderful all the same.

The thought had her staring out the window so he couldn't see her face. It would be agony when it ended. She didn't want it to, but Teagan was nothing if not a realist. It would happen in the end. She had to be prepared. Keep a little bit of insulation around her heart.

Rough knuckles touched her cheek. When she turned, Lucas had his sparkling gaze on hers. He winked and her insides did a gigantic roller-coaster lurch, shooting her heart from the very top of her chest to her stomach and back up again.

Reminding her there was no insulation for this. No vaccine, no preventative, and definitely no cure. This was love.

Vanessa helped Penny out of the car. Carefully, they made their way to the steps. Penny remained very weak. Vanessa wasn't sure she should have been released, but the hospital needed the bed, and Vanessa was more than capable of looking after her sister. Plus Bunny had promised to come around later to take a look. A vet was better than nothing.

'Where's Teagan?' asked Penny, sounding bewildered when they found the house empty.

'She probably had to work late for Nick. He's short-staffed again.' A white lie, but Penny wasn't well enough to hear what Vanessa really thought her niece was up to. Lucas was a considerate boy. He wouldn't keep her too long.

Penny became impossibly teary at the sight of her scrubbed room. 'I'm so sorry.'

'Don't be. You were ill. You couldn't help it.'

Vanessa could understand her sister's humiliation. Penny had been unable to control herself and the smell alone had been horrendous. The stains worse. But Vanessa took to cleaning up the way she did everything – as a task that had to be done. She'd never seen the point in complaining. The sheets had been stripped and washed in hot water, the mattress dragged outside to rest behind the shed, out of sight. The bedroom rug had been shampooed and draped over the verandah rail to dry. The new mattress she'd ordered yesterday afternoon had arrived that morning as promised, and been remade with a new underlay, pillows and manchester. No odour remained, banished by the lemon-myrtle-scented candle she'd burned that morning and now relit for its soothing scent.

She tucked Penny into bed with a full glass of water and a jug on her nightstand.

'What did Graham say?'

Vanessa had been avoiding mention of Graham but now she had to answer. 'He hopes you get well soon.'

'Did he . . .' She blinked, her lashes suddenly covered in teardrops. 'Did he say he missed me?'

Vanessa considered a lie and couldn't do it. Graham had been a mess when she'd called. Blubbering into the phone and talking of driving up to see Penny. A folly Vanessa had immediately cautioned against. Penny needed time to recover, not only from her ill health but from everything else he'd put her through.

The silly man had made all sorts of promises about changing. But when Vanessa had angrily asked what he was doing to ensure that, he'd had nothing to offer. A contact in Levenham had revealed he'd been seen playing pokies at a local pub. Vanessa had considered Teagan's interpretation of trading contracts for difference as gambling as too narrow. Certainly it wasn't for the unsophisticated investor, but they had a place among financial derivatives. But she could see now how in the hands of someone like her brother-in-law that it was no different to pressing the button on a poker machine or lodging any other form of bet.

She stroked her sister's forehead. 'He misses you very much, but enough of that. Sleep now.'

'I should go to him. It was a mistake to come here. Teagan doesn't need me.'

'That's just exhaustion talking. Remember how good you felt last week? And, darling, you're wrong. Teagan does need you. We all need each other. That's how families work.'

She left, mulling over their conversation. Penny had never once needed her. In fact, after Vanessa left home there were occasions when Penny had been downright hostile, but families were families. The bond existed whether it was wanted or not and Vanessa didn't have children of her own. She only had Teagan and Owen, and she hadn't seen Teagan's brother in years.

In all its complicated dysfunction this was still her family. One she had every intention of protecting. Which meant if Penny still loved Graham, she'd have to do something about him, too.

She sighed and padded outside with her cup of coffee and some hummus and bread for lunch. She'd make soup later. Something easily digestible for Penny with plenty of vegetables.

Saffy came to sit by her side, expecting food. She stroked the dog's head, grateful the Labradoodle hadn't found anything stinky to roll in today. Blanche eyed them both from her perch on the verandah rail. With all the dramas of late the animals had been neglected. She really ought to give them more attention.

The thought made her think of Merlin and what was happening with Callum. Both Bunny and Dom had promised her she'd be fine, but she couldn't help worrying. Now Lucas had been inadvertently dragged into it, responsible for hiding Merlin. The gorgeous man hadn't complained, but she could see he wasn't comfortable.

She was finishing off the last of her coffee when Dom's Mercedes purred through the gate. Vanessa's stomach tightened at the sight of his tired movements. This was all her doing.

He kissed her cheek. 'How is she?'

'Sleeping. Poor darling's terribly upset about causing trouble.'

'Tell her not to be.'

Vanessa studied his haggard face. 'Is there a problem I should know about?'

'Nothing we can't handle.'

She raised an eyebrow.

'Someone at the hospital went to the media, citing Penny's stay at the centre. We'll be fine. PR's onto it. What about you? How are you holding up?'

'Oh, you know me. Keep calm and carry on smiling.' Except the smiles were hard to produce at the moment and she was bottling up concern. 'Everyone else has far bigger worries than me.'

'Maybe, but that doesn't mean you should neglect yourself.'

'Are you telling me I'm not looking my best, Domenic?'

He chuckled, suddenly back to his usual self. 'You could never look anything less than amazing.' The chuckle faded. 'Don't worry about Albright. I'll take care of him.'

Although it went against everything Vanessa believed in, the idea of ceding control to Dom was a relief, even if it left her feeling uneasy. 'You don't have to do this.'

'I do.'

She splayed her hands. 'I have nothing to offer you in return. I need you to understand that.'

'I'm not doing this because I expect anything in return. I'm helping because I want to.' He was quiet for a moment. 'I'm not like your exes, Nessie. You matter.'

But he was. He was so very like them, that's why she was beginning to love him so strongly. The way he was standing by her was twisting her heart.

She didn't want this conversation. Not now. Penny was inside, Teagan would be home soon. And the way Vanessa was feeling, the longing in his regard, she'd be too weak to resist any move he might make. Once that happened her carefully built walls would crumble. A disaster she couldn't allow.

She traced a finger over the saucer of her coffee cup. 'Have you heard any more about the assault?'

'No.' Dom rubbed his forehead, his tension returning. 'It's not looking good though.'

'It was him?' She twitched an apologetic smile. 'Sorry. I shouldn't have asked.'

'I meant from an overall PR perspective. I had some opposition before, but it's strengthening.'

'I'd better warn you that you're not likely to get a warm reception from Teagan either.' The scars Graham's betrayal had left were deep and her niece, she'd learned, wasn't one to let something like this drop. Even with a distraction like Lucas around. 'She's very distressed about what happened to her mother. She blames herself. But she also believes that the centre is equally at fault.'

Dom stiffened, immediately transforming into corporate speak. 'While I'm as upset about Penny becoming ill as everyone else, the Wellness Centre took every precaution with regards to her treatment and health, fully disclosing the benefits and risks of the cleansing program. She was also advised both verbally and in writing as to the proper administration of said program. That she apparently failed to follow those instructions is most unfortunate, but not the fault of the centre.'

'Dom.'

He blinked and frowned.

'This is me you're talking to. Not a reporter.'

He slumped back in his chair and rubbed his hand over his mouth and chin. 'Sorry. It's been a tough morning.'

'I'm the one who should be sorry for dragging you into this. You and poor Lucas with Merlin.'

'Don't fret about Lucas. I'll make sure he's kept out of trouble.'

Vanessa studied him. 'I didn't think you liked him.'

'Let's just say we're warming to one another.' Dom nodded towards the drive. 'Speak of the devil.'

Teagan alighted first, throwing Dom's Mercedes and then the verandah a filthy look, before marching purposefully for the steps.

'Teagan, wait,' Lucas called from behind, but she didn't falter.

Alarm at her niece's expression had Vanessa turning hurriedly to Dom. 'Please be kind. She's just feeling scared and guilty.'

He nodded and sat up.

Teagan stomped up the steps, homing in on Dom. 'What do you think you're doing here?'

'Teagan, please. Dom is my guest and a very welcome one.'

But her niece was only getting started. 'Come to check the results of your centre's handiwork?'

Dom stood, his hands spread. 'I'm sorry Penny became ill, I really am.'

'You're sorry? Like that means anything. She ended up in hospital!'

Catching the argument, Lucas took the steps two at a time. Nodding at Dom and throwing an apologetic look at Vanessa, he wrapped an arm around Teagan's shoulders. 'Come on.' He kissed her temple as he attempted to steer her inside. 'Go say hello to your mum.'

Teagan wasn't to be budged. 'Places like yours just sucker in the vulnerable. Profiting from people's weaknesses.'

'That's quite enough,' said Vanessa.

Dom remained calm. 'The Wellness Centre genuinely helps people. We wouldn't still be in business if we didn't.'

Lucas tried again. 'Come on. I'm sure your mum's waiting.'

She shrugged him off. 'Helps? You call making people sick helping?'

'That was unfortunate.'

Teagan gave a bark of humourless laughter. 'Unfortunate? What a pathetic description. But I guess that should be expected from someone like you, someone who values money over people.'

With that final accusation Dom's expression turned to granite, his blue eyes direct and cold. 'I'd be careful who you criticise, Teagan.

Perhaps if you'd been more proactive with your father your mother wouldn't need any of the centre's services.'

'You bastard!' She lunged towards Dom but Lucas locked her arms. She fought and twisted against him, her eyes blazing.

Vanessa shot Dom a disgusted look. She'd warned him and all he'd done was make things worse.

He briefly closed his eyes, breathing hard, before addressing a still spitting Teagan. 'I apologise. That was uncalled for.'

'Stop this.'

They all turned to the door. No one had noticed Penny's approach. She pushed the door open a little further and took a careful step outside.

Vanessa leapt up to steady her arm. 'You should be in bed.'

Penny wasn't listening. Her focus was on her daughter. 'You're wrong to blame Dom. It was my fault. No one else's.'

Teagan was crying now, sagging against Lucas's hold. 'You should never have gone to that place. All those idiot treatments.'

'I should have. I felt wonderful.'

'Then you ended up in hospital! Can't you see? All those therapies are a con. They get away with it because the people they're dealing with are too gullible and weak to be rational.'

Penny gaped at her daughter. 'Is that how you see me? As weak?'

Vanessa held her breath, praying for Teagan not to answer. But Teagan was in too much of a fury to hold back.

'Christ, Mum. Dad didn't get away with all he did because you were strong.'

Penny's voice was barely above a whisper. 'I thought you'd forgiven me for that.'

Sudden realisation crossed Teagan's face. 'Oh, God. Mum, I'm sorry. I didn't mean it.'

But Penny was already slowly creaking her way back into the house.

Vanessa stopped at the door, attention on her niece. Teagan's tears and apologies were too late. She had no sympathy. For any of them. Almost all the compassion Vanessa was renowned for had been burned by the fire of this confrontation. Enough remained for her sister. But no more.

Shame hung thick on the verandah. No one could hold her gaze. Vanessa's jaw ached from holding in her anger. Anger at all of them, and at herself for permitting this to escalate.

Teagan caught the worst of her withering glare, head dropping as Vanessa fired her words. 'I hope you're ashamed of yourself. Deeply ashamed. Because there is no reproof adequate enough for what you just did.' Next she addressed Lucas. 'I think it'd be best if you took Teagan away from here before she does any more damage.' She switched focus to Dom. 'You'll have to excuse me, Domenic. My sister needs me.'

With a final shot of displeasure at them all, she strode inside.

TWENTY-ONE

SINCE STUMBLING to the edge of her bed several minutes ago, Teagan hadn't moved. She didn't feel capable. She didn't even feel human.

Her body was rigid, but inside everything thrummed as if in the aftermath of a shock, loud in her ears. Mouth partly open, she stared at the wall, her senses focused inwards, listening for the dark slick, that first sweep of drowning, endless night. It didn't arrive. Instead her mind continued empty, as if it had detached itself and floated away.

Lucas stood at the bedroom door, saying nothing. Teagan supposed there wasn't much to say. Apart from censure. And Ness had done a good job of that already.

'Teagan?'

The concern in Lucas's voice snapped her back to reality. She buried her face in her palms, the heat in her cheeks like a fire. She'd hated herself plenty of times before but nothing quite like this. Cruelty to one's self was one thing, but cruelty to others, especially someone as defenceless and ill as her mother, was quite another.

He stepped into the room.

'I'm okay.' She glanced around, working out what to pack. All of it, she supposed. Ness hadn't said she wanted her out in so many words but it seemed clear. She wasn't welcome at Falls Farm.

She had little to pack anyway. She'd left Pinehaven with only half the ute tray loaded. Other than the white bikini and a few other treats from Ness, her clothing and other possessions remained the same. 'I'll just grab a few things. You go . . .' She swallowed at the words. They had a prophetic feel. After what she'd done she wouldn't blame Lucas for not wanting anything to do with her. 'Check on Ness and Mum,' she finally mumbled.

For a heartbeat she held a faint hope that Lucas might come to her and comfort her in his steady hold. The steps remained unwalked, the embrace ungiven. With his hands fisted in his pockets, he turned away. She was left staring at the doorway, her heart hollow of everything but shame.

She didn't even feel love anymore.

It took her less than fifteen minutes to pack her bags. She kept her mouth closed hard against the ache in her throat. The onslaught of tears was only a sob away. She had to keep them at bay or they'd never stop.

Lucas frowned as his eyes swept the emptied bedroom and Teagan's heart plummeted further.

'It won't be . . .' Permanent is what she wanted to say.

'It's all right,' he said, bending for the bags. 'I'll take these to the car. Vanessa's in the kitchen.'

She didn't know if it was a suggestion she talk to her aunt or if Ness had requested to see her. It didn't matter. Teagan needed to apologise anyway. Again. There could never be enough sorries.

Ness was chopping onions with aggressive, hacking strokes, her eyes watery and red from the fumes. Or tears of fury. Teagan couldn't tell. She suspected both.

She stood on the other side of the bench. Ness didn't look up. Her grip on the knife was fierce, the skin over her knuckles stretched and white. She was clearly trying to hold her temper.

'I'm sorry,' said Teagan. 'I don't know what came over me.'

Ness put the knife down, placed her hands on either side of the chopping board and bowed over it with her head down. She regarded the board for a long moment. 'You may not but I do. And it's beyond time you saw a doctor about it.'

The tears Teagan was holding in threatened to burst. So many times over the last year Em had said those same words, but Teagan had resisted. She had a solid idea what the doctor would say, and it terrified her.

'I'm getting better.' And that was the truth. The Falls, Ness, Lucas, were all helping. She'd had entire days where she felt normal.

'So you acknowledge there's something wrong?'

Teagan looked away. She didn't want to talk about this. She could barely talk about it with her best friend. She wasn't going to share this with her aunt. And she *was* getting better. So much better. It was just that sometimes the pain inside became too huge to control.

Vanessa's face softened. 'Teagan, being depressed is nothing to be ashamed of.'

'I'm not depressed.'

'No?'

'I'm not.'

Ness came from around the bench, wiping her hands on a tea towel. She stopped in front of Teagan and placed her hands on her shoulders. 'I want you to listen to me. Just for a minute.'

Teagan licked her lips and nodded warily.

'The Wellness Centre has counsellors you can talk to.' She held up a finger. 'No, don't. Hear me out.' Despite Teagan's set jaw and mutinous expression she kept going. 'I'm serious. A counsellor, Teagan. Not a naturopath or any of the other therapists you think so poorly of. A trained clinical psychologist with experience in dealing with people with your issues.'

'I don't have issues.'

Ness cocked an eyebrow.

'I'm getting better.' If she said it enough it would happen. 'Lucas makes me laugh.'

'I've no doubt about that but it's not enough.'

'It is.' It would have to be because Teagan sure as hell wasn't going to the Wellness Centre.

Ness sighed and let her go. 'I can't help you if you refuse to help yourself.'

'I'm doing okay.'

'Really? Then why is your mother in her room with her heart breaking because her own daughter not only thinks she's weak and gullible, but blames her for losing a farm that was never hers in the first place?'

'I put my soul into Pinehaven. And money.'

But Ness had lost all sympathy. 'Then who's the weak one, Teagan?'

She needed to leave. This was hurting too much. She looked towards the door. Lucas was hovering with the last of her bags, his expression crumpled with worry.

Vanessa saw the bags and pursed her lips. 'You're moving out?'

'Yes.'

'I didn't mean for you to do that.' She sighed wearily. 'Although perhaps it's for the best. Goodness knows my efforts haven't worked. Maybe Lucas will have more luck with you.' Ness's tone made it sound as if Teagan was a hopeless cause. Maybe she was.

She swallowed and glanced towards the back of the house. 'I'll say goodbye to Mum.'

'No. You've done enough damage for one day. Your mother needs rest. Save your apology for another day, when you've come to mean it.'

Teagan's legs felt like concrete blocks as she walked to the door. She turned back, hoping to wave to Ness, but her aunt had returned to her onions. Teagan stood staring in defeat until a strong arm circled her shoulders and guided her outside.

'Are you right to drive?'

She sniffed and nodded. 'Fine.'

Lucas peered at her. 'You sure?'

'Yes.' Using the bottom of her shirt, she wiped her cheeks and sniffed again. 'I'll be fine.'

The keys were dangling in the old ute's ignition. She stared at them. A turn. A release of brake. A press on the accelerator. Normal things she did every day. Only today she didn't want to. It felt too final.

She glanced through the ute's side window. Lucas was already in his car. He was staring at her, a frown creasing his brow, waiting for her to reverse away from the fence.

He lifted a hand off the steering wheel as if to say, well?

With a last regretful look at the house, Teagan started the car.

Lucas spent the journey to Astonville fretting over Teagan. The way she'd sat on her bed, facing the wall with a thousand-mile stare, her fingers making scary jerky movements like a suddenly severed robot's hand. Her face was so vacant and elsewhere, even the memory frightened the fuck out of him.

He'd caught snippets of her conversation with Vanessa, the mention of the centre setting his ears on alert. That Teagan had serious problems wasn't a surprise. He'd begun to figure that out himself. But what had got Lucas in the guts was the way she'd said his name. The hope in her voice when she said he made her laugh. That he was enough.

He had to keep making sure he was.

She was silent as they carried her things to the house. When she hesitated in the hall, he stepped past and placed the first of her bags in the spare room. She stood staring, unable to look at him, her mouth jammed closed and her eyelids spread unnaturally wide as though her life depended on keeping them open.

He hadn't meant it to mean anything. The house was old, the rooms small. There was simply no room in his bedroom for all her stuff.

He touched her cheek. 'It's okay. This is just until I can clean out some cupboard space for you.'

She nodded but the stare remained.

On his return from fetching the rest of her belongings he found Teagan sitting on the edge of the bed looking at her hands.

'Can I get you anything?'

She shook her head.

'Why don't you have a lie-down in my room. I have things I want to do in the shed anyway.'

'Okay.' She didn't look up.

He followed her slow tread to the master bedroom, wishing he knew what to do, what to say. Right now leaving her to rest seemed the best option. With dull movements she removed her shoes and sat, not once meeting his gaze. 'Help yourself to anything you need.'

'Thank you.'

Lucas hesitated, unsure. Finally, when Teagan curled onto her side and tucked her hands under her cheek, he left.

The shed provided no solace. Lucas was too distracted to craft anything. He looked at his main furnace. With all the time he'd been spending at Nick's and Falls Farm it felt like he hadn't fired it up in weeks. Ever since Teagan's arrival his life had changed, and now it was changing again. She would be living under his roof, and not because last night had turned friendship and want into something special. But because he'd taken in another exile.

Only this time he wasn't dealing with a knuckle-headed ram. This time his guest was all too human, and judging from the conversation he'd overheard, very, very fragile. A kick in the arse wasn't going to work.

He walked outside to where Merlin was grazing. At his approach the ram looked up and bleated throatily before resuming his graze. Lucas rested on the gate and watched him for a while. Then he pulled his mobile from his pocket and searched for the number he never thought he'd dial.

The call was answered on the third ring.

'Lucas. Everything okay? I wanted to stay but Vanessa insisted I leave.'

'Teagan's with me, at Astonville.'

'Ah. Look, I'm sorry for what happened between us. I should've held my temper.'

Lucas reached down to pick at a runner of kikuyu that was worming its way up the strainer post. 'Vanessa says she's depressed.'

'Yes, it's been worrying her since Teagan arrived.'

'Is she?'

'It's possible, but without a clinical diagnosis we can't know for certain. Is that what you're calling about? Getting her to see someone?'

'No. I mean, I'll try, but from the way she spoke to Vanessa I don't think that's going to happen. My worry is how to handle her.' He stared back at the house. 'She matters. A lot. I don't want to fuck this up.'

'You love her.'

'Yeah.' Although right now he was scared shitless over what that might mean.

Several beats passed before Dom spoke again. 'I can arrange a counsellor, for you or Teagan.'

He gave a sad half-laugh. 'I think she needs it more than me.'

'I couldn't agree more. I'll talk to Meredith. She's our senior psychologist, and very experienced. She'll have some ideas. But we still have you to worry about. This isn't easy.'

'I just need a mate.'

'Then I'm here.' Dom paused. 'Like I always wanted to be.'

Lucas hung up and leaned back on the fence. He wasn't sure about what he'd just done but he had no one else to turn to. Dunks had his own problems with Bunny and his ex. Vanessa was too close to it all, which left Dom. His father.

His father.

Somehow, those words gave him a weird sense of safety.

Lucas was going through paperwork at the kitchen table when Teagan walked in. He'd checked on his return to the house and found her curled up in the foetal position, her cheeks pale and tearstained. He'd spent a long time studying her, his heart aching for her. He badly wanted to help. But he didn't know how.

She pulled out a chair and sat down, her hands cupped in her lap and her head bowed. Lucas wished she'd smile, just a little.

'Can I get you anything? Cuppa? Something to eat?'

She shook her head.

He glanced at the invoice he was holding and put it down. 'Do you want to talk?'

'Not really.'

At a loss, he picked up the invoice once more. Perhaps he would need to talk to Dom's counsellor. In the face of her distress every word seemed wrong.

'I've been thinking,' Teagan said after a while. 'I think maybe I should go back to Levenham. I have friends there. Astra – my horse – she's there.' She bit her lip and stared towards the window, wincing a little. 'I've made too much of a mess of things here to stay. I should never have come in the first place. I should've had the guts to stick it out instead of running away.'

The thought of her leaving made his heart constrict. She couldn't go. She couldn't. 'What about us?'

Her hollow gaze slid to his. She smiled sadly and shook her head in dismissal.

Anger flared inside him. 'So last night and this morning meant nothing then, did it?'

'You know as well as I do it would never have lasted.'

'Don't tell me what I do or don't know.' He thrust out of his chair and began to pace. Jesus. What the fuck had he done to make her think that? They'd been amazing together. Funny, sexy, happy.

In love.

'You deserve someone better than me.'

He scraped his hand through his hair and forced himself to override the panic building inside. Losing it wouldn't help. 'No, I don't.'

She stared at him in disbelief.

'Okay, what happened between you and your mum was shitty, and I know everyone was upset, but that doesn't mean you can just bugger off back south because you think you've screwed things up too much here.'

'Ness and Mum are better off without me.'

'And me? Don't I matter?'

She stared back at her hands. 'You matter more than anything.'

'Then stay.'

She bit her lip. A tear escaped and trailed her cheek. She swiped at it angrily. 'Why? When I'll only disappoint you and everyone else again?'

'You didn't disappoint me. You just, I don't know, lost your temper because you were scared. Said something you didn't mean. It can be fixed.'

Her mouth twisted. 'I'm not sure that it can.'

He closed his eyes, wishing she'd stop frightening him. 'I don't want you to go. I want you to stay. I want you to start laughing again, like you did that day with Vanessa and your mum. Like you did only a few hours ago, with me. I like that person.' He swallowed, tossing over whether to reveal what lurked in his heart, and decided he needed to hold onto it a bit longer. 'I like that person a lot.'

'I can't be that all the time.'

'Why not?'

'Because.' She dug her teeth into the side of her lip. 'Because I don't know how.'

He breathed out, his panic easing. She was starting to have second thoughts. 'Then let me help.' He smiled. 'I managed okay earlier.'

'That was different.'

He moved to crouch in front of her. He took her hands, surprised to find them cold, and cradled them in his big warm ones. He looked up, and his heart lurched at the longing in her gaze. 'Do something for me?'

'What?'

'Trust me.'

Another tear fell. God, she was gorgeous. Even pale and tear streaked, her skin had a luminous tone. But it was how she looked at him that did him in.

Like he could be her saviour.

'Please?'

Finally, she nodded.

TWENTY-TWO

TEAGAN FOUND Lucas in the forge. The day was hot, the temperature even higher in the shed thanks to the burning furnace. He was pounding a piece of glowing steel, sparks exploding with every hit. Behind him, the furnace heat turned the air shimmery, as though something from an invisible realm was trying to push through, causing the space to swell and bend.

Lucas was wearing his blacksmithing clothes: leather apron, goggles slipped up on his head, long-sleeved shirt and jeans. Sweat soaked the cloth and streaked the sides of his cheeks. He rippled with sexy masculinity and the kind of grace unique to expert craftsmen. She propped against the door, where a little breeze cooled the moisture on her own back, to watch.

It had been a week since he'd held her hands in Astonville's kitchen and asked her to trust him. She was trying, but the relationship had an eggshell fragility. Teagan found herself tiptoeing, not knowing how to act. Still ashamed of what she'd done and not understanding why he would want her to stay. The tension in her body refused to ease. Sometimes she'd halt and stare at nothing, her concentration inward, listening to the crazy whispers telling her it was all false. Dread would frost her skin. Her heart would thud and the effort of stopping herself from howling would make her throat swell and ache.

Lucas had caught her a few times and done his best to soothe her with promises that everything would be okay. Distracting her with his touch, his tender kisses, the intimacy of sex. But she couldn't shake the feeling that it wasn't real. That it was more to keep her craziness at bay than because of any deeper feeling he had for her.

Teagan's relationship with Ness and her mother was even more fraught. It had taken her three days to summon the courage to return to Falls Farm and apologise again. An apology that was accepted by her mother with good grace, less so by Ness, who had been watchful and thin-lipped throughout. Though her aunt had called in each day since, she hadn't invited Teagan once to stay for cocktails. In a way Teagan understood. Her record with alcohol wasn't great, but it still hurt not to be included in what had become an anticipated and fun Falls Farm ritual when she'd resided there. Although not as hurtful as catching a glimpse of Lucas's ute in the yard during cocktail hour when she'd driven past the following evening.

Work helped to keep her mind occupied, but even the most inno-cent of looks from Nick, Erin, Bart or the other staff left her paranoid. She was sure they could all see through her carefully constructed facade. The constant anxiety was beginning to wear her down, which only added to her internal fear that one mistake would see her crack apart forever. Today, Nick had kept her at Belgravia well past her normal time to help set up another of his riding schools that was beginning the following day, leaving her even more fatigued and down.

Which is why it was nice to spend a few secret, tension-free moments watching Lucas.

He plunged the worked steel into a bucket. The resulting steam added to the pressure-cooker atmosphere of the shed. He pulled it out and inspected his workmanship, and grunted to himself.

'Very cave man,' said Teagan, wandering inside.

He grinned and waved the elegantly formed scroll. 'Like it?'

She inspected it, aware of keeping her distance from the hot metal. She'd been around Lucas's shed enough now to understand the safety requirements, and she liked watching him. It was one of the sexiest scenes imaginable. Earthy and elemental, and very, very masculine.

'It's lovely.' She meant it. He'd made coarse metal into something artistic and beautiful. She pointed to where the tip twisted outwards, like a strange animal horn. 'That looks dangerous.'

He screwed up his nose as he inspected it. 'It probably is, but I like it.'

'So do I. What's it for?'

'I was thinking of using it as decoration for a birdcage.' He shrugged and placed the rod down. 'Just an experiment. Have you had lunch?'

'Not yet. I grabbed us some pies from the bakery. They're in the oven.'

'That must've been fun.'

Fun wasn't the way Teagan would describe it. The moment she'd walked in, Kathleen Ferguson was on her. The Falls Union Progress Association was meeting that night. In secret. Kathleen Ferguson wanted her to come.

Teagan had greeted the invitation with suspicion, but the old lady was insistent, needling her with Penny's illness, the way Dom was taking advantage of villagers who needed local employment. Buying loyalties and quashing disquiet with his sponsorship and false charm. A few weeks ago she would have brushed Kathleen off, but now Teagan didn't have the strength. Plus she was curious.

'Not exactly,' she said in answer to Lucas's question. 'Mrs Ferguson kept me waiting so long I couldn't avoid Col. It appears the rise in temperature has also brought a rise in Col's shorts.' She made a face. 'What sort of man wears orange jocks?'

'I have a pair of orange jocks.'

'They're trunks. And Col doesn't fill his the way you do.'

Lucas's expression took on that teasing look she adored. The one that signalled where his interest was heading. 'And how's that?'

'Impressively.'

He shut down the furnace and began to strip off his apron.

'I thought you were busy.'

The goggles went to the bench. He approached and stood in front of her, his body hot and shiny from heat and exertion. Closing her eyes, Teagan breathed him in. He smelled of metal and man. Of everything she longed for.

Of hope.

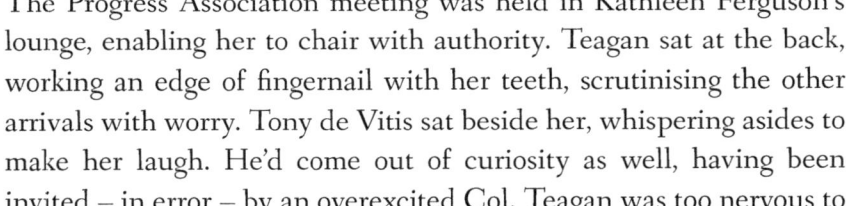

The Progress Association meeting was held in Kathleen Ferguson's lounge, enabling her to chair with authority. Teagan sat at the back, working an edge of fingernail with her teeth, scrutinising the other arrivals with worry. Tony de Vitis sat beside her, whispering asides to make her laugh. He'd come out of curiosity as well, having been invited – in error – by an overexcited Col. Teagan was too nervous to do more than twitch a smile, afraid that someone would dob her in to Ness or Lucas. Tony had promised to keep mum. Whether he would remained to be seen.

For Ness, Teagan's attendance would be just another disappointment, but for Lucas it would be a betrayal. She hadn't lied as such. She'd simply gone out late that afternoon and not returned, hoping Lucas would assume she was visiting her mother. When he'd sent her a concerned text, she'd replied that she wanted a bit of time on her own, which had only resulted in a flurry of more worried texts. Now her phone was shut down to ward off any calls, the last message promising she was fine and that she'd be home around eight. A white lie that only made her feel sicker.

The invitees were crowded into a pristinely kept and decorated fifties-style lounge. Uncomfortable chrome-and-vinyl chairs had been brought in from the kitchen and it was on these that Teagan and Tony sat while others took the sofa, armchairs and tapestry pouffes. Kathleen Ferguson took position in a queenly pose in front of an ancient built-in oil heater, Col hovering sycophantically alongside. Faint blotches of yellow marked her cheek and chin, otherwise she appeared fully recovered from her assault.

According to gossip, the police had a suspect but were keeping tight-lipped as they continued the investigation, which made Teagan suspicious of another cover-up. Dom would do anything to protect his investment and with his development application before council, the timing was critical.

Besides Col and Tony, Teagan didn't know anyone else, although she recognised Bunny's frightening receptionist, Janice. Except for a younger woman, her belly swollen with mid-term pregnancy and appearing even more nervous than Teagan, most of the dozen or so people appeared eager.

The mantle clock behind Kathleen began to bong out its seven-pm chime. At the final stroke, Kathleen clapped her hands together. 'Attention!'

Everyone sat up like an obedient primary-school class. Teagan half expected them to start chanting, 'Good ev-en-ing, Miss-us Fer-gu-son.'

Their host gave a cold smile. 'Welcome to the inaugural public meeting of the Falls Union Progress Association.'

'Public, my arse,' whispered Tony.

'Thank you for coming. I understand for some of you this has posed some difficulty.'

Colin gave a significant nod. According to Tony, Col wanted the meeting held at his place, but his daughter, Maggie, had been made furious by the idea. That he was involved in the Fuckuppas was bad enough, holding an anti-Dom meeting on her property was going too far. She'd been so incensed she'd railed at him for a solid thirty minutes about bored old men with nothing to do except create mischief, ending the tirade with a threat to cut off his caravan power if he even thought of attending such a meeting. The encounter had left him severely rattled, but being far more afraid of Kathleen Ferguson than Maggie, and tizzied by all the drama, he'd come along anyway.

Ignoring Col's puffed-out chest and martyred countenance, Kathleen began to point out others in her audience. 'Antonio, I'm sure you're worried about your business and how taking sides may upset some of your customers.' The finger moved to the pregnant woman. 'Carol, I appreciate your husband is a gardener at the centre and your presence could cause problems between you. Janice, given your boss's friendliness with Vanessa and the centre's proprietor, I imagine you have fears for your position.' A claim that sounded rather odd when Bunny's fierce assistant appeared to harbour anything but fear.

Kathleen continued on, pointing out each of her guests in turn and the risk they'd taken to be present. Finally it landed on Teagan. 'No doubt your aunt would have something to say about your presence here, too, Teagan.'

Teagan shrivelled in her chair as everyone turned to look at her.

'But we are fighting to keep our rural village free of riff-raff and drug addicts. Thanks to that centre we not only have our roads laden with ridiculous vehicles, sporting blacked-out windows and driven by eastern European gangsters, but a hideous fence hiding some of our most magnificent countryside from view. If that wasn't enough, land that should be producing prime cattle is instead being kept for a coterie of rich, over-pampered starlets. Now the centre has brought crime to our peaceful village. Not petty thefts. Armed robberies and assaults. On defenceless elderly people such as myself.'

Murmurs went around the room. Heads bobbed in agreement. The fading bruises on Kathleen's face seemed to take on a deeper, more sinister tinge. Colin was nodding like a bobble-headed toy.

She slammed her fist into her palm with a smack. 'A line must be drawn.'

A chorus of hear-hears tumbled around the room.

'I'm worried for our children,' said the pregnant woman.

'And our property values,' said another.

Others joined in with their concerns. Tony sat back with his arms crossed, shaking his head and muttering about small-mindedness, but as Teagan listened to the complaints she began to wonder if some weren't valid. Admittedly, Kathleen's rant about gangsters and violent crime was completely over the top, but the other villagers appeared genuine in their concerns.

Kathleen held up her palms to shush the group. She scanned faces until her eyes found Teagan's. 'We've also had reports of people becoming ill from the centre's quackery. Illnesses that were quickly covered up by Domenic Ashe's public relations machine. More proof that the centre serves only one purpose: to make its callous owner richer than he already is. He has no feelings for his clients, just as he has no feelings for this precious village.'

'He's sponsoring the cricket club,' called Tony. 'Pretty generously too.'

Kathleen's gaze turned arctic. 'A ploy. Propaganda, like the Nazis used.'

Teagan blinked. Tony let out a snort. A few of the others shifted uncomfortably.

The pregnant woman put her hand up. 'I don't think Domenic Ashe is a Nazi.' She glanced to her side for support. 'I mean, that's a bit . . . you know.'

Kathleen ploughed on. Dissenters weren't to be tolerated. 'He is a man of great means and we are but simple villagers. We must be alert for schemes to break our alliance. And watchful of moles.' With the word she threw a meaningful glance at Tony and then the pregnant woman, who coloured deeply. 'And root them out. If we are to defeat this man, we need to maintain a war footing.'

'Santo cielo,' muttered Tony, rolling his eyes heavenward. 'Now she's channelling Churchill.'

'The Falls was once a community. Now a divide has split us.' Kathleen raised a fist. 'We must return to the old ways, the days when the land was open and used for productive purposes instead of pampering the rich.'

'Returning to the old days?' whispered Tony. 'I thought this was a progress association.'

Teagan bit down hard on her lip.

'So,' said Kathleen. 'What can we do? Petition. And petition hard. Make the council see that we don't want Domenic Ashe and his misnamed Wellness Centre.' She reached for a wad of papers and held them up. 'These are our weapons. Use them.'

The meeting was over. Teagan fled but not before having a dozen petition forms thrust into her hand. They sat on the ute's passenger seat as she made her way through The Falls until, unable to stand the evidence of her lie to Lucas any longer, she stopped at the servo and dumped them into the bin. No matter how she felt about the centre or Dom, she should never have gone to that meeting. She had no business involving herself in village politics and her attendance was bound to be revealed. Lucas would find out, so would Ness, and her mother and Dom. She stifled a sob at the thought. Why was she doing this to herself? To them? It was if she *wanted* to ruin her life in The Falls.

Her guilt only worsened when she found Lucas in the darkness, pacing the yard.

She alighted, ready to explain, but he got in first.

'Where have you been? I've been worried sick.'

'I'm sorry. I didn't mean to —'

He shut her up with an embrace that felt almost desperate. 'Jesus,' he breathed. 'Jesus.' Finally he let her go. 'I'd better call Vanessa.'

'What for?'

'So they can all stop worrying.'

She stepped back, guilt making her snappy. 'For God's sake. I'm an adult not a child.' At his dismayed expression she looked away. 'I'm sorry. I didn't mean to snap. It's just . . .' She raised a hand and let it flop down. 'I'm not used to this.'

'To what? People caring about you?'

She bit her lip and stared towards the road. 'I've always looked after myself. Then, with what Dad did . . .' She trailed off again. How to explain how hard she found it to trust? To believe anyone could act, not in self-interest, but with selflessness. Especially towards someone so undeserving.

'I'm not your dad, Teagan.'

'I know.' She curled her fist against her chest and rubbed her sternum in an attempt to soothe the ache that pulsed behind it.

'Hey.' A big arm went around her shoulders and she was hugged against Lucas's solid body. With a kiss on top of her head, he began to lead her to the house. 'We'll work it out. I promise.'

At his kindness, the urge to cry rose thick and strong. She held it back in. She'd cried too much in front of him already. 'I really am sorry for worrying you. I honestly didn't mean to.'

'I probably over-reacted. It's just that when you said you wanted time alone it freaked me out a bit.' The next words were said with slow carefulness. 'Teagan, I know there's stuff you might not be able to talk to me about but Vanessa said the centre has a psychologist that could help.' He paused. 'With your depression.'

'I'm not depressed,' she said quickly. A painful knot tightened in Teagan's stomach. Now Lucas thought she was crazy, too. Everyone probably did. She bet they were all talking about her, how nuts she was. The thought made her want to tear from his hold and run. Anywhere. As long as it was away from here. Instead, she breathed in deeply. She might not be able to run but she could hide, within herself. Pretend there was nothing wrong. It had worked in Levenham. Mostly. 'I'm fine. Really I am. You're all worried about nothing.'

Though his expression was doubtful he let it drop and pulled open the kitchen door. 'You must be starving.'

'A bit.' She caught the smell of curry and spotted the wok on the stove. 'You didn't wait for me, did you?'

He shrugged. 'Didn't feel like eating.'

'Oh, Lucas, I'm sorry.'

'It's okay. You're back. That's what matters.'

She set the table, pretending not to listen in on his phone conversation as it carried from the lounge. Though Lucas spoke softly she caught snatches of phrases. A few 'I don't knows', an 'I don't want to push', a few straight 'I knows'. Teagan filled in the gaps: Ness asking where Teagan had been. Whether she'd agreed to see Dom's counsellor. Blunt statements of 'she's crazy' and 'she needs help'.

By the time he'd finished her hands were shaking and she had to escape to the bathroom to calm herself down. The anxiety lingered, and several times during dinner her cutlery clattered loudly against her plate. She caught Lucas's tightened mouth and tried to cover up the awkwardness with inane talk. Faking her way through was better than addressing a subject she feared.

'Shower?' he asked when the last dish was stowed and the benches and table cleaned.

She glanced up and was astonished to see desire in his gaze. She'd done nothing to deserve this and yet he still wanted her.

'Are you telling me I smell?'

Smiling, he moved closer and slid a finger up and down her waist. 'I'm telling you I want to see you naked.'

Heat pulsed in her groin, pushing away all other feeling. She toyed with his shirt buttons and slid the top one undone. 'Again? You saw me naked this morning.'

'That was hours ago.' His hand drifted to the button of her jeans. With an expert flick it sprang open.

'Surely you haven't forgotten what I look like during that time?'

'That's the problem. I haven't.' He placed a gentle kiss on her neck and moved his lips along the sensitive line to her ear. A delicious shudder went through Teagan as she heard the quickening of his breath. 'It's been driving me crazy.'

She gasped as he pushed the zip of her jeans down and slipped his fingers into her underwear. 'You drive me crazy.'

'Good. I like crazy.'

Teagan closed her eyes. It was a joke. A sexy bit of banter.

But one she desperately wished was true.

Vanessa leaned forward, concern for her sister crinkling her face. 'Oh, Penny darling. Are you sure?'

Penny nodded. 'He's my husband. The only man I've ever loved.'

Vanessa sat back. She'd suspected this was coming. Fearing the disruption he might cause to both his wife and daughter, Vanessa had done her best to keep Graham at a distance. But she wasn't home all the time. Graham had the house number and had been calling, and now the worst had happened. He'd convinced Penny to take him back.

She sighed. Penny loved him, that much was clear, but the man had a problem. A major problem, but then the entire family had problems. The only person without them was herself. Although that wasn't quite true either. She still had that tiny-penised prat Callum threatening her. And her deepening feelings for Dom to sort out.

'But he let you down so badly.'

'I know. But he's sorry.'

Sorry, in Vanessa's opinion, wasn't enough. Apologies were easy things. It was action and change that was hard, and from what she'd heard Graham had done neither. He was currently surviving on the kindness of an old family friend who'd offered him a room until he found his feet. The problem was that Graham's feet kept taking him towards poker machines. If Penny returned there could be only one outcome and that was disaster. The broken woman she'd picked up from the airport weeks before was too fresh in Vanessa's memory to allow her to return to that life so soon.

'And I didn't help with my issues.'

'Don't you dare blame yourself. Don't you dare.' Vanessa breathed through her nose in an attempt to calm down. 'Look, darling, this is all very sudden. Why don't you think on it for a few

days? Perhaps talk to your counsellor. There's no need to rush,
is there?'

'No,' said Penny, sounding uncertain. 'I suppose not.'

'Good. Now how about some sangria to brighten us up?'

Vanessa was chopping orange segments when she spied Dom's
Mercedes through the window. Her heart gave a little skip of anticipation. The sun caught his blond hair as he stepped out and she
wondered when he'd start to go grey. Only yesterday she'd noticed
how much her own hair was losing its rich colour. The years were
catching her. Her body was changing, yielding to middle age. Had
she stayed, her ex-husbands would have traded her in long ago.
Perhaps that time would come soon with Dom, too.

She ceased chopping and stared at the window, swamped with
despair at the idea of her life without Dom. His friendship
mattered. So did his unconcealed want. When she was near him she
felt young and desirable. She liked his charm, his intelligence, his
sophistication. And she liked his decency. The way he conducted
his business honestly, but without compromising his determination
to succeed.

It would hurt badly when he moved on. She needed to be
prepared.

'I have some good news for you,' said Dom, breaking off his chat
with Penny as Vanessa pushed open the screen door and stepped
onto the verandah. He took the drinks tray from her and kissed her
cheek. He smelled of the aftershave she'd bought him for his birthday
– a delicious citrus scent underpinned by a woody base that seemed
even sexier on him than the famously hunky actor used to advertise
the brand.

'Merlin has had a reprieve?'

'Not yet, but Bunny's gone over Montague's head and arranged
for his boss to inspect Merlin.'

'But what if it backfires and he declares him dangerous?'

'He won't. Bunny knows him. Apparently he thinks the claim is
spurious anyway. Bunny said he would've quashed it already except

Montague's an officious type who'd cause trouble if process wasn't followed.'

Relief made Vanessa uncharacteristically weepy. 'I so hope you're right. I don't think I could cope if Merlin had to be destroyed.'

'Hey,' said Dom, putting down the tray. He placed warm hands on her upper arms and studied her face. 'What's this?'

She stroked a fallen tear away. 'Nothing. I'm just being silly.'

'You've shouldered too much lately.'

'Oh, I'm fine.' She smiled, wanting to press herself into his chest and let his safe arms comfort her but aware it would send the wrong signal. To him as well as her traitorous heart. 'Now, I think good news deserves a drink. Sangria?'

Although under doctor's orders to avoid fruit juice for a while, Penny was still off alcohol. She left them to it to play with Wilma.

'Penny mentioned just before that Graham rang,' said Dom when she was out of earshot. There was concern in his voice.

'He did. He asked her to come home. She's thinking about going.'

'Ah.'

'It's awful.' Vanessa closed her eyes briefly at the thought. 'I can't let her go back to him.'

'She's an adult. Difficult to stop her.'

The teary feeling welled again. 'It'll end in disaster. I have to find a way to protect her.'

'Can I help?'

She shook her head. 'No. I'll talk to Kevin again, the friend he's staying with. See if he can't convince Graham to call the gambling hotline.'

'And Penny?'

She looked towards her sister. 'I've told her to talk to her counsellor. I hope you don't mind. It seemed the only way to stall her.'

'Of course I don't mind. We'll book her in for another stay. It'll give you a break, a chance to stop worrying.' He pulled out his phone and began tapping.

'Dom.' Her tone was severe. She knew what he was doing.

'What?'

'I'll pay this time.'

'We'll work that out later. Let's just get her booked in.'

Irritation had Vanessa rubbing her eyebrow. She knew him too well. This was a bill that would never come; another IOU on a list that had been building alarmingly of late. His generosity left her with the feeling she was being bought, no matter how many times he rejected the accusation.

This was how it had started before. The almost paternalistic taking care of her, solving her problems. The charming promise that she didn't owe anything when there was always a cost in the end. A big one.

She studied Dom's profile as he worked, hungry for a sign that he was different. That for all his likeness to the men of her past he could be the man of her future. The one who wanted nothing in return except her love. Who adored her mind, her character, even her imperfections, as much as he did her body and grace. A man who never used her to achieve his own ends because she was the end.

Sensing her scrutiny, he looked up and smiled. It was tender and open, and laden with an emotion that made her heart flutter.

In that moment, the scales shifted and a dangerous thought began to form. One she needed to control fast before it built and took over. Yet with each breath, each heartbeat Vanessa held his gaze, it grew until it sat fat and frightening in her mind.

Against the heaviness of losing Dom, her independence weighed little.

TWENTY-THREE

TEAGAN STRETCHED and rolled onto her side, tucking her hands under her cheek as she opened her eyes to gaze at Lucas in the faint Friday pre-dawn light.

'Hey,' he said. Gently, he smoothed a lock of hair away from her face.

The house was quiet, only their shallow breathing and bed creaks filling the space. Teagan had come to treasure these times. The hushed minutes in which she felt truly calm and relaxed. Her and Lucas, cosy from sleep, their skin brushing in intimate whispers. The way he looked at her, as if she were the most precious thing in the world. A night fantasy experienced awake.

'Sleep well?' he asked.

'I did. You?'

He smiled lazily. 'I had dreams.'

'Oh, yes?'

He held eye contact, the smile still in place, and for a moment she believed that what lived behind those blue eyes was real. That it would stretch beyond the bed and into the day.

'I have something for you.'

'I'm sure.'

'Mind out of the gutter.' He rolled over. The bedside drawer slid open. Teagan assumed he was fetching a condom, but when he rolled back he kept his fist closed. He smiled again as he rested his hand on the sheet between them, and slowly opened his fingers.

A pendant lay in his palm. It was silver, with a fine leather thong threaded through a delicate clasp at the top. The metal shone like starlight, slowly brightening as the rising sun hit the side of the house. The outer edges had been worked into organic curves that swept up to form tiny curlicues. Between the swirls of moulded silver shone enamel inlays in blue, green and indigo. The effect was like a stylised peacock feather, except Lucas had somehow improved on nature and made it more.

'It's incredible.'

'It's for you.'

She swallowed, the urge to cry welling thick and inconvenient. Teagan kept her eyes on the pendant, breathing the pressure away.

Finally, she felt calm enough to look up. 'Thank you.'

He touched her cheek, the gesture tender, like his gaze.

'You're so talented.' She stroked the pendant. The warmth of his hand had left its smooth surface feeling strangely soft. As more light touched the room, the inlays seemed to glow as though lit from within. 'Everything you make is an art piece. Like you take the best of nature's design and turn it into something even more exquisite.' She scanned his face with a kind of awe. 'You must see things so differently to the rest of us. Like a . . .' Teagan hunted for the right word. 'Like you can see another dimension beneath the world.'

Suddenly she blushed. It was a silly thing to say. She had no idea what he saw, only that it must be amazing.

'Come here.' Lucas fed the leather thong around her neck and tied a knot. The pendant hung just below her throat, still warm from his body heat. He stroked the skin around its edges before cupping his big hand around her chin and swooping in to kiss her breathless.

They made love in the glitter of sunrise, every object around them shining and sparkling with slanted light. Teagan felt touched by it, special. And for once the hope that she woke with lingered, carried into the dawn locked in silver and enamel, and the passion in Lucas's eyes.

The feeling remained with her throughout the morning, following her on the drive to Falls Farm. With the afternoon still ahead and Lucas tied up, she'd packed her bikini in case Ness invited her to swim. Perhaps later she might even be asked to stay for cocktails. That would nice. A little awkward, given that Dom was likely to turn up, but still nice.

'Teagan,' called her mother happily from the verandah when she alighted in the yard. 'You're just in time. We've a new addition to the family.'

Teagan blinked in surprise, then watched as Penny descended the verandah steps carrying a ridiculously long-eared fawn rabbit.

Teagan glanced up to where Ness stood against the rail, one hand on a straining, narrow-eyed Blanche. Her aunt shook her head but there was amusement on her face.

Penny held out the rabbit. 'She's an English Lop. Aren't her ears amazing?'

They were. The rabbit's ears fell down either side of its face far below its chin, giving it a maudlin look, like a basset hound. Teagan gave the rabbit a dutiful stroke, then another as she felt its soft fur. 'Another of Bunny's rescues, I take it?'

'Yes. Poor thing was going to be put down. Nibbles belonged to a little girl over Emu Plains way, but her dad has a new job in Queensland and keeping pet rabbits is illegal there. No one else wanted her so Vanessa kindly agreed to adopt her.'

'Temporarily,' said Ness. 'Until we can find her a good home.'

Teagan smiled. 'Like Betty and Wilma and Claudia and Mouse were temporary?'

Vanessa's chin lifted. 'I mean it this time.'

Teagan gave Nibbles another pat and climbed the stairs. She nodded at Blanche, now stalking along the rail, following Penny and

Nibbles's progress around the yard with her shoulders hunched like a hunting leopard. 'Looks like Wilma's lost her place at the top of Blanche's menu.'

'Yes.' Ness moved to settle into one of the chairs. She elegantly crossed a leg and tilted forward to place her forearms over her knee. 'I hear you went to a meeting Tuesday night.'

Teagan stared at the ground. Tony must have broken his promise and dobbed her in. Then again, it could have been Col or any of the others. Ness knew a lot of locals and Teagan's attendance would have been impossible to keep secret.

She expected admonishment, perhaps even disappointment, but Ness surprised her.

'I appreciate you have strong feelings about the Wellness Centre, and I'm not one to tell anyone what to think. You're an adult perfectly capable of forming your own opinions. But Kathleen Ferguson is not your friend.'

'I know.'

'Be careful, darling. This could get very unpleasant. You don't want to get caught up in it.'

'It's just petitions. I threw the forms away.'

Teagan tried not to squirm as Ness contemplated her for a long moment, then her aunt let out a doubtful 'mmm' noise and changed the subject. 'You're looking happier today. Astonville seems to suit you. Perhaps leaving here was a good idea.'

The reminder that Falls Farm had been her temporary home dampened Teagan's feelings. 'I really am sorry for how I behaved. I didn't mean it.'

'We know.'

Vanessa's smile was kind, but it was clear apologies weren't enough. Teagan had to prove her contrition, and that meant making sure she didn't lapse again.

Her mother returned to the verandah, Nibbles cuddled in her arms. Immediately Blanche leaped down from the rail to curl around

Penny's feet, her body sinuous and mesmerising, as if this would entice the rabbit from her arms.

Ness sighed. 'That cat's going to give poor Nibbles an ulcer. Which reminds me, I'll have to buy a bigger cage. It's too crowded with Betty and Wilma.'

'Ask Lucas,' said Teagan. 'I'm sure he wouldn't mind making one.'

Penny looked up from her rabbit cuddle. 'How are you and Lucas?'

Teagan touched the front of her shirt, feeling the outline of her necklace beneath. 'Good.'

Ness and Penny exchanged a glance that made Teagan's cheeks heat, as if they knew exactly what she and Lucas had been doing that morning.

'Did you bring your bathers?' asked Ness. 'We should all have a swim.'

'I did,' said Teagan, hoping that didn't make her sound presumptuous.

'Good. An invigorating dip followed by margaritas will be just the ticket.'

Which was how Lucas found them all when he arrived – bar Nibbles, who was safe with Betty and Wilma in their hutch. He stood at the side of the pool wearing a pair of thongs, bright-red board shorts and a blue T-shirt that stretched tight across his chest, with his hands on his hips and an admiring smile. Almost a white-toothed Hollywood caricature of the perfect boy next door. And though his grin bounced from Ness and Penny, Teagan couldn't help the flutter of her heart when it remained anchored mostly on her.

'Isn't this a sight for a bloke on a hot day.'

'You should come and join us,' said Ness, stroking her way to the shallow end, and pulling herself out of the water. Even with her skin lightly age-crinkled, Ness filled out her fifties-style bathers like Marilyn Monroe. Penny followed with her businesslike breaststroke. 'Go on. Us oldies will leave you to enjoy the water in peace.' Grabbing up her towel, she raised an eyebrow at Lucas. 'Just remember the rule.'

Teagan almost melted with embarrassment, but Lucas only laughed and began pulling off his T-shirt. 'Spoilsport.'

He dived into the deep end as Penny and Ness left, and stroked to the midpoint where Teagan was resting with her back to the pool's edge. He emerged dripping and sexy in front of her and angled in close for a long kiss.

'I missed you.'

'A part of you certainly did.'

His eyes sparkled like the sunlit water drops shimmering on his skin. 'I really hate Vanessa's rule.'

'I'm not sure I do. Getting caught having sex in a pool by my aunt or mother would be death by mortification.'

He rested his forehead against hers. 'We could always head home.'

'And miss cocktails?'

'You've been invited?'

Teagan nodded. She bit her lip. 'I think Dom's coming.'

'Don't worry about him. He'll be fine. He'll have me to deal with if he's not.'

'Hero.'

He winked at her. 'Glad you think so. I do try my best.' He touched her necklace. 'You're wearing it.'

'I don't want to take it off.'

He continued to touch it. 'What you said this morning. About seeing things.'

'I'm sorry. It was a silly thing to say.'

'No. No it wasn't. It meant a lot.' He studied her face in a way that made her think he wanted to say more, then his focus dropped to her mouth and he was kissing her with a passion that left her too brain-scrambled to interpret anything, other than the overwhelming longing for this to last.

They swam and groped and kissed and mucked around for

another half an hour before reluctantly getting out. By the time they made it to the verandah, Bunny had arrived along with Domenic. All of them had their heads close together, jumping apart the moment the door squeaked open. From their guilty looks Teagan knew they'd been talking about her.

Lucas must have sensed it, too, for he took her hand and gave it a quick squeeze.

Dom nodded at Lucas before returning his attention to Teagan. 'Enjoy your swim?'

Teagan swallowed, still unnerved about being talked about and flummoxed by the tone of Dom's voice. This was their first encounter since their confrontation, yet he didn't sound remotely censorious. 'It was good, thanks.' She took a deep breath and stepped closer. Ness was occupied pouring drinks, Bunny and Lucas had launched into a discussion about small-animal cage design, while Penny had lifted Nibbles's enormous right ear and was whispering in it. Teagan doubted she'd get another chance to have a quiet word. 'I'm sorry for what I said the other day.'

'As am I,' said Dom. 'You were only concerned for your mother. It must've been very distressing seeing her so ill.'

'It was.' She wished she owned the grace to say that it wasn't his or the centre's fault, but the words wouldn't come. Like the hospital doctor, Teagan simply couldn't approve of what the centre practiced. Not that side of it.

He gave her a look that said he knew exactly what she was thinking. 'If you'd ever like to take a tour, I'd be more than happy to show you around. It might alleviate some of your concerns. It's an offer open to all members of the Progress Association.'

The comment left Teagan cringing inside. So Dom knew she'd been at the meeting, too. Talk about awkward.

'Thanks. But I'm a bit busy myself with work and . . .' Her eyes flicked to Lucas, golden and handsome. 'Things.'

Dom nodded in Lucas's direction. 'It's good to see him happy.'

Teagan frowned. Since when did Dom care about Lucas?

As though sensing their attention, Lucas looked up. He quickly crossed to drape a possessive arm around Teagan's shoulders. 'You'd better not be trying to steal my girl.' Despite the words there was no threat in Lucas's tone.

Dom laughed. 'I'd say you're safe. I'm far too old and grizzled to be attractive to a woman as young and pretty as Teagan.'

'Good,' said Lucas, kissing her temple.

Ness interrupted with drinks. She handed a margarita tumbler to them each before picking up her own and sipping. She listened for a moment to Bunny's and Penny's animated chat and smiled wryly at Lucas. 'Careful, darling, or they'll have you building the Taj Mahal.'

'I don't mind.' He took a sip of his drink. 'It mightn't be a bad business idea. Plenty of people with pets around the place. Horse types don't usually stop at equines and dogs. They have all sorts of animals.'

Dom nodded. 'Custom-made hutches. Not a bad concept.'

The discussion moved to how Lucas could expand from there, into dog kennels and bird cages. Ness thought the idea brilliant, pointing out local sales points like produce stores and agricultural supplies. Bunny was even more encouraging, promising free advertising in the clinic.

Teagan could tell from the way Lucas's face lit up that the prospect appealed to him enormously. He would be good at it, too. Not only with his blacksmithing skills, but because of his creativity and innate empathy for the needs of animals.

Once again she felt the glow of hope and happiness, feelings that for so long had been elusive and impossible. For Lucas mainly, but also for herself. The way he kept including her in his ideas as if she was at Astonville to stay left her breathless.

'By the way,' said Ness, when the discussion moved on and the group had split into pairs again. She glanced to where Dom was resting against the rail with Lucas. The two of them talking too quietly for Teagan to hear, although both appeared to be watching their conversation closely. 'Penny has decided to return to the Wellness Centre for a few days.'

Disbelief seared across Teagan's brain. Her fingers went tight around her tumbler, a tick flickering in her jaw. The expression she held felt as brittle as old bones, as though one false move would see it splintering. Her mother back at the place that had landed her in hospital. Were they mad?

She concentrated on her breathing. She would not comment. She would not.

Ness was watching her closely. Lucas and Dom had stopped talking. In the yard, alerted by the break in conversation, Penny and Bunny looked up from settling Nibbles in for the night. Teagan lowered her head and closed her eyes, digging for strength. She had to say something. Words to prove she could think of others' wellbeing more than her own selfishness.

She took a shaky sip of margarita to moisten her throat and lifted her head, her smile rigid but in place. 'I'm sure Mum will enjoy that.'

Teagan could have sworn a breeze was created from the simultaneous exhalation of breaths.

Ness patted her shoulder as though she'd done well. 'Yes, I'm sure she will.'

The horribleness of it made tears burn. She couldn't let them see. Keeping her eyes down, she mumbled something about needing the loo and bolted inside.

She sat on the toilet lid with her face in her hands, feeling juvenile and angry. Juvenile because it was clear now how carefully they'd been inching around her, like an over-hormoned adolescent capable of exploding at a single wrong word. Angry because her mother was going back to that place and there wasn't a thing Teagan could do to stop it.

A tap sounded on the door. 'Teagan, are you okay?' Lucas asked.

'Yep. Fine. Just needed the loo.' She stood and flushed, even though she hadn't used it. She took a few seconds to run her damp

palms down her thighs and settle her shoulders, before opening
the door.

Lucas was leaning against the wall with his arms crossed.
'All right?'

'Yep. Yep. Fine.' She slipped into the bathroom to wash her
hands. Her reflection showed how red her cheeks were, the crazy
burn in her eyes. The thinness of her mouth. She spent a moment
trying to force calm through muscles that were locked with tension,
aware that Lucas was at the door, watching. Teagan licked her lips,
nervous under his scrutiny.

She dried her hands and turned.

He jerked his head. 'Come here.'

She stepped into his hold and let his muscular arms fold
around her.

'Your mum will be fine.' He tilted her head back to gaze at her.
'And so will you.'

Her throat roughened even further. She wanted to believe him, to
clutch at all he offered.

He smiled. 'You know why?'

'Why?'

'Because you have me.'

'That'll fuck All-dim,' said Bunny, slapping her hands together.

Lucas watched the council ute as it laid a dust trail down the
drive. Montague's boss had spent five minutes observing Merlin
before declaring his underling's report a farce and spending the next
twenty minutes trying to chat up Bunny.

He couldn't blame him. In jeans and a T-shirt she looked broad
shouldered, athlete fit and magnificent. Dunks must be having a hell
of a time.

'Vanessa will be happy.'

'All-dim deserves a good kick in the gonads for the stress he's caused.' She sniffed and draped her arms over the fence rail. 'I've told Cherub to cut him from the Falcons. Can't have an idiot like that in the side. He'll only ruin morale.'

'We don't have enough players to go cutting people.'

'We will.'

'You're confident.'

'With good reason.' She gave him a smug smile. 'Vanessa and I have discovered an ace hidden in the Falls pack.'

'Who?'

'Oh, you'll find out soon enough.'

Lucas could guess but decided to let Bunny enjoy her game. If he was right in his suspicions, it wasn't a bad coup. Certainly surprising. 'I hope Dunks appreciates how lucky he is.'

Bunny's smile dropped. She stared at her boots, her lips pursed. 'He's asked me to marry him.'

'But that's great.' Lucas's happiness at the news faded as he caught Bunny's expression. 'Okay, what's up?'

She crossed her arms. 'I'm too old for him.'

'Yeah, and he has two girls and an ex-wife who wants to screw him over. We've been over this. You love him, don't you?'

'It's not about love. I'll be old when he's still young. He won't want to be wiping slobber from my chin.'

'Jesus, Bunny. That's years in the future. You're so fit you'll probably end up taking care of him.'

She said nothing.

'Don't do this to him. He loves you.' He sighed and scratched his head. 'So you'll sacrifice happiness now for something that might happen in the future? Come on. You could get hit by a bus tomorrow.'

Bunny squinted into the distance. 'I don't want to disappoint him.'

'That's never going to happen. He's in awe of you.' He joined her at the fence. 'What does Vanessa say?'

'That I should say yes.'

'There you go.'

She threw him a wry look. 'Easy for you to say.' Her expression turned serious. 'Speaking of love-lives, how's yours with Teagan?'

'We're kicking along.'

Which was the truth. Sort of. After a few upbeat days, Teagan had faded into quiet again. This morning he'd kissed her goodbye only to check outside five minutes later when he hadn't heard her ute start and catch her staring blankly at the forge door, her head slightly tilted as though listening for something. At the sound of the screen door closing she'd started and broken out of the trance, then fobbed off his worried questions as she always did by promising she was fine.

She wasn't. He knew it. So did Dom, Vanessa and everyone else.

'You know she went to the Fuckuppa meeting.'

'Yeah.' He didn't want to talk about that. The discovery that she'd lied still cut, but the way she was acting meant he couldn't bring it up.

'You'd best keep a close eye. Vanessa's worried enough about her as it is and getting mixed up with that lot won't do her any good either.' Bunny checked her watch and gave his back a comradely pat. 'I'd better get going. Janice is probably savaging my waiting room.'

'What're you going to tell Dunks?'

Smoothing her palm over her spiky blonde hair, Bunny released a tired sigh and grimaced. 'No idea.' With leggy strides she headed for her car, tossing over her shoulder, 'Whatever the answer, you won't be first to hear.'

TWENTY-FOUR

VANESSA KISSED her sister on the cheek and passed her over to one of the Wellness Centre's perfectly coiffed and made-up receptionists. Worry tightened her insides as Penny was escorted down the hall towards the Bourke Wing. It was ridiculous, but she couldn't help herself. Her sister desperately wanted validation that returning to Graham would be best for everyone. What if counselling gave her that?

'Come have a drink,' said Dom.

She liked the feel of his palm on her back, the gentlemanly care, and wished she could linger a while longer. But if Vanessa was nervous for Penny, she was even more nervous for herself. Maintaining decorum in Dom's company was becoming increasingly troublesome with each passing day.

'Tempting, but I should get back to the farm. Blanche has probably frightened poor Nibbles to death and I have no idea where Saffy's disappeared to.'

'Your animals will look after themselves.' He lowered his voice seductively and bent close. 'Be a devil. Say yes.'

The tickle of his breath on her ear shot Vanessa's willpower somewhere near her groin. 'You know me too well, Domenic Ashe. I never could resist being devilish.'

Dom's quarters at the Wellness Centre were typically masculine; sleek stainless steel and glass, and soft furnishings in impractical arctic white. It had a hard, cold feel, and while it suited the man others considered Dom to be, it was nothing like the man Vanessa knew he was.

His Tamarama apartment was a better reflection, with a softer decor of honey-coloured timber and blue suede furnishings, bookshelves laden with everything from business tomes and biographies to fantasy novels, and a state-of-the-art stereo for listening to music while he did paperwork or relaxed.

She wondered why he hadn't furnished the centre's living quarters the same and supposed that, until recently, he rarely spent enough time here to warrant it. Vanessa tried not to let the thought of him returning to live permanently on the North Shore bother her, but it did. Knowing he was close, seeing him every day, made her life at Falls Farm feel complete.

'Wine? Cognac? Gin?'

'Wine will do fine, white if you have it.'

He buried his head in the fridge before looking up in apology. 'None cold I'm afraid. Plenty of red though.'

Vanessa shook her head. 'Don't worry about it. I shouldn't be drinking anyway. I have to drive home.'

'You should. It'll make you feel better. And help take your mind off Penny.'

'Interesting comment coming from a man who owns a Wellness Centre renowned for its rehabilitation programs.'

He grinned at her before pulling a bottle from a rack and two glasses from an overhead cupboard. 'I never said I was a saint.'

'No. And, as everyone knows, saintliness is completely overrated.'

She accepted a glass of wine and followed Dom to the lounge. He indicated for her to sit then settled close alongside. Too close, but

Vanessa felt it rude to shift away and the truth was she didn't wish to. The way his breath had felt against her skin lingered like a tease. She wanted him that near again.

He pressed the edge of his glass against hers. 'To unsaintliness.'

Their eyes met over the toast and Vanessa once again felt her willpower slide south.

Dom reached aside to place his glass on the occasional table next to the sofa's arm, then leaned his elbow on the back of the sofa and rested his head on his fist to look at her. 'I have a confession.'

Vanessa eyed him warily. 'Oh yes?'

'Graham's here. I had him flown up this morning.'

She jerked upright so fast her wine slopped.

Dom rose with her and quickly removed the glass from her hand. 'Nessie . . .'

Her fingers pressed to her forehead, Vanessa stepped away to pace back and forth on the other side of the coffee table. After three laps she halted. 'I think you'd better explain.'

'I wanted to help. You said he had a gambling problem and that you couldn't risk Penny going back to that life. So I brought him here, where he could get treatment. So you'd know she was safe.'

'You did this for me?'

'For you and your family.'

'Why?'

'I think you know why.'

For once, Vanessa didn't know what to say. She placed her hands to her cheeks and lowered her head as fatigue washed over her.

'Come sit with me, please.'

Vanessa tilted her head back, her lips rolled together, blinking as she tried to work out what to do. Everything hinged on this moment.

'Please.'

The fight against herself was too much. She breathed out, and slowly returned to her seat. Dom draped his arm across the back of the sofa, not touching. With a sigh she let her head flop onto his chest and briefly closed her eyes. It had been too long since she'd felt like this. Protected. Loved.

His voice was rough with sincerity. 'I know I took liberties, but I also know how much you love your family. I wanted to protect them for you. Even if they don't deserve it.'

She lifted her eyes to catch his.

'You told me once that they disapproved of you.'

She relaxed again. 'They did. Penny especially. But they're all I have.'

'No. You have me.'

They lapsed into silence. Vanessa wished she could decide what to do. The longer she stayed with him the harder it would be to leave.

The quiet lingered, stretched across them like a delicate veil neither wanted to raise. Dom's fingers were gentle on her hair. He kept swallowing, his focus never leaving her face. Finally, he spoke, an uncharacteristic fragility adding a tremor to the deep timbre of his voice.

'There's something else.'

Vanessa inhaled and didn't let it out.

'I have a son, Nessie.'

The revelation caused Vanessa to sit up. Once more Dom had left her speechless. A son? As far as she knew he hadn't been in any relationships. Of course he must have had women but she'd tried not to dwell on it. They were friends. It wasn't her business.

'I didn't know he existed until a few years ago. He's a man now. A good man. The sort a father would be proud of.'

'But that's wonderful.' She inspected his face. 'Isn't it? That you've found him.'

Dom nodded. 'It wasn't for a while. He didn't want anything to do with me. I wasn't good to his mother.' He grimaced. 'It was a long time ago. I was different then, ambitious. I never knew she was pregnant and she never told me. I think it was her way of punishing me.' He smiled bitterly. 'But she ended up punishing the both of us.'

'I'm sorry.'

'Don't be. It wasn't your fault.' He reached for his glass and took a sip. Lamp shadows highlighted the lines in his face, the regret there.

'But you have a relationship now, you and your son?'

'We're building one. It's hard to make up for the lost years. I was never there for all the important moments.'

'Keeping him from you was cruel.'

'It was. But I guess she had her reasons.' He said nothing for a moment. 'Do you ever wish you had children?'

She reached for her own glass of wine. 'Yes. I wanted them.' She rubbed the bowl back and forth between her hands, staring at the contents. 'It never worked out.'

'I'm sorry.'

'I was pregnant once, when I was young. I'd only been in Europe a couple of months. It was the last thing I wanted. I had an abortion.' Tears stung her eyes. Even now the hurt was still there. 'I don't have many regrets about my life, but that . . .' She took a shaky sip of wine. 'That one is with me forever. I'll never forgive myself for robbing that baby of life.'

'You didn't try again?'

'With Timoteo. He knew how much I wanted a baby, but it never happened. He was so much older than me, and busy. We were going to try IVF, but by then I was worn down and had had enough of whoring myself and wanted to come home.'

'You didn't whore yourself.'

'Perhaps not, but it felt that way sometimes. Even with Timoteo, who was a darling man and genuinely loved me.' Embarrassed, she puffed out a breath and looked at him sideways. 'I don't know why I told you all that. I must be tired.'

'It's a day for confessions.' He stroked her hair. 'It hasn't been an easy time for you. First Teagan and then Penny.'

'And now Graham. That was naughty of you.'

'Are you angry?'

She stared into her wineglass and considered. 'A little.' She sighed and rubbed her eyebrow. 'Actually, that's not true. I was, but now I'm thankful. What you did was thoughtful and kind.' She held his gaze. 'I'm pleased for you about finding a family of your own, even if it is belated.'

'You could be my family, too.'

The earnestness of his appeal choked her up. She looked away in case he saw the longing there.

'I mean it, Nessie.'

'I know you do.' Her voice was barely a whisper. 'I can't.'

'Why not?' When she didn't answer he plucked her wineglass from her hands and set it on the table before returning to cup her face, gaze searching. 'I'm not joking about this. You know how I feel about you.'

'It's not that simple.'

'Why isn't it?'

'I don't want to be another rich man's trophy. I want my independence.'

'And me loving you would stop that?' He sounded incredulous.

She pulled out of his grip and stood. He'd broken the rules and said it. Now the admission hung in the thickened atmosphere of the room, dangerous and tempting, hovering between being snatched and cherished or cast down. 'I can't do this right now. I'm tired. I need to think.'

'Did you hear what I just said?'

Her hand went to her forehead where a headache was starting to pound. 'Please, Dom.'

'I love you. Why do you think I'm doing all this?'

She took a step back. Those words were too reminiscent of her past life. The gifts she'd naively accepted, thinking they were tokens of love when the reality was they had meant nothing. Throwaway trinkets and insignificant favours designed to impress and make her beholden.

'You think that you can make someone love you by buying them?'

'No. That's not what I meant and you know it.' Dismay twisted his face. 'Why are you being so obtuse? I'm doing these things because I don't like seeing you hurt. Because your family matters to you. And yes, I admit it. I'd hoped you'd come to see me in a different light.' He stepped back as well, suddenly stiff and cold. 'Obviously I was wrong.'

Vanessa swallowed. The headache was pounding now. How had this happened? One moment they were on the couch, Dom's arm warm and comforting around her shoulders, and now they were shattering with heartbreak.

She surveyed the room; the barrenness of it seemed fitting now. A reflection of how the day had turned. Of what their relationship really was. 'I should go.'

He didn't object. This time there was no warm palm on the small of her back. Dom had become as aloof as his surroundings.

In reception, he left her to speak to one of his staff. Vanessa walked to the doors and watched them slide quietly open. She hesitated then stepped outside. The wind had come up, rustling the trees, their leaves trembling like her insides. As she drew her car keys from her handbag Dom returned to her side.

'I've arranged for a car to take you home, another driver will follow in yours so you won't be without.' He held out his palm as if it were a fait accompli. 'Please.'

She stared at him in disbelief.

'Keys, Vanessa. I know it's only five minutes, but I won't have you driving when you're upset.' His tone and expression brooked no argument, and the truth was Vanessa didn't feel she could cope with even the short journey to Falls Farm. All she wanted, right this second, was her verandah, her dog, a gin and tonic the size of a bucket, and plenty of tissues to mop up the tears she planned to shed.

She slapped the keys into his hand. 'Thank you.'

Vanessa expected him to stride off. Instead he waited with her. Within minutes one of the centre's Humvees had pulled up in the circular drive. Dom strode ahead to open the rear door for her.

She nodded and went to climb in, then stopped herself. Dom

deserved more than a silent goodbye. Their friendship did. She turned to examine his face, a last check of what really lay there.

His blue eyes were weary and sad. Sorrow tilted the corners of his mouth. But what upset her most was the sag of his shoulders, the defeat there. He didn't want her to leave any more than she wanted to. Yet he was willing to let her go.

Because he wasn't like the others.

This man truly loved her.

Vanessa didn't think. She stepped forward, placed her hand on his chest and lifted herself on tiptoe to place a careful kiss on his mouth.

For a second he didn't respond, then his lips moved and softened into a tender kiss that was made more meaningful for its briefness.

'I don't want . . .' He cleared the gruffness from his throat. 'It's not necessary for you to thank me that way.'

'That wasn't thanks.'

He raised his eyebrows.

A sudden feeling rushed over Vanessa. Euphoria from the kiss and a deep liquid fire that had been simmering inside her for months and now refused to calm. 'That was a test.'

'Did I pass?'

'It seems you did. Very well.' She glanced towards the front of the car but a panel separated the driver from his passengers. Behind the glass walls of the reception area, the receptionist quickly looked down as though she hadn't been spying. Vanessa grinned. 'Can I interest you in a cocktail?'

Relief and much, much more broadened Dom's smile. 'I thought you'd never ask.'

'Hey, did I tell you? Dom's joined the cricket club,' said Lucas. He was at the stove, stirring spiced-up mince for the tacos they were making for dinner.

Teagan ceased chopping lettuce. 'What? As a player?'

'Yep. Bunny and Vanessa talked him into it.'

'Can he play?'

'No. But without Callum we only have ten players. Even a dud number eleven is better than none.'

Teagan thought on that for a while. 'I bet he's hired a coach. He's too competitive to let himself be made a fool of.'

Lucas concentrated on the mince. He wanted to tell her that it was him who had offered to help Dom. They'd been practising the last couple of mornings, early, after she'd gone to work, on the parkland surrounding the centre. He wanted to tell her that his dad showed talent, which made him wonder if that was where he'd got his own natural sportsmanship from. He wanted to tell her that he'd learned Dom played rugby and basketball as a boy, the same as Lucas had.

But he couldn't say any of these things. Not yet. Not until he was convinced she could handle it. He had selfish reasons, too. The need to get to know Dom without interference or judgement.

There were other matters he couldn't bring up either. The news that Dom and Vanessa were lovers. That her own father was at the centre, enrolled in a gambling-treatment program. Dom had also resumed discussions with Nick and Stacey about leasing horses for equine therapy, or for clients who simply wanted to go for a ride. The centre's large acreage meant there was plenty of room for day yards, a manège and riding trails, but Dom didn't want the hassle or the expense of dedicated facilities.

Then there was their chat about Dom lending Lucas the money to establish a proper blacksmithing business. So he could give up being a farrier and work on his creations. It was only a pipe dream at the moment, and an offer he wasn't sure he'd take up, but it tempted him all the same.

He glanced at Teagan as she continued to chop. All these things he couldn't tell her yet. Things she might be hurt by because she didn't know Dom like Lucas was coming to. Because of the way she still stared hollow-eyed into space when she thought no one could see, and continued to fake cheerfulness when she sensed anyone watching. The way she clung to him when they made love, as if each time would be their last.

He had to make her happy. So happy none of it would matter when she learned of all the secrets they'd been keeping from her.

'Are you going to come to cricket on Saturday?' he asked when they'd settled down to their meals.

'Of course. I wouldn't want to miss all the fun. Nick said he'd let me go early, too.'

'Good. Vanessa's coming. So's your mum and Bunny if she's not called out. Be nice to have a cheer squad.' He ate for a minute, wondering how to phrase his next question. 'You know your horse, the one you left behind in Levenham?'

'Astra?' She screwed up her nose. 'She's not mine anymore. Em bought her. I don't have the money to buy her back.'

'I thought you said Em would let you have her whenever you wanted?'

'She would. But I'd still have to pay her back the money.'

He tried to keep his tone casual. 'I could lend it to you. You could keep her here. There's room.' To his dismay her eyes began to glisten. Shit. This wasn't what he'd intended at all. 'It was just an idea. I didn't mean to upset you.'

'You haven't.' She regarded her half-eaten taco. 'It's just that you make it sound like you want me to stay.'

He reached across for her hand and squeezed it. 'That's because I do.'

She looked up, gaze searching his face as though she didn't believe him.

'I mean it, Teagan.'

Other words were right there, waiting to be said. Words he believed, in his heart. When she slept he whispered them quietly, hoping they'd slip into her subconscious and give her comfort. Except now wasn't the time. They were eating tacos, talking about her horse. Hardly romantic.

Besides, how could he tell her he loved her when he was keeping so much to himself? When she was doing the same. Lying about how she was, drifting, untouchable, to her own hidden world, away from him and everyone else who loved her.

He tried to make a joke to cover up. 'Unless you start farting in bed. Then you're out.'

She laughed, though it had a forced edge. 'I'll try to remember to hold it in.'

'The reverse doesn't apply though.'

'Nice.'

He grinned. 'That's me.'

That brought on a smile but, like the laugh, it wasn't quite real. She picked at a piece of shredded lettuce, unwinding it from the taco and letting it fall to the plate. 'Some would say too good to be true.'

'Who? Tell me and I'll go belt them one.'

She laughed and then sobered, searching his face again, worry pinching her brow. 'You're not, are you?' Her voice hardly broke a whisper and her tortured eyes once more turned liquid. 'Tell me this isn't some joke.'

'It's no joke.' He left his chair to kiss her, hard, and press his forehead to hers. 'Would I lie to you?'

'I hope not.' She swallowed and lowered her eyes. 'But I have to you.'

A leaden feeling dug into his stomach. 'What about?'

'Where I was last Tuesday. I was at Kathleen Ferguson's.'

'For the Progress Association meeting. I know. The Falls isn't an easy place to keep secrets.' Although he and his father were managing. So was Vanessa, come to think of it.

She looked glumly at her plate. 'I suppose I shouldn't be surprised, but when you never mentioned it . . .' That empty look he hated crossed her face, like she'd looked inside herself and found nothing worthwhile. 'I'm sorry. For not telling you.'

'You have now.'

'No more secrets?'

Instead of replying, Lucas kissed her until she couldn't remember he hadn't answered.

TWENTY-FIVE

VANESSA HAD NEVER FELT SO amazing. Dom was, as she'd fantasised on many occasions, rather spectacular in bed. Each morning found her waking with a sense of delight and anticipation that even when she was young she'd never experienced.

Oh, how she'd missed sex. And intimacy, and all the other wonderful relationship things – small and big – that Dom was proving so adept at. Seduction. Silly, sexy lover's babble. The simple act of listening when Vanessa wanted to talk. She could kick herself for waiting so long. All those worries she'd once considered huge and insurmountable had become petty in the dwarfing shadow of Dom's love.

It was proving contagious, too. Falls Farm itself seemed to fizz with excitement. Penny had returned home from the Wellness Centre fairly skipping, and this time it had nothing to do with black cohosh or coffee put in places it never belonged. It was all due to discovering that Graham was in treatment at the centre. The husband she had never wanted to leave in the first place. Who, with her big loyal heart, she'd forgiven for all his many sins.

Everyone was finding light in their personal darkness.

Except Teagan.

Yesterday afternoon, Lucas had called in for a candid chat. He'd sat on a cane chair with his hands held prayer-like against his mouth and worry carving lines in his brow.

'I can't do this anymore,' he'd said. 'I hate lying to her. Especially about —' He caught the word before it could be said and Vanessa softened in sympathy.

'Dom. I know, darling. He told me.'

Why she hadn't clicked before Vanessa still couldn't fathom. Dom's and Lucas's relationship was so obvious now – their extreme physical beauty, the blue-eyed blondness, Lucas's unrestrained and unfathomable dislike of Dom. They were akin in nature, too, both driven in their own, unique way. Both considerate. Both protective of the women they loved.

He leaned back and blew air between his lips. 'She'll flip when she finds out. Not just about me. About you, about her dad being at the Wellness Centre.' He scraped his hand down his face. 'Jesus.'

'So we tell her.'

'Right. When?'

'Perhaps Sunday. When she's not so tired from work. We'll have lunch here. You, me, Dom, Penny. Afterwards we'll sit together and explain.'

Lucas hadn't liked it. The memory of Teagan attacking Dom was too fresh. That and the aftermath, when she'd frightened him so terribly with her absent stare and thoughts of leaving. But Lucas was right, none of them could keep hiding like they were. At least he'd come up with a distraction. Buying Teagan's horse back was a genius idea.

Which was exactly what Vanessa had just done.

Honestly, her family were sending her broke. But better Vanessa spend her money when it could do good than leave it to them when she was dead. Plus now that she had official confirmation that Merlin was safe, she didn't have to fret. Insurance would take care of that tiny-penised twerp Callum.

Emily had been delighted to help. She'd even offered to bring the horse up herself, but Vanessa didn't want to put her out and suggested they organise specialist transport. Horses were moved around the country all the time, and with the many racing and equestrian facilities in the area there was bound to be someone coming by. With practical matters resolved, they'd fallen into a conversation about Teagan. Having suffered family dramas of her own, Emily hadn't been in contact as often as she would have liked and was eager for news that Teagan was settling in well after the trauma of losing Pinehaven. Vanessa had prevaricated, feeling it wasn't her place to reveal too much, but was left in no doubt that Emily was as worried for her niece as the rest of them.

They'd exchanged numbers, promising to sort Astra out as soon as practicable.

Her immediate problems solved, Vanessa sat back with her hands across her belly, feeling smug. Smug and more than a little horny. Something she found rather surprising given that Dom had left only a few hours before. She hoped he wasn't too exhausted, poor darling. Lucas apparently didn't give any quarter when it came to cricket training. Dom was already covered in bruises from being smacked by Lucas's powerful bowls.

Tomorrow would be such fun. The Falcons' first home game. Vanessa had decided to make it a proper English-style picnic day at the cricket, while Dom had promised to provide Humvees to shuttle the Falls Farm contingent to the ground and back, so no one had to worry about drunk driving. A few champagne cocktails, some lovely finger food, and an afternoon of slightly sozzled cricket watching. Perfect.

The phone rang. She picked it up, thrilled to hear Bunny's greeting. Five minutes later she put the phone down and smiled even more happily.

Oh, yes. Tomorrow was going to be a good day.

Erin had once again failed to turn up to work on Saturday, causing Teagan to take the load and making her too late to catch the Humvee shuttle to the cricket oval. By the time she arrived the ground was buzzing. Players in coloured clothes dotted the field, throwing balls, doing stretches and practising blocking manoeuvres with their bats. Lowering her head to see properly through the ute window, she hunted for Lucas, amused to spot him catching for Dom, who was bowling what appeared to be a highly unorthodox version of spin.

Lucas filled out his blue-and-gold Falcons uniform beautifully. To be fair, Dom didn't look bad either. Leaner, but with the same broad-shouldered, narrow-hipped physique. Both wore blue floppy hats against the sun and zinc cream on their lips, but where Lucas looked sexy, Dom looked a bit of a dill. Though uncharitable, the thought gave her a catty frisson of pleasure. It was in that moment that Dom and Lucas broke into laughter over Dom's latest unconventional bowl and Teagan experienced a lurch of unease. The similar way their blue eyes crinkled was uncanny. Almost as if they. . . but no, the idea was ridiculous. It was just the uniform making them look alike. Forcing the thought away, Teagan scouted for a spot to park.

She found the last remaining patch of shade under the bordering line of old gums and alighted. The day was already warming, the temperature forecast to be in the low thirties. With nothing else to wear, Teagan had donned an ancient halter-neck chambray sundress. Normally she would have worn shorts and a singlet or T-shirt, but for some reason she felt an afternoon at the cricket warranted a dress. Though old, it was pretty and showed off her shoulders and legs.

She picked her way around the outside of the field towards the small besser-block clubhouse. A line of portable shades formed a bright string along the boundary, beneath which the teams' various supporters had laid out picnic rugs, card tables and deck chairs. Someone had fired up a barbecue and the stomach-grumbling scent of frying onions and sausages filled the air. Eskies and ice buckets dotted the landscape. This was a crowd clearly up for an alcoholic afternoon.

Spotting her, Lucas waved and made a take-five type of gesture towards Dom before jogging to the fence. Teagan stopped, thrilled when Lucas reached across to pull her into a kiss. Sunshine lit his blue eyes and made them vibrant.

He looked her up and down, the sunlit glow turning hot. 'I like that dress.'

'Maybe I shouldn't have worn it.'

'Why not?'

'I wouldn't want to put you off your game.'

He grinned, gloriously sporty and handsome. 'Not a chance. Anyway, it'll give me something to aim for.'

She raised her eyebrows.

'If I score a century will you wear it to bed tonight?'

'If you score a century I promise to do that thing you like. In the dress.'

His grin flashed even broader. 'You're on.' He glanced back at Dom. 'I need to get back to warming up. If I stay talking to you any longer I won't be able to get my box on.'

'Can't have that. I rather like your crown jewels.'

'I rather like you.' He grabbed her and kissed her again.

She watched his progress as he crossed the field, clutching her pendant and feeling surreal. As Lucas approached, Dom turned and waved at her and she was surprised to find his smile seemed genuine. Confused, Teagan gave a weak lift of her hand in response.

She kept her attention on Lucas as she walked the rest of the fence line. Happiness bubbled inside. This wasn't a fantasy. He really wanted her. She could have hugged herself with joy.

'Teagan!' Ness waved from under one of the shades. As always, her aunt looked stunning. With each movement, her rich dark-blue sateen dress caught the sun and flashed like a fishing lure. The figure-hugging top was cut like a love heart, and though modest, it moulded her ample breasts and showed off their lush roundness. Her skin was creamy and lightly freckled. Her softly waved red hair was held away from her face by pushed-up bug-eye sunglasses. Bright lipstick stained her lips with screen-siren perfection.

Penny stood with her in a button-fronted green-and-white polka-dot sundress that would have been very flattering had she not been standing next to her luminous younger sister.

'Drink?' asked Ness, waving a bottle of expensive pink champagne at Teagan.

'Why not?'

'That's the right attitude.' As Ness poured she eyed Teagan's outfit. 'You look lovely. That dress suits you.'

'Thanks. You're looking unfairly glamorous as always. You look nice too, Mum. Is that new?'

'Yes. Vanessa found it for me.' Penny smoothed her hands over the skirt. 'It's a bit more colourful than I'm used to.'

'I think it looks great.' Teagan accepted the glass and held it up. 'To a win for the boys.'

Ness sipped, leaving a scarlet kiss of lipstick on her flute. 'I do so hope they aren't trounced. Dom would be very disappointed. Men are so competitive.'

'At least they have a full side,' said Penny as Mark Dunkerton jogged out to Dom and Lucas for a chat.

Teagan's gaze followed and once more she was struck by the similarities between the two men. She'd considered their likeness previously, but Dom's metro smoothness and Lucas's country ruggedness had made their differences seem vast. Now, stripped of their usual clothing and wearing matching Falcon's uniforms, they could easily be uncle and nephew.

'Good of Dom to step in when he's never played before,' continued Penny.

'Lucas says he's quite talented.'

Disquiet tightened Teagan's stomach muscles. 'They've been practising, have they?'

'Mmm,' said Ness, not meeting her eye before smiling sunnily. 'Have you had lunch, darling? You must be starving after working all morning. We've made all sorts of canapés.' She hurried to an esky. 'Or would you prefer something more solid? I've some roast beef and Branston pickle sandwiches.'

'Whatever you prefer. Although I'm tempted to pinch a sausage off that barbie. They smell unreal.'

'Best you don't.' Ness began laying out plates. 'It belongs to the opposition.'

Leaving Ness to her preparations, Teagan moved alongside Penny and pointed to the ground's pristine white picket fence. 'This is all very English and civilised.'

'Vanessa said it used to be quite run down. As part of his sponsorship Dom paid for a new fence and roller for the wicket. Apparently the ground has never looked so good.'

'Generous of him.'

'He's that kind of man.' Penny eyed her. 'No matter what you think.'

Right now, Teagan wasn't sure what she thought. All she understood was that the more she observed Dom and Lucas, the more troubled she felt.

'Perhaps he is,' she said, not taking her eyes off the men. Lucas even stood with his legs spread and arms akimbo the same way as Dom. 'But he's also a businessman trying to curry favour with the local community. His generosity won't be all due to altruism.'

But Penny wasn't to be budged. 'Really, Teagan. Must you see underhandedness in everything? You have no idea how kind that man has been. To me, your aunt, and especially to us as a family.'

Without warning, a plate was shoved between them and pushed aggressively towards Penny's chin. 'Vol-au-vent?'

Looking startled, Penny snatched one off and quickly stuffed it in her mouth, smiling stiffly as she chewed, while Ness smiled with equal rigidity.

'Oh good,' said Ness, lowering the plate. 'Bunny's made it.'

Like a blonde Amazon in Falcons colours, Bunny strode towards the clubhouse, eyes fixed on Mark Dunkerton. Men, women and dogs stepped aside as she marched determinedly under the awning. Without a pause for breath she kissed Mark firmly and long on the mouth to the whoops and teasing of his teammates.

'Yes,' was all she said.

Mark gaped at her.

Bunny grinned at his stunned expression and ruffled his hair. 'Play well, Cherub. And don't get hurt. You and I have a whole lot of loving to do.'

Ness squealed and did a little jig. The Falcons erupted. With a bow and a wink at a still speechless Mark, Bunny strode over to Ness.

'Right.' Bunny slapped her hands together and rubbed them. 'A celebratory drink is in order.'

Laughing and still jigging, Ness threw herself at Bunny, hugging her hard.

Penny and Teagan looked at one another.

'What's going on?'

'I,' said Bunny proudly, unwrapping a happy-teared Ness from her neck, 'am getting married.'

Teagan grinned in delight. From under the awning the Falcons boys broke out into more whoops and backslaps as they congratulated and teased their captain.

'Win or lose,' said Bunny, grinning hugely, 'it's going to be a big night at the bowlo.'

It was going to be a big day at the cricket, too. Mark lost the toss and the opposition chose to bat. Teagan, Penny, Bunny, Ness, the other wives and girlfriends and several villagers stood by the fence clapping and cheering them on as the Falcons filed out.

The team huddled in the centre of the ground as Mark barked out instructions and pointed to field placings, mouth working as he channelled former Australian test captain Ricky Ponting and chewed nervously on gum. Lucas was sent to slips, while Dom jogged towards the outfield. Peter Somersby, not a limp wrist in sight, jogged easily to mid-on. Realising how close he was to the batsman at short square leg, Tony de Vitis's Italian swagger took on a distinct wobble.

The crowd wandered back to their various sunshades. Nick and Stacey arrived with baby Olly and another esky rattling with ice and booze. Gus and Debbie Anderson from the IGA brought a tray of hot party pies and sausage rolls, which Teagan, desperate for quick sustenance to soak up too many gulps of celebration champagne, tucked into. Soon Vanessa's shade was spilling with people, drinking, laughing and chatting. High on a glorious day, community spirit and Bunny's good news.

Mark opened with his fastest bowler, a storky-looking man Ness said was a local carpenter and who Teagan had met briefly at the trivia night. The Falls contingent groaned as he was hit for four on the first ball. Mark shouted encouragement, Lucas following suit.

More balls followed. Another boundary followed by three dot balls and a single. The game was underway.

Teagan settled into a deck chair with a plate full of Vanessa's sandwiches. Any attempt to avoid a champagne refill had been thwarted by Bunny, who insisted everyone celebrate on her behalf. Teagan supposed it didn't matter. The Humvee shuttle would see her home and her old ute would be fine left overnight at the grounds. Still, Teagan warned herself to be careful. A little bit of alcohol was fun, and helped her forget her worries for a while. Too much made her thoughts turn dark and roused the nasty whispers in her head. Today was for Lucas, not her screwed-up mess of a mind.

She looked around, at the people she had now come to call friends. At her mother looking the best she ever had, at her generous, vibrant aunt. At Bunny who couldn't stop grinning and toasting everyone who came near. At her boss, his wife and their chubby-faced baby, the Andersons and their easy smiles.

At Lucas, crouched in slips. Talented, athletic, sexy, kind and maybe, just maybe, truly hers.

The Falls Farm crowd left their seats to line the edge of the shade when Lucas was called into bowl. He had a sublime action, smooth and powerful. When the first ball was hit for a four he stood in the middle of the wicket with his hands on his hips and a grim expression, his eyes narrowed at the batsman. He walked back, catching the ball as it was thrown to him with ease. At the end of his run-up, he turned, the ball twisting in his hands, before exploding towards the wicket. This time the ball was right on stumps and fast.

The batsman played at it. The sound of the snick had Teagan holding her breath. The ball flicked up, ricocheting towards Mark, who cupped his hands and caught it with barely a bobble. The ball went flying back into the air as he whooped in triumph. Lucas accepted the head rubs and back slaps of his teammates, Dom's lasting longer than any of the others. Bunny crowed from the sidelines like a rooster.

Lucas bowled another over, finishing with an impressive one for five as the incoming batsman treated him with more wariness.

'Cherub will swap the bowling around now,' said Bunny, nodding sagely. 'Ed next, I think.' She smiled as Mark did exactly that. 'Good man.'

The afternoon swung between indolence and drama. The Falcons' tactics kept the opposition in check. As the overs ticked by, the frustrated batsmen ceased blocking and took to playing at anything close to being off line. Bunny kept everyone amused with her insightful but massively biased commentary.

'You should be out there,' Nick told her.

'I might make it out yet if someone gets injured.' As soon as the words were spoken Bunny hunted for something wooden to touch, sighing in relief as she laid fingers on one of Vanessa's serving boards.

'Do you have a uniform?' asked Penny.

'Cherub has a spare. I can borrow that in a pinch.' Bunny tapped the board again. 'Quit tempting fate.' Suddenly her attention shifted towards the carpark. '*Achtung*, babies. The Fuckuppa Führer and her pendulous pet are approaching.'

Teagan couldn't help her laughter. She really needed to lay off the champagne.

Kathleen Ferguson strode under the shade as though invited. Col was red-faced behind, whiskered chin scrunched up in consternation as though he wanted to call her back but was too scared. Kathleen's hard gaze fell on Teagan, making her squirm and reach for a calming drink.

Ness hid her displeasure well. 'Can I offer you a glass of champagne, Kathleen? We're celebrating an engagement.'

Both Kathleen and Col looked at Teagan. 'Not me.' She pointed at Bunny, who was grinning triumphantly. 'Bunny.'

Col seemed genuinely thrilled. He bustled over to kiss her cheek. 'Well, that's wonderful news, Bunny. Wonderful. Good to see you're being made an honest woman at last.'

'I was honest before, Colin.'

'Congratulations,' said Kathleen without a hint of sincerity.

'Thank you,' replied Bunny with equal disdain. 'I'd invite you to the wedding but it'll be a private affair, probably in the Wellness Centre's gardens. Dom says they're very beautiful.'

Kathleen's mouth puckered.

Ness waved the champagne bottle. 'Fizz?'

As Col opened his mouth to accept, Kathleen butted in. 'Best we don't.'

'It is?' said Col, clutching his hands and looking bewildered.

Kathleen ignored him, twitched a smile and strode off, tossing back a 'Come along, Colin' when he continued to linger.

Col threw a last look of deep longing towards Ness before scuttling off behind his leader.

'Those two are up to no good,' said Penny, frowning at their backs, but no one paid much heed. The Falcons had just taken another wicket.

TWENTY-SIX

'WELL, THIS IS GOING MARVELLOUSLY,' said Vanessa, clapping her hands together and smiling. Anything to cover her anxiety and ensure the day progressed as planned.

She wished Dom was by her side. Since Kathleen's entrance she'd struggled to maintain her poise. The woman's sly expression had threaded worry through her veins and Colin had seemed more agitated than normal. As expert collectors of local gossip they could be harbouring all kinds of information. Information Vanessa would rather remain secret for a day longer. But she knew that pair too well. The chance to make mischief during the Falcons' first home game and Dom's debut for the team would be too exquisite to miss.

At least Teagan and Penny seemed to be enjoying themselves, although there was a rather fraught moment early on when Penny began to defend Dom. Fortunately, Teagan seemed too wrapped up in Lucas to notice and Bunny, bless her, had saved the day completely with her engagement.

Vanessa smiled at her friend. Despite the celebrations, congratulatory hugs and multiple toasts, Bunny's focus had rarely left the game. As soon as drinks were called she'd gathered up a basket of sports bottles and jogged out. Now she stood in the centre of the pack, pointing animatedly at the field and players while Mark looked on with a mixture of awe and adoration. The two of them made Vanessa's heart skip with delight.

The thought had her seeking out Dom. He was standing next to Lucas, drinking as he listened to Bunny. An unflattering cotton hat was on his head, similar to Lucas's, and she was warmed by how well they fitted together. And how pleasing for Dom, who wanted the relationship so badly, that Lucas was thawing. The resentful man was slowly morphing into a friend. One day he would be a son, too.

Somehow, her troubled niece had brought not one, but two families together.

Vanessa glanced around for her. Cold seeped across her back as she spotted Kathleen and Col deep in conversation near the clubhouse. As though sensing her scrutiny, Col glanced towards the Falls Farm shelter. He caught Vanessa's eye before his focus shifted to a point behind. Vanessa followed his line of sight to where Teagan stood with her glass of wine, chatting to Stacey. When she looked back, Kathleen was watching. For a moment the woman's mouth crimped into a catty smile, then was hidden as she deliberately turned her shoulder.

Teagan was in that mild state of buzzy drunkenness that made her feel marvellous. She'd never been much of a cricket fan, but she'd never enjoyed a game like this either. A glorious day, great company, good food and wine, an engagement to celebrate, and a man on the field she was beginning to believe might honestly love her.

Wrapping her arms around her waist, she gave herself an indulgent hug as she made her way to the loos. She'd have to be quick.

Already the boys were downing the last of their drinks and slapping backs in encouragement, ready to take the innings by its throat.

She smiled at the mirror as she washed her hands. The champagne had put pink in her cheeks and her eyes had lost their haunted dullness. The chambray dress might not be as expensively elegant as Vanessa's sleek blue job but it made her look pretty and young.

Claps began to sound. The teams were filing out. As the yelled barracking, occasional whistles and good-humoured sledges faded, other voices filtered in from outside the toilet block. Recognising Col's, Teagan cocked her head and listened in as she tore off a stretch of paper towel and dried her hands. From his tone he sounded overexcited about something.

'But she came to the meeting.'

'Spying, no doubt. Along with Tony.' The voice was Kathleen's. 'No question whose side she's on now that Vanessa and Dom are together.'

Teagan stilled, her heart thumping.

There was a pause before Col spoke again. This time his voice was almost wistful. 'I think it's nice she's found someone. Very attractive lady. Shame for her to be on her own.' His words began to fade as he moved away from the toilet block. 'They do make a good couple. Wonder why they've been keeping it secret.'

Teagan tried to process the conversation but, tossed around by alcohol and disbelief, the words wouldn't settle. She closed her eyes, breathing hard in an effort to focus. Ness and Dom were together? It had been clear from the beginning that Dom had strong feelings for her aunt, but Ness had always held him at arm's length. If Kathleen and Col's conversation was true, then clearly that had changed.

And no one had told Teagan.

Who else knew? Her mother? Living at the farm she had to know. Lucas? From the way they were acting on the field, he and Dom were pretty thick these days. So why hadn't either of them mentioned it? The memory of her attack on Dom and her mother reared. She swallowed as tears pricked and her throat turned rough.

No one trusted her. Given her past actions she couldn't blame them, but it was as though they thought she was so mean she would begrudge her aunt happiness. Teagan would never do that.

Hauling in a shuddery breath, she blew her nose on the towel and tossed it in the bin, before checking herself in the mirror. A little bedraggled and too wide-eyed, but she'd pass. Enough at least for no one to corner her before she'd had a chance to talk to Penny.

She slipped from the building and, keeping behind the spectators, made her way to the back of the Falls Farm shade. Smiling at Debbie Anderson and ducking past Stacey who was burping Olly, Teagan tugged on the back of her mother's dress.

'Can I talk to you for a minute?' she whispered when Penny turned. Teagan darted a look at the others. 'In private.'

Penny threw a pensive glance Vanessa's way, but her sister was busy watching the cricket with Bunny. 'Is everything all right?'

'I just need to ask you something.'

Her mum frowned before nodding reluctantly and following Teagan towards the dusty road that separated the spectator stands from the car-parking area. 'What is it?'

'Are Ness and Dom lovers?'

'Oh, Teagan.' Her mum reached out.

Teagan stepped back, biting her lip as hurt flooded her. 'Why didn't anyone tell me?'

'We didn't want to upset you.'

She gazed at the field, blinking. Lucas was stepping in from the outer as the bowler made his run. 'By we, I guess you mean Lucas too.'

'Teagan, sweetheart, it's not how you think.'

'Then how is it, Mum? Did you all think I was so mean-hearted that I wouldn't be happy for Ness?'

Was she really that awful a person?

'No!' Penny held out her palms in a pleading gesture. 'Come back into the shade. Let Vanessa explain.'

The crowd let out a cheer. Teagan jerked her head towards the field and stared as Dom sprinted up to Lucas and slapped him on the back. Still triumphantly holding his catch, Lucas turned and man-hugged him. A tiny groan escaped her mouth as all the little hints and clues merged together and realisation finally hammered home. Lucas and Dom were related. Most likely father and son. The father he had once hated, who'd caused his expression to darken and whom he'd described as an arsehole. Who Lucas was now best mates with, and never said a word to her about.

A clenching pain swelled beneath her ribs. Balling her fist, Teagan jammed it against her chest but the ache kept growing.

'What else are you keeping from me?' She could barely get the words out, they hurt so much.

Tears swamped Penny's eyes. 'We were going to tell you every-thing tomorrow.'

'Tell me what?'

'Your dad . . .'

Her tongue felt thick, her mouth sticky. Fiery sun pounded her head. 'What do you mean, my dad?'

'He's at the Wellness Centre.' At the blood-draining shock on Teagan's face Penny began to gabble. 'Dom had Graham flown up on Monday. He's in the gambling program. Dom says it's one of the best there is. I've been to see him. He promises he'll work hard to get better.'

The words faded into a jumble. Teagan took another staggery step back. Her own father, here, in The Falls.

And no one told her?

Slowly, she faced the cricket ground again. Lucas and Dom were side by side, waiting for the new batsmen, united. She shifted focus to the shelter and locked eyes with Vanessa. Her aunt lifted a hand to her mouth as it widened in dismay.

The lies crowded in on her, one after the other. Ness and Dom. Lucas and Dom. Her father at the centre. How many more were there? How much worse did they get?

'Teagan, come on, please. It'll be okay. Talk to Vanessa. She'll explain.'

Explain? Teagan didn't need any more explanations. Her worst nightmare had come true. They all thought she was crazy, an unkind, ugly-hearted person not to be trusted with anything. And given the horrible, insane thoughts rioting through her mind, they were probably right.

Teagan took another step back, then another. Swivelling forward, she broke into a jog.

When she reached the oval's gates, she began to sprint.

⊸⊷⧓⊶⊸

'Where's Teagan?' asked Lucas, scanning the shades and spectators. He thought he'd heard her cheering when he took that catch but hadn't heard anything since.

The opposition were all out for a hundred and fifty-nine. Now it was the Falcons' turn to chase runs. The team were gathered under the clubhouse awning, kits open, bats and pads and helmets ready for strapping on. As opening batsman, Lucas was already preparing. Any moment he'd have to head out. He wanted a kiss for good luck.

Vanessa answered in a weird, high voice. She'd been tucked at Dom's side ever since they'd come off the field, the pair exchanging whispers. 'I'm sure she's around. Probably the loo.'

Lucas noticed her grip on Dom's arm. He looked at his father's face. Something was wrong.

'Come on,' said Dunks, slapping his back. 'Get those pads on.'

But Lucas didn't want to get his pads on. He wanted to know where Teagan was. He stared around again and caught the excitement on his teammates' faces as Bunny revved them up. There was cricket to play and Teagan was a big girl. She'd be fine. Probably in the loo, as Vanessa said.

He finished padding up and shoved his box into place, thinking of

Teagan and their deal. She'd looked amazing in that dress. Girlish and sexy. But best of all, when she'd smiled, it'd been real, reaching her eyes and lighting them in a way that had his heart leaping.

His gloves went on. He grinned as Dom ruffled his hair and handed him his helmet and bat.

'You'll do great.'

Pride surged through Lucas. It had taken years, but the longed-for little-boy dream was coming true. His dad was here, watching him. Playing on the same team like he'd once fantasised.

The calls of good luck faded as he and Dunks walked out to the wicket. Lucas glanced back, hoping to see Teagan. Hoping to hear her voice, see her smile, but again there was nothing. Sickness lurched in his stomach. He tried to put it aside but it lingered all the way to his stumps.

As he took his mark he scanned the crowd one last time. Then all Lucas could think about was the ball coming straight at his head.

'I don't know where she's gone,' Vanessa hissed to Dom. She'd dragged him to the side of the clubhouse away from the others. When Penny told her what had happened they decided to let Teagan be, confident she wouldn't miss Lucas's innings. A little time to work out her temper and for Vanessa and Penny to coordinate their approach would do them all good. Except it had been half an hour now, Lucas was at the crease, and she still hadn't returned.

Dom rubbed her shoulder. 'She'll turn up. It's fine.'

Vanessa wasn't so sure about that. The look Teagan had given her as she'd retreated from her mother had been one of complete disbelief and deep hurt.

'How did she find out about us? We've been so careful.'

Dom shrugged. 'Maybe someone saw my car at the farm.'

'But that's hardly unusual.'

'It being parked there all night is.'

Out of the corner of her eye, she caught the tall figure of Kathleen Ferguson and remembered the catty smugness of her earlier expression. Vanessa's lip curled slightly. She bet it was her. Not much happened in The Falls without Kathleen hearing about it. Her and Col were like bowerbirds when it came to gossip. Anything colourful was snatched up with glee, and against their grey daily life in The Falls, she and Dom would glow very colourfully indeed.

Vanessa scanned the grounds again, desperate for Teagan. All they needed was a chance to explain. For her to understand they'd only wanted to protect her.

Dom followed her gaze. 'She can't have gone far. Her ute's still here.'

'That doesn't mean anything. She's had too much to drink to drive. We all have.' Vanessa wrung her hands. She had guests to get back to. Dom had his son and team to watch and cheer on. She pressed her lips together to hold back worried tears. 'Oh, this is awful. Teagan was having such a lovely time and now it's all gone so wrong.'

He frowned, at last looking as worried as she felt, then softened at Vanessa's distress. 'Hey,' he said, kissing her temple. 'Stop fretting. It'll be all right.'

'But I can't just stand around doing nothing.'

Dom's mouth thinned. 'I know. But bar starting a search party I don't know what else we can do except wait and see if she turns up.'

It was getting dark now, the air cooling. Teagan's feet hurt. She'd busted a strap on her sandal during the sprint away from the cricket ground and the rough edge had rubbed a raw patch over her toes.

She'd run a long way. A long, long way in her search for somewhere safe. But there was nowhere in The Falls that was safe, not when the danger lay inside her.

She stared at the waterfall and pool, hunting for a way out of this mess, only for her vision to blur with more tears. They hadn't stopped. Each time she thought they might dry up, the overwhelming feeling of betrayal and uselessness flattened her again, squeezing more out.

Why hadn't she trusted her gut and returned to Levenham when she had the chance? At least there she had Em and Jasmine, friends she knew she could rely on. And Astra, with her solid warmth and big horsey heart. She could have found a job easily enough, fended for herself. The Falls would have been a memory.

Lucas would have been a memory.

Lucas. God, it *hurt* to think of him; his smiling, promise-filled eyes. His ardent, almost angry plea for her not to leave when she'd wanted to go. Teagan had hoped it was because he truly felt something for her, but she could see now it was just another ruse to keep her here, the depressed mean-girl who needed help.

Help, no doubt, in the form of the Wellness Centre.

An icy shiver ran over her skin at the thought of that place. She couldn't go there. The risk was too great. The counsellors would get inside her head and see the awfulness there, and then everyone would know how truly crazy she was.

She didn't want to be like this. All she wanted was to be her real self again, for the whispery darkness to stop.

The tears and sobs came again. Convulsive and loud, bouncing off the rocks before being absorbed into the green bower. When the fit had passed, she sniffed and wiped her sodden cheeks on the bottom of her dress. Deep fatigue dragged at her bones and flesh. She was so tired. So sick of crying, of not knowing what to do. And so scared of a future that contained only more of this misery.

A noise sounded from her dress pocket. Recognising her phone's 'feed me' bleep, she dug it out and stared at it. The screen had sported a 'Connect to Charger' message for a long while now. Unsurprising. She'd been gone for hours.

More tears began to fall. God, were they ever going to stop? She closed her eyes tightly. She wanted to go home, to the place where she was once normal. Recapture the girl that had become so lost. Except she didn't know how, and there was no one she could trust to help anymore.

Apart from . . .

She hit 'call' on Em's number before she could stop herself.

'Teagan? How are you? I've been meaning to call.'

The kindness in Em's voice, the genuine delight at hearing Teagan's voice had her breaking down again.

'Teagan? Teagan talk to me. What's wrong?'

But the sobs were coming too hard and hoarse to answer.

'Where are you? Teagan? I'm here for you, Blissbomb, like always. Tell me where you are and I'll come find you.'

'It's too far.'

'Nowhere is too far. You're my friend, I love you. Jas loves you. Astra misses you like crazy.'

Teagan sniffed.

'Come on, where are you?'

'The Falls.'

'Are you at your aunt's place? Teagan? Talk to me. Where in The Falls are you?'

Teagan lowered her head and caught sight of her reflection in the pond. A hollow-eyed crazy person stared back. She kicked out, destroying the pool's mirrored surface. But the waves settled and the image returned, haunting and horrible.

She let out a sad, exhausted sigh. 'How's Astra?'

'She's good. Missing you, like we all do. Did you know we're bringing her up to you? It's all arranged.'

'When?'

'I spoke to your aunt. It's all worked out. Lucas – that's your boyfriend's name, isn't it? – he says there's plenty of room at his place. He must love you very much. Like we all love you.'

Teagan went cold. More conspiring behind her back. Lucas. Ness. And now her best friend.

Without another word, she hung up. For a long while she stared at the phone. Finally it beeped at her. The familiar 'you've run out of time' beep that sounded before it went dead.

Her expression like stone, she threw it in the pond, killing the connection for good.

TWENTY-SEVEN

VANESSA HANDLED the Alfa Romeo like a rally car. Penny was in the passenger seat, urging her to go faster. The panic in her voice was contagious, but Vanessa was at her skill limit for the windy dirt road.

Thank God for Emily Wallace-Jones. Without her call they'd still be searching. Lucas was out scouring The Falls, Dom doing the same. Everyone else was at the bowlo, getting plastered. Vanessa had honestly thought Teagan would turn up. Lucas had batted brilliantly and only just missed his ton. To his and Vanessa's delight, Dom had taken a wicket. As had Peter Somersby, who had turned out to be a rather sneaky swing bowler. Everyone from the Falls Farm cheer squad, apart from Stacey who was on baby duty, was drunk and now getting drunker celebrating the Falcons' first victory.

From the moment Lucas came off the field and learned what had happened he'd taken charge. Still padded up, he'd dragged Dom, Penny and Vanessa aside and ordered them to start searching for Teagan properly. Though it was obvious to everyone that something was wrong, Vanessa had waved off their enquiries and offers of help. The Falcons had a match to win. Plus this was Bunny's special day, and she didn't want her friend's celebration spoiled by something that could turn out to be a silly panic over nothing.

On Lucas's instruction Penny had called the police but little could be done. Teagan was an adult. She'd been gone only hours. Chances were she'd turn up when she'd calmed down. Which left the four of them to hunt.

After searching all the obvious places – Astonville, Falls Farm, Belgravia, even the bowling club and village shops – they'd regathered on Vanessa's verandah to try to decide what to do next. It was then that Col had arrived. Everyone had groaned. He was the last person they wanted interfering but Col had been genuinely distressed to hear Teagan was missing and wanted to help. Besides, he knew The Falls better than anyone.

'We have to find her.' Vanessa's voice was tremulous with anguish. What if she'd been hurt? But worse was the worry that Teagan might hurt herself, that her depression was even deeper and darker than any of them imagined.

Penny let out a sob. 'It's all my fault.'

'Shh, stop that. It's nobody's fault.' She looked at Dom and then at Lucas. Guilt ran across their faces. The secrets they'd kept had become furrows of fear in their skin. Except this was not the time for self-reproach. What they needed was to find Teagan. The rest could come later. Curbing her own anxiety, Vanessa injected practicality into her voice. 'She'll be all right. We'll find her.'

'We need to get back out there,' said Lucas, scraping his hand through his hair and staring towards the road. 'But where to start?'

'She was on foot,' said Vanessa. 'Wearing sandals. That has to narrow it down.'

'Can't have gone too far,' agreed Col. 'Not too many footpaths in The Falls.'

'Somewhere in the village?'

Lucas snapped his fingers at Dom. 'You search the south streets. I'll search the north.' He turned to Vanessa. 'I'll have my phone. Anything, anything at all. Call me.'

She nodded and bit her lip.

As Lucas jogged for his ute, Dom lingered beside her. He touched her face. 'I love you.' Then he kissed her lightly, nodded at Penny and was off.

Fifteen minutes after they'd gone Vanessa's mobile rang. Expecting either of the men or perhaps, sickeningly, the police, she snatched it up and answered without checking the screen. It was Teagan's friend, Emily. The panic in her voice made Vanessa's heart race. Then she registered the words.

Teagan had called her, only a few minutes before.

'She said she was at The Falls,' said Emily. 'When I asked where exactly she changed the subject then hung up. But there was a noise, in the background. Like . . .' She could hear Emily breathing hard as she thought. 'I don't know. I'm sorry. But it was distinct. Loud. Not a road but . . .' She made a frustrated sound.

A sharp cold feeling crept down Vanessa's spine. 'Could it have been a waterfall?'

'Water? Oh, God, yes. That's it. Please, you have to hurry.'

The Alfa skidded around the last bend, its headlights flooding the canopy of green that surrounded the watercourse. They swept towards the pool. A forlorn figure was huddled by its edge. Then Teagan turned her pale face and huge eyes on the car.

Penny's door was open before Vanessa could slide to a halt.

Vanessa pressed her forehead against the steering wheel and gave into a quiet sob of relief. When she looked back up, Teagan was in her mother's arms, the pair of them hugging and crying and apologising.

By the time they made it to the car, Teagan had quietened. She sat in the back wrapped close to her mother and a hollow, gone-elsewhere stare to her gaze. Vanessa tried to get her attention in the rear-vision mirror, succeeding only when the car turned onto the steadier surface of the main road.

'We just wanted to help.'

But Teagan shook her head and looked away.

Vanessa swallowed at the pain in her throat. How badly she'd judged this, and how arrogant she was to think she could help Teagan on her own. A person in her niece's mental state needed professional treatment, not homespun remedies. Not an error she would make again.

'Teagan?'

Her niece looked up.

'I'm going to call Dom.' She hesitated. 'The centre has an on-call GP and psychologist. I can ask them to come to the farm.'

Teagan closed her eyes.

'Sweetheart,' said Penny, stroking her head. 'Please. It's for the best.'

'I don't want anyone to know.'

'Know what?' Penny stopped her stroking, and stared at Teagan's crumpling face. 'Know what, honey?'

When Teagan remained silent, Vanessa answered for her. 'You don't want anyone to know how depressed you are?'

Slowly, she nodded.

'But they can help you. Don't you want help?'

Teagan dropped her head and turned away.

Catching Vanessa's eye, Penny nodded. Grim-faced, Vanessa made the call to Dom, while in the back seat, Teagan quietly resumed her sobs.

Lucas was at the main gate when they arrived. Desperate to check on Teagan, he followed them up the slope, jogging alongside the car, but the sight of him only made her hunch further in on herself and bawl even harder. He broke off halfway up the drive, hands on his head and looking as if he, too, wanted to cry. If Vanessa weren't in such a state herself, she would have cried for him.

She pulled up near the fence and turned off the engine, unlocked her seatbelt and took a deep breath before twisting around to check on her sister and niece. Penny was stroking Teagan's back, making soft *shh*ing noises. She locked eyes with Vanessa and gave a tiny, helpless shake of her head.

Vanessa responded with an encouraging smile. They'd get through this. Whatever it took, she would see her broken family whole.

With a final glance at Teagan, she stepped out and bumped straight into Lucas.

'She's all right, isn't she?' He was panting from his sprint up the drive, attention lasered on the Alpha's back seat. 'She's not hurt?'

'Only inside.' Vanessa squeezed his arm. 'I think it'd be best if you kept your distance.'

His eyes were limpid in the moonlight, his voice autumn-leaf fragile. 'But I love her.'

'I know.'

Penny was helping her daughter out of the car. Teagan's head remained bowed, her shoulders curled in, clawed hands raised to protect her throat, arms jammed against her chest. As Penny began to guide her towards the house, Lucas brushed out of Vanessa's restraining hold and tried to put his arm around Teagan.

With an angry noise she jerked away from him. Lucas halted, mouth agape, and stared with agonised impotence as the woman he loved moved out of his reach.

'I'm sorry,' said Vanessa, giving him a last pat before following Penny and Teagan up the stairs.

Lucas had never understood the description 'dead-eyed' until now. But that's what he'd glimpsed in the second Teagan had lifted her head and stared at him from the back seat of Vanessa's car. She was there, he saw her. Tangled red hair and waxen, tear-stained face, but it was a shell. A shell that had instantly crumbled and given way to a sobbing woman that couldn't stand the sight of him.

He didn't know which scared him more.

Love and disbelief at her reaction had made him ignore Vanessa's advice and attempt to go to her. But she'd made that bitter noise and shrunk away from him as if his intention was to hurt not help.

He loved her. He'd never hurt her.

Yet he had.

Lucas sank onto the stairs and covered his face with his hands. Grief and fear gripped his heart and made his throat tight. He was going to lose her. And it was his own fault for not being honest. For keeping things from her. Just like her dad had done.

The screen door banged. Stupidly hopeful, Lucas dropped his hands and looked up, but it was Dom. He trudged down the stairs to sit next to him.

'How is she?'

'Not bad, given the circumstances.'

'What did the doctor say?'

'The usual, which is very little.' He smiled to soften the lack of information. 'Doctor Johar isn't one for breaking patient confidentiality. For now he's given her something to help her sleep. Meredith will stay with her until she does. She's in good care.'

They were reassuring words, giving Lucas hope that maybe sleep would bring Teagan back from wherever her hurt mind had transported her. He looked away. What a stupid thought. It would take more than sleep to make Teagan better.

'Now what happens?'

'Meredith and Penny will take her to see Doctor Johar in the morning. They'll talk about medication and treatment. It's pretty clear she's clinically depressed. Meredith thinks there might be anxiety issues as well.'

'And then?'

Dom scraped a palm up and down his forearm. 'I've reserved a room at the centre for her, should she wish to take it.'

'She won't. Not after what happened to Penny. Anyway, I can look after her.'

Dom regarded him. Several heartbeats passed before comprehension finally dawned. Unless Teagan had an overnight change of heart, there'd be no return to Astonville. Or to him.

Lucas took several long breaths, trying to control his emotions when all he wanted was to run into her room to clutch her to his pain-filled heart.

'Shit.' He stood, fists tight, frustrated with helplessness. '*Shit.*'

And all because of their stupid secrets.

TWENTY-EIGHT

'THE FIRST THING I want you to understand,' the woman who'd identified herself as Meredith Burns said, 'is that you're not going mad.'

A thousand times Teagan had reflected on those words. Without them she would have been truly lost. It was the simplicity of them, the hope they held, that had brought her to make the most important decision of her life. A decision she should have made a long time ago.

She'd asked for help.

Teagan stared around her. The Wellness Centre's rear garden was nice this time of day. Cool in the shade but dappled with light from the hot spring sun. At first she'd baulked at the idea of coming here but after listening to Doctor Johar outline her medical treatment, and Meredith's suggestion for therapy, it had seemed the smart decision. Anti-depressants took time to take effect. Individuals could experience unique responses to dosages and types, and often finding the right drug was a matter of trial and error. Some reportedly made people worse before they got better, and the centre offered the safety net of twenty-four-hour medical supervision and counselling.

What it also offered was a place to hide.

Neither her mother nor Vanessa pushed, but Teagan didn't miss the relief in their faces when she told them. A reaction that had cut deeply at the time, and made her feel even more useless and unwanted. But it was either Falls Farm or the Wellness Centre. Against the thought of becoming a zoo exhibit at Vanessa's, with people tiptoeing around her and every move and mood fussed over and judged, the privacy-obsessed centre seemed the perfect sanctuary.

For two weeks now it had been that. The peace she was beginning to feel here made Teagan almost wish it could be forever.

She still struggled to remember the day of the cricket match. The details – exact words, exact faces, the run – remained fuzzy. The emotional pain didn't. That remained vivid and mostly centred around Lucas and his betrayal. Except it wasn't really betrayal. She understood that now. He was trying to help, like the others, but for some reason that scab remained itchy and unhealed.

She looked sadly towards the tree canopy. Lucas was over now. The Falls was over. As soon as she felt strong enough she was heading back to Levenham. Like the Wellness Centre, it was safe there. No one bar Em knew what had happened in her time away. No one would look at her with mockery or pity. There'd be no contempt for causing a fuss and ruining a cricket victory.

Teagan jerked as a twig cracked behind her. Her fingers gripped the timber seat's arms. She clenched her teeth, wishing he'd leave her alone. This was all his fault. Why couldn't he see that? Having him come talk to her was like suffering an encounter with the two-faced god Janus. One face a mask of contrition, the other secretly laughing.

She breathed hard through her nose and said nothing as he dragged a chair close and set it at right angles to her.

'Lovely day.'

Teagan looked deliberately in the other direction. When she'd brought up his visits with Meredith she'd said that it would help if they talked. But Teagan didn't want to talk, not to him.

He never seemed to mind that she ignored him. The words kept coming regardless, as if she was actually listening instead of humming in her head to block him out.

'Penny said Emily called. She's going to bring up Astra for you next week. That'd be good, wouldn't it? Seeing Astra.'

Despite herself, a tear slipped down Teagan's face. Astra. She missed her horse so much. Sometimes she thought that it was leaving Astra behind that had worsened her depression. The lack of her silky coat to cry onto, the comfort of her soft nuzzles as Teagan poured her heart out, the understanding in Astra's kind brown gaze, had led to bottling up her fears and emotions until they turned rancid.

'Lucas said he's building a stable for her. Well, not really a stable, more a three-sided shelter with a yard, but it'll give her a bit of shade and somewhere to stand in a storm.'

At the mention of Lucas, Teagan breathed even harder. They all talked about him as if the two of them were still together, when she knew that was impossible. He'd visited once, in the early days. She was fragile and unwell with side-effects from the anti-depressant she'd been prescribed, and the visit was hard to remember clearly, but it was here, in her favourite place on the grounds. She'd been sitting down, staring at nothing. Imagining herself a different life. One in which she'd copied Ness and disappeared overseas instead of burying her soul in Pinehaven's rich soil.

He'd crouched in front of her and taken her hands, his eyes very blue and strangely liquid. He'd licked his lips, his chest moving up and down from his shallow breaths. 'How are you?'

Sad, she'd wanted to answer. Sad and hurt and guilty and miserable and worst, worst of all, still in love with him. Instead she'd blinked and let the tears slide.

He'd seemed to take it as some sort of positive signal. He'd said her name in anguished tones and tried to embrace her. For a moment she'd let him. Her eyes had closed and she'd seen sweet white light behind the lids. Then she'd remembered all he'd kept from her. The collusion. The lies. In a rush she'd thrust him away and stood, panting. Checking left, right, left again. Not knowing where to run. Only knowing she had to before the hurt shredded her further.

He'd stepped back, apologising, his hands spread. 'I'm sorry. I just needed to see you.'

His voice was thick and caught her attention. She'd stared at him, the ponytailed hunk who'd voiced his attraction on first meeting and never took it back, and for a wonderful second the dark curtain of her heartbreak and sickness had parted and she'd believed. Sweet white light. Hope.

'I'll come back another time.'

Too much. Too many words. None of them the right ones because there were no right ones. The curtain had closed back over.

'No other time. No more.'

His expression had collapsed. He'd stood helpless the way she felt helpless. Then he'd nodded and walked away with his hands on his head and his head tilted back. She'd followed his progress, certain from his body language that he was going to turn back. When he'd reached the path he'd paused, but it was only to look at her. She'd taken a step towards the shadows, not wanting him to see how hard she was crying. His hands had fallen, his shoulders had slumped. Without another glance he'd trudged on.

Teagan still didn't know what to make of that memory.

She threw a look her father's way. Why didn't he get the message and do the same?

'Shouldn't be too bad a run for them,' he said, still talking about Em. 'Couple of days at most. Dom said they can bring Astra to the grounds here for you to say hello. That'd be good, wouldn't it?'

He did that a lot, her dad. Adding 'wouldn't it?' to the end of statements, like a verbal tic. One of these days, just to shock him, she might answer.

'Emily and Josh – they're getting married, did you know? – plan to stay with Vanessa for a few days. Apparently Josh wants to check out a few shops in Sydney. Custom-furniture-design places, that sort of thing.'

Teagan knew about their engagement. Her mum had told her. She'd been pleased for Em. Josh was a good man. Both she and Jas had always suspected that neither Em nor Josh had ever got over their teenage love affair and breakup. Josh was probably living out at Rocking Horse Hill now, helping Em around the farm. Most likely having sex in every corner like she and Lucas used to at Astonville.

She swallowed. Lucas, Lucas, always Lucas.

A movement had her sliding her eyes towards her dad. He was glancing at his watch.

Catching her peek, he smiled sheepishly. He looked better these days. Cheerier. No sign of the desperate cheat that had skulked and snapped around Pinehaven as he'd secretly destroyed his daughter's world.

'Meredith wants to see me at eleven. I don't want to keep her waiting.' He rose and patted his pockets, a habit he'd always had, although Teagan never understood what he was checking for. 'Best get going. Good to talk to you, Teagan. You take care now and don't stay out too long. Can't have you getting burned.'

She watched him ready himself to shuffle off with another pocket pat. 'Why do you do this?'

His eyebrows rose. 'Can't a father talk to his daughter?'

'You stopped deserving the right to be called father the moment you started lying to me.'

His expression clouded. The smile he'd been trying to keep fixed flattened. 'You're right. I did. I made a lot of mistakes. Especially with you.'

'And now what? You think you can just act like it all never happened? That you didn't gamble Pinehaven away? My home, the place I loved like nothing else.' She slapped a hand on her chest. 'You emptied me of everything, even my dreams. And I didn't see it coming because there was no way I could believe my own father would do that to me. But he did. And that made me the biggest fool on earth because I not only believed your lies, I helped you perpetuate them.'

He took her spat words with his back straight and eye contact unwavering. 'I did all those things. I hurt you, your mother, your brother. Friends. Everyone. I acknowledge that.'

'Well, bully for you.' Teagan looked away. She'd had enough. No doubt he'd try to apologise again. She was sick of hearing it.

'You and I are too alike, Teagan.'

She made a 'pfft' noise. 'I am nothing like you.'

'Then why are we both here?'

Him she had no idea about, nor did she care. But Teagan's goal was to get better. Walk out strong and return home to a safe place and start again.

'Go away,' she said tiredly. 'Just go away.'

She may as well have not bothered speaking.

'When your brother said he wasn't coming home,' said Graham, 'something broke in me. With no son to pass Pinehaven on to, all that I'd worked for, that my father – your grandfather – had worked for, seemed wasted.'

'Right. And I was nothing, was I?' The tear sting was back. She breathed deeply through her nose in an attempt to ease it only to find the effort made her throat ache. She gave up. The tears were going to come anyway. 'You had a daughter.'

'I know. But I thought that as soon as you married you'd go off somewhere else.'

'Married? Jesus, Dad. I was working so hard on the farm I didn't get a chance to even go on a date!'

'I know.' He lowered his gaze. 'I'm sorry. I should've realised you loved Pinehaven more than Owen ever could. Penny tried to tell me, but I didn't want to believe her. I was too upset that Owen had chosen another man's farm.'

'That's ridiculous. Owen didn't choose anything. He fell in love, that's all.'

'No more ridiculous than you thinking no one loves you.'

Teagan swiped at her eyes, angry she'd started this conversation. She should have let him walk off.

'It didn't start out as gambling. It was a way to help make the farm prosperous. The salespeople promised that if I followed their program I could make money. Good money. It seemed easy, not much risk. They had testimonials, charts. I was going to use the extra income to make the improvements the place needed. Finally buy the new tractor I'd been promising.' His jaw wobbled. 'I thought if Owen saw what he was missing out on he'd come home.'

Of course Teagan never figured in that plan because she didn't matter. She'd never mattered to him. But she'd been too dumb to see it.

'He was never going to come home,' she said, rubbing her face. 'Why do you think he went away in the first place? He didn't want to be stuck at Pinehaven anymore.'

He hadn't wanted to turn out like his parents, is what Owen had actually said. She remembered it clearly. They'd been in the wool-shed, getting ready for shearing. Teagan loved that time of year. The smell of it. The productivity. The shearing team and the way the sheep looked bright and new afterwards. Owen had been working permanently at home for four years by then and growing more disgruntled by the day. He'd worked hard – it wasn't in their Bliss genes not to – but he'd resented it. The way his life seemed to be already decided for him, mapped by a father's expectations.

He'd told her then of his plans to escape. He was going to travel. Have adventures like Aunt Ness. Thanks to Penny's parents being English he was eligible for a British passport, enabling him to stay and muck around the EU all he liked.

'But what about the farm?' Teagan had asked, struggling to comprehend why he'd want to leave Pinehaven.

Owen's face had set with stubbornness. 'No way I'm staying here to stagnate like them.'

She hadn't understood. To be like her parents was what Teagan wanted. They worked together, managed things, went through good and bad standing stoically by each other's side. It's what farming people did – they withstood. Owen wanted to run to something unstable, something unknown.

She should have run with him.

Her father sagged into a seat and stared bleakly at the ground. 'I didn't know that. He never said. I just assumed . . .' His mouth turned down even further.

'Like you assumed I'd leave.' The scorn Teagan felt was incredible. 'You could've asked.'

'Never been one to pry.'

'No. You like secrets. Even when they could ruin us all.'

He looked up, strength returning to his face. 'We're not all ruined. We still have each other. We're still a family. We still have that love. These are rich things. All you have to do is see them.'

He glanced to the side. Meredith was walking towards them.

'I thought I'd find you two here.' She looked around at the lush bower. 'Such a gorgeous garden. Peaceful.' Her focus went to Teagan. 'It's a nice place to rest, and talk.' She waited for her to respond but Teagan wasn't playing. 'Did your dad tell you about Astra?'

'Yep.'

'We'll arrange for her to visit.' She tilted her head. 'Or you could go to see her, at Lucas's.'

Teagan shook her head, her throat feeling strangled. 'I can't.'

'That's all right. We'll bring her here for you to say hello.'

Meredith turned to Graham. 'Penny will be joining us this session.'

Her father's face changed at the news. He stood, patting his pockets, eager.

Meredith nodded to Teagan. 'Don't stay out too long. I know it's shady here but you can still burn.'

They walked off, leaving Teagan to her shaky thoughts.

When they were out of sight she dug into her shorts pocket and pulled out Lucas's pendant. She turned it over in her hands, watching the light catch the silver. Pondering the craftsmanship. The way the enamel had a depth to it.

Rich things she couldn't see.
But longed to.

TWENTY-NINE

'THAT HORSE IS A TOTAL NUTJOB,' said Lucas as Astra whirled around Emily for the tenth time, whinnying loudly.

'Actually, she's pretty good compared to what she was.'

Josh reached out to grab the horse's halter. 'Em's put a lot of work into her.'

'Not that much.' She smiled kindly at Lucas. 'But I tried for Teagan.'

Unlike Teagan's glamorous, highly strung filly, Lucas had liked Emily and Josh immediately. They were good people and caring friends. Emily seemed a bit aloof at first; one of those posh haughty horse sorts he knew only too well, but her reserve had gradually thawed. Last night over dinner and wine at Falls Farm, encouraged by Vanessa, she'd opened up with stories about Teagan. The shows they'd competed at, the girly evenings they'd shared, their adolescent antics. Penny had added more stories from Teagan's childhood, her love of horses, mischief on the farm. Times from when Teagan was happy. A girl Lucas had sensed but only caught glimpses of. Enough to fall in love.

Josh was like him. A working bloke doing pretty well for himself.

Although truth was Lucas wasn't doing great at all. Not in his heart. Astonville, The Falls, everywhere, was empty without Teagan. He never thought he'd miss her so much, but he did. She was an aching wound that wouldn't heal.

She'd been at the centre three weeks now, with no sign of leaving. Vanessa promised Teagan was making excellent progress but refused to elaborate further. When Lucas had asked Dom when she might be well enough to come home he'd prevaricated, softening his answer with a fatherly grasp of Lucas's shoulder. That was up to Teagan herself. A probe about the cost garnered an equally oblique response. As far as Dom was concerned, she could stay as long as it took. She was his guest, the way Penny and Graham had been guests. The cost was irrelevant.

More than once Lucas had considered washing his hands of her. She'd made it clear the day he visited that the split between them was too deep to ever close over. As time passed his heartbreak worsened, driving his pessimism about their future. If they'd even had a past beyond what he'd fabricated in his wishful mind.

Dom kept telling him to hang in there. Some women – even the difficult ones – were worth the wait. Vanessa advised him to do what his heart told him was right, but Penny took him aside and begged him not to abandon her daughter. No matter how she'd acted Teagan loved him. But they were just words, assurances from a protective mother. Then she'd revealed something that had made him rethink: Teagan still had his pendant. She didn't wear it, but she kept it always close, like a talisman.

Like it mattered.

Astra let out another high-pitched whinny. Lucas rolled his eyes. What was it with him and high-maintenance women? He should stick with males. At least, bar the occasional ram raid when Lucas forgot to pay attention, Merlin caused no trouble. Eat grass and bleat a lot, was all the ram did and Astonville allowed plenty of scope for both. Which was why Vanessa had asked if Lucas would mind keeping him on, adding that with every other animal and human at Falls Farm being female, perhaps Merlin's misbehaviour was because he felt his masculinity was threatened. Lucas suspected the real reason Vanessa wanted him to keep Merlin was because with Teagan gone she was convinced he needed the company.

He let out a sigh and patted Astra's neck. 'Let's get this done.'

For a fractious animal the filly floated quite well. She walked up the ramp with little more than a few sniffs and a head shake, hardly moving on the drive to the centre despite the serpentine road.

Perhaps she was as paralysed by the thought of seeing Teagan as he was.

Emily had visited her the day before. Lucas had been so anxious for news that on Emily's return to Astonville he'd found it hard to hold back from interrogating her like a captured spy. She'd understood though, and after making a cuppa had sat with him outside to talk while Josh made phone calls inside.

The vines had sprouted in the warmer weather and Lucas was slowly training the canes up the pergola posts. Every day new leaves unfurled and the vines reached out with exploratory tendrils, like blind lovers learning to touch. Each time he sat there he thought of Teagan and the way she'd admired it. He thought of other things, too. Good things. The first time they'd slept together; Teagan curled up on the bed, self-conscious and tentative before coming sexily, sweetly alive under his tender caresses. The day they'd had sex in the forge; him cracking up afterwards at her soot-covered bum as she'd skipped naked in front of him back to the house. Quiet evenings on the couch, her head in his lap, idly tracing the planes of her face with his fingertips as they'd zoned out in front of the telly, feeling contented and right.

'She still loves you,' Emily said.

'She said that?'

'She didn't have to.'

His heart sank again. Kindness was making Emily lie. He stretched back to stare at the vine leaves.

'Lucas, I've known her since we were thirteen. Believe me, she loves you.'

'How do you know?'

She smiled. Teagan's friend was an attractive woman, classy, with an articulate voice and an intelligent gaze. 'It's in the way she avoided any mention of your name. I played along. Then at the end, when I said I'd better go, she asked how you were. Then she wanted to know everything, which was difficult when we've only just met. So I told her she should ask you herself.'

'And?'

She hesitated before answering. 'She said there was no point.'

With her words, the ember that was Lucas's hope lost the last of its glow.

Emily toyed with the handle of her cup. 'I suspect she thinks you've given up on her.'

Given up on her? How the hell could he ever do that?

'Christ,' he said, rubbing his hand over his face. 'So what do I do?'

'Tell her you still love her,' said Josh, walking up to them.

Emily caught Lucas's expression and her eyes widened. 'You had told her, hadn't you?'

'Not exactly.'

Emily regarded him as though he was a complete idiot. Probably because he was.

'Better hurry up then,' said Josh, stroking Emily's hair in that absent but caring way that showed he did it often, with love. 'Not saying it nearly cost me Em.' He sat down, picked up his fiancée's coffee mug and took a sip, before settling his gaze on Lucas. A small intimacy between a devoted couple that made Lucas feel his emptiness even more. 'My old man has this saying: nothing sucks a man's soul drier than regrets. It's true. You love her, you tell her. Can't make things worse.'

Emily leaned forward. 'Teagan needs to hear it, Lucas.'

Which was why he was in his ute now, guts churning as he towed Emily's horse float towards the Wellness Centre. Astra was his safety net. Teagan could push him away, but she wouldn't push away her horse.

He hoped.

Teagan checked her clock for the twentieth time. Eleven was when Dom said Astra would arrive. It was now ten to. Someone would come and fetch her. Meredith, she supposed, a professional to offer guidance.

Yesterday, after Em had left, Teagan had revealed to Meredith her deep fear that Astra might reject her. That her horse would have bonded with Em and forgotten the mistress who had adored her. But Meredith had a way of taking a question and using it to probe deeper. Discussion moved on to why Teagan's friendship with Emily remained intact when others had fractured, despite initially feeling her friend had betrayed her. Teagan hadn't had a solid answer for that. All she knew was that it had been Em she'd run to when she'd learned the truth about Pinehaven. Em who'd sat up all night listening. Em who'd promised to keep Astra safe.

The trust of an almost lifelong friendship was hard to break. Which was why Em wanted Teagan to be her bridesmaid. Giving Teagan another reason to think about leaving the centre and start rebuilding her life.

The clocked ticked to eleven. Teagan began to pace. Why wasn't anyone here? She chewed her lip. Maybe Astra wasn't coming. Maybe something had happened and they didn't know how to tell her.

The thought made sweat spring across her brow. She glanced at the clock again and then at the door. In a few strides she was out.

Her favourite spot in the garden was empty. Knowing how much she liked it, she'd expected they'd direct Em to lead Astra there, but there was no sign of either her friend or her horse. She stopped in the centre of the bower and wiped her hands down her hips. If Astra rejected her she wouldn't know how to cope.

She stood for a long while breathing hard, trying to control her growing anxiety. The birds were active today. Noisy miners bounced among the groundcover, chattering to one another. From further away, a bellbird began to call, and others joined in. The sound reminded Teagan of her first day at Falls Farm, when the future had lain ahead. Her new life.

She remembered how she'd found Lucas with Claudia. The way her breath had caught at seeing him. How he'd fooled her, by not being the wanker she'd thought but a good man. Easygoing, funny, kind. A man who'd made her smile, who'd not seen the depression that she hated and dreaded so much, but an attractive, if skinny, redhead he wanted to know better.

Rich things.

A whinny broke her thoughts. She listened, unsure if it was real or if her desperate mind had conjured the sound. Another whinny came. She grinned. Astra.

Teagan jogged out of the bower. From the whinny's carry she could guess where Astra was – the flat land at the bottom of the hill that Dom had once earmarked for specialised treatment facilities and accommodation for drug addicts. Those plans were scrapped now. He'd withdrawn the development application in favour of establishing another property on the tablelands, near Orange. More privacy for his clients was the excuse. Teagan suspected that it had more to do with keeping peace in the village for Ness than any business reason.

She ducked around a tree and spotted the back of a horse float and recognised it as Emily's. Excitement had her stepping out again only to falter. The car attached to the float wasn't her friend's. It was a late-model ute, sparkling chrome trunks lining the back tray. She scanned left to where the parkland opened to a grassy clearing.

Her heart pounded. Lucas was quietly leading Astra in a large circle. He was hatless, his ponytailed blond hair as glossy as Astra's short summer coat. Both muscled, both magnificent. The pinnacle of beauty for their species.

But more importantly, blazingly, vividly real.

Two things she loved, together.

Voices drifted, catching her attention. Dom and Ness walking back up the hill towards reception, hand in hand. Walking to fetch her, most likely. Teagan raised her hand, about to call out, and stopped. This was something she needed to get through on her own. She watched them disappear into the gardens, hoping they wouldn't panic when they found her room empty.

She turned back to Astra and Lucas. He'd paused in the centre of the clearing. Astra's head was up, her ears pricked. Teagan could see the flare of her pretty nostrils as she scented the air. The horse took a step forward and whinnied.

And Teagan knew that it was a welcome. For her.

She headed down the slope. Her feet crunched on dropped leaves and dried twigs, the sounds like her nerves, fragile and easily shattered. With each step she breathed in slowly, willing herself calm but braced for any setback in her thoughts. But the closer she approached, the more intense the sweet white feeling became. There was trepidation, certainly, but not darkness. He was here. That had to mean something.

Slowly she crossed the grass, leaking happy tears as Astra strained against her lead and stretched towards her mistress, whickering in delight. A few steps and Teagan was cupping Astra's jaw, kissing her long nose and stroking her silky neck, while Astra blew warm air from her soft nostrils over Teagan's face and into her hair.

Tears smeared her cheeks as she whispered nonsense. Stupid talk about how beautiful the filly had become, how shiny her coat was, how clever her eyes. The horse had filled out in the time she'd spent at Rocking Horse Hill. The lush pastures had made her put on weight. Em had trimmed her mane and tail. Her hooves were neat. Everything about her shone with good health and vitality.

Finally, she stepped back. Lucas was standing as far from them as the lead would allow. He wore a small smile as though he found the reunion touching. Even though the morning sun had bite, he wore jeans and his scuffed steel-capped boots. A polo shirt stretched across his torso, the open collar exposing a lightly tanned triangle of his chest. The sun shot golden streaks through his hair like a celestial blessing.

Teagan suddenly felt stupid and shy. What to say to this man?

'She obviously missed you,' he said, taking a step closer.

'Thanks for bringing her.'

'That was Emily and Josh. They drove her up here.'

Teagan stroked Astra's nose, hunting for the right words. She didn't know where to start and apprehension kept her silent. The white sweetness was still pulsing, but she couldn't prevent the worry that one wrong utterance could see it vanish.

'How long can she stay?'

'As long as you want. All day.' He shrugged. 'It's up to you.' He looked around, squinting in the sun, and gestured towards the ute. 'Your tack's in the car. Emily thought you might want to go for a ride.'

'No, not today. Maybe another day.'

'Dom will be pleased about that.' At her puzzled look he smiled. 'He doesn't have the insurance to cover it.'

Lucas took another step forward and stroked his hand down Astra's neck. 'She was a bit ratty earlier but she's calmed now. Must be because she's with you.'

'I suspect she just likes the attention.'

They fell silent. Teagan continued to scratch and stroke Astra. Her horsey smell filled Teagan's nostrils, along with something else. Something as warming. And reminiscent.

Lucas.

She watched him out of the corner of her eye. He kept fiddling with the end of the lead, looping and unlooping quick-release knots. Catching her looking, he stopped. The quiet became awkward.

He scratched the side of his nose. 'Josh helped me finish the yard off yesterday. Everything's set for her now.' The fidgeting stopped and Lucas shifted a little to stand with his shoulders straight and chin raised. His gaze locked on hers. 'And you, for when you want to come home.'

She frowned. What did he mean for when she wanted to come home? Home wasn't Astonville, it was . . . She didn't know. Home was something she had still to figure out.

'I love you, Teagan.'

Her breath caught at the words. Words she'd wanted. Words so hard to believe. She hugged herself as longing and memory punched her chest, and looked away. 'You don't mean that.'

'I do. I should've said it from the moment I realised the truth instead of waiting.'

'You can't. I'm a screw-up.'

'No, you were depressed.' He smiled, a radiant, perfect Lucas smile. 'Now you're getting better.'

The sight of that smile had her heart flipping. God, she'd missed it. She'd missed everything about him. His sincerity, his kindness, his sexy masculinity.

He sobered. 'It's been driving me crazy, not seeing you.'

'It's been driving me crazy, too,' she whispered. Ten minutes ago she would have denied the truth. Now it was rushing over her in a cascade. Her words tumbled out, desperate to be free of the locked cage in her head. 'I wanted to see you but I was scared. That day, when you came and I pushed you away? I thought you wouldn't want anything to do with me after that.'

'No.' He reached for her hand, the way he'd always done, like it was the most natural, perfect thing in the world. 'I want everything to do with you. The good, the bad, the completely screwed up. It doesn't matter. As long as you're with me.'

She stared and stared. 'You mean it?'

He smiled and bent close, breath brushing her lips. 'Told you I liked crazy.'

'You said you like redheads, too.'

'Yeah, but those I don't just like. Those I love. Especially ones with the last name Bliss.'

'Is that so?'

His mouth caressed the corner of hers. She closed her eyes, inhaling him. 'Teagan?'

'What?'

'Shut up and kiss me.'

THIRTY

TEAGAN ROUSED and rubbed the back of her hand into her eye. She breathed in the morning, her first away from the centre in nearly four weeks.

'Oh, God,' she said, wrenching upright and opening her eyes onto a pale-blue alien gaze. Teagan screwed her nose up. 'I'd prefer to wake up to something more attractive, you know.' Lucas, ideally, who was not only very attractive but smelled of man and metal and other delicious things. Unlike Vanessa's evil-minded cat.

Blanche meowed. They exchanged glares, waiting. When Teagan failed to tip her off Blanche settled onto her lap. Her tail whipped a few times and stilled. Teagan maintained her grumpy face for a few more seconds before picking up the cat and cuddling it to her chest. Blanche's happy purrs vibrated against her skin.

Teagan almost felt like purring herself.

A tap sounded at the door. Teagan called a 'come in' and waited to see who it was. They were all nervous for her – Mum, Dad, Ness, even Dom, but Meredith wasn't. Neither was Lucas. His confidence in her was ridiculous in its intensity. She loved him for it though.

Knowing he thought she could cope made her believe she really could.

Vanessa's luscious red waves appeared around the door's edge, her morning smile dropping as she spotted Blanche. 'Oh, you rotten thing.'

'She's fine,' said Teagan, stroking Blanche's bony, wrinkled head. 'Funny, but I've kind of learned to appreciate her qualities.'

'I'm glad someone likes her. She's in the dog house for attacking Nibbles. Have you any idea how much surgery on a rabbit costs? Even at a discount?'

Teagan held the flaccid cat up under the armpits and glared at her. 'Not cool, Blanche.'

Blanche yawned.

Teagan's eyes met Vanessa's and they laughed.

'Your dad's cooking us bacon and eggs for breakfast. It'll be ready soon.'

Teagan returned Blanche to her lap and stroked her, saying nothing.

Ness crossed the room and sat on the edge of her bed. 'Don't be scared.'

'I'm not.' She pressed her lips together, trying to hide her nerves with a wry smile. 'Maybe a little.'

'It's only family.' Ness reached out to tuck a lock of hair behind Teagan's ear. 'Everyone who loves you.'

Only family. No Lucas. The disappointment hung. He'd come for a little while last night. They'd stood on the verandah with Ness and Dom, Penny and Graham, talking trivia. To Teagan's relief no one toasted her return. They carried on, sipping gin and tonics as though it was normal for her to be there, while Teagan sipped water, feeling anxious and a little suffocated. The worry about what they were all thinking of her hadn't waned, not completely.

Lucas had taken her hand and cocked his head towards Claudia's paddock. 'Feel like a walk?'

She'd nodded, grateful to escape the claustrophobic feeling that was getting worse with each minute. The Wellness Centre had been full of people, but she'd kept to herself for most of her stay, only emerging from her shell in the last week. Meredith had orchestrated a lot of it. Chance meetings here and there. Some group sessions focusing on managing alcohol dependency during which Teagan had spent most of her time gawping at the extremely famous movie star sitting opposite.

She'd been aghast that someone as composed, talented and rich as this woman could be as depressed as herself.

'Depression doesn't discriminate,' Meredith had said afterwards. 'It can happen to anyone.' She'd smiled at Teagan and given her an encouraging hug. Not very professional perhaps, but to Teagan it had meant an enormous amount.

Lucas's hand had remained secure on hers as they walked down the track. It was still hot and the cicadas were in full song, chirruping in piercing surround sound across the landscape. The dry track threw up red dust that stuck to the back of her legs where they'd become sweaty from the chair. They needed rain. A good storm to soak paddocks and fill the creeks and dams.

He wore a small smile, the sort that comes when people know a good secret or they're feeling smug with happiness.

They leaned on the fence, watching Claudia and Mouse together.

'Remember when we first met?' he said.

'Yes.'

'You thought I was a dickhead. And in love with your aunt.'

She laughed. 'I did.'

'Now?'

She fiddled with her pendant, unable to look at him. It frightened her to admit how intense her feelings were. Sometimes, it was like he was the calcium that made up her bones and kept her standing. That, without him, she'd never cope with the world, never find independence. No matter how many times Meredith told her that she'd grow into her own strength, the vulnerability of it was scary.

'I don't think you're a dickhead.'

'That's something, at least.' He rested his head on his arms and looked sideways at her. Sunset was far off. His eyes glowed in the bright day. He was, as he had been back then, utterly beautiful. 'Do you want to know what I thought?'

Teagan could guess. 'That I was rude and prickly. And skinny.'

'Not rude. Skinny, yes. But I thought you were the sexiest woman I'd ever met.'

Teagan didn't know what to say.

'I still do.' He tugged her towards him, changing position to brace against the fence and nestle her between his legs. His gaze swept appreciatively over her. 'Even more.'

'Despite everything?'

'Despite everything.'

She wanted to plaster his face with kisses when he looked at her like that. Instead, she sighed and tucked her head against his big shoulder.

He brushed his cheek against hers. 'I wish you were coming home tonight. It's been lonely without you. Merlin's a thug and Astra's already sick of my attentions. And I need a muse.'

She lifted her head. 'A muse?'

'Yeah, someone to inspire me. I have orders for bird cages up the yin-yang.' His hands coasted lazily to the tops of her shorts and up her T-shirt to stroke the soft skin of her waist. 'I need some more curves to give me ideas.'

She pressed closer to him. 'From the feel of it you already have ideas.'

'Always, when it comes to you.' He sobered and shifted his hands to lock them at the small of her back. 'I love you. I mean it.'

The words, so sincere, simple and honest made her chest feel huge with feeling. She breathed in, fortifying herself, and held his loving gaze. Though he'd said it several times now, she'd yet to say the same to him.

She toyed with the pendant around his throat. It was different to the one he'd worn when they'd first met, a smaller, less ornate version of hers. She frowned and inspected it closer. The blue-and-green enamel inlay wasn't abstract as she'd thought but formed into a stylised T.

She looked up. The tenderness in his expression was still there.

'So you're by my heart,' he said.

She touched her own pendant. 'Like you're by mine.' She took another long breath and felt all her anxiety drop away. 'I love you.' Then she smiled. 'Like a crazy person.'

'You're not crazy. You're just you. And that makes you perfect.'

They'd kissed for a long, long time.

A kiss that Teagan had reminisced about that night while she lay in bed, listening to the sounds of the house and the breeze rustling the trees. A kiss that she thought of now as she dressed and padded out to the kitchen, redolent with the scent of bacon and the sound of spitting fat.

Her dad turned and waved a spatula at her. 'Won't be long.'

She busied herself with the espresso machine, watching him as it went through its cycle of bean grinding and milk frothing. He was different to the father she remembered. There was life about him now. Even the lines that had seemed permanently etched in his face had softened.

And he was cooking breakfast, something he hadn't done since Owen had left.

Her mother bustled in. Spotting Teagan, she rushed over for a hug. 'Sleep well?'

'Pretty good.'

Letting her go, Penny crossed to the stove and regarded the pan critically. 'Vanessa likes them runny don't forget.'

He screwed up his nose and poked around in the pan a bit. 'I'll do some more.'

Teagan and her mother exchanged a look. Graham had never been capable of cooking runny eggs. Penny raided a shelf, pulled down several bottles and began counting out pills. Teagan smiled

wryly. She'd been convinced to try a few of the milder natural therapies on offer at the centre, surprised to find they weren't as bad as she
imagined. Not that she was about to share that around too loudly.
And she sure as hell wasn't going to admit to anyone about the
enema. Ever.

The espresso machine finished its cycle. She retrieved her latte
mug and took a sip as she observed her parents squabbling some more
over the eggs.

There was happiness in the air.

'Pie time, I think,' said Nick, hands on his hips and surveying the hay
they'd just unloaded into a neat stack in the hayshed. Apart from a
few trail riders, Belgravia was quiet. Everyone was gearing up for
Christmas and most of the horses were turned out. There was still
plenty of work. Time to attack the many chores that had been
neglected during busy times and staff shortages.

'I'll go,' said Teagan.

Lucas pulled off his gloves. 'I'll come with you.'

She put her hand on his arm. 'It's okay. I can manage.'

He studied her with apprehension. Nick walked off, giving them
privacy. Three weeks had passed since Teagan had returned to work,
almost eight weeks since the day at the cricket ground, and she still
hadn't done a pie run. She'd been to the shops to collect mail, visit the
IGA and pick up Belgravia's veterinary supplies from Bunny, but she
had yet to set foot in the bakery.

Out of all The Falls locals, it was Kathleen Ferguson who she was
most nervous about. Everyone knew what had happened. The
majority had been kind, asking how Teagan was faring, and bringing
up family member's or close friend's – even their own – experiences
with depression. Revealing how common it was. With Kathleen, as a
woman prone to self-righteousness, Teagan felt as though she had

something to prove. Mostly to herself that she'd recovered enough to be beyond the narrow-minded judgements of people like Kathleen.

Col had been particularly sweet, a little bit bored-old-man fussy perhaps, but genuinely sympathetic. Gossip was that he'd had a falling out with Kathleen caused by her lie to the police, which had resulted in an embarrassing caution and much chuntering by villagers. Apparently the bakery break-in was real enough – the work of a scabby local out for easy cash – the assault, however, wasn't. Kathleen's bruises were caused by a fall the night before, when she'd slipped on some flour. She'd taken one incident and added it to the other for her own ends. The rumour that a famous soapie star had recently entered rehab couldn't have been more opportune. She'd used his description to put pressure on Dom and discredit him in the eyes of the village. Unfortunately for Kathleen, the soapie star wasn't at the Wellness Centre but far away, at an exclusive Chiang Mai facility.

Now the entire Falls knew she was a liar. Business had eased off, but not enough to put the bakery at risk. As Ness so often said, regardless of the people who ran them, the village needed its businesses to keep the community vibrant. If that meant giving patronage to places they'd rather not, then so be it.

Plus the bakery did make the best pies.

Teagan's hands were sweaty on the wheel as she made her way into the village. She parked the car and took a few moments to breathe. Glancing towards the veterinary clinic's door, she wondered if she should poke her head in. Get a Bunny no-nonsense pep talk. But Bunny was probably busy with a patient. Or organising her wedding.

There was nothing for it. She opened the door and stepped out. The carpark felt humid and thick. She paused, wishing she'd let Lucas come after all, then scolded herself for her fear. One step at a time, Meredith had advised. Eventually those steps would turn into strides.

She straightened her shoulders and pushed into the shop.

Kathleen Ferguson locked eyes with her. 'Here for some pies, I take it.'

'Yes. Two plain, a curry pie, a potato pie, a cheese and bacon, and a couple of sausage rolls.'

Unlike any other time, Kathleen set about filling the order without so much as a 'do you want sauce?'.

Teagan studied the pastries as she waited. The vanilla slices looked good. She might add a couple to the order for Lucas and Nick. Maybe an apricot tart for herself. Though nothing like Vanessa's voluptuous figure, much to Lucas's appreciation, Teagan was developing proper curves. She planned to keep them cultivated.

'Do you want a plastic bag?' asked Kathleen.

'Thanks. I'll grab a couple of vanilla slices and an apricot tart as well.'

When Kathleen rang up the total she handed over a note and waited for the change.

The old woman hesitated before passing it. 'I hear your aunt has moved into the old Fowler property with Domenic Ashe.'

'She has.' And Ness couldn't be happier. With its modern Tuscan design, stunning view of the mountains, and large courtyard for entertaining, Ness was in her element. Most of all, with Dom, she'd found the love she'd always sought.

'Your parents are looking after Falls Farm now.'

'For the time being.' They were still tossing that up. Mum missed Levenham, but both had developed a liking for the relative luxury of the farm. Plus someone had to look after Claudia and Mouse, and the other animals. The guilt of preying on Vanessa's generosity had eased now that Dom had given them both jobs to keep them busy – Mum as a cleaner, Dad working on the grounds. Teagan suspected that in a few months they'd be so entrenched there'd be no move back to South Australia.

'And you're at Lucas's.'

'I am.' If the old cow expected more she wasn't going to get it.

'You happy?'

Teagan blinked at the intrusive question. The urge to answer 'none of your business' was enormous but she bit her tongue. Kathleen Ferguson didn't matter. What mattered were the people she loved.

She held out her palm and waggled it. 'Can I have my change please?'

Grudgingly the old lady handed it over. Teagan walked out with her spine straight and a grin of pure accomplishment splitting her face.

Lucas smiled into the back of Teagan's neck and placed a soft kiss on the fuzzy surface of her skin. At his touch she stretched and rolled over into his arms.

'Hello,' she said sleepily.

'Hello,' he said, stroking her hair away from her face so he could kiss her properly.

'What time is it?'

'About four.'

She smiled and stretched again. 'We've been naughty.'

'We have.'

She tucked herself in closer under his arm. Her fingers went to his chest to toy with the hairs there. 'You spoil me.'

'I hope so.'

'We should get up.'

'Probably.'

He kissed her hair again when she didn't move. Afternoon sex was becoming a habit of theirs, one he wasn't keen to give up. He'd joked that it was his muse time. That he needed inspiration from Mother Nature's best achievement before he could create. It was bullshit, of course. He just couldn't keep his hands off her.

Teagan thought that was funny. She thought a lot of things were funny these days, and each time she laughed or smiled or made a joke his chest would balloon with pride. She had her moments. He could tell when they arrived. Hollowness would drape her face and she'd quieten as her mind condensed around a negative thought. At those times he'd take care to tell her how much he loved her, how special she was, how sexy and clever and gorgeous. How she'd turned his, and everyone else's, world upside down.

It was happening less and less now. Soon, he hoped, those moments wouldn't come at all.

'Lucas?'

'Mmm?'

'Are you looking forward to being best man again?'

He considered for a moment. With Dom and Vanessa's wedding this would be his second best-man gig in a matter of weeks. Bunny's and Dunks's nuptials had been casual and fun, but this was a bit special. 'Yeah, I am.' He gave her a tickle. 'I'm especially looking forward to getting down and dirty with the bridesmaid.'

She giggled beneath him, all sexy smooth skin and warmth. His heart began to pound as a thought came over him. He shifted his weight so she was below him and he could look down at her. She was smiling, happy.

'You know what?'

'What?'

'I'd rather be the groom.'

Her mouth parted slowly as understanding dawned.

Apprehension made him clumsy as he tried to cup her face. She searched his eyes, her own wide.

'Marry me?'

He didn't need to hear the words to know her answer.

Rocking
HORSE HILL
CATHRYN
HEIN

A Levenham *Love* Story

Rocking HORSE HILL
CATHRYN HEIN

Who do you trust when a stranger threatens to tear your family apart?

When Emily Wallace-Jones's brother Digby arrives home with a secretive new fiancée, no one knows how to react. The Wallace-Jones are old-money rural aristocracy and Felicity Townsend is from a very different side of the tracks.

But Em is determined not to treat Felicity with the same teenage snobbery that tore apart her relationship with her first love, Josh Sinclair. A man who has now sauntered sexily back into Em's life and given her a chance for redemption.

As Felicity settles in, suspicions are raised about her intentions toward Em's beloved Rocking Horse Hill, the historic family property that Digby owns but has promised will be Em's home for as long as she wishes. Though worried for her future, Em sides with her brother and Felicity, until a near tragedy sets in motion a chain of events that will change the family forever.

An emotional story of family turmoil and second-chance love played out against the dramatic landscape of rural South Australia.

Order your copy in ebook or paperback from your favourite retailer today!

DEAR READER

Thank you so much for reading *The Falls*. I hope you enjoyed Teagan's and Lucas's journey to love and happiness. If you did, and you have a few moments, I'd be very grateful if you could leave a rating or few words in review on your favourite book site to help others discover my books.

If you'd like to know when my next release comes available plus gain access to exclusive content, news and other goodies, please subscribe to my newsletter via my website.

More information about me and my books, including the inspiration behind *The Falls*, along with plenty of other fun stuff, can be found at cathrynhein.com.

Web: cathrynhein.com
Facebook: facebook.com/cathrynhein
Twitter: @CathrynHein

Lightning Source UK Ltd.
Milton Keynes UK
UKHW01f1206220618
324641UK00012B/1406/P